The

Legends *&* Lore

of

Illinois

By

Michael Kleen

Black Oak
M E D I A

To order copies of this book contact:

Black Oak Media
Rockford, Illinois
www.blackoakmedia.org
orders@blackoakmedia.org

Printed in the United States of America.

Contents

Introduction   **5**

Case Files

Behind the Scenes

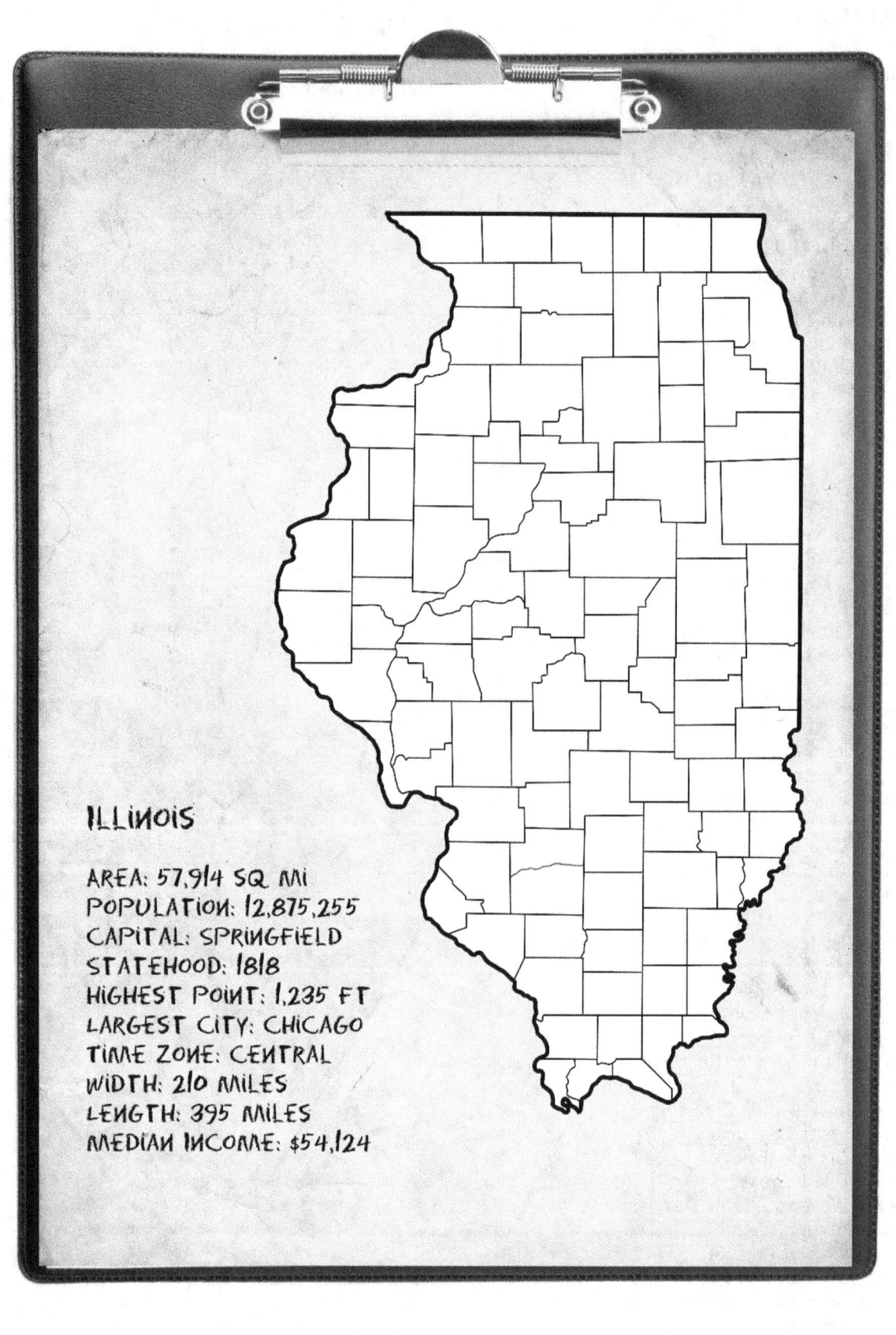

ILLINOIS

AREA: 57,914 SQ MI
POPULATION: 12,875,255
CAPITAL: SPRINGFIELD
STATEHOOD: 1818
HIGHEST POINT: 1,235 FT
LARGEST CITY: CHICAGO
TIME ZONE: CENTRAL
WIDTH: 210 MILES
LENGTH: 395 MILES
MEDIAN INCOME: $54,124

INTRODUCTION

Over the past several years, the website that grew out of a small electronic publication called the *Legends and Lore of Illinois* has become one of the most popular of its kind. At a time when paranormal investigation was the dominant lens through which the public encountered the strange and mysterious, this website's motto was "leave science to the scientists." It decided to throw out the question, "is this ghost story true?" and instead focused on the question, "how do ghost stories enrich our lives?" Playing freely with fact and fiction, it embraced a philosophy of creativity while earning the respect of fans of folklore and ghost stories all over the Prairie State.

How did the *Legends and Lore of Illinois* go from being a relatively obscure e-zine to one of the most visited websites about the paranormal in Illinois? For the answer to that question, we have to start at the beginning.

The Beginning

"I have an idea for a newsletter about haunted places in Illinois," I told my friend Donna as we sat in a Taco Bell along Rand Road in Prospect Heights in the winter of 2006.

Or maybe it started months earlier in the basement of Booth Library at Eastern Illinois University, when I created the prototype of a website called "The Legends and Lore of Illinois."

Or maybe it was in my friend Adam's house on Henry Street in Des Plaines when, at the age of nine or ten, we formed a club to look for ghosts in his parent's attic.

I actually do not know when the idea first came to me to start writing about ghost stories and the (allegedly) haunted places of Illinois. I have always been interested in the more unusual side of life. In high school, when others were playing sports or going to parties, I sat squirreled away in the public library reading Ursula Bielski's *Chicago Haunts*.

During those long evenings after school, I never would have dreamed that one day I would be sharing the stage with my favorite authors. Ursula Bielski, Richard Crowe, Dale Kaczmarek, and Troy Taylor were the top names in the paranormal world at the turn of the last century. Twelve years later, their work has given birth to dozens of writers, researchers, and other paranormal enthusiasts.

Over the past four years, I have interviewed more than thirty of those enthusiasts, including some of the big names themselves. My website, trueillinoishaunts.com, has received more than 931,800 visits since January 2009. The story of the *Legends and Lore of Illinois* goes back further than that, of course.

Its direct decedent was the *Legends and Lore of Coles County, Illinois*. During my undergraduate career at Eastern Illinois University in Charleston, friends and acquaintances introduced me to a variety of local legends and stories that had never been written about in a book before. Places like Airtight Bridge, "Ragdoll" Cemetery, Ashmore Estates, and the St. Omer Witch's Grave. I decided to do some research on them and write up a series of short monthly newsletters. I posted these newsletters in PDFs on my website for anyone who was interested to download.

In creating these newsletters, I tried to think about what would have been helpful to me in my search for information. What I wanted to see were pictures and facts. Stories were easy enough to come by. What was the *history* behind the story? What did the location look like? Most books and websites only gave their readers a vague description.

A PDF (electronic file) was the perfect format because it could contain several color photos and text that could be downloaded, printed out at home, emailed, or stored on a flash drive. I made sure that each issue of the *Legends and Lore of Coles County* contained at least five or six photos.

In addition to visiting each location and taking pictures, I used the skills I learned as a graduate student to do in-depth research on the history of each location. Research involves looking through primary sources such a property records, newspaper archives, birth and death certificates, court records, and even conducting interviews with eyewitnesses. Those sources are then used to piece together a story, a story that is (you hope) as factual as possible.

Because very few people had ever really looked into some of these stories, accurate information was difficult to come by. I spent hours searching through microfilm archives trying to get to the bottom of the stories and rumors I had been told. The result was nine issues of the *Legends and Lore of Coles County*. I even created little commercials on YouTube for the series.

After that project ended (around October 2006), I decided to begin publishing a monthly electronic publication about haunted places in Illinois. I obtained an ISSN number and called it *Legends and Lore of Illinois*.

Legends and Lore of Illinois is Born

The subject of the first issue of this new publication was Bachelor's Grove Cemetery. I picked that place because it is, without a doubt, the most well-known haunted location in Illinois (perhaps even in the United States). It seemed like a logical place to start.

One thing that would distinguish this electronic serial from the last was the inclusion of a fictional story set at the location being discussed. The idea was to stimulate my readers' imaginations and give them something unique that no other book or publication had done before. Instead of inventing whole new protagonists for these stories, I decided to use characters from previous short stories I had

written, a group of paranormal investigators called "the Fallen."

As it turned out, including these stories was so new and different from what people expected, it created a lot of confusion. I actually received emails from readers who thought the Fallen were real and that what they experienced in the stories actually happened. After a presentation at the Rockford Public Library in 2009, one audience member asked me, "Where are the Fallen?"

So why did I include the other characters in the stories? Why the P.C.P.R.S., Zealots, Satanists, and others? They are not just there for the sake of an interesting plot. Their origin is in Raymond Moody's book, *The Last Laugh*. Raymond Moody, Jr. is the doctor who first publicized the phenomenon of near-death experiences in his groundbreaking book, *Life After Life*.

The Last Laugh was a post-script to *Life After Life*. The premise of *The Last Laugh* is simple but revolutionary. Throughout recent history, there have been three main players in the discussion of the paranormal: parapsychologists, professional skeptics, and fundamentalists. Not only have these three perspectives not advanced our knowledge very much on the issue, but Moody contends that neither actually wants to resolve the debate, because in resolving the controversy they would eliminate their bread and butter.

According to Moody, fundamentalists in particular believe that everything involving the paranormal is evil and the work of the Devil. The Zealots and Satanists in my stories were meant to represent this perspective. The P.C.P.R.S. represented the parapsychologists, and also satirized many paranormal investigation teams in general. Emmer, one of the characters in the Fallen, represented a professional skeptic.

I draw other elements of the Fallen stories from Lovecraftian horror and from some of my own experiences. All of those elements came together on a stage set with the haunted and mysterious places of Illinois, creating a unique set of tales I hoped my readers would appreciate.

Touring the Mysterious in Illinois, 2007-2011

The *Legends and Lore of Illinois* premiered on the website of my publishing company, Black Oak Media, on January 1, 2007. The first issue featured an appeal for letters from my readers, a factual account of the history and folklore of Bachelor's Grove Cemetery, a short story set at the cemetery, and a couple of fictional "personal experiences." From there, the publication grew to include trivia, games, book reviews, and interviews.

I tried to get the word out as best I could. Those were the days of Myspace, YouTube, and Blogtalkradio. One of my first interviews was on an Internet radio show called Joliet Paranormal Radio. I spoke with the hosts, John and Brian, from my cell phone in a Taco Bell parking lot in Prospect Heights. I was still in graduate school at the time and had returned home to the Chicago suburbs for the summer.

I scouted locations for the *Legends and Lore of Illinois* about a year in advance, so I had all the pictures ready to go in case I was too busy to visit every location as I was writing the issue. I never knew how heavy my work load was going to be at school, and new issues always threatened to be postponed. I took great care to make sure each issue came out on time around the first of every month.

For the first two years, I posted new issues on the Black Oak Media website. In 2009, I premiered trueillinoishaunts.com, a website to be exclusively devoted to the *Legends and Lore of Illinois*. At first, I only posted links to new issues, teasers for upcoming issues, and photos. Then I added content that first appeared in the issues themselves: interviews, book reviews, games, etc. I also posted the occasional news story, if it pertained to something particularly interesting. One of my most popular series of posts was about the scandal at Alsip's Burr Oak Cemetery. In the summer of 2009, a cemetery manager and his crew dug up dozens of bodies to make more room and deposited their bones along the fence, where they were discovered by passersby. Relatives of the deceased were outraged.

My life went through a lot of transitions during those four years. I always seemed to be on the move, first from Charleston, then to Rockford, then Macomb, and back to Rockford. All the while, I only missed one issue, in November 2011. In all, I produced 47 issues of the *Legends and Lore of Illinois*. Month after month, my audience grew, from 71 average daily visits in January 2009 to 2,338 average daily visits in October 2012.

Sometimes, the most widely read issues were a surprise to me. The issue concerning Chanute Air Force Base, an abandoned air base in Rantoul, has been one of the most popular. There are over 277 comments on its webpage, mostly from former servicemen who were stationed at the base. Their friends and family have joined the discussion as well. It has become something of a message board for them, and that is wonderful. It is a great feeling to know my work has brought so many people together.

I kept a lot of bars and fast food restaurants open while writing new issues of the *Legends and Lore of Illinois*. I find it difficult to write at home, so every month I would take my notebook, post-its, and story outlines to whatever my favorite watering hole happened to be at the time. In Charleston, I alternated between Jimmy John's, Lincoln Garden, and Taco Bell. In Rockford, I would usually write at McDonald's, and in Macomb, I spent a lot of time at Hangovers Bar & Grill and Buffalo Wild Wings. That is probably why places like Taco Bell are mentioned more than once in the Fallen adventures. Of course, what is a trip to your favorite haunted place without stopping to pick up a cheap meal along the way?

It is impossible to finish this section without talking about the people who helped me along the way. Sometimes I explored the locations alone, but often there was someone who went along for the ride. I will not mention any names for the sake of privacy, but these are the folks who spent hours driving across Illinois and trudging through woods with me, who play tested the Fallen board game, sent in their personal experiences and photos, and who provided the illustrations of the Fallen characters. The time we spent together made writing and doing the research for the *Legends and Lore of Illinois* so much more enjoyable.

New Beginnings

I posted the last issue of the *Legends and Lore of Illinois* in December 2010, although I brought it back for two issues in the beginning of 2012. I have no way to know how many times each issue was downloaded in the e-serial's first two years, but between January 2008 and December 2012, various issues of the *Legends and Lore of Illinois* were downloaded over 25,500 times. Bachelor's Grove (our very first issue) remains in the top ten most popular.

Even though the *Legends and Lore of Illinois* was over, trueillinoishaunts.com grew by leaps and bounds. Most of this newfound acknowledgment was due to our top ten lists. I have been a fan of Cracked.com's lists for years, and I decided to do a similar thing for the haunted places of Illinois. I was not disappointed. "Top 10 Most Haunted Churches in Illinois" remains one of the most popular posts on trueillinoishaunts.com, thanks to a link appearing on the front page of Fark.com in June 2012. "Top 10 Creepiest Places in Illinois" has received more visits in two years than our home page has in the past four.

In transitioning away from the electronic publication, I kept up a monthly schedule of posts ranging from interviews, to top ten lists, to breaking news stories, reviews, trivia games, opinion polls, and more. I also began to include stories and personal experiences submitted by my readers. Of course, there were spotlights on previous issues of the *Legends and Lore of Illinois* as well. All-in-all, I tried to continue to highlight and be creative with the various ways in which we encounter the paranormal in Illinois.

The future still looks bright. In 2012, trueillinoishaunts.com had visitors from 161 countries, including Canada, Great Britain, India, Germany, and Australia, demonstrating that you do not have to live in Illinois to find this is a fascinating place.

In 2013, trueillinoishaunts.com evolved into Mysterious Heartland. After more than four years, I felt it was time to expand the website's geographic boundaries to include other Midwestern states. Mysteriousheartland.com will focus on unsolved mysteries, true crime, ghost stories, folklore, and books and movies about those topics. It is for everyone in the Midwest who is interested in learning more about the places, history, and events that make our hometowns unique. I hope you join me for this exciting new adventure.

INVESTIGATION FILE 001

BACHELOR'S GROVE
Midlothian, Illinois

Bachelor's Grove has been an enigma of southwestern suburban Chicago for over three decades. Like most such locations, it started out with a mundane existence. Over one hundred years ago, picnickers dressed in their Sunday best lounged under oak trees in the park-like atmosphere of the cemetery. Two of the grove's neighbors heated their small homes with coal burning stoves and drew water out of their brick wells, while horse drawn buggies trotted down the dirt road. It was a much different scene from today.

Much of the origins of Bachelor's Grove have been obscured by the passage of time. Even its name is a mystery. Some say it was named after a group of single men who settled in the area around the 1830s, but a family named Batchelder already owned the land. According to Ursula Bielski, author of *Chicago Haunts*, the cemetery itself was originally named Everdon's. Its first burial was in 1844, and the cemetery eventually contained eighty-two plots.

In the early half of the 20th Century, the Midlothian Turnpike ran past the cemetery, over the stream, and beyond. Today, the broken road appears to end at the cemetery gates, but closer inspection of a long ridge across from the stream reveals a roadbed that has been nearly reclaimed by the forest. The road was closed in the 1960s. Locals say that was when the trouble began. According to the *Chicago Tribune's* Jason George, the body of a teenage girl was found in the woods in 1966, and in 1988 a man, who had been murdered by a former girlfriend, was found in the cemetery. Aside from those gruesome incidents, grave desecration regularly occurred. Bodies were dug up, animals were sacrificed, and headstones were moved or stolen.

Then the ghosts came.

One of the most controversial sightings involved a phantom house. In the 1970s, Richard T. Crowe, a local ghost enthusiast, collected stories from dozens of eyewitnesses who claimed to have seen a white farmhouse complete with a glowing light in the window at various places in the woods alongside the trail.

UPDATE

Richard Crowe died on June 6, 2012, from complications of pancreatic cancer.

However, "there is no house on the property, nor anywhere near the site," Ursula Bielski wrote. "No property records exist to suggest that there ever was."[1] She does mention that "most anyone familiar with the area will offer to show you the foundations of a house that they claim did exist."[2]

There are in fact two separate foundations, one east of the cemetery and one west of it. Although the two are hidden in plain sight, both of them are very real. As www.bachelorsgrove.com has well documented, two wells also exist near these foundations. Hundreds of visitors have probably seen these and later reported them as "houses." Time and imagination took care of the rest.

Another popular ghost is the White Lady (or Madonna) of Bachelor's Grove. Cemeteries in the Chicagoland area are overpopulated with these women, who are almost always searching for their lost infants. Bachelor's Grove contains a monument to an unnamed 'infant daughter,' which has become a shrine for visitors and adds fuel to the story. This ghost, or one very much

---

[1] Ursula Bielski. *Chicago Haunts: Ghostlore of the Windy City* (Chicago: Lake Claremont Press, 1998), 59.
[2] Bielski, 61.

like it, was supposedly captured on a now famous photograph taken using infrared film. Unfortunately, the "ghost" in the picture casts a shadow on the headstone she sits upon, suggesting that she is not very transparent.

Visitors also commonly report seeing orbs or ghost lights, a staple of haunted locations everywhere. These bright will o' the wisps are patriotic, appearing in red, white, and blue colors. Although I have been to the cemetery nearly a dozen times, I have yet to see one.

The pond adjacent to the cemetery has its own share of legends. Stories say it was one of the hundreds of places scattered around Illinois where mobsters dumped their victims during the roaring '20s. One of these victims apparently grew a second head and has been known to crawl out of the water. Lastly, a number of years ago a policeman reportedly saw the apparition of a horse, followed by a man and a plow, walk out of the pond and cross 143rd Street. The ghost is said to belong to a farmer who drowned in the pond when his horse decided to take a swim one day.

Disappearing cars, sometimes sleek, black 1920s and '30s style, or the sound of car doors slamming, have been reported along that stretch of 143rd Street. Richard T. Crowe has written that he personally witnessed two of these phantom automobiles. Although the number of visitors to Bachelor's Grove has declined, and vandalism has trickled off (there is not much left to vandalize), the curious still routinely travel to Midlothian to snap pictures, leave cryptic notes, or place offerings at the stone of the infant daughter.

The mystery of Bachelor's Grove may never have been cracked had it not been for the timely release of the investigation files of the Fallen, a secretive team of paranormal investigators only equaled in their knowledge of the esoteric by their unyielding quest for the truth. Not much is known about the group, but their research has yielded some of the most exciting information hitherto unavailable to the public. What follows is an actual account put together from their private files...

BACHELOR'S GROVE

THE FALLEN INVESTIGATE

JAN. 3

3:15 PM

28° F

The five walked stealthily down the cracked cement road under a canopy of barren oak trees. At their head stood a stout man in an oversized black trench coat. His piercing eyes scanned the tree line as he swept the glass lens of his VHS-C video recorder from moldy trunk to moldy trunk.

Emmer, the tallest and leanest of the group (and the most skeptical) was the first to speak. "What are we looking for again?" he asked with a slightly sarcastic laugh.

"Evidence of a house," Mike, at the head of the group, replied. He stopped walking and zoomed in on the depths of the woods. "People keep seeing a phantom house out there. If there was a house, we should find some evidence of it."

"But all the books that mention Bachelor's Grove say there's no evidence that a house ever existed here," Davin, the youngest of the five, interjected through chattering teeth. "Why would they lie to us?"

"I don't know," Mike replied. "Are you sure we read everything carefully? They had to have said something else about it." Aurelia, or Aura for short, rolled her eyes and folded her arms across her chest. She was short, with tightly tied back charcoal hair. She wore a long, black skirt and heavy, platform combat boots. Her foxlike gaze barely hid her contempt.

"Hey guys," Greg interrupted, waving his cane through the air. "This is the fourth time we've been here. Maybe it's somewhere we've never looked before?" Greg never parted from his cane, which he had bought at a voodoo shop in New Orleans. He was a head shorter than Aurelia, and he always wore cargo shorts no matter what the temperature.

"Maybe it's down this trail we pass all the time," Emmer suggested while he pointed to a small deer path that diverged from the main road to the cemetery. "We've never looked there before."

"Good idea," Mike announced. He swung himself around and marched into the woods with his camera leading the way. The four followed him while Davin shivered and rubbed his hands together.

"It's really cold," he said, but the only response he received was a sharp kick to the shin by one of Aurelia's boots.

Not more than three yards down the trail, Mike stopped dead in his tracks. "Wow!" he yelled. "Hey, guys, come look at this!" He zoomed in on a twenty square foot hole in the ground, littered with rocks, old branches, and ceramic dishes of every kind. Rusted, metal pipes jetted from the ground. It was obvious to the trained investigator's eye that this was a house foundation.

The four, who had lagged slightly behind, picked up their pace and joined Mike at the edge of the foundation.

"I don't believe it," Davin exclaimed when he saw the debris. "Oh man. This is unbelievable!"

"I don't get it," Mike said as he kicked a frosted bottle out of his way. "How could no one have found this before?"

Emmer thrust a stick with an old, red tank top dangling from the end of it into the group, who jumped back in surprise.

"Call me crazy but I don't think we're the first ones to have found this place," Emmer said. He tossed the stick aside and kicked an empty can of Ice House at his friends.

Mike was speechless. He shook his head and walked around the perimeter of the depression, making sure to film all the pieces of ornamented plates, cups, saucers, old glass bottles, and metal pipes he could find.

"Maybe there's more further down the trail," Greg ventured, and then started down the winding path.

His friends caught up after taking one last look at their amazing find, but on their way down the path the five heard another group of people heading towards them. The crash of underbrush was distinctive.

"Hold up," Greg said, and held out his cane.

Two kids, a boy and a girl who looked like they were locals, soon joined the Fallen and passed with nervous smiles. "Hey," the boy said. "If you guys want to see a well, there's one just around this bend."

"Thanks," Mike muttered, and waited to curse until the two were out of earshot. "What is this, a theme park?" he asked rhetorically. "Everyone knows about this place."

"Look on the bright side," Davin said in between violent sneezes. "At least we're not in our nice, warm houses watching TV in the loving embrace of Jack Daniels."

Aurelia aimed a frustrated sigh at Davin, while Mike marched down the worn trail, over collapsed logs and through piercing, wild raspberry bushes looking for the well. Just as they had been told, it loomed a few feet off of the path. Constructed of stacked, moldy bricks, it was slightly asymmetrical.

"This is the last straw," Mike grumbled. "I'm never believing anything I read anymore."

"I told you all of this is crap," Emmer scolded him. "The only reason I come on these trips is because I would be sitting on the Internet doing nothing all day if I didn't."

"Hold on," Greg protested. "It's obvious this is a place locals know about, but you can't expect writers to know everything. I mean, they have book signings to go to. They don't have the time to actually come out here."

"Let's get out of here," Davin said. "It's freezing. I think I'm getting sick."

The five agreed, snapped some pictures, and slogged back to the main trail where they ran into the members of the Pan-Continental Paranormal Research Society, who were unpacking boxes full of equipment on the cracked cement.

"Look at them," Mike grumbled, "they have their own t-shirts and everything."

"Don't bother going down that trail guys," Greg said as the two groups passed each other. "There's nothing there, we already checked."

The professionals shot the Fallen dirty looks. "Get out of here," one shouted. "You're disrupting the energy!"

"Whatever," Mike muttered. "Do you follow us everywhere we go?"

INVESTIGATION FILE 002

GREENWOOD CEMETERY

Decatur, Illinois

Greenwood Cemetery is rumored to be one of the most haunted locations in central Illinois. According to Troy Taylor, a popular author on haunted locations in the Midwest, the land that would become Greenwood was originally an Amerindian burial ground, and then was later used by the first white settlers to bury their dead until the late 1830s.

These graves have since disappeared. The oldest visible marker on the grounds dates back to 1840, and Greenwood Cemetery was officially established in 1857. Between 1900 and 1926, the cemetery was the premier location to be buried in Decatur, but by the end of the '30s the cemetery association ran out of money and the grounds were barely maintained.

In 1957, the city of Decatur took over ownership of the cemetery in an effort to save it, but they estimated that repairs would cost around $100,000. Volunteers gathered, and after much effort, the cemetery was restored. Vandals plagued the grounds, however, and rumors circulated regarding ghost lights and eerie sounds that emanated from the old public mausoleum. In an effort to control who went in and out of the cemetery, the city sealed two of the three entrances and closed a road that ran through the woods west of the cemetery.

The public mausoleum was a failed project from the start. Built in 1908, poor construction led to leaks and subsidence in the walls. Rumors soon spread that visitors occasionally heard strange sounds coming from inside, including screams. In 1957, the building was declared unsafe, closed, and completely removed a decade later. The foundation of the building can still be seen just beneath the grass.

According to Troy Taylor, there are many stories regarding the lost souls of Greenwood Cemetery. One of the most interesting concerns the ghosts of dead and dying Confederate prisoners who were dumped at the cemetery on their way to a prison camp and buried in the hillside under what is now a memorial to Union soldiers. Years later, heavy rain collapsed part of the hill, mixing the bodies together. The hill was repaired and the bodies reburied, but many believe their spirits were permanently disturbed.

Another popular legend concerns the so-called "Greenwood Bride," who wanders the grounds in her wedding dress searching for her fiancé, who was murdered by bootleggers. Greenwood Cemetery is also haunted by phantom funerals, ghost lights that flicker in the southeastern hills, and other, more sinister apparitions. Old mine shafts are also said to exist beneath the cemetery. Rumors of collapsed graves and strange protrusions in the lawn add fuel to that legend.

Despite the manicured condition of the cemetery today, vandalism does still occur. More than a decade ago, miscreants opened the crypt of George Wessels and pulled his casket out. Unfortunately for them, his casket featured a glass covering, and they were treated with a sight they will never forget.

The Fallen conducted several investigations at Greenwood Cemetery, but for a more in-depth look at the history and hauntings of this interesting location, visit www.prairieghosts.com on the web or check out Troy Taylor's book *Where the Dead Walk* (2002).

THE FALLEN INVESTIGATE

FEB. 11

12:30 PM

43° F

The Fallen's 1991 dark blue Toyota Corolla puttered through the white, metal gates of Greenwood Cemetery with Mike, Greg, Aurelia, and Emmer inside. Their rusted muffler hung inches from the road.

"Did anyone notice that it smelled like rotten eggs on the way in here?" Emmer asked over a remix of calliope music that blared from the car speakers.

"I don't know what was worse," Greg interrupted, "Mike screaming at anyone who wasn't going over sixty-five miles per hour or the fact that we had to listen to the Insane Clown Posse all the way down here."

"Alright just calm down," Mike instructed the two as he steered the car down a side trail that ran through a cluster of mausoleums.

Greg ignored him. "Where is Davin again?"

"He said he refused to go on any of these trips until it got warmer," Mike explained. "Luckily I can message him on my cell phone if we need him to look anything up for us."

Their Corolla crested a ridge and broke into the open. A wide valley spread out before them, and the character of the cemetery seemed to abruptly change. At the bottom of the hill, adjacent to a row of leafless bushes, sat a crisp, black van with the letters "P.C.P.R.S." painted on the side. A team of six men and women wearing identical t-shirts stood on a patch of lawn and appeared to be scanning the area with sophisticated technology, followed by a television camera.

"Darn it!" Mike cursed and struck the steering wheel with the palm of his hand. "I don't believe this. How could the Pan-Continental Paranormal Research Society know we were going to be here today?"

"It's just a coincidence," Emmer suggested. "How many of these places are there? We have to learn how to share."

"Shut up," Mike replied bitterly, and he pulled the steering wheel sharply to the right. "We're going back up into this terraced area. I don't want to deal with them today."

"Is there anything up here?" Aurelia asked from the backseat.

"Let me text Davin."

Mike: Davin, get online and see is anything is haunted in this hilly area.

[›/LoRdOfDarKnesS\‹]: Let me get out of bed first.

"What's he saying?" Greg demanded.

"He has to get out of bed first." Mike set his phone down in the change tray and steered the car around a sharp curve. The phone buzzed after a few moments.

[›/LoRdOfDarKnesS\‹]: OK. Head up the road a little wayz. U R going to see a cement staircase with the name Barrackman on it.

Mike: What's the story behind it?

[›/LoRdOfDarKnesS\‹]: Hang on.

"We don't have all day here," Greg interrupted. "Tell him to hurry up."

[›/LoRdOfDarKnesS\‹]: K. There isnt much online, but according to this book, a woman in a dress appears on the stairs at sundown. No one knows why.

"He says he read in a book that there's a staircase up here where the ghost of a woman appears," Mike informed everyone as he jerked the steering wheel to the left and then screeched to a halt as he nearly flew past the short, moldy steps labeled 'Barrackman,' which were set into a slight ridge at a three-way intersection.

"Is this it?" Aura asked.

"I guess so," Mike replied. "It doesn't look very haunted." He closed his cell phone and slid it into the pocket of his cargo pants.

"It was in a book," Greg shot from the backseat. "Anything in a book has to be true. Like *Jurassic Park*."

The four opened the Toyota's doors in unison, then slammed them shut and positioned themselves around the staircase.

"Are you going to tell me when the ghosts get here?" Emmer asked sarcastically.

Greg ignored the comment and turned towards Mike. "Get the instrument out," he urged. "Let's see if it picks anything up."

Mike reached into the pocket of his trench coat and produced a small crystal that hung from the end of a black string. He dangled it over the staircase and it began moving. "My hand is shaking," he said in a characteristically monotone voice. "It's too cold out."

He looked over at Aurelia, who appeared to be deep in thought. "Aura," he shouted. "Ask your spirit guide if there are any other ghosts here."

"You mean her imaginary friend that she made up because her boyfriend is in jail again?" Emmer interrupted.

"I don't want to talk about him right now," Mike growled.

Aurelia stuck her nose in the air and turned her head with a defiant snap. "Humph!" she angrily exhaled.

"Great, look at what you did," Greg said with a poorly concealed laugh.

"Alright, fine," Emmer grudgingly replied. He removed his blue Chicago Cubs hat and folded the rim. "Sorry."

"Aura," Mike yelled again. "Please. We need your help."

Aurelia sighed and placed her hands on her wide hips. "Give me a second. You distracted me."

Emmer rolled his eyes while Aurelia concentrated. After a few minutes, she spoke. "He says the woman is lonely. She wants to get home but she can't. She feels rejected by everyone and afraid because the other spirits ignore her."

"She's kind of like one of us," Mike interrupted. "The Fallen."

Greg and Emmer both laughed.

"Alright, what else is here?" Emmer asked. "I hope we didn't drive all this way just to look at some old stairs."

"What about those tunnels we read about," Greg suggested. "Let's go over there."

The four piled back into their car and drove to the top of the hill, where the statue of a woman overlooked a trimmed lawn filled with rows of nearly identical headstones.

Mike stopped the car and got out. His three compatriots followed. "This looks like where those Civil War ghosts are seen," he announced. "Let's leave the tape recorder here while we look for the entrance to these tunnels." He produced a small recorder out of the pocket of his trench coat and placed it on top of one of the stones, while Greg snapped some pictures.

Suddenly, Aurelia called out from the edge of the hill. "I found something!" she screamed.

Mike, Greg, and Emmer rushed to her side and peered into the valley that lay beneath the steep slope. At the end of a long, straight ridge, behind the cemetery fence, a broad, brick chimney jutted from the ground. A manhole lid covered the top.

"Good work," Mike said. "Now how are we going to get down there?"

"Looks like there's only one easy way," Emmer said with a grin. He jumped off the edge, barely landed on the soles of his shoes, and slid the remainder of the way down. The rest of the Fallen hesitantly followed him, until

GREENWOOD CEMETERY

all four stood facing the chain link fence and the suspicious ridge of grass.

"Well, this is a pickle," Greg muttered. "Are we going to climb the fence?"

"It wouldn't be too hard," Emmer replied.

"It looks like that manhole has been cemented shut," Aurelia cut in. "Maybe we can dig into the tunnel from here."

"Yeah, that's a great idea," Greg sardonically retorted. "Let's dig into the tunnel."

Mike kicked some of the dirt away with his boot and struck something hard. "There are bricks under this grass," he announced from the top of the ridge. "I think they're loose." He kicked downward, and suddenly his foot broke through the wall. He almost fell down in surprise, but kept his balance, then carefully withdrew his foot. A potent, musty odor spewed forth.

"I would move if I were you," Aura prophetically warned as suddenly half a dozen large, brown rats poured from the opening and screamed in anger.

Mike jerked away and began running back up the hill towards the car, followed closely by the rest of the group.

"We can't just leave," Greg protested between heavy breaths as the four collapsed around the base of a cannon that was nestled among the Civil War graves.

"I ain't going down in there," Aurelia yelled.

"She's right," Mike said. "Maybe next time. For now, let's just see if anything comes up on these tapes."

INVESTIGATION FILE 003

DEVIL'S GATE
Libertyville, Illinois

The truth behind the mysteries of Devil's Gate, located near the Independence Grove Forest Preserve in Lake County, is elusive. What may or may not have happened there has been lost in the minds of the older generation, who have so far not come forward with the real story.

According to legend, sometime in the distant past a school stood behind the set of iron gates off of a sharp bend in River Road, about a mile north of Libertyville. One day, a maniac broke into the school and abducted several of the girls. He killed each one and mounted their severed heads on the spikes of the gate. Every full moon, the heads reappear on the rusted spikes.

Like most legends, there are very few facts to back up the story. There is no doubt, however, that an institution once stood on those grounds. According to the *Chicago Daily Tribune*, construction on what was known as the Katherine Kreigh Budd Memorial Home for Children began in the early spring of 1926. Britton I. Budd, the president of the Chicago Rapid Transit Company, funded the project. The institution itself was to be run by the Sisters of St. Mary, an Episcopal organization, and was expected to house around 150 children in its first year.

The Reverend Sheidon M. Griswold formally dedicated the home late in June 1926. At that time, fifteen buildings, including a pool and a "large farm," had been erected on the premises. In 1931, the home began to also accept destitute children and their families.

In my own research, I discovered that the three fire hydrants located on the premises were one-piece barrel model Eddyvalve Hydrants. That business was purchased in the 1940s by James Clow and Sons, the company name that is stamped on the sewer covers also scattered around the area.

Sometime in the late 1950s, Katherine Kreigh Budd Memorial Home for Children closed down. It was reopened several years later in the early 1960s as a summer camp known as St. Francis Home for Boys. Tragedy accompanied the transition. On May 11, 1961, a two year old boy named Glen Bottorff drowned in the Des Plaines River adjacent to the grounds of the not-yet-opened camp. According to the *Libertyville Independent Register*, he had been playing nearby with his sister, who ran home to ask permission to eat lunch outside. Depending on which version of the story you read, either two men who had been searching for the boy discovered his body, or his own loyal dog led them to it.

I do not know when St. Francis Home for Boys shut down, but I do know that the Park District owned the land in 1992. At some point, all of the buildings were knocked down and their contents buried on the premises. Today all that remains are cement foundations, rusted metal, and glass bottles that are slowly being reclaimed by nature, protected by a sign that proclaims it to be an "ecologically sensitive area." My own hunch is that the ghost story regarding the severed heads dates back to when the boys camp was in operation. Many summer camps have their own ghost stories. It may very well be that this one has outlived the camp itself.

NOTE

A man who attended the camp later wrote to us. His experiences appeared in the October 2008 issue of the *Legends and Lore of Illinois*.

THE FALLEN INVESTIGATE

MAR. 3

11:23 AM

36° F

The three stood in front of the spiked iron gates, dusted by cold mist that trickled from the thick, gloomy clouds above. Mike pulled his trench coat tightly around himself as Greg adjusted his knit cap. Emmer, who nearly towered over the other two, looked unconvinced as Mike explained why they were there.

"There isn't much information on this one," he said. "But the general story is that a guy went crazy, kidnapped and killed some girls who supposedly went to a private school here, and hung their heads from these gates. If there was a school, there's got to be evidence. Just like that house at Bachelor's Grove."

"But why are we here today, in the rain?" Emmer asked with annoyance in his voice.

"It's March," Greg replied. "It's always gonna be cold and rainy."

Avoiding a few puddles, the three walked off the pavement and onto the long horse trail that led into a deceptively well-maintained forest preserve. After about fifty yards, the unexpected appearance of an old fashioned, rusty fire hydrant took them by surprise.

"What's this?" Mike asked rhetorically. "Why is this just sitting in the woods?"

"Forest fires?" Emmer replied.

"Look how old it is," Greg interjected. "This was here long before the forest preserve."

"You're right," Mike said. "Let's get a picture and keep moving. We can look it up later."

"Maybe we won't get rained on so much in the woods," Emmer suggested.

The three headed off to the right-hand side of the trail, where a stand of pine trees suspiciously stood out from the rest of the forest. With an eye for the out-of-place, Mike spotted a gap in the undergrowth surrounded by weeds not more than two yards off the trail.

"I think we have something over here," he announced, but didn't wait for his companions to investigate. Parting the tall, wet grass, he stumbled onto a rectangular patch of cement, covered by patches of moss and small, chipped rocks. "Over here!" he yelled.

Greg and Emmer quickly joined him, and Greg tapped the cement with his cane. "Looks like there was something here after all," he said. "This can't be all of it though. This building was too small to be a school."

"Let's look over there," Mike replied, pointing in the direction of a small, open field that was sparsely populated with thick maple trees. The three fanned out, and not long after, Emmer stumbled upon a second fire hydrant. But Mike took the most direct route along the edge of the woods, and the sight of two strands of rope dangling from the outstretched arm of one of the trees stopped him dead in his tracks.

"Uh, guys," he called out. "Come here."

Greg wasn't far, and he also noticed the ropes, which gently swayed in the icy breeze. "That looks like it used to be a swing," he said.

"Yeah," Mike confirmed. "A child's swing. Right in the yard behind whatever building that cement slab used to be." A knot formed in his stomach, and the feeling that the story had an eerie truth behind it started to settle in.

"It's just rope, guys," Emmer suddenly said from behind them. "I found another fire hydrant over there." He stared up at the branch intently.

"Let's go back into the woods," Greg suggested after a moment of silence. "Maybe we can find something else."

Mike wiped the rain off of his glasses and followed his friends into the tree line.

Despite the fact that the weeds had yet to replenish after the winter, dead branches and raspberry bushes covered the ground. Thorns tore at the Fallen's clothes.

At long last, the three burst into a small clearing and fell off a cement ledge that rose a foot from the ground. As they looked around, they realized that the dirt under their feet was not the natural forest floor.

"I think we fell into a swimming pool," Greg suggested while examining his surroundings. "Look at these walls. They have rounded corners and are lined with blue tiles. Where else would you see that?"

"It could have been a bathroom or a shower room," Mike suggested.

"Whatever it was, it got filled in," Emmer interjected. "They probably knocked the buildings down and plowed the debris into the pool."

"Well, let's get a sample of this tile and go deeper into the woods," Mike suggested. "I have a feeling."

"It's a good thing Davin didn't come with us," Greg quipped as he climbed back onto the forest floor. "He'd get pneumonia. Then he'd die and we'd have to look for his ghost."

"That's what happens when you sit inside and play videogames all day," Mike replied. He chipped off a piece of the sky blue tile and carefully placed it into a plastic bag.

The three walked westwards through the forest until they came to a clearing, where a deer trail snaked through the slick crabgrass. In the distance, under the cover of more trees, Mike, Greg, and Emmer spotted what appeared to be a block of cement. On closer inspection, they discovered the cement supported pipes and what looked like a pump of some kind.

Emmer kicked at the thick, brown leaves that carpeted the ground and uncovered a coil of dense, flat fabric.

"Look at this," he said. "It looks like an old fire hose."

Greg was busy examining some wires that protruded from the pump. He pulled out his electro-magnetic field detector, or EMF

meter for short, and aimed it at the wires. To his surprise, the needle jumped. "Hey!" he called out. "There's still juice flowing through here."

"You have to be kidding me," Mike replied. "This hasn't been used in decades."

"Look for yourself."

Mike took the EMF meter from Greg and confirmed that there was indeed a weak current flowing through the wires. "I'll be damned," he swore. "I don't think there's any doubt anymore whether a school or camp of some kind existed here."

"But why hide that?" Greg asked. "Unless there were murders."

"Maybe they aren't hiding anything," Emmer interrupted. "Maybe they just don't give a crap. This stuff is just garbage to the park district. They've probably never even heard the story."

"I find that hard to believe," Mike replied.

"Not everyone cares about this as much as you do," Emmer countered. "Rich yuppies just want to ride their horses and roller blade down the trail. They don't want to remember what used to be here before they were even born. Hell, neither do the people who were here when it existed because if they did they would have put up a plaque or something."

Mike opened his mouth to protest, but then shut it bitterly. "You're probably right," he grudgingly admitted. "Let's head back. Maybe we can check the other side of the trail before this rain gets too bad."

"That's a good idea because I'm just about soaked," Greg complained.

The three trudged back toward the clean, wide path while the sky above them slowly darkened. In the woods on the other side of the trail, they stumbled upon a collection of rusted metal drums, broken toilets, bedsprings, and bottles of every shape and size. Emmer picked up a piece of a child's play set—a small teeter-totter. It was difficult for him to imagine someone once playing on the bent and fragile aluminum.

DEVIL'S GATE

"Look at this stuff," Mike exclaimed. "There's enough here to fill a museum."

"Unfortunately we don't have the means to haul it out," Greg said from a few yards away. "I would hate to see this crap just thrown away."

"Yeah, that would be a tragedy," Emmer muttered sarcastically. He tossed the teeter-totter aside and pulled up the collar of his damp coat. "Hey, guys, I don't mean to cut this party short, but can we get the heck out of here?"

"Good idea," Greg seconded.

Mike hesitantly agreed after taking a few minutes to sort through a small pile of bottles. "I wonder if we'll ever solve the mystery of this place," he asked rhetorically as he turned one around in his hand. "Something bugs me about it. It just ain't right. We've been here for over an hour and I have more questions now than I did before." He placed the bottle back in the pile, covered it with leaves, and rushed to join his two companions.

The drops of rain came heavier and faster, and the three raced down the trail to their car. As he ran, Mike glanced at the large field to his right and wondered what kinds of secrets were hidden in the golden-yellow grass.

"Has anyone heard the new Tristania album?" Emmer asked as the group piled into their beat up, blue Toyota Corolla.

"No," Mike said. "Is it any good?"

Emmer's voice faded into the background as Mike's thoughts dwelled on the group's discoveries that day. He knew that one day the Fallen would uncover the truth.

INVESTIGATION FILE 004

CHESTERVILLE CEMETERY
Chesterville, Illinois

Chesterville is a small Amish and Mennonite community that consists of no more than a few dozen houses located a couple of miles away from Rockome Gardens. If you are traveling from the direction of Arcola, you will have to cross the Kaskaskia River twice to get to Chesterville cemetery, once on Route 133 and once over an old one-lane bridge just north of town.

Within the neatly trimmed grounds of Chesterville Cemetery, an old oak tree stands at the edge of the woods that separates the graveyard from the river. The peculiar thing about this tree is the iron fence that surrounds it, and the old stone marker that no longer bears a name.

According to Troy Taylor, our Central Illinois ghost expert, this is the grave of a woman who turned up dead after being accused of witchcraft in the early 1900s after she challenged the conservative views of the local Amish church elders. The town planted a tree over her grave to trap her spirit inside and prevent her from taking revenge (picture something like the opening scene of *Ernest Scared Stupid...* "and here ye shall be buried..."). Her ghost can still be seen from time to time hanging around the area.

However, an alternative theory exists that the grave's occupant was a young woman who lived during the mid-1800s and was reputed to possess healing powers, as well as the ability to control humans and animals. When she died of natural causes, her father planted a tree near her grave to preserve her spirit. This is not an unlikely story, as there are a few other examples of the graves of girls around Illinois who allegedly possessed healing powers, such as the grave of Mary Alice Quinn in Holy Sepulture Cemetery in Worth, Illinois.

Planting an oak tree over the grave of a loved one has Biblical roots, and would have been reserved for someone who was especially cherished by the community. In Genesis 35:8 Deborah, Rebekah's nurse, died and was buried under an oak tree. The deeply religious Amish would certainly have been familiar with this practice.

As Chad Lewis and Terry Fisk pointed out in their book *The Illinois Road Guide to Haunted Locations* (2007), how-ever, Chesterville Cemetery is not an Amish cemetery.[3] They also have their own take on the version of the story involving the girl with healing powers. In that version, the girl was shunned for her abilities.

Like the "witch's grave" in St. Omer Cemetery outside of Ashmore, and the "warlock's grave" in Ramsey Cemetery, Effingham, the grave in Chesterville Cemetery is probably the victim of a few active imaginations. It seems that every particularly unique gravesite has a story about it, and accusations of witchcraft have just enough ambiguity to keep the tale alive. After all, it would be very difficult to prove the person buried there was not accused of witchcraft.

On the other hand, Troy Taylor alleged to possess convincing testimony from people in the community who not only corroborated his version of events, but who also claimed to have seen the ghost of the woman! Until more people come forward, we may never know for sure.

---

[3] Chad Lewis and Terry Fisk, *The Illinois Road Guide to Haunted Locations* (Eau Claire: Unexplained Research Publishing Company, 2007), 17.

THE FALLEN INVESTIGATE

APR. 11

4:23 PM

50° F

The rickety bridge groaned as Manowar's "All Men Play on 10" blared from the speakers of the dark blue, Toyota Corolla. Mike, with his thick, furled brow, nervously played with his keys behind the wheel, hoping the bridge over the swollen Kaskaskia River would hold. Davin, dressed in a plain black hooded sweatshirt and jeans, gazed out of the back window as Aurelia, with her characteristically tired face and matted hair, sat in the front passenger seat.

"Do you think it's healthy to go to these cemeteries all the time?" Davin yelled over the music.

"I don't know," Mike replied in a steady voice. "Do you think it's healthy to sit on your computer all day?"

The reply went unanswered as the three cleared the bridge and made it safely to the other side. The road curved harshly. Beyond an old, abandoned car in a small dirt quarter off to their left, sat a long, neatly trimmed graveyard. A white farmhouse and barn stood on the other side of the road, and a forest grew behind the two structures. Several horses hugged a nearby fence to get a look at the strange visitors.

Mike pulled his car off to the side of the road and handed a jar to Aurelia. "Here," he said. "Put this blueberry jam somewhere."

"Why did you buy that?" Davin asked with his own brand of excited distain as the engine and music cut off simultaneously.

"That's small-town-America jam," Mike shot back. "You can't get that just anywhere."

Aurelia rolled her eyes and placed the jar on the floor.

As the four climbed out of their car, the cemetery unfolded in front of them. It was a typical rural cemetery; rectangular and park-like, with the older graves in the back and the newer graves sprawled out near the road. A chain-linked fence surrounded the acreage, which was pressed up against the Kaskaskia River.

Mike stopped next to the gate and spread out his arms. "Listen," he said. "Silence. No Paranormal Research Society with their TV cameras anywhere."

"What are we looking for again?" Davin inquired as he pushed his way past.

"A tree with a fence around it," Mike replied. "Supposedly a woman spoke out against the Amish community in the early 1900s and was accused of being a witch. She turned up dead one day and she was buried in this cemetery. A tree was planted over her grave so that she couldn't rise up and take revenge."

"I think that's the tree over there," Aurelia interrupted.

"I don't know if I buy that story," Mike continued as the three headed toward a tall oak near the back of the cemetery. "The Amish are pacifists. They don't believe in violence under any circumstances."

Aurelia stepped around the short iron fence that surrounded the trunk of the tree. "Well, whoever was buried here we'll never know," she said and pointed at the base of what used to be a headstone. The letters 'ML' had been carved into the old granite. "Someone stole the top of her marker."

"Maybe you can try and sense something," Mike suggested.

"God," Davin sighed. "Aren't we too old for this?"

"What?" Mike responded with irritation in his voice. "No. I've been doing this for my entire life. Why should we stop now?"

"Yeah," Aurelia cut in. "Remember when we were kids and you used to pretend Lydia from Beetlejuice was your girlfriend?"

"You shut up about that," Mike shot back. "Winona Ryder is a goddess."

Davin rubbed his forehead and turned away while Aurelia took a few deep breaths and closed her eyes.

"I can just sense someone saying 'hi,' that's all," she laughed. "Just 'hi'."

"Great," Davin interrupted. "Can we leave now?"

"Stand a little closer to the tree," Mike suggested. "Let's try something."

Aurelia moved closer until she nearly touched the fence, then rested her left hand on the trunk.

"Okay. You're going to ask questions, and if the answer is 'yes' we'll hear a knock. If the answer is 'no' we'll hear two knocks."

Aurelia thought for a moment. "Are we alone?" she asked. For a long moment the three heard nothing but the wind. Then, very faintly, two hollow taps emanated from the oak.

With a grin, Mike encouraged her to continue.

"Is the ghost of the woman buried here with us now?" she asked. A quick tap followed her question, but before she could say anything else, two more hollow taps quickly issued forth.

"That doesn't make any sense," Mike said.

Aurelia shrugged her shoulders and Davin broke out in laughter.

"What's so funny?" Mike demanded.

Davin pointed up at the treetop, where a series of sharp sounds rang out. "It's a friggin' woodpecker," he chuckled. "All that time watching the Discovery Channel has finally paid off."

Mike grumbled to himself and folded his arms across his chest. "Fine, whatever," he spat. "Let's get out of here then. Maybe something will show up on the pictures."

"Probably more birds..." Davin mused as the three walked out of the lonely cemetery.

CHESTERVILLE CEMETERY

INVESTIGATION FILE 005

DUG HILL ROAD
Jonesboro, Illinois

Both *Haunted Illinois* (2004) and *Field Guide to Illinois Hauntings* (2001) erroneously place "Dug Hill Road" (or perhaps the nearby Dug Hill Lane) off of "State Highway 126." It is, in point of fact, located off of Highway 146 in the western portion of the Shawnee National Forest, nearer to the tiny town of Berryville than Jonesboro. To be fair, Highway 127 (not 126) splits off from 146 in the vicinity of that point, so there may have been some confusion over the numbers.

At any rate, this publication is not about cartography, it is about ghosts. To picture what this road must have once looked like at the time of the hauntings would take an active imagination, since the banality of its flowering fields, woods, and serine pond seem to evaporate any sense of foreboding.

There are several strange stories concerning the area. The first is a classic haunting, and according to Beth Scott and Michael Norman's *Haunted Heartland* (1985), it is "the most notorious ghost in Southern Illinois." As they described the incident, Union army deserters ambushed and killed a provost marshal named Welch in 1865. There are two versions of the story, one involving three deserters, the other involving a dozen or so. In the second version, Welch's own friend betrayed him and led him into the ambush.

Carl L. Stanton, in his collection of Illinois' Civil War stories *They Called it Treason* (2002), recounted the story of Welch's murder, which actually occurred on April 15, 1863 just outside of Anna, Illinois. Welch was killed while escorting a group of Union Army deserters that he had captured.[4]

Storytellers claim that Welch's ghost has been seen on at least one occasion. In the late 1800s, a man driving a horse-drawn wagon found the ghost lying face down in the road. According to Beth Scott and Michael Norman, the man tried to pick up what he thought was the body of a flesh-and-blood person, then returned to his wagon and drove over it(!). He never looked back, they wrote, but the authors of *Field Guide to Illinois Hauntings* claim that when the man looked back the body had disappeared. Also, a "half idiot" named Bill Smith reportedly witnessed a spectral wagon pass over his head along Dug Hill Road.[5] The wagon was a typical ghoulish fare—pulled by a pair of black horses. That is the only reported encounter with this particular phantom.

A third story pertaining to the Dug Hill area concerns a creature known as "the boger." The boger, or the boger-man, was something cooked up by parents who wanted to scare their children, according to *Haunted Heartland*. Two men have reportedly seen this boger along Dug Hill Road in the past. The creature appeared as a nine-to-eleven foot tall man who wears black pants, a white shirt, and a long scarf. No one has yet come forward to explain where this creature found someone to tailor his gigantic clothes.

Today, according to Kristina Dailing in her article "A Hill of Haunts," (*Daily Egyptian*, 2002) Dug Hill is used as a local drinking spot. Many who live in the area are skeptical of the stories. Paul Morgan, a longtime resident of Jonesboro and on whose testimony she relied heavily for her article, said he believed the stories had simply been invented.

---

[4] Carl L. Stanton, *They Called it Treason: an Account of Renegades, Copperheads, Guerrillas, Bushwhackers and Outlaw Gangs that Terrorized Illinois During the Civil War* (Bunker Hill: by the author, 2002), 83.

[5] Beth Scott and Michael Norman, *Haunted Heartland: True Ghost Stories from the American Midwest* (New York: Barnes & Noble Books, 1985), 41.

THE FALLEN INVESTIGATE

MAY 4

1:26 PM

76° F

"**T**his can't be it," Greg yelled from the front passenger seat of the Fallen's ancient Toyota Corolla as gravel cracked beneath its wheels and picturesque scenery rolled past the window.

"Look at the sign," Mike replied. He turned the hard, plastic steering wheel and the car passed under the unassuming green road sign that proclaimed 'Dug Hill Ln.'

Halting laughter erupted from the back seat, where Emmer sat beside Aurelia but distantly enough to avoid physical contact.

"We must have made a mistake somewhere," Greg insisted.

"Do you see any other Dug Hill Road around here?" Mike asked. "Look at the friggin' map." He tossed a folded sheet of paper at Greg, who made a halfhearted attempt to catch it.

Greg threw the piece of paper at the floor once it was in his grasp. "What do you want me to do with that?" he asked without expecting a response.

"Hey, there's an old barn," Aurelia announced. "Is that part of the story?"

"No," Mike shot back. His knuckles turned white as Greg and Emmer continued to laugh. Suddenly, he jerked the car over to the side of the one-lane, gravel drive within sight of a wooded hill and abruptly depressed the breaks. "We're getting out," he announced.

"But what if that booger—or whatever—thing attacks us," Greg snorted. "It's a good thing I brought my cane."

"You're going to have to be more worried about me in a minute," Mike grumbled under his breath as he threw open the door and slammed it shut.

"What is this thing supposed to be anyway?" Emmer asked. He stumbled down the grassy incline on the right side of the car, but quickly regained his footing. "Is it like Bigfoot?"

"No," Mike replied. "It was an unnaturally tall man wearing normal clothes. It could have been an Archfay. John Michael Greer says in his book *Monsters* that they sometimes inhabit hills like this."

"Yeah, or it could have been just some guy who was hitchhiking," Emmer interrupted.

"Anyway, there are also ghosts along the road."

"Well, where are they?" Greg asked impatiently. He cupped his hands around his mouth and shouted, "Heeere ghosty-ghosty-ghosty!"

Aurelia gave him a sharp kick in the shins with her black, platform shoes.

"Maybe it would help if we went to these places at night," Emmer suggested as he removed his baseball cap and smoothed his hair. "Or, maybe we would see these ghosts if we smoked some weed beforehand."

"No," Mike spat. He removed his 35mm camera from his pocket and began taking pictures of the area.

"Relax, man," Emmer said. "I was just kidding."

"Here's an idea," Aurelia interrupted. "Let's go in the woods. Didn't that article you found say something about the woods?"

"I don't remember," Mike replied. "But that's not a bad idea. Greg, do you have the video camera?"

"Yeah, I got it right here." Greg raised the camcorder up in his right hand. His left hand rested on the cane he had bought in New Orleans several years before. He believed it contained powers of attraction, but it seemed to be faulty of late.

The quartet trudged into the sparse woods, but the thrill of discovery seemed to lag far behind. After about five minutes Mike, Greg, Aurelia, and Emmer stumbled upon a pile of empty beer cans and an old, moldy sleeping bag.

"Ew," Aurelia announced.

"I don't see any ghosts here, Mike," Greg said as he zoomed the camera in on the sleeping bag. "Except maybe the ghost of virginity."

"I can't believe we drove all this way to see this," Emmer laughed.

Mike was not amused. "Darn it," he cursed. He hunched his shoulders and walked toward the car.

"Stop!" Greg yelled. "We must have made a mistake somewhere. Maybe we misread the directions."

Mike halted just inside the forest perimeter. "No," he responded. "No. This is the only road called Dug Hill anywhere around here."

"But the book says Dug Hill Road was a shortcut to the Mississippi River," Greg explained. "That means it had to run east-west. This road goes north-south. Maybe the old Dug Hill Road was a part of the highway."

"That's impossible," Mike shot back. "If it was why didn't they just say that? Why do these books have to be so darn vague all the time?"

"Maybe we should just wait until the ghosts show up," Emmer interjected with a grin. "Then we'll know if we're in the right place or not." His attention was only partially focused on the conversation. He tried to lift up the discarded sleeping bag with a branch, but the branch, which was quite rotten, broke.

"Man," Greg continued. "If this was Buffy the Vampire Slayer some creature would jump out of nowhere right about now. No one can have a conversation on that show without something crazy happening."

"Well this is real life," Mike replied bitterly.

Neither Emmer, Greg, nor Aurelia commented. Instead, they turned and walked silently back to their car.

INVESTIGATION FILE 006

RESURRECTION CEMETERY
Justice, Illinois

Resurrection Mary is undoubtedly Chicagoland's most famous ghost, hitching rides from unsuspecting commuters in the southwest suburbs for decades. Folklorists and ghost enthusiasts alike claim that Mary's story dates back to the 1930s, when the ghost of a burgeoning Polish girl was first seen along Archer Avenue near Resurrection Cemetery. According to Kenan Heise, who would later go on to write a novel about the ghost, "she is a minor cult, a shared belief and an initiation rite for teenagers. When you learn to drive... you test the myth's reality."[6]

Richard Crowe originally popularized the story in the 1970s, when he began collecting firsthand accounts and theorized that the real-life Mary had perished in a car accident in the early 1930s. "Mary supposedly was killed in a car wreck 40 years ago, and she's been coming back and going dancing ever since," he remarked in a May 13, 1974 article in the *Chicago Tribune*. Later, he elaborated that the sightings usually occurred around 1:30am.

In July 1979, the *Tribune* published a letter that claimed the last time the ghost of Mary had been seen was in August 1976 or '77, by two policemen near the gate of Resurrection Cemetery. That anonymous writer was probably referring to the most intriguing event of all related to this saga: the night that Mary left physical evidence behind.

Although most accounts of the incident vaguely refer to a "man" or "someone" at "sometime" having seen a woman in white clasping the bars of the cemetery gate, Richard Crowe revealed that the man in question was none other than Pat Homa, a Justice police officer who had responded to a trespassing call

the night of August 10, 1976 and discovered two of the bars burnt and bent irregularly, with what looked like finger impressions melted into the bronze.[7]

As crowds began to gather, the Cemetery Board tried to smooth the bars with blowtorches, which only made them more conspicuous. Finally, they removed the bars altogether and sent them off to be straightened. According to Crowe, the bars were put back in December 1978, but the discoloration remained.

Mary's paraphysical appearance has been disputed over the years. According to Peter Gorner of the *Chicago Tribune*, Mary materializes as "a pretty Polish girl, about 18, with long blond hair, wearing a white dancing dress."[8] Michael Norman and Beth Scott more or less agreed, calling her specter a "captivating, blue-eyed, flaxen-haired girl in her late teens" who wears a "long, off-white ballgown and dancing shoes."[9]

According to Ursula Bielski, however, Mary "wore a beautiful white party dress and patent leather dancing shoes."[10] In the mind of Jo-Anne Christensen, Mary is a "breathtaking blonde with light blue eyes, dressed elegantly in a snowy white cocktail dress with matching satin dancing shoes."[11] In his *Haunted Illinois*, Troy Taylor added a "thin shawl" to her appearance.

Which of these descriptions is correct? Either these authors are taking creative license, or there is a supernatural Macy's somewhere. However, it is not uncommon for eyewitnesses to give varying descriptions of living persons

---

[6] *Chicago Tribune*, 29 October 1982.

[7] Richard T. Crowe, *Chicago's Street Guide to the Supernatural* (Oak Park: Carolando Press, 2000), 219.

[8] *Chicago Tribune* (Chicago) 13 May 1974.

[9] Scott and Norman, 1.

[10] Bielski, 23.

[11] Jo-Anne Christensen, *Ghost Stories of Illinois* (Edmonton: Lone Pine, 2000), 48.

they had just seen moments ago, let alone ghosts, so there is plenty of room for speculation.

Despite these disagreements, it is generally acknowledged that Mary sightings first began in the 1930s. In 1936, a man named Jerry Palus picked up a mysterious girl at the Liberty Grove Hall and Ballroom in Brighton Park. She instructed him to drive her down Archer Avenue, and asked to be let out near Resurrection Cemetery. The young woman reportedly told him something to the effect of, "where I'm going you cannot follow," before she disappeared through the gates. Years later, Jerry's brother Chester would claim that a friend, and not Jerry, had been driving the car that night.[12]

Other early sightings included the specter of Mary causing a scene as she threw herself at passing cars. Over the years, Mary would resort to materializing as an accident victim, always vanishing as the bewildered drivers got out of their cars to survey the damage. This bloody behavior either shows two ghosts at work, as Richard Crowe suggested in *Chicago's Street Guide to the Supernatural*, or it shows that the ghost of Mary cannot be pigeonholed so easily as just another urban legend.

Mary's earthly origins are as elusive as her ghost, and several historical candidates have been put forward. A commonly articulated, but just as commonly dismissed, candidate was a 21 year old woman named Mary Bregovy, who died in a car accident while (allegedly) returning home from the O' Henry Ballroom on March 11, 1934. Mary Bregovy died in downtown Chicago, however, nowhere near Resurrection Cemetery, even though she was interred there. Also, this Mary had short, dark or brown hair, and was buried in an orchid dress. According to Ursula Bielski, a cemetery worker had told a nearby funeral director that he had seen Bregovy's ghost in Resurrection Cemetery during the 1950s. Apparently the two stories became enmeshed and Bregovy was

henceforth regarded as Mary's physical and historical counterpart.[13]

Another candidate was one Mary Miskowski, who was struck by a car and killed on her way to a Halloween party sometime in the 1930s.

The least likely candidate for Resurrection Mary was a 12 year old Lithuanian girl named Anna Norkus, who took on Marija, "Mary," as a favored middle name. She was killed in a car accident on her way to the O' Henry Ballroom on July 20, 1927. Her existence as a ghost, according to Bielski, largely depends on a "what if" scenario that might have resulted in her body being mistakenly laid to rest in an unmarked grave in Resurrection Cemetery.

Whoever or whatever Resurrection Mary was in the past or is today, her legacy will always remain as one of the most beloved specters of Chicagoland. As long as the wind whips down Archer Avenue, writers, musicians, folklorists, ghost hunters, and surprised motorists will continue to reinvent her story for generations to come.

---

[12] Bielski, 17.

[13] Bielski, 16.

THE FALLEN INVESTIGATE

JUN. 6

5:59 PM

80° F

An elderly woman scowled as she sauntered past the dark blue Toyota Corolla and eyed a bumper sticker which proclaimed 'Necrophilia is Dead' in skeletal lettering. The five members of the Fallen scarcely noticed. Mike, Aurelia, and Davin's attentions were concentrated on the seaweed-green cemetery fence while Greg and Emmer chuckled behind them.

"Let me know when you find those two bars," Emmer shouted.

"Darn it," Mike yelled back. "They could be any of these."

"Don't you have a picture of it?" Aurelia asked in her characteristically dismissive manner. She folded her arms below her chest and blew her bangs away from her eyes.

"If I had a picture I wouldn't be standing here like an idiot, would I?" Mike shot back.

"You wouldn't look like an idiot if you weren't wearing those combat boots with those shorts, buddy," Emmer laughed.

The five stood inside the yawning gates of Resurrection Cemetery. Cars honked and whooshed past along Archer Avenue not more than a few yards away.

"Why do we always do everything the hard way?" Greg asked. "Why don't we just go ask?"

"Yeah that's a good idea," Mike replied, his voice dripping with disdainful sarcasm. "Let's just go ask."

Before Mike could continue, Emmer and Greg piled back into the car and gestured for the group to follow. Aurelia sighed deeply and threw open the back door. Mike reluctantly took the driver's seat.

The Corolla puttered down the blacktop until it screeched to a halt inside the visitor center parking lot, and its four doors simultaneously swung open. Mike climbed out and strolled up the sidewalk. He stopped at the entrance to the Romanesque building. "I ain't going in alone," he yelled back at the quartet who had taken positions around the front of the car. Aurelia did not wait for the others before she marched to join him. Greg, Emmer, and Davin stayed behind.

Mike and Aurelia entered the lobby of the imposing structure where several mourning widows stood and scanned maps of the cemetery. The man behind the main desk glanced with disgust at the two as they strode up to him. He was an elderly gentleman who wore a dark gray suit and a red boutonnière.

"Excuse me," Mike said with feigned enthusiasm. "I have a question."

The old man coughed violently, cleared his throat, and adjusted the button on his shirt cuff. "Yes?" he asked in drawn out syllables.

"I'm sure you're familiar with the story of Resurrection Mary?" Mike began. "In the '70s she supposedly bent bars on your main gate and they were straightened out afterwards. Do you know which bars that happened to be?"

With a sound like a flooded engine turning over, the elderly gentleman cleared his throat again. "There's nothing like that here," he gargled. "I don't know what you're talking about."

"Yeah, right," Mike replied. Without looking at his friend, he scowled and walked out of the building with his hands thrust deep into the pockets of his jean shorts. Outside, he found Greg and Davin pointing at a family assembled on the other side of the parking lot. They ogled the oldest daughter, who was dressed more for a day at the beach than a funeral. Mike glanced to his left and to his right; Aurelia was nowhere to be seen.

"Now where the heck did Aura go?" he asked.

Davin grinned. "Who cares," he said brusquely.

Suddenly, Aurelia's shrill voice broke through the air. "I'm right here!" she announced from a few steps behind Mike, who quickly spun around.

"Let me guess," Emmer piped up. "They didn't know anything about the bent gate."

Mike rubbed his temples with his fingertips. "Nope," he sighed.

"They obviously painted over it," Greg interjected. "Why would they want that kind of publicity? This is a cemetery, not a tourist attraction."

"It is to us," Davin said.

"Well, we're not going to get anywhere standing here," Mike said. "Why don't we go across the street to that bar and see if the owner knows anything?"

"Let's do it," Emmer seconded. "I could go for a Corona."

With no protestations, the five piled back into their blue Toyota, drove out of the front gates of the cemetery, and screeched onto the crowded street, nearly missing an oncoming van. Greg tightly gripped the panic handle until they were safely on the cracked and worn out asphalt of the parking lot adjacent to Chet's Melody Lounge.

"I guess I'll just wait in here," Davin muttered.

"Oh yeah," Mike said as he threw the gear shift into park. "I forgot you're not twenty-one."

"No one is going to care," Emmer interrupted. "Just as long as he doesn't order anything. We don't want him sitting in here alone. He's going to start cutting himself again."

Davin glanced down at the expiration date he had written on his arm and laughed. "Hey guys, I'm expired," he proudly announced.

Mike rolled his eyes and climbed out of the car.

The five tramped up the handicap ramp under the dark awning and entered Chet's Lounge single file. Once inside, Emmer removed his Cubs baseball cap and folded it into the back pocket of his shorts while the bar

RESURRECTION CEMETERY

patrons turned their heads in unison to gape at the interlopers.

Mike walked straight up to the bar and ordered a beer, sliding his driver's license over the damp counter. "Has anyone in here seen a ghost?" he asked with a grin.

"Are you one of those guys from TV?" the sweaty bartender replied as he slammed down an equally perspiring bottle.

"Nope," Mike said. "We're just tourists."

Emmer thrust his hand across the bar. "Before my friend makes a jerk of himself, could I get a Corona?" he interjected. The bartender motioned for his ID and Emmer produced it from a wallet thick with single dollars.

"You might want to talk to Łukasz over there," the bartender suggested as he examined Emmer's driver's license. "He claims to have seen Mary one night a few weeks ago. Ain't that right, Łukasz?"

The Fallen focused their eyes on an aging man who was hunched over the bar with three empty shot glasses lined up in front of him. Greg, who had come in behind his friends, had the pleasure of obtaining the adjacent stool.

"That's right," Łukasz confirmed with a Polish accent so thick Greg could smell the pierogi. "I saw her. February I think. Must've been February." He took a deep breath. "Can't remember any details."

"Would ten bucks jog your memory?" Mike asked.

"Whoa," Greg cut in. "Relax man. Let the guy think."

"I think..." Łukasz wheezed. "She was standing on the side of the road, plain as day. Just like you're sitting right there now. The next thing I know, she's gone. It was the damnedest thing."

"Are you sure it wasn't just someone crossing the street in the dark?" Emmer asked as he squeezed his lime wedge and pushed it into the yellow bottle of Corona resting in his left palm.

Łukasz belched. "Nope. She disappeared."

After a few minutes, the bartender leaned over the counter and nodded his head at Aurelia, who had been looking around contemptuously.

"So, you live near here?" he asked.

"Excuse me?" Aurelia replied.

"Do you live near here?" the bartender repeated. "Are you looking for a dog? I sell Rottweilers, you know."

"Okay..."

Mike threw the bartender a dirty look and removed the quarter he had left for a tip. "Let's get out of here," he whispered to Emmer, who chugged the remainder of his beer.

Greg tossed a few dollars on the counter and spun off of his stool. "Let's go!" he yelled.

"You kids stay out of trouble!" Łukasz shouted after them as the group followed Greg out the door.

"Why can't we ever see anything like that?" Davin asked once the five were safely in the parking lot.

"I can think of a few reasons," Emmer replied.

Mike simply sighed and shook his head.

INVESTIGATION FILE 007

"CEMETERY X"
Clarksdale, Illinois

"Cemetery X." The name conjures up images of a foreboding and desolate graveyard—a secretive place known only to an elite cabal of paranormal investigators who made an arrangement with local authorities to keep its location a secret. From then on, only a privileged few would have access to one of the most haunted cemeteries in Illinois. A romantic—but silly—story. "Cemetery X," or "Graveyard X," as it is known, is actually Thomas Anderson Cemetery, located south of Taylorville near the tiny town of Clarksdale. Of the long list of cemeteries that claim to be the "most haunted" in Illinois, this is the least likely candidate for the position.

Attempts to keep its identity a secret have been mediocre at best. In Troy Taylor's book *Beyond the Grave* (2001), Anderson Cemetery, buoyed by a background story lifted from the pages of a Christian County cemetery record, was featured in a section entitled "Mysteries of the Grave."[14] That same year, the *Field Guide to Illinois Hauntings*, published by Taylor's press, Whitechapel Productions, included an entry for "Graveyard X" with the very same background story.

Additionally, passages describing Anderson Cemetery in *Beyond the Grave* are identical to those describing "Graveyard X" on Troy Taylor's website. Compare this passage from Beyond the Grave: "Anderson cemetery is not a place you are going to find on any maps. It is a typical rural cemetery that is well hidden by curving back roads..." and this passage from www.prairieghosts.com/ander.html:

"Graveyard X is not a place you are going to find on any maps. It is a typical rural

cemetery that is well hidden by curving back roads..." Aside from the name, they are identical. Even the web page for "Graveyard X" has the first five letters of "Anderson" in its address.

This cemetery's claim to fame seems to be its inclusion in a documentary called *America's Most Haunted*, which Troy Taylor highly dramatized in *Beyond the Grave* as well as *Confessions of a Ghost Hunter*. Dozens of amateur pictures of mists and orbs taken here have circulated the Internet as well.

Somewhere near the cemetery is another interesting location that I have since had difficulty finding a second time, known as "Rober's Court [sic]." It is located near a small bridge and consists of a graffiti-covered boulder and a stone cabin. Troy Taylor makes brief mention of this place in *Beyond the Grave*, but I am unaware of its history.

UPDATE

This cabin, once located near a "witch's bridge," has been moved to a park in Rochester, Illinois.

Christian County locals undoubtedly know the location of Anderson Cemetery, and it is unlikely that anyone would drive several hours just to tip over headstones. If you plan on taking the trip, please be respectful and observe posted hours.

NOTE

There are apparently two cemeteries in close proximity to each other called "Anderson." Controversy rages as to which is the real "Cemetery X."

---

[14] Troy Taylor, *Beyond the Grave: The History of America's Most Haunted Graveyards* (Alton: Whitechapel Productions Press, 2001), 191.

THE FALLEN INVESTIGATE

JUL. 11

1:45 PM

85° F

The Toyota's tires deposited a layer of rubber on the road as its breaks locked and it skid to a halt about ten yards beyond the cemetery. Mike's knuckles turned white as he gripped the steering wheel.

"What was that?" Davin asked from the backseat. "Was that the cemetery?"

Greg turned around in the front passenger seat to get a better view through the rear window. "No. It couldn't be," he replied.

"The sign says 'Anderson Cemetery,' right?" Mike attempted to confirm while also straining his neck. "This is where that old man back in town said it would be." He threw the shift into reverse and began driving backward toward the cemetery entrance. The dark blue Toyota Corolla came to a stop in front of a large, rectangular sign labeled 'Thomas Anderson Cemetery.'

"Check the book," Mike yelled at Aurelia, who sat in the seat next to Davin.

Aurelia tossed the paperback on Illinois hauntings to him, which bounced off the headrest and landed on Greg's lap. "You look at it," she yelled back.

"Jesus," Mike muttered and grabbed the book from his surprised friend. He flipped it open and began scanning the pages. "Yep, this is the one. The background story is identical to the one on 'Graveyard X' in that other book."

"It doesn't look very haunted," Davin piped up.

"Yeah I know," Mike agreed with a concerned expression. He turned the wheel and guided their car beyond the cemetery fence. He parked along the side of the gravel drive, but before the four were able to leave their car, a black van with P.C.P.R.S. plastered across its side in bold lettering appeared on the main road and pulled into the cemetery.

"Crowley's arse," Mike swore. "It's the Pan-Continental Paranormal Research Society! They must have followed us here."

"You're always so paranoid," Greg said. "They couldn't have known we'd be here. We haven't seen them since Greenwood Cemetery, over four months ago."

"Maybe they hacked into the forum," Aurelia suggested as she opened her door.

"They're not smart enough to do that," Mike said bitterly. He pulled himself out of the vehicle and ran his right hand through his knotted hair.

The four waited until the black van parked and its six occupants slid the side door open to begin unloading their equipment.

Mike took a few steps forward and yelled. "Hey! What do you think you're doing here?"

A potbellied man wearing a P.C.P.R.S. shirt turned towards him and frowned. He wore an intricately designed metallic claw on one of his fingers. "We're conducting a serious investigation," he said. "You guys need to leave."

"We're not going anywhere," Mike said.

"Man, they outweigh us forty-to-one," Greg whispered.

"Do you have permission to be here?" the man asked as he removed a small case from the van.

"Permission?" Mike replied. "We don't need permission. We're the Fallen."

"Don't you kids have some Dungeons and Dragons to play or something?" the man asked, hardly hiding his condescension.

"Okay," Greg interjected. "Why don't we both just do our things and not get in each other's way? There's plenty of cemetery here for all of us. You guys should just not stand too close together around any fresh graves. We're not digging you out if you sink."

One of the members of the P.C.P.R.S., a middle aged woman with long, brown hair who carried a tape recorder and a microphone, snorted as she walked past.

Davin, who had been standing behind his three friends during the confrontation, began walking towards the other end of the cemetery. Mike, Greg, and Aurelia soon followed.

"Can you believe them?" Mike fumed when they were far enough away not to be heard. "They should ask permission from us to be here. We always have to clean up after their mess."

"Okay, calm down," Aurelia said.

"She's right," Greg grudgingly admitted. "Let them play with their toys. Who cares? They'll never find what we came for anyway."

Mike glanced over his shoulder and then produced a small crystal on a black string when he was sure no one was watching.

"Maybe we'll find something with Emmer not here," Davin muttered under his breath.

Mike held his arm outstretched and dangled the crystal nearly a foot off the ground. It did not move. "Aura," he said, "are you getting anything?"

"Nope," Aurelia replied.

"This is supposed to be one of the most haunted places in central Illinois," Davin interrupted. "There has to be something here."

"Maybe that's what they want us to think," Greg countered. "It seems to me that some of these places just magically become haunted when someone needs something to write about."

"Well, there has to be a gateway somewhere in Illinois," Mike explained. "That's why we came out here to begin with, remember?"

"It would help if we had a diagram or something," Greg said. "We don't even know what one of these things looks like. How will we even know when we find it? How do we even know it exists?"

"Trust me," Mike replied with a grin. "It exists. Look, this isn't Buffy the Vampire Slayer," Mike said. "The solution won't just become obvious suddenly. Like 'oops, there it is, the ethereal portal! It was under the library the whole time!'"

"If this was Buffy the Vampire Slayer," Davin interrupted, "one of us would be in a band and Aura would have to become a lesbian."

On the other side of the cemetery, some of the members of the P.C.P.R.S. turned their heads towards the Fallen.

"*I am in a band*," Greg whispered.

"Whatever. Are we just going to leave then, or what?" Davin asked.

"Crap," Mike spat. "Let's poke around by the tree line for a bit. On that website someone wrote that at certain times the trees will open up into a secret part of the cemetery. Maybe there's some truth to that."

"Or maybe it's just methheads again," Aurelia suggested.

The group moved toward the weed-choked trees, which were separated from the cemetery by a woeful wire fence. Mike dangled the crystal again, but this time it began to rotate slowly.

"What is it doing?" Greg wondered aloud. "It's not pointing at anything."

"Maybe because we're already standing where we need to be," Mike replied. He glanced at Aurelia, who closed her eyes. A gust of cold wind blew past.

Suddenly, she snapped her eyes open and clutched her stomach. Her face strained to suppress the look of pain. "Something is here," she gasped. "It's hiding something."

"Alright everyone back off now," Mike ordered, and the group retreated a few feet. "This isn't what we're looking for."

"How do you know?" Davin asked.

"Because if it was, stomach pains would be the least of our concerns..."

INVESTIGATION FILE 008

SHOE FACTORY ROAD
Hoffman Estates, Illinois

The most distinctive feature on Shoe Factory Road in Hoffman Estates is an old, derelict Spanish Colonial revival style building. Just down the street, in the direction of the Poplar Creek Forest preserve, sits an abandoned farm. Both are rumored to be haunted.

The unique stone house was at one time the Charles A. Lindbergh School, named after the famed aviator and American patriot. According to John Russell Ghrist, who has written on and researched the school extensively, the current structure was built in 1929 to replace the Helberg School, named after a neighboring farmer, after it burnt down.

The Lindbergh School's first enrollment consisted of 29 students from the surrounding community. Their teacher was named Anne W. Fox, who would be employed there for most of the school's existence.

The institution was closed in 1948 when rural schools began to be consolidated into the modern Illinois public school system. The stone structure spent the next 30 years as a residence, until it became abandoned sometime during the 1970s.

According to the *Daily Herald*, an archeological survey of the property in July 1998 yielded pottery shards that could have been used by Amerindians over one thousand years ago. The archeological firm that conducted the survey for Terrestris Development Company described the shards as "weathered and hard to classify."

In 2001, the development company offered to donate the former school to the village of Hoffman Estates, but the village board was unable to find anyone who would shoulder the cost of bringing the building up to code.

By 2007, the effort to save the building had gained momentum and a small sum of money had been raised. In May, the village board debated a plan to turn the former school and residence into a museum. According to the *Daily Herald*, a final vote on the structure was put off until July, and then extended to August. As of today, the fate of the old Lindbergh School is undecided.

The only source of information on the alleged hauntings of Shoe Factory Road come from the Shadowlands Haunted Places Index. One entry claims that the stone house became abandoned after a child killed his parents. The ghost of the child, who plays with a knife, can be seen sitting on the steps.

The haunted farm, and its nefarious barn, are associated with several stories. One story has the farmer going insane and murdering his family, burying them at the middle of a circle of trees. The other has the family being murdered and hung in the barn by a mental patient.

None of these stories, to my knowledge, can be substantiated.

For more information on the Charles A. Lindbergh School, visit www.lindberghschool.org.

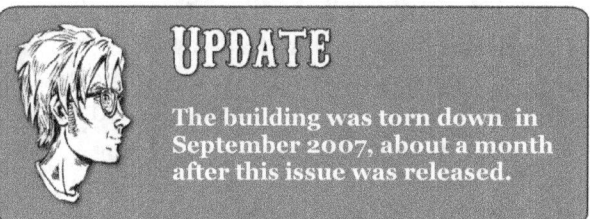

UPDATE

The building was torn down in September 2007, about a month after this issue was released.

THE FALLEN INVESTIGATE

AUG. 15

7:40 PM

80° F

"So, explain to me why we're trespassing on private property," Emmer said as Mike, Aurelia, Greg, and he climbed the stone steps of the abandoned, chapelesque home.

"We're not trespassing," Mike shot back as he took the lead and entered through the open door and into the narrow hallway. "Obviously no one owns this place."

"Man, there was clearly a sign back there," Greg said as he glanced over his shoulder at Shoe Factory Road, only a sliver of which could be seen through the rotting doorframe. The interior of the house was small and poorly lit. The aroma of mold and mildew hung thick in the air over the carpet and emanated from the peeling wallpaper. With every breath, the Fallen inhaled hundreds of noxious spores.

As Emmer and Aurelia poked around the interior, Greg pulled Mike into a small room off to the side of the main hallway. The colorful, infantile wallpaper seemed to indicate its previous use as a nursery or a child's bedroom.

"Do you really think we're going to find anything here?" Greg whispered as though it was possible to obscure his voice in such a tightly enclosed space. "We could be arrested."

"No one ever said this was going to be safe," Mike replied. "Besides, we have to explore every possibility. They could have hidden this astral portal anywhere, but they couldn't hide the fact that it would still be a magnet for the supernatural. There's no way to find it other than to investigate every single rumor of supernatural activity in the state."

"So, whoever it was that created it hid the portal in plain sight?"

"Exactly. If you want to hide a black marble, put it in a pile of a hundred black marbles."

"There's got to be a better way," Greg countered. "It would take forever to look into every possible rumor of a haunting. We can rule some of them out. Like this one."

"We can't be sure," Mike said dismissively. He forced his way past his friend and joined the rest of the group further down the hallway.

"I don't know what you guys were hoping to find here," Emmer said when Mike appeared by his side, "but all I see is a bunch of dirty carpet and spider webs."

"Why don't we check the basement and then move on to that barn?" Mike suggested. "There's supposed to be a group of dead trees that forms a pentagram on the property. Maybe that's what we're looking for."

"You guys are nuts," Emmer chuckled as he pushed his way past and carefully climbed down the narrow staircase to the basement.

The stairs were lit by sunlight that streamed in through a side door, so Emmer turned off his flashlight. Bits of broken plaster, wood, and wiring had already been ground into the spongy carpeting by whoever had been there last. He was forced to turn on the flashlight again once he stepped onto the basement floor.

The basement was nothing more than a vacant square filled with piles of debris. Graffiti covered the cement walls. Greg moved closer and inspected the neon markings. A large, yellow Latin Kings crown was intermixed with professions of love, as well as the occasional misspelled proclamation such as "we warned u not 2 com down," "northwest syde 4 lyfe," and "take notice: this property belongs to Clan Exodus."

"Most of this is just gang related," Greg said. "Nothing genuinely occultic."

Mike dangled a quartz crystal from a black cord clenched in his fist, but it did not move. "I'm not getting anything," he replied with a heavy sigh. "Let's go check out that barn."

Aurelia coughed. "Please," she said. "My asthma is starting to act up. This dust is horrible." Without waiting for the others, she climbed back up the stairs and exited through the side door. After a few minutes, the quartet stood under the shade of the trees alongside the slab rock dwelling. They quickly marched across the road and towards the abandoned farm located no more than one hundred yards away. A teetering, two-story house, the side of which had been painted orange by the setting sun, greeted them. A large barn and a cement silo stood at the end of the gravel driveway.

"That must be the barn," Mike announced as he approached the gaping, weed draped entrance. "The barn of death."

"I hope it's not the barn of death," Greg joked, "because we're the only living things around here."

"Heads up," Emmer shouted as the grinding of gravel under the wheels of a car told him they were no longer alone. A sleek, white Ford Explorer crawled up the driveway.

"Son of a—" Mike cursed. "Wait a minute. That's not the P.C.P.R.S.. Who the heck is that?"

"I think we're about to find out," Greg said as the sport utility vehicle stopped a few feet away and the doors swung open. Two men and two women, all middle aged and wearing white sport coats and pants, climbed out. The only color in their wardrobe belonged to the black sunglasses that covered their eyes. "Looks like the circus is in town," Greg added.

The two groups squared off and faced each other like characters in a Leonard Bernstein musical. Mike opened his mouth to speak, but one of the women in white cut him off.

"Good evening," she said in a deep but pleasant voice. "What are you kids doing out here?"

Offended by the woman's use of the word 'kids,' Greg sneered. "We're on a play date," he shot back.

"What do you care what we're doing?" Aurelia asked as she dug her fists into her brawny hips. The slim, black bracelets on her forearms slid down and bunched together angrily.

"Why don't we just cut to the chase," one of the men, an older gentleman with silvery hair, replied. A Rolex Daytona watch, one of the most sought after watches in the world, dangled from his wrist and his fingers were adorned with rings. "We know who you are and what you're trying to find. We've been shadowing you for quite some time."

"You're probably the ones who've been tipping off the P.C.P.R.S.!" Mike spat.

The man grinned. "Naturally. But now we feel we must come out and absolutely forbid you from continuing your search. What we're looking for is too valuable to fall into your hands."

"Excuse me?" Aurelia venomously interjected.

"What the heck is wrong with you people?" Emmer cut in, referring to the entire ensemble. "You don't actually believe the tripe that he says, do you?" He thrust a bony thumb at Mike, who returned the favor with an irritated glare.

"Thanks, Emmer," Mike responded. He turned back toward the pristinely clad interlopers. "And how do you plan on using the portal if you find it?" he demanded.

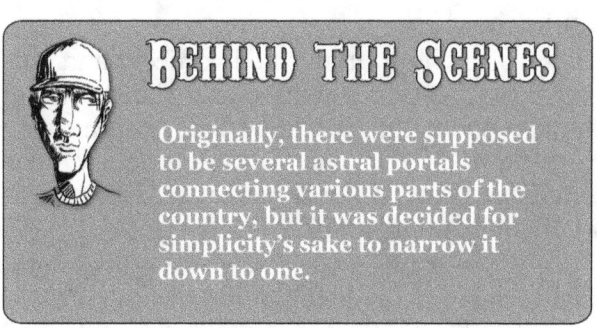

BEHIND THE SCENES

Originally, there were supposed to be several astral portals connecting various parts of the country, but it was decided for simplicity's sake to narrow it down to one.

"To spread the word of our God, of course," the silver haired man said. "Once we have unlocked this secret, all will be witnessed. We shall spread Yahweh's message of obedience

CHARLES LINDBERGH SCHOOL

everywhere, and we will not let the sacred portal and its secrets fall into the hands of evil. It conceals things the world is not ready to know."

"Knowledge is only evil to tyrants," Mike snapped back.

Before anyone could respond, a sharp siren cut through the air and a police cruiser pulled up behind the SUV.

"I thought I smelled bacon," Greg muttered.

The blue uniformed officer and his partner strolled up the driveway. The shorter of the two spoke into his radio before addressing the crowd. "This is private property," he announced after a brief exchange. "Can I ask what you're doing here?"

"Sorry, officer. We were just telling these kids to leave. It looked like they were about to cause trouble," one of the women in white said with a smile. "Especially this *witch*," she whispered.

Aurelia balled her hands into fists and sneered at the woman. With the growing redness in her face the only warning, she sprang at the woman.

The policeman was quick to react, and intercepted Aurelia before she could do any damage. His partner quickly handcuffed her and ordered the rest of the Fallen to put their hands above their heads.

The group reluctantly complied.

A short time later, through the police cruiser window, Mike saw the silver haired man smile at them as they were carted away.

"Nice going," Emmer whispered. "How are we going to get out of this mess?" He received an elbow to the ribs from Aurelia in response.

INVESTIGATION FILE 009

RIDGE CEMETERY
Tower Hill, Illinois

As far as I can tell, Troy Taylor was the first person to write extensively on Ridge Cemetery and Williamsburg Hill (not to be confused with Tower Hill, the closest town). He devoted sections to the area in a number of his books, including *Haunted Illinois* (2001), *Haunted Decatur Revisited* (2000), and *Beyond the Grave* (2001).

Williamsburg Hill is the highest point in Shelby County and is accessible by 1100 E, a road that horseshoes around the tiny community of Cold Spring. Visitors can pick up 1100 E just west of Tower Hill on Route 16, and it will lead them straight to the hill and the cemetery.

As Troy Taylor explained, the hill that Ridge Cemetery occupies once also sheltered a town, one of the many that sprung up and disappeared during the 19th Century in central Illinois. Williamsburg, as it was known, was platted in 1839 by two men, Thomas Williams and William Horsman. Many Horsmans can be found buried in Ridge Cemetery to this very day. The village disappeared in the 1880s as the railroad bypassed its inconvenient location.

The legends surrounding Ridge Cemetery involve occult rituals, spook lights, and the ghost of an old man who disappears upon approach. "There is little evidence to suggest these stories are true," Taylor wrote, "but once such rumors get started, they are hard to stop."[15]

In *Haunted Decatur Revisited*, he reported two chilling stories that a woman who lived on the hill had related to him. When she was a young girl visiting a relative's grave with her father, she said, she had apparently witnessed a phantom funeral in broad daylight.

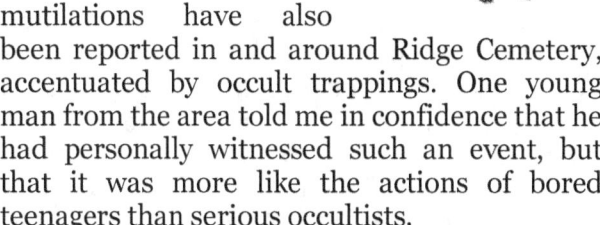

Years later, when she had a daughter of her own, her daughter developed an imaginary friend named "shadow" and had once told her that "the people in the ground" wanted her to "come and stay with them." Obviously a disconcerting episode.

Animal mutilations have also been reported in and around Ridge Cemetery, accentuated by occult trappings. One young man from the area told me in confidence that he had personally witnessed such an event, but that it was more like the actions of bored teenagers than serious occultists.

To my knowledge, Troy Taylor is the only person to have done any sustained investigation into the origins of Ridge Cemetery. I was unable to independently verify any of his information, although the Shelby County Genealogical Society would more than likely contain much of the same information.

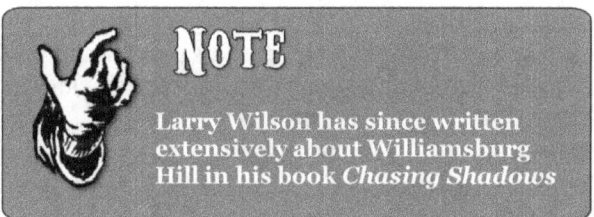

NOTE

Larry Wilson has since written extensively about Williamsburg Hill in his book *Chasing Shadows*

Ridge Cemetery is one of the more mysterious places in central Illinois. Of all the rumored haunted cemeteries, this, with its secluded location and remarkable past, is among the more respectable.

---

[15] Taylor, *Beyond the Grave*, 212.

THE FALLEN INVESTIGATE

SEP. 5

11:36 AM

84° F

Iron Maiden's "Fear of the Dark" blared from the speakers of the rickety Toyota Corolla as it transported its five occupants up the gravel road and under a giant microwave tower. The Fallen sat in their usual configuration—Mike in the driver's seat, Greg in the passenger seat, and Aurelia, Emmer, and Davin in the back. Davin appeared as though he might pass out at any time, and Emmer repeatedly wiped the sweat from his forehead.

"Hey, it beats being in jail, huh?" Greg asked jocularly. "So Mike, I guess this means you can't make fun of Aura's boyfriend anymore."

"I think our situation was a little different," Emmer chimed in while Mike merely grit his teeth angrily. "Aurelia's boyfriend was arrested for selling meth to kids at a skating rink. We only trespassed. If that's the worst thing we ever do, I'd say we're alright."

"You guys are missing the point," Mike blurted out. "If we don't find this astral portal soon those zealots will."

"Oh, here we go again," Emmer interrupted. "Can't we ever go anywhere anymore without that coming up?"

"*It's important*," Mike insisted.

"It's stupid," Greg said as their car came to a stop at the chain link fence in front of the cemetery. "We don't even know this thing exists."

"Well, those guys in the SUV seemed to know about it, so it must have some basis in reality," Aurelia chimed in.

Davin leaned against the door and didn't participate in the conversation. The engine shut off. Emmer shoved Davin out of the car and headed for the gates.

"Wait a minute," Greg said as he took off toward the tree line. "I have to take a leak." He went no more than a few steps when he stumbled upon a gruesome scene. A corpse in an advanced state of decay lay sprawled in the leaves and gravel at the edge of the forest.

Moments later, Mike arrived at his side. "That doesn't look human," he said. "It's too big, and it has hooves. Look at the skull too. It's obviously a deer."

"I know it isn't human," Greg replied, "but look at the way it's arranged. Its limbs are laid out in an 'X.' It didn't just die that way."

Aurelia elbowed her way between the two. She cleared some of the leaves with a stick and revealed several melted nubs of black candles. "Someone tried to perform a ritual," she theorized. "A sloppy ritual, but interesting anyway. I don't know of any covens around here."

"Could have been anyone," Greg said.

"It could mean we're on the right track," Mike replied.

Emmer laughed. "Yeah," he said. "It could also mean that someone around here has been listening to a little too much Cradle of Filth."

Mike snapped a few pictures, then suggested that the group move on.

The five walked into Ridge Cemetery. Emmer and Greg stood and talked under a tree while Mike and Aurelia scoured the area. Davin loitered alone near the chain link fence.

"Please tell me you think this whole portal thing is not just stupid, but a little crazy," Emmer said to Greg as he watched Mike, holding a string with a crystal attached to the end of it, pace in the distance.

"I admit that we're probably wasting our time," Greg replied. "Is it possible an astral portal exists somewhere? Sure. I just don't think we have enough information to find it."

"Where the heck did he come up with this idea?"

"It started when we were all back at College at St. Sebastian's," Greg explained. "Mike found a few loose pages in one of the old books in the library. The only problem was that it was written in Latin, so it took us a while to figure out what it said. Apparently the religious order that founded the college believed they had discovered a number of gates that could transport you anywhere on earth, or anywhere on the astral plane.

"The trouble was that they based their information on Indian legends and stories from French fur traders. Mike decided that they were describing a location somewhere in what is now Illinois, but it could have been anywhere in the Midwest, or it could have just been a rumor."

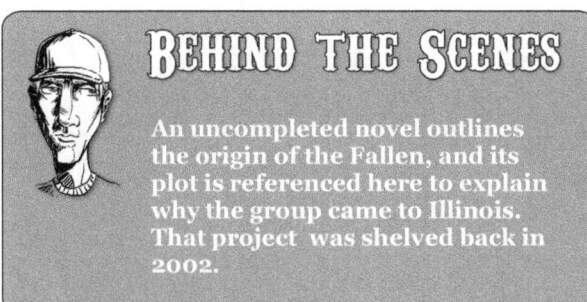

BEHIND THE SCENES

An uncompleted novel outlines the origin of the Fallen, and its plot is referenced here to explain why the group came to Illinois. That project was shelved back in 2002.

"So that's why he insisted on coming out here," Emmer interjected. He chuckled. "Poor guy. We come all this way, he goes on a wild goose chase, and Aurelia hooks up with a scumbag. Now we're being stalked by religious nut jobs."

"Man," Greg said, referring to Aurelia. "That girl is frightening."

At the other end of the cemetery, Mike and Aurelia paced near some of the older headstones. Aurelia, wearing her usual summer attire of camouflage pants, a black tank top and platform boots, made sure to stay within a few paces of her companion.

"I think Emmer might have a point," she said as Mike growled in frustration at the instrument in his hand, which showed no results.

"Not you too," he whined.

"Look, we went to Bachelor's Grove—"

"And found a couple of foundations," Mike interrupted.

"Greenwood Cemetery," Aurelia continued as though Mike had said nothing. "Resurrection Cemetery. Some of the most haunted places in Illinois, plus a bunch of obscure places that had nothing there. We've found nothing. Maybe there's nothing there to find."

"You need to be patient," Mike said. "You can't expect everything to just unfold immediately."

"Screw that," Aurelia countered. "I want it now." She laughed and gave her friend a playful shove, which sent him stumbling.

Suddenly, Greg's voice rang out across the graveyard. "Mike!" he shouted. "Get over here!"

Mike rolled his eyes and pocketed his crystal instrument. "Let's go see what they want," he grumbled.

As Mike and Aurelia neared the rest of the group, they found Greg and Emmer laughing and examining Davin superficially.

"What's wrong with him now?" Aurelia demanded.

"He said he got the chills suddenly, like the temperature dropped to below zero," Greg explained. Davin appeared pasty and pale, but that was not necessarily out of character.

"Maybe this has something to do with that corpse we found earlier," Mike wondered aloud.

"Davin gets sick twenty times a week and this time it's due to supernatural causes?" Emmer snapped. "Do you realize how crazy that sounds?"

"I'm just throwing out possibilities," Mike defensively retorted.

"Yeah."

Davin's teeth chattered and he visibly shook. "I think I need to go home, guys," he stuttered. "Something isn't right here."

"Oh, great," Emmer said. "Now he thinks he's cursed too."

"Wait a minute," Greg interrupted. "Do you hear something?"

The Fallen fell silent. Oddly, the usual background noises—birds, crickets, cicadas, etc.—were absent. The wind blowing through the nearby trees was the only audible sound, until, very faintly at first, an electric hum pierced the air. The clamor did not seem to come from any easily discernible direction.

"Okay, now that's creepy," Emmer admitted.

"Maybe it's those zealots," Greg suggested.

Mike shook his head. "No, they would never do anything like this. It's too Satanic for them. They would rather be martyred than attack anyone."

"Clearly we should leave," Emmer said. "Whatever the explanation. Davin needs to go lie down."

At his words, the chain link gate, which they had left open, swung shut with a clatter. The five jumped and spun around.

"I told you guys!" Mike shouted triumphantly. "The closer we get the more hostile things seem to become. We're on the right track."

"I wouldn't count your chickens before they hatch, buddy," Emmer laughed.

Helping Davin, the Fallen climbed over the fence and headed for their car.

INVESTIGATION FILE 010

CUBA ROAD
Lake Zurich, Illinois

Cuba Road has received some attention from writers of ghost lore. Two of the original and most authoritative writers on Chicagoland ghosts, Richard T. Crowe in *Chicago's Street Guide to the Supernatural* (2001), and Ursula Bielski in *More Chicago Haunts* (2000), have selections of work on it. Scott Marcus devoted an entire chapter to the road in his book *Voices from the Chicago Grave* (2008).

Cuba Road sits nestled between the towns of Lake Zurich and Barrington, both upper and upper-middle class retreats. The main portion of the road runs between Route 12 and Route 14. Its legends are numerous. White Cemetery, located on the eastern half of the road, has its spook lights. The avenue itself hosts a phantom car (or cars), a pair of spectral lovers, and a vanishing house. Rainbow Road, a side street, formerly had the distinction of being home to an abandoned mansion or farmhouse that some believed was an old asylum.

White Cemetery is usually the focal point of this lore. The small, rectangular graveyard is said to date from the 1820s, undoubtedly a local family plot at the time of its establishment. Mysterious, hovering balls of light are most often associated with White Cemetery, but other unusual occurrences have been described as well. Richard Crowe related the story of a young man who witnessed the gates unexplainably change position, from open to closed depending on when he drove past that particular night.[16]

The vanishing house of Cuba Road is said to appear in the woods near White Cemetery. It is a small dwelling, apparently occupied by an elderly woman. Legend says that the house burnt down long ago, but it still makes an appearance on some moonlit nights. Apparently there is concrete evidence that a house did actually burn down along the road at some point in the past, but I have not seen it.

In the summer months, according to Ursula Bielski, "a mysterious couple walks arm and arm along the deserted stretch of roadway, vanishing into the horizon."[17] I have never heard an explanation of who this couple is or what event propelled them into the afterlife.

Phantom automobiles also make an appearance along the road. Bielski believes the ghosts of gangsters are the occupants, but other accounts point to a popular urban legend as the origin of this tale. Friends familiar with the Cuba Road folklore have informed me that a pickup truck, blaring its headlights, tries to run unsuspecting drivers off the road. Most likely, the same urban legend that inspired that tale also inspired the opening scene in the movie *Jeepers Creepers*.

Then there is the "asylum" off Rainbow Road, which is accessed via Cuba Road. This abandoned mansion, or perhaps a large farmhouse, inspired many trespassing attempts. The property has been recently reclaimed, however, and is being sold as "Kaitlin's Way."

As long as gas prices do not discourage the traditional weekend drive, I believe Cuba Road will continue to draw ghost and curiosity seekers alike.

---

[16] Crowe, 166.

[17] Ursula Bielski, *More Chicago Haunts: Scenes from Myth and Memory* (Chicago: Lake Claremont Press, 2000),158.

THE FALLEN INVESTIGATE

OCT. 8

10:20 PM

74° F

The inarticulate shrieks of Alexi "Wildchild" Laiho reverberated around the cabin of the dark blue Toyota Corolla. Aurelia registered her disapproval of the music with a loud groan while Mike swerved onto a darkened side street.

"Will you turn this crap off," Aurelia demanded as she reached for the volume dial.

Mike intercepted her hand as it crossed over the cup holder. "Man," he said, "you can't turn off Children of Bodom."

Aurelia twisted out of his grasp and dug her fingernails into his forearm. "Yes, you can," she insisted.

Tearing his arm away, Mike braked just in time to avoid two raccoons that scampered across the road. The Toyota's brakes locked and its two occupants jolted forward.

Aurelia screamed, but quickly regained her composure when she realized that no damage had been done.

"Jesus," Mike blurted. "You almost made us crash!"

"Oh, go screw yourself," Aurelia replied. "Are we almost there?"

Mike turned down the volume on the tape deck. "Well," he said, "this is Rainbow Road. I'm not sure where the entrance to the asylum is."

The dark blue Toyota carefully navigated several more curves in the road, until a gate appeared along the left hand side. Overgrown weeds and shrubbery indicated that it had nott been used in many years.

"Something tells me we just found it," Mike whispered as he slowed the car down to a crawl and guided it to a stop on the gravel shoulder.

"We're not going in there are we?"

"Of course we are," Mike responded. "Why do you think we came all the way out here?"

"Wasn't getting arrested for trespassing once this year enough for you?" Aurelia asked as she unbuckled her seatbelt and opened the passenger door.

"We're not going to get arrested," Mike insisted. "It's already past ten, who is going to be on this road?" He exited the Toyota and slammed the door. "Just because those other jerks bailed on me, don't bail on me too."

"Greg, Emmer, and Davin bailed on us because this little quest of yours is leading nowhere," Aurelia corrected him.

"Ye of little faith," Mike retorted. With a press of his thumb, the electric torch he held in his hand lit up. He scanned the perimeter of the gate, and discovered that it was not immediately connected to a fence.

"I have a bad feeling about this," Aurelia whispered as she followed him through the gap and onto the property.

The chirp of crickets was the only sound that greeted them as they made their way down the tenebrous driveway. The beam of their flashlights traced the contours of trees and bushes, looking for any sign of a building.

At last, the two found themselves adjacent to a small pond. Across the pond, on the other side of an old silo, stood an unusually large farmhouse. All of its windows were missing, and its white walls were covered in dirt and graffiti.

"Jackpot," Mike whispered.

Aurelia tossed her head back to see if anyone had followed them onto the property. The drive was as dark and lonely as it was when they had first entered. Never the less, she felt a shiver crawl up her spine.

"Something doesn't feel right," she said. "I think someone else is here."

"Nonsense," Mike responded. "We're not going back. If anyone else is here, let them come out and cause a problem."

Putting one boot steadily in front of the other, Mike marched towards the front door of the farmhouse while a cold wind rushed past.

The large porch wrapped around the front and side of the house. An old swing lay shattered on the porch, but it was, aside from a generous collection of empty beer cans, otherwise barren.

Mike and Aurelia climbed the stairs and found that the front door had been removed from its hinges. Inside, the yellow circles projected from their electric torches fell on empty rooms and more graffiti.

"It doesn't look like anything is here," Aurelia said.

"Thanks," Mike replied sarcastically. "Maybe there's something further in, or on the second floor."

Suddenly, he stopped dead in his tracks and his eyes strained in the darkness to take in the whole picture. A deep red pentagram had been painted onto the hardwood floor in the living room. He estimated that the symbol was several yards in diameter.

"Is... is that blood?" Aurelia blurted.

"Let's not jump to conclusions," Mike said, "but it sure looks like it to me." His voice failed to hide a kind of excitement. "What did I tell you? Didn't I say we were on the right track?"

As his mouth closed, a family of opossums scurried through the living room and almost ran into Aurelia, who shrieked.

"Blast it!" she screamed. "Why do these freaking animals keep coming around us?!"

"Maybe they smell something," Mike offered, but before he could finish his thought, the stairs creaked.

Mike and Aurelia trained their flashlights on the interloper, whose pressed, white suit and sunglasses immediately gave her away.

"Not you again," Aurelia groaned.

The middle-aged woman with curly, brown hair and rosy cheeks thrust out her hand, which clutched a large, wooden cross. "Stay where you are," she ordered.

"We're not vampires, you idiot," Mike spat.

"What were you doing here?" the woman demanded as two silver-haired men entered the living room from the direction of the back of the house. "What were you going to do with this pentagram?"

"What?" Mike said. "We didn't make this."

"Right," one of the men replied. "The days of you scum taking over old buildings like this are over."

"Look, man," Mike attempted to reason, "we didn't do any of this. How do we know that you didn't do it to set us up? You were obviously here waiting for us this whole time."

Another woman dressed in white stepped through the front door. The group now had all of the exits blocked. Aurelia, who had been quiet since the first one appeared, spun around and grit her teeth.

"There are no cops around this time," she hissed. "Do you really want to find out what would have happed if they didn't stop me?"

The woman in the doorway seemed to hesitate and took a few steps backwards. She looked up at the matron on the stairs for help.

Aurelia smiled.

"What are you going to do?" Mike said defiantly. "Jesus preached compassion and nonviolence. If you are really Christian, you'll just let us walk out of here."

"Don't you dare tell us what it means to be Christian!" the brown haired woman yelled, but her companions exchanged confused glances.

Mike and Aurelia were unhesitant in their reaction. The two bolted for the front door, straight at the woman who blocked their way. Working in unison, they shoved her aside. She stumbled and fell against the porch.

Halfway down the stairs, Aurelia faltered. "I twisted my ankle!" she cursed.

Mike doubled back and slung Aurelia's arm around his shoulder. As the two men and two women in white suits and sunglasses spilled out onto the porch, Mike and Aurelia turned off their flashlights and steadily made their way back down the driveway.

"Crowley's arse that was close," Mike panted. "How the hell did they get in there without us knowing?"

"I told you I sensed something," Aurelia replied as she winced in pain.

Moments later, the two were safely in their car and on their way home.

INVESTIGATION FILE 011

MT. PLEASANT CEMETERY
Claremont, Illinois

Mt. Pleasant Cemetery is one of those places, like Shoe Factory Road, that has developed its legends within the past decade or so. This means that it is an exciting prospect for folklorists. The ingredients are all there: one out-of-the-way rural cemetery and one abandoned church, add a dash of imagination and a couple of mischievous nighttime visits, and there you have some brand new legends and lore.

There may be little to no history behind the location, just a parade of stories with no real basis in fact. Still, outsiders wonder. Why did the church close? When did the church close? Are these paranormal experiences credible? Where can I find more information?

I am going to teach you, dear reader, how to investigate and research a location like Mt. Pleasant Church and Cemetery.

"Olney – Mt. Pleasant Cemetery - An old church stands at the front of the cemetery. This church is said to be haunted. When the front door is knocked on sounds are heard within the church, sometimes choirs, footsteps and strange lights. On some nights funeral sessions are seen at the church. Although no funerals have taken place there since the 50's."

You come across this entry in the Shadowlands Haunted Places Index for Illinois. How do you proceed from there?

First, you know nothing if you do not know exactly where the cemetery is located. The entry says it is located in Olney, but do you know that for sure? Before you get into your car and go on a wild goose chase, you need to check the Internet. There are several GPS sites that allow you to locate place names. You will discover that Mt. Pleasant Cemetery is not in Olney, but is, in fact, several miles southeast of there.

Print out the map. Take it with you when you go there (you would be surprised how many people forget this essential step).

Once at the location (in the daytime), try to confirm as many facts as possible. Yes, there is actually a cemetery and an abandoned church. But what do you know about the church? Nothing right now, so you might want to venture inside. This carries risk because you may be breaking the law, so it is a good idea to get permission from the owners. But, keep in mind that they might not give you permission and might be openly hostile to you when they find out why you want to go inside.

You discover an old calendar on the wall while snooping around. It is open to September 1990, which is an excellent indication of when the church closed. Finding nothing else of note, you leave, making sure to take pictures for reference.

Now comes the fun part—research. The local genealogical society (often part of the public library) might have basic information on the church. They would be able to tell you when it was built and what denomination worshiped there. To find out the circumstances surrounding its closure, however, you will want to find microfilm archives of the local newspaper.

Any library worth its salt will have at least one microfilm machine. In this case you will have to go to Olney. Search the archives for September 1990 and see if you can find an article on the closure. That might also dredge up names for possible interviews.

You will be well on your way to becoming an expert on any haunted location with these basic tools. Have fun—be your own detective.

THE FALLEN INVESTIGATE

NOV. 5

3:00 PM

56° F

"Well, I'm glad that a few more people decided to join us this time," Mike said to the sparse gathering at the top of the hill, "considering what almost happened last month."

"I'm only here because I want to see you humiliate yourself again," Emmer chuckled.

Aurelia bit her bottom lip in a failed effort to prevent herself from smiling as Mike glared angrily at his two companions.

The trio stood at the edge of the small, crab grass infested gravel parking lot kitty corner to a gray, one room church. Two country roads converged at the bottom of the hill, several yards away. The frosty wind assaulted the few remaining leaves on the trees that lined the roads.

Mike pulled his heavy, leather trench coat taught around his waist. With a determined glare, he turned toward the chipped, off-white wooden doors of the church.

"If you two are done," he said, "prepare yourselves to witness what we've been searching for all these months. You doubted me before, but I am almost absolutely certain that this is the place where we will finally open the portal to the astral plane."

"Alright, let's see it," Emmer said impatiently.

Mike cracked his knuckles and seized the door handles. The lock seemed as though it would give with a minimal effort.

The doors shook violently as Mike attempted to force them open. As he stepped back to prepare for another attempt, a faint buzzing sound filled the air.

"Do you guys hear that?" Aurelia asked with detached concern as a handful of tiny wasps lumbered past her head.

"What?" Mike snapped.

Suddenly, a deep crack in the siding above the door came alive with hundreds of tiny wings.

"Look out!" Emmer shouted. He stumbled backward toward the car.

"It's only a bunch of bees, stop being a baby," Mike scolded.

"I'm allergic to them, jerk," Emmer shot back.

"It's November. I'm surprised they're not all hibernating."

Aurelia swatted away the stray wasps with a wrist full of bracelets. "There, they're gone," she said. "Let's just get this over with. We didn't come all this way to get scared off by a bunch of insects."

"You're right," Mike heartily agreed. "Everyone step back. We don't know what's going to happen when I open this door."

Mike leaned in and on closer inspection discovered that the padlock holding the door closed was not even secured. He slipped the lock from its position and grasped the door handles.

Aurelia's voice cut through the air. "What are you waiting for?" she demanded.

"Are you sure you're ready?" Mike replied.

"*Just open the darn door already,*" Emmer interjected.

With a forceful tug, Mike yanked open the double doors and a gust of wind blew out from the opening. Nothing but dust and a nearly empty room greeted him.

Emmer burst into laughter.

"Now hold on," Mike shouted. "You can't expect this thing to just manifest itself. It has to be called forth."

"Alright there buddy," Emmer said. "I think we've done enough for today."

Mike glared at his friend and procured a piece of yellowed paper from the pocket of his trench coat. "I need to recite this incantation, jerk off," he hissed.

Clearing his throat, Mike began. *"Anail nathrach, uatha bha'is, bith thonn du'iseacnt,"* he chanted, his voice growing steadily louder, *"le de'anamh E!"*

Thick clouds gathered high above the church, but nothing happened. Poorly contained laughter reverberated throughout the interior.

Mike stepped resolutely inside the building and recited the ancient words once more. *"Anail nathrach, uatha bha'is, bith thonn du'iseacnt, le de'anamh E!"*

Again, nothing.

"Come on, let's go before we get arrested again," Emmer said. He pulled his baseball cap from his head and ran his fingers through his stringy, blonde hair. Standing nearly a foot taller than the others, he would have had a commanding presence if not for his poor posture and nervous demeanor.

Aurelia stepped out of the way as Mike stormed past. He tucked his trench coat beneath his rear and sat under a tree.

"What, are you pouting now?" Aurelia asked.

"What did you expect, man?" Emmer cut in. "You knew it wasn't going to work. You've never even seen a picture or an illustration of this thing you're looking for. You've never seen it located on a map or even heard it mentioned anywhere else. I hate to be the one to break it to you, but the invisible and the non-existent look very much alike."

"I hate to admit it, but he has a point," Aurelia added.

A long period of uncomfortable silence followed, then Emmer chuckled nervously.

"So," he stuttered, "did anyone see the game on Sunday?"

Mike slowly turned his head, his face contorted into a look of anger.

Before he could open his mouth, a black van crept up the gravel drive toward the cemetery's meager parking lot. It did not seem possible, but his face turned an even deeper red.

He rocketed to his feet as the van came to a stop. The letters P.C.P.R.S. were plastered across its side.

"Uh oh," Aurelia whispered.

A middle aged man, his face and fingers smeared with orange Cheetos dust, climbed out of the driver's seat. One other man and two women quickly joined him. Each wore a crisp, new windbreaker with P.C.P.R.S. emblazoned above the breast pocket in yellow. One of the women held a small dog at the end of a leash. It growled and barked at the Fallen.

"You've got to be kidding me," Mike snapped. "How did you know we were here? Did those zealots tell you?"

"Oh look, they're out of jail," the man covered in Cheetos dust said.

"As a matter of fact," his companion added, "they did. Not that it's any of your business. We're sick of you amateurs giving us a bad name."

"Amateurs!?" Mike repeated.

"We've reported you to the paranormal police for violating our code of conduct," one of the women condescendingly informed the trio.

Emmer burst out laughing. "The paranormal police? Give me a break! Don't you people have jobs and families?"

"Who are you?" the woman demanded. "And why are you here if you don't believe in any of this?"

"God made me an atheist," Emmer replied. "Who are you to question his wisdom?"

"Enough!" Mike yelled. The two groups fell silent, equally surprised by the uncharacteristic burst of emotion. "I am sick of you following us around and then accusing us of getting in your way. I don't care how many times you've been on TV or how many books you've written. You have no right to tell us what to do or where we can and can't go. You don't have any more claim to this place than we do. If the owners want us gone, that's one thing, but screw your 'paranormal police' and screw your rules."

The man covered in Cheetos appeared flabbergasted.

"You can tell that to your friends too," Mike added. "I don't know who has been leaving those Satanic markings around, but it ain't us. I'm sick of you people blaming us for everything just because we don't conform to your idea of what we should be doing."

"Maybe we should get out of here," one of the women attempted to whisper.

"Don't bother," Aurelia said, "we were just leaving."

As the Fallen made their way to their car across the parking lot, the leader of the P.C.P.R.S. struck Mike with his shoulder. "This isn't over," he whispered.

Mike grinned.

INVESTIGATION FILE 012

ST. JAMES-SAG
Lemont, Illinois

St. James of the Sag Church and Cemetery, abbreviated as St. James-Sag, sits on a bluff overlooking the juncture of the Chicago Sanitary and Ship Canal and the Calumet Sag Channel. Two roads, Archer Avenue (Route 171) and 107th Street also converge at this point. It is the tip of a heavily forested triangle in between Palos Hills to the east and Lemont to the southwest.

The area has a long history. According to Richard T. Crowe, there is evidence that French explorers used the bluff as an observation post as early as the 1690s, and before that, Amerindians camped there and may have lived nearby.[18]

The church and cemetery also have distant origins. One burial can be traced to 1818, but the graveyard began to be heavily used in the 1830s when Father St. Cyr built a log chapel to accommodate the spiritual needs of the Irish canal workers. St. James-Sag was in fact the second Catholic house of worship founded in the Chicagoland area. The limestone building that exists today was built in 1850.

As the geographic focal point of the area, St. James-Sag also happens to be the supernatural focal point, if you believe the stories.

In her book *Chicago Haunts* (1998), Ursula Bielski claims that phantom monks have been seen at the location since at least 1847, but failed to share more information.

The earliest substantiated encounter at the church involved two musicians, William Looney (no pun intended I'm sure) and John Kelly, who spent the night at a dance hall located at the base of the bluff along Archer Avenue in September 1897. That night, William awoke to a commotion outside. The sounds of a horse and carriage were clearly audible from the road, but there was none to be seen.

William woke his friend, and this time a woman in white, who looked like she was in a state of despair, appeared in their field of vision. She seemed to be impatiently waiting for something. After a moment, the two men claimed that a carriage materialized on the road. The woman merged with it and disappeared. The scene reoccurred twice before fading completely.

John and William's story appeared in local newspapers and apparently went forgotten until recently, when it was rediscovered by folklorists.

The phantom monks continued to make appearances over the years. According to Richard T. Crowe, a police officer by the name of Herb Roberts encountered nine of the monks in the early morning hours of the day after Thanksgiving, November 1977. The officer reported that the robed figures ignored him when he ordered them to stop from behind the gates of the cemetery. The figures seemed to disappear as he pursued them inside.[19]

Several sources have also reported that a priest stationed at the church had observed the ground moving up and down as though it were breathing.

There are plenty of theories as to why this location attracts paranormal phenomenon, but none have adequately explained the presence of such a wide and diverse variety. One thing is for sure, we have not heard the last of St. James of the Sag.

---

[18] Crowe, 239.

[19] Crowe, 240.

THE FALLEN INVESTIGATE

DEC. 29

4:30 PM

21° F

"**Y**ou see," Greg explained as he traced a line across the map with a shivering finger, "I didn't notice this until just the other day. I think you were on the right track last time, picking a church as the location of the portal, but you missed these indicators."

Mike, Greg, Aurelia, and Davin stood outside of their rusted Toyota Corolla under the arching sign that greeted visitors to St. James of the Sag Church and Cemetery. A foot of thick, pillowy snow covered the ground. Mike folded his arms across his chest, his black leather trench coat making it appear as though his upper body was disproportionately large.

"Look at how all these haunted places follow the contours of the landscape," Greg continued. "Everything comes together here, at this bluff. This cemetery is the apex, and I bet you this is the location of your astral gate."

"Good work," Mike complimented. "You've been busy lately."

"You didn't think I gave up on you, did you?" Greg replied with a grin.

"Let's get this over with," Davin interjected through chattering teeth. "I'm going to catch pneumonia out here."

"Not again," Aurelia groaned as she gave him a hard shove. "I'm not wearing half of what you are, and do you hear me complaining?"

"*That's because you're insane,*" Davin shot back.

"That's enough, you two," Mike shouted. He spoke with authority, but his tone betrayed a gnawing eagerness. "We don't have time for that today. We need to get up to that church and open this gate."

The four piled back into their car and pulled into the main parking lot, which lay under the watchful eyes of the administrator's residence. Trying not to attract attention, the Fallen quietly stepped out of the Toyota and shut their doors. Aurelia stubbornly slammed hers, drawing sharp looks from the others.

"Nobody cares," she said defensively.

Greg rolled his eyes and marched toward the gate that led into the cemetery. "There's no telling where this portal is," he announced, "so we're going to have to fan out. Wave if you feel anything out the ordinary. We all have crystals, right?"

"I don't think splitting up is such a good idea," Mike interrupted. "We don't know what kind of things might happen if one of us stumbles upon the astral gate alone. From what I read, we don't want to find out. The monks at St. Sebastian's destroyed their monastery trying to master this, remember?"

"Yeah, but that was them, and this is us, the Fallen," Greg smirked. "We've faced worst things before."

"Don't remind me," Mike grumbled.

"Fine, we'll split up into groups of two," Greg suggested. "I'll take Davin and you take Aura. We'll make a loop around—"

"I'm not going anywhere with you," Davin interrupted.

"Crowley's arse," Mike swore. "Fine. I'll go with Greg and you two pair off. We'll look around the church, you go through the cemetery and we'll meet in the back. Shout if you encounter anything unusual."

While Mike and Greg took off toward the imposing, yellow church, Davin and Aurelia headed up the trail into the sprawling graveyard.

The snow had been plowed off the trail, but the wind had blown a fine layer over the ice that had solidified on the asphalt, making it difficult to navigate. "We'd probably have an easier time walking on the grass," Aurelia groaned as the two groups became further and further apart.

"Do you sense anything?" Davin asked as he struggled to maintain his balance.

"Yeah," Aurelia replied as she shuddered. "I sense that it's freezing outside."

"I thought you said you weren't cold—"

The temperature had dropped significantly in just a few steps as an ominous cloud appeared over the tree line at the back of the cemetery. With each passing moment, it headed inexorably closer.

"Come on, let's go," Aurelia insisted as she continued to slog forward.

Devin hesitated, but then followed.

By the time they reached the top of a small hill near the tree line, the dark cloud had eclipsed them and now hovered directly over the church. Davin and Aurelia were so transfixed by the sight that they nearly missed the group of robed figures emerge from the woods and glide briskly in their direction. Nearly.

Something told Aurelia to turn around. She dutifully obeyed just in time to grab Davin and throw him out of the way. The figures, three

of them in all, wore dark brown robes that concealed their faces. They rushed past, obviously intent on scaring the trespassers.

It worked for one, but not the other. Davin took off toward the church, but Aurelia stood her ground. Seeing herself now outnumbered three to one, however, she turned around and ran after her friend.

The phantom monks followed close behind.

On the other side of the cemetery, Mike and Greg strolled alongside the imposing edifice of the church. Mike dangled a crystal, which was suspended by a black string, about a foot ahead.

"Does that thing even work?" Greg asked as the dark clouds gathered overhead.

Mike stopped in his tracks. "You know, I don't know," he replied. "I always just assumed it would."

It was then that they saw the commotion. As the two reached the back of the church, they heard Aurelia call out.

"Darn it, what's up with them?" Mike

ST. JAMES-SAG CHURCH

cursed, but it did not take him long to determine. The three figures dressed in dark brown stood out against the white snow like Star Jones at a Republican convention.

"They're coming right for us," Greg announced.

Mike reacted quickly, and his eyes examined the terrain. To their right, the ground dropped off into a terraced section of the cemetery before it dropped off again, this time going down about fifty feet to the road below. He noticed, under the thin layer of snow, a stone staircase that led precariously to the edge.

"I have an idea," he said. "Give me your cane. You lure them over to this staircase and I'll do the rest. If we're lucky, we should be rid of them and not minus one or two of us."

Greg understood, but hesitated before handing over his cane. "I got this in New Orleans," he said, "if you lose it I'll kill you."

Mike glared at him until he let go of his cane and bounded up the slope.

Pressing his back against a concrete wall alongside the stairs, Mike positioned himself so that he could barely see over the edge of the grass. A sheet of ice covered the stairs.

Out on the hilltop, Davin and Aurelia rushed toward Greg, who waved his arms wildly.

"Heeere monky, monky, monky," he called out as though he was summoning a cat to dinner.

As Davin and Aurelia passed, Greg ordered them to keep running toward the ledge, and they seemed to intuitively understand.

The monks (if that is what they really were) followed in hot pursuit. At the last moment, Greg, Davin, and Aurelia leapt off the ledge and landed onto the grass, rolling into a pile against a headstone. Mike allowed the first two monks to pass him on the stairs. Before they knew what was happening, Mike thrust Greg's cane in between the legs of the third and he or she fell into the others. In a whirling mess of brown, the monks tumbled down the stairs and disappeared over the edge.

After they collected themselves, the Fallen quickly assembled in front of the church doors. "This has got to be it," Mike shouted, still gasping for breath. "We've gone through too much."

"Speak the words," Aurelia urged. "Hurry before they come back."

Mike closed his eyes and stretched his arms out wide. "*Anail nathrach, uatha bha'is, bith thonn du'iseacnt, le de'anamh E!*" He repeated the ancient Gaelic phrase a second time, stressing every syllable. His trench coat whipped in the icy wind.

Thunder crackled in the clouds above and the ground around them seemed to heave with energy. Suddenly, the doors of the church burst open, but instead of the interior, only a tenebrous pool of swirling energy greeted the quartet.

Mike and Greg exchanged nervous glances. Aurelia grasped Mike's hand in hers, and the four stepped into the portal.

INVESTIGATION FILE 013

ARCHER CEMETERY
Justice, Illinois

Archer Woods Cemetery sits near Archer Avenue and shares many similarities with the more infamous Resurrection Cemetery. Both feature a tavern across the street, and both host the ghost of a woman in white. Some researchers believe this is no accident—that the two locations are inexorably linked in the beyond.

Ursula Bielski is one of the few credible folklorists to have examined this site in detail. As she pointed out in *Chicago Haunts* (1998), Archer Woods is easily passed over in favor of the more famous haunts that dot the area.

In the past, she assured her readers, Archer Woods Cemetery was one of the most notorious of the local cemeteries as a result of its resident specter, a lonely, sobbing woman. Like the sobbing woman of Bachelor's Grove, it is likely that this spirit is in search of a lost child or lover. These apparitions are so common that they warranted their own category in Trent Brandon's *Book of Ghosts* (2003).

According to Brandon, the sobbing woman of Archer Woods Cemetery is known as a "Broken Heart" because "the feelings of guilt have become so overwhelming that this ghost believes that it must suffer forever to make up for her child's fate."[20]

What links Archer Woods Cemetery to the other locations along Archer Avenue, besides the predominance of ghostly women, is the appearance of a terrifying black hearse pulled by a team of mad horses. The vehicle has no driver. If you have read the previous issue of the *Legends and Lore of Illinois*, the connection to St. James-Sag should be readily apparent.

In 1897, two musicians claimed to see a spectral woman and a similar black carriage near the grounds of St. James-Sag, which is located only a couple of miles southwest of Archer Woods. Stranger still, local legends have placed the body of Resurrection Mary inside the hearse. They claim that the driverless carriage is trying to transport her spirit into the afterworld.

On the grounds of the cemetery there is a strange-looking monument called the "Garden of Hymns." It is a block of sandstone slabs with several metal pipes jutting out from it, which were fashioned to look like part of a pipe organ. Local rumors claim that organ music can be heard coming from the area on clear nights.

Back in 2002, on a visit to Archer Cemetery, I talked to a groundskeeper who had a strange tale to tell. I had noticed a hole in the fence and asked how that came about. The man told me that he did not know, but that out of the four people employed at the cemetery, he was the only one who had been coming into work lately. A lot of press had been snooping around as well. Could this have been related to the hole in the fence, or was there something else? That was one mystery that I never solved.

Whatever the truth to these stories, Archer Woods Cemetery is a nice excursion for any folklore enthusiast looking to get off the beaten track.

---

[20] Trent Brandon, *Book of Ghosts* (Zerotime Publishing, 2003), 87.

THE FALLEN INVESTIGATE

JAN. 2

1:00 AM

18° F

When we last left them, the Fallen had appeared to unlock the gate that would allow them to travel on the astral plane, but they were unaware of what awaited them on the other side. Exhausted, cold, and hungry, Mike, Greg, Aurelia, and Davin were violently deposited in the woods across from an old cemetery. The snow stung their cheeks and a dog barked angrily in the distance.

"Ugh, I feel like I just ran through the Kama Sutra with Rosie O'Donnell," Davin groaned from his position at the bottom of the pile of bodies.

"Thanks for the image," Aurelia retorted, her left leg stuck somewhere between Mike and Greg.

The four had fallen into a tangled mess at the edge of a forest preserve parking lot in the middle of a circle of wooden stakes that poked just above the snow.

Greg was the first to ask the obvious question. "Where are we?"

Mike pealed himself off the frozen ground and looked around. "I don't know, but at least we're still in the same century," he said, having noticed the parking lot, paved road, and power lines directly in front of them.

Leaping to his feet, Greg dusted himself off and retrieved his cane. "Let's see if there's a sign on that cemetery gate," he suggested.

Aurelia and Mike nodded in agreement and started walking toward the road, but Davin hesitated.

"Did anyone notice where we landed?" he asked, but none of his companions turned around.

As he approached the gate, it became evident to Mike that the group was not far from where they had entered the portal. "Crowley's arse," he cursed. "This is Archer Cemetery. St. James is only a couple of miles away from here."

"Geez, we have to walk all the way back to the car?" Greg complained.

"More importantly," Mike added, "what happened to that portal? And how long were we in it? It was only seconds to us, but who knows how long that was on earth."

"As I was trying to tell you," Davin interrupted, "we fell out inside some kind of circle back there. Maybe that was an accident, but I doubt it."

"I think you're right," Aurelia said under her breath as, for the first time, she noticed that they were not alone.

Three figures dressed in black stood blocking the entrance to the cemetery. Two were men and one a woman, but all three sported long, black hair. They were of varying sizes ranging from Ashley Olsen thin to Kirstie Alley in her 'fat actress' stage, with one in between. Their clothes hung loosely from their bodies and pentagrams dangled from their necks. The largest of the group repeatedly stroked his tangled goatee.

"Now who the heck are they?" Davin exclaimed.

"Who cares," Greg replied, yawning.

"It looks like someone watched *The Craft* one too many times," Mike added as the Fallen cautiously approached the interlopers. "Let me guess," he yelled from across the street, "you're the ones who have been leaving all those Satanic markings everywhere."

"Congratulations," the thinnest of the trio, the other male, bellowed. "You're even dumber than your reputation led us to believe. You led us right to the portal and even got rid of its guardians, those pathetic middle-aged zealots. How could you have been so blind?"

"Well, the shoddy work and Hollywood nature of your magic rituals made me think you were a group of pathetic losers trying to blow off some steam," Mike retorted. "I see that I wasn't too far off."

The man stopped stroking his goatee and frowned. "Tell us how you opened the portal," he demanded.

"Make us!" Aurelia retorted before anyone else could respond. Without a second thought, she bolted across the street and headed directly toward the three. Mike and Greg exchanged quick glances and ran after her.

The man with the goatee did not move, but the smirk on his face vanished when, without hesitation, Aurelia grabbed his Adam's apple in one hand and kicked him in the left shin with one of her steel toed, platform boots.

"Jesus," his male companion swore and began to back away while the man with the goatee turned blue and began to cough violently.

Mike and Greg quickly arrived. Greg took out the other male by striking him behind the knee with his cane. The young man cried out in pain as his entropied tendons buckled and he sunk to the ground. Their female companion turned and ran into the cemetery.

The Fallen ignored the two men and ran after the girl, who was having a difficult time on the slippery path. She made it about ten yards before collapsing into the snow. Aurelia, Mike, Greg, and Davin quickly surrounded her.

She feebly kicked and flayed into the air with her limbs.

"Hold her down," Mike commanded, and Greg and Davin all too eagerly complied. "Where are those other two?"

"It looks like they're running away," Aurelia reported as her wolfish eyes scanned the horizon.

"Did you hear that?" Mike said. "Your friends left you here. Now stop struggling. We won't hurt you, you have my word."

"It doesn't surprise me they left," the girl said bitterly as she stopped squirming. "Assholes!"

"What's your name?" Davin asked.

Before the girl could answer, Greg noticed scars on her wrists when he released them. "Hey look," he said. "You two have something in common."

"Cute," Davin shot back.

"Let her talk," Aurelia aggressively interjected. She shoved Greg off balance and he fell over with a cry of surprise.

"My name is Emily," the girl said, quickly pulling her sleeves down to cover her wrists. She dragged herself to her feet as everyone else stood up as well. Her face, aside from some redness from either the cold or from embarrassment, was as white as the snow that blanketed the cemetery grounds.

"So what's the deal?" Mike demanded. "As if we don't have enough problems with the P.C.P.R.S. and those zealots, now we have you people shadowing us and trying to curse us and steal our research?"

"They thought they could use the gate to bring Satan into this world," Emily coughed.

"Yeah, well, we don't even know what that thing does, or if we're going to be able to open it again," Mike explained. "We were in the process of figuring that out when you... interrupted us."

"I'm sorry," the young woman said. "I thought it was a joke. I mean—I didn't think it was real until we saw you guys go through it. I couldn't believe it. That's when I knew what we were doing was terribly wrong."

"You got that right," Greg interrupted. "You guys couldn't pour pee out of a boot with instructions written under the heel."

Davin rolled his eyes. "They did a pretty good job of ejecting us from that portal, remember?"

"Beginner's luck," Mike retorted.

"Anyway, screw them," Emily said bitterly. "If they want to leave me here that's fine. I'll just walk home." She hesitated. "I mean, can I get a ride?"

Greg smirked, but held his tongue.

"No," Mike replied while throwing Greg a look of disapproval. "But only because we're stuck here too. Our car is still at St. James-Sag."

"Oh, right," Emily said sheepishly. "About that... We kind of trashed your car before we came over here. You know it's been almost a week. It's 2008 now."

"What, we missed New Years?" Greg blurted.

Mike's face turned crimson. "You did what!?" he shouted.

"Relax," Aurelia said. "You promised we wouldn't hurt her, remember?"

Fists tightly clenched, Mike turned around and began to trudge out of the cemetery. His companions heard him angrily mutter to himself all the way to the main gates.

"I guess this means you're one of us," Davin muttered to their new companion. "For now."

INVESTIGATION FILE 014

SUNSET HAVEN
Carbondale, Illinois

Up until around the mid-1950s, people who could not take care of themselves; orphans, the elderly and infirm, epileptics, and alcoholics, often found themselves on a county farm known as a "poor farm." A superintendent and his family would look after the residents while the residents earned their keep by farming the land, if they were able. Most of these institutions closed down when our modern welfare system came into maturity. The land was sold and the buildings were often turned into psychiatric hospitals or homes for the developmentally disabled.

Sometimes poorly managed, and not very profitable, those institutions frequently closed their doors and were taken over by vandals and thrill seekers. Sunset Haven, or "Building 207" as it is known today, is one such place.

The Jackson County Poor Farm (its original name) has a somewhat unique history. According to Troy Taylor's *Haunted Illinois* (2004), it became known as Sunset Haven during the 1940s before it was converted into a nursing home. It was finally closed in 1957 when Southern Illinois University purchased the property to expand its agricultural program.[21] It then became known as the Museum Research Corporation.

During the 1970s, the research corporation made an effort to locate all the unmarked graves of the dead that had been buried during Sunset Haven's years as a poor farm. The graves are supposedly located in a grove of trees behind the building. Sometime later the name was changed again, this time to the "Vivarium Annex," where, according to

Taylor, SIU used it for animal research. The building is currently abandoned, although the university occasionally stages emergency drills on the property to test its medical students.

The building's final closure and decay inevitably led to stories of ghosts and other horrors. The atmosphere inside the structure lent itself to rumors of medical experiments gone awry. According to Troy Taylor, "stainless steel cages and medical equipment are scattered throughout the place, giving it the ominous feel of some mad scientist's lair."[22]

Those who ventured down the long driveway at night for a look inside the notorious building got more than they bargained for. "Rumors about the place get bigger and bigger each year when some brave crowd of teenagers gather up the courage to walk the 2.5 miles all the way down the back drive in absolute darkness," Courtney Cruse wrote in her high school newspaper, the *Terrier Times* (October 2005). "The ones who do stay... are almost mesmerized at how many scary artifacts are left in the eerie building."

Visitors today will not find very much worth seeing inside those halls. Most of the aforementioned equipment has been stolen or removed by the university, and the walls are covered with graffiti. Sunset Haven is a shell of its former self.

NOTE

A man who briefly lived at Sunset Haven when it was a laboratory later wrote to us. You can read his experiences in the May 2008 issue of the *Legends and Lore of Illinois*.

---

21 Taylor, *Haunted Illinois*, 42.

22 Ibid., 43.

THE FALLEN INVESTIGATE

FEB. 2

11:45 AM

35° F

With the paved road less than fifteen yards behind, Mike, Davin, Aurelia, Emmer, and their new companion Emily strolled up the dirt trail toward the summit of a small hill. Fallow cornfields flanked them on both sides, and a stand of trees obscured the brick building at the end of the trail. The unobstructed wind assaulted them.

"While you guys were out doing who-knows-what over New Years, I was doing some serious research," Emmer explained as he led the group toward the distant brick building. "I found something real for us to investigate, for a change."

"This looks like private property," Davin interrupted. "I hope we're not going to get arrested again. The last time that happened I got stuck in a cell with that pervert who kept flashing me."

"Weren't you in there with Greg?" Mike asked.

"Who did you think I was talking about?" Davin replied.

Emmer forcefully cut them off. "Anyway, as I was saying, I discovered something interesting. All of you have heard of coydogs, right? Half coyote, half dog? Supposedly the coyotes have been breeding with domesticated dogs that their owners have abandoned along the road out in the country. Nasty critters. I was always skeptical of that explanation, and now I have reason to believe that the appearance of these coydogs wasn't by chance."

"You mean someone bred them on purpose?" Emily asked from the rear of the group.

"Who the hell is that?" Emmer whispered to Mike, but without much concern for the volume of his voice.

"Never mind," Mike replied. "You were saying?"

"Right. Anyway, I think someone bred them on purpose. That building up there is owned by the university and used to be used for animal research. They closed it down years ago—I have no idea why. I read in an old newspaper article that they were conducting genetic experiments."

"That's quite a leap," Aurelia said as she pulled her coat tighter to insulate herself from the thrashing wind. "There are probably dozens of places in Illinois where that kind of research goes on."

"Yeah, but how many closed mysteriously?" Emmer cut in.

As the group approached the summit of the hill, their throats tightened. The simple, rectangular building appeared to be nothing but a shell. Sheets of aluminum covered its windows and broken branches were strewn around the lawn.

"Who wants to go in first?" Mike dared.

Aurelia shook her head and marched up the cement stairs, past a dead tree tangled with vines, to the door. A wire mesh had at one time covered the doorway, but a gaping hole had been torn in the links, allowing for easy entry. She stopped and signaled for the rest of the group to follow.

Once inside, a stairwell presented the Fallen with three choices. The basement looked promising, but there were two other floors besides that: the ground floor and the second floor. Mike, who was easily confused by more than two options, scratched his head.

Emmer sighed and shoved his way to the front of the group. "The most likely place we'll find anything is in the basement," he said.

Suddenly, the group caught movement just inside their peripheral vision. In the adjacent room, twin branches covered with dead leaves jutted like monstrous cockroach antenna through the wire mesh that coved the broken window. The tips of the branches caressed the wall below the windowsill.

But it was an object outside the window that caught Mike's attention. From between the branches and the metal links, he noticed a blue tractor that slowly lumbered toward the building along the dirt road a few dozen yards away.

"Crowley's arse, everyone get down!" he hissed.

"What is it?" Davin yelled.

"Shut up!"

Mike and Aurelia grabbed Emily and pulled her against the wall, while Emmer and Davin dropped to their knees. There they waited while they heard the tractor engine rumble closer.

Suddenly the engine stopped. The torn aluminum that covered the windows on the top floor scraped together, making a high pitch squeal that was almost indiscernible from the chirp of a two-way radio.

For several moments the Fallen held their breath while they heard a pair of shoes crush the orange and brown leaves strewn outside.

Mike signaled to Emmer and Davin that they should make their way deeper into the building. Once they had carefully crept into the hallway, Mike, Aurelia, and Emily followed.

Minutes passed. The footsteps climbed onto the porch and skidded on the dirt in the foyer. There they stopped.

"Hello?" a man's voice called out.

A shuddering wind blasted through the corridor, but all else was silent.

"I don't get paid enough for this," the Fallen heard the man grumble. He waited a few more moments before he turned around and walked out of the building. Mike, Emmer, Aurelia, Davin, and Emily stayed frozen against the hallway wall until they heard the tractor engine turn over and rumble into the distance.

Davin looked as though he was seconds away from passing out when he finally exhaled.

"That was close," Mike whispered.

SUNSET HAVEN

Emily shivered and wiped tears away from her eyes, but no one seemed to notice.

"Alright, who's ready to check out the basement?" Emmer asked with an inappropriate cheerfulness.

Mike smirked and led the group back to the stairwell, where they switched on their electric torches and pointed the beams into the darkness below. Wires hung from the ceiling and the peach paint pealed in every direction. Leaves were piled up on the floor in some places. The obligatory graffiti covered everything.

Rats squeaked and scurried away as the five descended the stairs. Emmer took the lead and went from room to room, carefully scanning their contents. Most were empty, but a few held benign objects or random debris. Trespassers had stolen anything that was not nailed down. Disappointed, Emmer scowled and turned off his flashlight.

The group noticed that sunlight poured into the boiler room and decided to check it out. At first they saw nothing out of the ordinary. The equipment in the room was old and rusty but it was, of course, just a boiler. The sunlight came from a door across from the equipment.

Davin made his way over to the door and peaked outside. "Hey, come here!" he shouted, although the other four were not more than a few yards away.

As Aurelia pushed Davin out of her way, she discovered that they were now standing in some sort of garage or vehicle bay. Leaves covered the cement floor, and a chain-linked fence topped with barbed wire surrounded the yawning entrance.

"Gross, look at this," she said as she brushed some of the leaves away with her boot, uncovering the skeletal remains of a canine.

"That looks like some kind of a weird dog," Emily piped up from the doorway.

"My thoughts exactly," Emmer said with a satisfied grin.

Mike leaned down to examine it closer and found that an old, decaying rope still clung to the vertebrae where the animal's neck used to be. "This skull looks strange," he muttered.

"Maybe it was just a stray," Davin said. "This doesn't prove anything. It could have gotten here any number of ways."

"True," Emmer concurred. "But it's still interesting that we found it here. I think we should take the skull home and run tests on it."

"Yeah, we'll run tests on it," Mike repeated. "I'll just take it back to my lab."

"You mean your bathroom?" Aurelia quipped.

"Right." Mike produced a large plastic bag from the pocket of his trench coat and gently placed the skull inside. He then tied the bag closed and stuffed it back into his pocket. "I think we have a lot of research to do," he said. "It's time to hit the books."

INVESTIGATION FILE 015

PEORIA STATE HOSPITAL
Peoria, Illinois

The ruins of Bartonville Asylum, or as it is more commonly known, Peoria State Hospital, are located west of Peoria in the small town of Bartonville, which lies directly across the Illinois River. Troy Taylor popularized this location via several books including *Haunted Illinois* (1999, 2004) and *Haunted Decatur Revisited* (2000), although it had long been an object of local curiosity. The property owners have not been amused by the asylum's growing notoriety, and police regularly patrol the premises looking for trespassers.

According to Taylor, Bartonville State Hospital began its life in 1885 as an empty shell and faux medieval castle. No patients were ever housed or treated in the building and it was torn down in 1897.

The institution was rebuilt and reopened in 1902 with a new name and a new superintendent. Now called Peoria State Hospital, a progressive physician named Dr. George A. Zeller took over the facility and instituted new, more humane treatments for mental illness. Small cottages were built to house the patients and a dorm housed the full-time staff. Essentially a self-contained community, the grounds also contained a store, a bakery, and a kitchen.[23]

The main story associated with Bartonville Asylum concerns the unusual circumstances surrounding the death of one of the patients, A. Bookbinder. Dr. Zeller assigned Bookbinder to the hospital's burial corps, and he performed his job admirably. Old Book, as he was sometimes called, mourned the passing of each and every person he helped intern in the cemetery.

When Bookbinder died, Dr. Zeller wrote that four hundred staff and patients observed his ghost mourning at his own funeral just as he had for countless others while he was alive. They even opened the coffin to confirm that Old Book was really dead. His corpse was securely inside.

The strange story does not end there. The elm tree on which Bookbinder had leaned and cried began to wither and die. Work crews attempted to remove it several times, but each time they were scared off by moans that seemed to come from within the tree itself. Years later, the elm finally succumbed to nature when it fell over in a storm.

There have been other reports of paranormal experiences at Bartonville, but none of them are very specific. In their *Field Guide to Illinois Hauntings*, Jim Graczyk and Donna Boonstra generically claim "numerous other events have been known to happen throughout the various buildings."[24]

The Peoria State Hospital for the Incurable Insane, along with many other similar institutions, closed during the 1970s. Since then, despite the owner's best efforts, it has been taken over by curiosity seekers and vandals alike. The hospital's fate is a familiar one. We can only hope that one day it is cleaned up and put to good use.

UPDATE

The building was recently opened to tours. Visit www.savethebowen.com for details.

---

[23] Taylor, *Haunted Illinois*, 216.

[24] Jim Graczyk and Donna Boonstra, *Field Guide to Illinois Hauntings* (Alton: Whitechapel Productions Press, 2001), 56.

The Fallen Investigate

MAR. 7

10:30 AM

31° F

The Fallen stood, thrashed by wind, in the shadow of the imposing stone building. Occasionally, a car rushed past on the nearby road and voices filtered from the parking lots of nearby businesses, but all were oblivious to the interlopers.

"Gentlemen, somewhere in there is the solution to this coydog mystery," Emmer announced, his hands perched defiantly on his hips.

A sharp noise of irritation pierced the air. "Ahem!"

Emmer rolled his eyes. "Gentlemen, and *other people*," he corrected, deliberately avoiding the term 'lady.'

Aurelia pushed him out of her way as she marched up to the ice-covered stairs in front of the long-abandoned Peoria State Mental Hospital. She shot a bemused glance at the small 'no trespassing' sign. "What does that say?" she asked sardonically.

"I don't know," Greg replied while he pretended to strain his eyes. "I went to public school. I never learned how to read words with more than two syllables."

"It must be nothing," Davin grinned.

"If you guys are done, I'd like to get this over with," Emmer interrupted. "Mike, tell them what you learned about that skull we found in Carbondale."

Mike cleared his throat as he followed the group into the dilapidated structure. As they forced their way inside, water dripped from the ceiling and pooled on the grimy, hallway floor. "I cross checked the skull against all known canines in North America and it doesn't match

any of them. It vaguely resembles a coyote, though. It might have belonged to a previously unknown breed."

"What would a coyote half-breed skeleton with a collar on it be doing in an old abandoned animal research hospital?" Emmer asked rhetorically. "Allow me to explain. In my own research, I discovered a newspaper article about a doctor who was employed at SIU in the 1960s named Dr. Wayne Gale. Dr. Gale worked in their animal research program doing cutting edge genetic research. He performed a lot of unnecessary experiments and the university eventually fired him for mental instability. Apparently the police found him back in the facility one night. He had been breaking in and continuing his experiments. He was arrested and found to be clinically insane. Guess where he wound up?"

"Bartonville?" Davin whispered.

"You get a gold star," Emmer smirked. "If we can find the medical files on Dr. Gale, we might be able to confirm what kind of experiments he was doing—if he in fact created our little coydog problem."

"What makes you think the files are still here?" Aurelia asked. Her shrill voice echoed down the long, empty corridor. "Look at this place. It's been closed for over three decades. People have torn it apart."

"I guess we'll just have to find out," Mike said with a satisfied grin as he flicked on his electric torch and pointed the beam into the darkness.

"I think you'd keep doing this even if there was nothing to find," Greg quipped.

"This is the fun part," Mike replied. "Where's the fun when it's over and everyone goes home?"

Suddenly the five heard a crash, followed by the distinctive clicking of nails on tile, coming from the floor above. The inhuman footsteps traveled the length of the ceiling and stopped directly above where the Fallen stood.

Everyone froze. "Uh," Mike whispered hesitantly, "those files are probably in the basement. I vote we go down there."

"Will you relax," Emmer said. "It's probably just an opossum or something. Maybe a homeless man with no shoes and really long toenails."

"Regardless, he has a point," Greg interjected. "Those files are downstairs... most likely."

Keeping their eyes and ears open, the five made their way to the stairwell and began their descent. The building, while quiet when they first entered, became alive with sound as though it resented the intrusion. Pipes rattled, the structure groaned, and unidentifiable clanks and clatters echoed throughout the deserted rooms.

"The ghosts don't want us here," Davin muttered.

Emmer quickly chastised him. "That's enough of that," he said. "I don't want to hear about any of that crap while we're actually trying to find something of substance for a change."

Mike clenched his teeth but refrained from responding as the group reached the bottom of the stairs.

The scent of mildew and dirt hung in the air. Now deep in the bowels of the building, Greg and Emmer switched on their flashlights. The beams explored the walls until they fell upon words stenciled in chipped paint: 'employees only.'

"I think the files were probably kept in this area," Aurelia said.

"Chalk another one up for the queen of the obvious," Greg sneered.

Aurelia retaliated by sending the steel toe of her boot into Greg's shin before Mike intervened and pushed the two apart. "Crowley's arse, that's enough out of you," he lectured.

"Here!" Davin yelled suddenly. Mike, Emmer, Aurelia, and Greg turned their heads in time to see Davin push open one of the doors. The door handle slipped from its mooring and clattered noisily to the floor. A sharp clank from the floor above followed closely behind.

"Okay, now even I'm getting nervous," Emmer admitted as he followed Davin into the room. "We better find these papers and leave."

Scanning the interior with the beam of his electric torch, Emmer discovered that Davin had unwittingly stumbled upon a jackpot. Rusted file cabinets were propped against the wall, and papers lay under a thick layer of dust on the floor. Luckily, perhaps even miraculously, the room was untouched by moisture aside from a few stains on the ceiling and along the walls.

"Well, I guess we got lucky this time," Mike grumbled.

"For once," Aurelia shot back.

The Fallen began opening cabinets and flipped through the crusted files, but an anonymous case number marked each one.

Greg growled in frustration, but then noticed a desk wedged between two of the cabinets. Tearing open the drawers, he found an old, blue binder and opened it. "Here!" he shouted. "This thing has a list of all the patients, serial numbers, and their room numbers!"

"Look for a Wayne Gale," Emmer ordered as he shown his flashlight on the pages.

"Wow, here he is," Greg said. "Gale, Wayne, Dr. # 0589 Room 206. I don't believe it."

Mike had already been thumbing through the filing cabinet, so as soon Greg read the number he anxiously pulled out the correct file.

"Patient #0589," he whispered. "Let's see what you've been hiding."

The file contained numerous note cards and loose sheets of lined paper. It took Mike a few minutes to decipher the scribbled handwriting.

"Hm," he said. "There's a lot in here about his mother. He seemed to be obsessed with never having been given any boundaries."

"Isn't that the problem these days?" Aurelia commented. "That doesn't tell us anythi—"

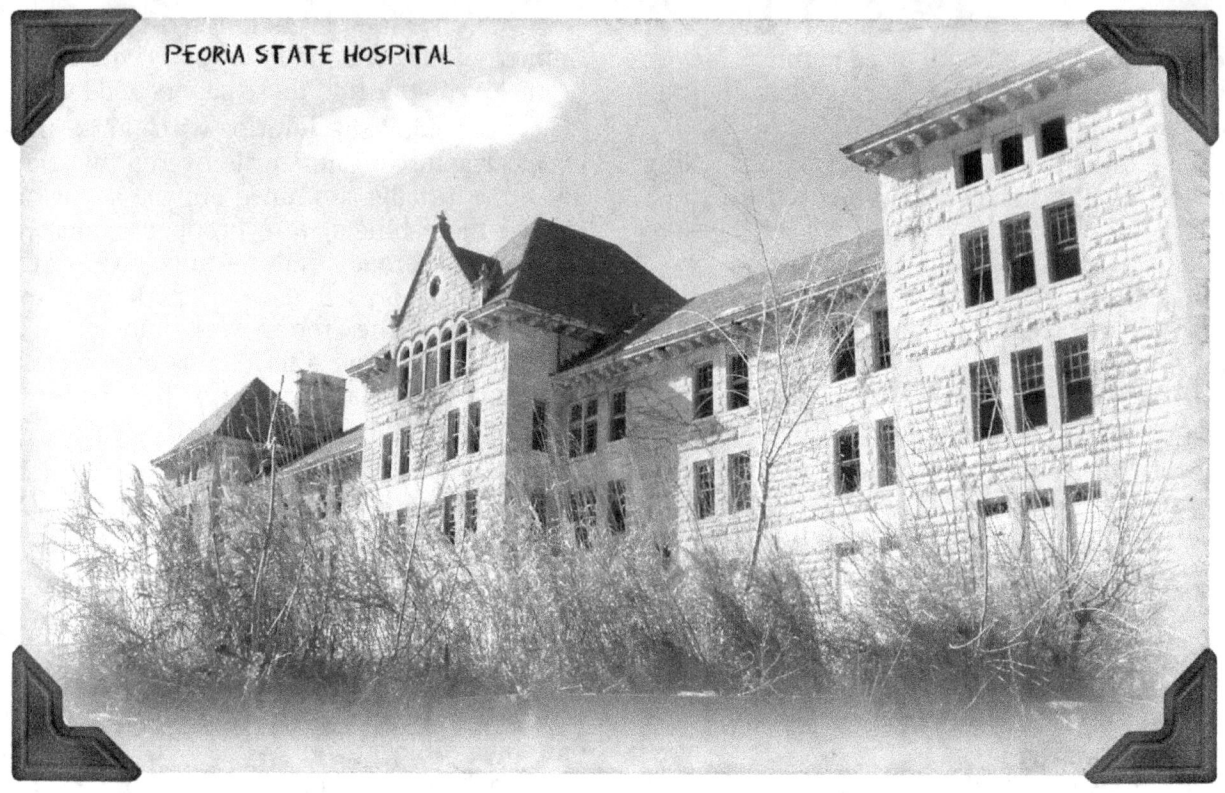

PEORIA STATE HOSPITAL

"Wait," Mike cut her off. "His shrink noted this: 'the patient is convinced that his work at the research center was important and lucrative. He claimed a security company was going to pay him a million dollars to breed a new kind of guard dog. Something that would be fearless but obedient. The company denies ever having known the doctor'."

"Son of a b—!" Emmer exclaimed before quickly composing himself. "That crazy... Do you think it's possible?"

"It's possible," Mike said. "But then again, anything is possible."

"Could you be any more cliché?" Greg sneered.

"Take that file," Emmer said. "We're going to get to the bottom of this if it's the last thing we do."

"Wait, have you ever heard of theft?" Davin said. "Don't you think we've broken enough laws today?"

Aurelia snorted.

"Fine," Mike replied. "We'll borrow the files, and you can return them when we're done."

Davin laughed nervously but kept his mouth closed. Mike took the file from Greg and slid it into his trench coat. "Let's get out of here," he said. "This place gives me the creeps."

INVESTIGATION FILE 016

AIRTIGHT BRIDGE
Coles County, Illinois

Airtight Bridge spans the narrow Embarras River in rural Coles County. It was designed by Claude L. James and built in 1914. In 1981, the bridge was added to the National Register of Historical places on account of "event, Architecture/Engineering."

Before this "event," the bridge was known as a drinking spot for local teens as well as students from Eastern Illinois University. Otherwise, the bridge, which even 26 years ago was described as "old" and "creaky," had a pretty mundane existence.

That all changed on the pleasant Sunday morning of October 19, 1980. According to newspaper reports, two men from rural Urbana spotted what looked like the body of a nude woman about 50 feet from the bridge as they drove past. A local man soon joined them at the scene and the three quickly discovered that the head, hands, and feet were missing from the cadaver. They called the sheriff's office, and 20 minutes later a full investigation was underway.

Police used scuba divers and dredged the river to find clues, but the body parts, which had been severed "fairly cleanly," were never found. There were several false leads in the case, including missing person reports, as well as a sack of clothes that was discovered north of Charleston. The cause of death, which probably lay in the head, was never determined.

Police described the woman as being in her 20s, "rather flat-chested," "not in the habit of shaving," about 5'9", weighing around 130lbs, with dark auburn hair. Her blood type was later determined to be A-positive, which is uncommon. The torso was shipped to Springfield to be examined by pathologist Dr. Grant Johnson, but nothing conclusive was uncovered because of the advanced state of decomposition.

After an extensive investigation, no killer was ever located (although Henry Lee Lucas became a prime suspect) and the identity of the woman remained a mystery for years. She was buried in Charleston's largest cemetery under the name Jane Doe.

Twelve years later, on November 20, 1992, the sheriff's department announced that the identity of the woman had been ascertained. Genetic tests determined that the victim was a 26-year-old woman from Bradley, Illinois, whose husband never reported her missing because, according to the *Mattoon Journal Gazette*, she had "left home on occasions before." Her biological family was separated across the country and did not learn that she was gone until years later.

According to Detective Steven Coy, she did not have a driver's license, so it was unlikely that she left Bradley on her own. Her family planned to replace the generic headstone in Charleston's Roselawn Cemetery, but it remains there to this day.

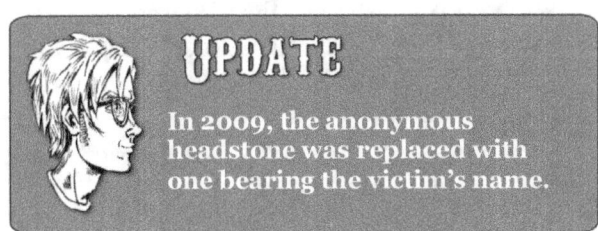

UPDATE
In 2009, the anonymous headstone was replaced with one bearing the victim's name.

Because of this gruesome story, its remote location, and its precarious condition, Airtight Bridge continues to capture the local imagination. There is little doubt that the bridge will continue to be a part of local folklore for generations to come.

THE FALLEN INVESTIGATE

APR. 15

6:00 PM

56° F

The Fallen's dark blue Toyota Corolla skidded around a sharp turn in the gravel road. Its black and yellow bumper sticker, which read "necrophilia is dead" in skeletal lettering, was sprayed with mud. Greg, Davin, and Emmer joked, shoved, and elbowed each other in the backseat.

"Hey, who do you think is the hottest of the women on *Charmed*?" Davin inquired.

Emmer, as usual, demanded clarification. "Season one through three or four through eight?"

"All of them."

"Paige, no question," Mike said from the driver's seat as he swerved to avoid a stray dog that bolted in front of the car.

"Piper," Davin countered.

"You would say that," Greg sneered. "How could you not like Rose McGowan? Haven't you ever seen *Devil in the Flesh*? I love homicidal tendencies in a woman."

"She's very pale too," Mike added. "My kind of woman can never be pale enough."

"You guys are all a bunch of weirdos and perverts," Aurelia interjected from the front passenger side. She rolled her eyes, sighed, and leaned disinterestedly against the door.

"First of all," Emmer added, "you're all morons. Alyssa Milano is way hotter than either of those two. Secondly, please explain what we're doing out here in the middle of nowhere."

"I'm glad you asked," Mike replied. "Since the trail has gone cold on that coydog mystery, and we still haven't figured out how to master that astral gate, I figured we would do something a little different. Up here around this bend is a place they call Airtight Bridge. A woman's torso was found here a couple of decades ago. Since then, people have reported strange occurrences."

"A torso?" Aurelia asked.

"You heard right."

"Would these 'occurrences' have had anything to do with drugs or alcohol?" Emmer interrupted with a chuckle. "I thought I had an occurrence once, but it was just some bad pot."

Feigning seriousness, Greg quipped, "The paranormal community frowns on your logic."

"Shut up," Mike demanded. "The bridge should be coming up at any minute."

Not a few moments after the words left his mouth, the road curved sharply and the rust-red trestles of the bridge loomed into view. The Embarras River, swollen from the recently melted snow, swirled only a few feet below. As the Toyota slid to a stop along the side of the road before it reached the bridge, it became obvious to the Fallen that they were not alone.

Emily, alongside two men who were donned in black Hot Topic apparel, stood in the middle of the bridge. A strong sense of déjà-vu permeated the scene.

"How did they know we were going to be here?" Mike growled as he threw the gear into park.

"Sorry guys," Davin stuttered. "I told Emily a few days ago we were coming here."

Greg and Emmer, who sat on either side of Davin, slowly turned to glare at their friend.

"I thought she was on our side now!" Davin insisted.

The Fallen piled out of their car and closed ranks. They marched to the mouth of the bridge but did not go any farther.

"Didn't you guys learn your lesson the last time?" Greg shouted. His voice echoed throughout the basin and was only rivaled in volume by the swirling water beneath.

"Tell us how you opened the portal," the largest of the three interlopers, an obese man with a tangled goatee and greasy, black hair, yelled back.

Aurelia burst out laughing.

Without warning, the thinnest of the three Satanists pulled a knife out of his pocket, grabbed Emily around the throat, and pressed the blade threateningly against the soft layer of skin protecting her kidney.

"This is not amusing," the man with the goatee snarled.

"Oh crap, Mike, you have to do something!" Davin cried.

"What do I care?" Mike replied with a shrug. "She chose to go back with those crazies."

Before anyone could respond, all eight were surprised by the sudden appearance of a shaggy, black dog that barked and drooled as it raced toward them from behind. It was the dog that Mike had nearly hit only minutes earlier.

Aurelia wasted no time in using the chaos to her advantage. While everyone else looked for a way out of the path of the feral animal, she bolted toward the obese man and shoved him against the metal railing along the side of the bridge. The top railing had fallen down long ago, leaving only the bottom one to catch his ankles and send him tumbling into the waters of the Embarras.

The man's scrawny friend shoved his hostage onto the broken pavement and turned the knife on Aura. Aurelia crouched to make ready for the attack, but before the Satanist could act, the black dog leapt at him and menacingly snapped its jaws. He fumbled with the knife and turned to run.

"Let's get the heck out of here!" Mike ordered from the other end of the bridge.

"What about Emily?" Davin insisted. "We never leave anyone behind."

"*That's the Marines*, you idiot," Emmer shot back, "and she's not one of us! She just sold us out, remember?"

A look of determination overcame Davin's face and he sprinted toward the middle of the bridge, where Aurelia had begun to backpedal away from the dog and its new toy.

AIRTIGHT BRIDGE

Davin quickly reached Emily, who was attempting to peal herself off the cement. Unfortunately for the two, the noise they made distracted the animal and it wheeled around to charge at them. Its giant tongue wagged as though it was enjoying the frenzy.

Mike sighed and raced toward the middle of the bridge, followed closely by Emmer and Greg. Arriving moments later, Mike tackled the dog while Emmer helped Davin and Emily get back on their feet. Greg struck the beast with his cane and it yelped in anger.

"Crowley's arse, it's drooling all over me," Mike growled as he attempted to force the canine's jaws closed with one hand while holding onto its body with the other. That proved to be too much, because the black dog wriggled free and barked and snapped at Greg's cane, which he was using to keep the animal at a distance.

Meanwhile, the overweight man with the goatee had managed to grab the branch of a tree that was mired in the floodwaters and pulled himself ashore. He emerged dripping wet, and his black eyeliner streamed down his face.

The Fallen were so preoccupied with fending off the enraged canine that they hardly noticed the two male Satanists retreat to their car, which was parked near the opposite end of the bridge, and peel away, leaving a cloud of white dust in their wake.

The wild dog, dim-witted and easily distracted, turned its attention toward the car and ran after it, barking and drooling until it disappeared into the smoke.

"Now would be a good time to get out of here," Mike said between ragged gulps of air.

"But we just got here," Greg complained with a smirk. "Haven't you been having any fun?"

Mike turned and looked disapprovingly toward Davin and Emily. "What the heck were you thinking?"

"I'm sorry," Emily begged. Nervous tremors shook her from head to toe. "They made me tell them! They threatened me!"

Mike eyed her suspiciously, but then turned toward the rest of the group. "Alright, Emmer and Greg, start filming and taking pictures of the bridge. Aura, write down your impressions. Maybe we can salvage something out of this disaster." He paused for a moment. "Oh, and watch out for that dog."

He took Davin and Emily aside. "You two seem to have a connection," he whispered. "That hasn't really worked out to our benefit yet, but never-the-less I want you to stick together. Davin, don't let her leave your sight until we figure out how to get rid of those guys, do you understand?"

"Yes," Davin replied. He looked over at the girl with relief.

Mike leaned toward Emily. "You need to earn our trust, do you understand? Otherwise you can just get out of here right now and I don't care where you go."

"I will," Emily gulped, and then clutched Davin's hand in hers.

INVESTIGATION FILE 017

UNIVERSITY OF ILLINOIS
Champaign-Urbana, Illinois

The University of Illinois was established as an industrial university in 1867 and first opened on March 2, 1868. It became the University of Illinois in 1885 and was renamed the University of Illinois at Urbana-Champaign in 1982. As one of the oldest public universities in the state of Illinois, the campus hosts a number of folktales and oddities. John Milton Gregory, the first president of the university, is buried on campus. His grave rests between Altgeld Hall and the Henry Administration Building, marked by an unsculpted stone and a plaque that reads, "if you seek his monument, look about you."

The University is home to a number of ghost stories as well. To my knowledge, Troy Taylor is the first person to have written about these ghosts in a book. His accounts can be found in several editions of *Haunted Illinois* (2001, 2004) and were reprinted briefly in *Field Guide to Illinois Hauntings* (2001) by Jim Graczyk and Donna Boonstra. Cynthia Thuma and Catherine Lower filled in some of the blanks in their book *Creepy Colleges and Haunted Universities* (2003).

Taylor claims that principal haunted localities on campus include the English Building, the Psychology Building, and the YMCA. If the other, scattered sightings are true, that would make the U of I one of the most haunted universities on the planet.

The English Building is purportedly haunted by the ghost of a student who committed suicide there during the time when the building served as a dormitory. Thuma and Lower tell us that the architectural firm of McKim, Mead, and White designed the structure in 1905 in a New Colonial style. I have been unable to determine when the dormitory was converted for its present use. The ghost is that of a young woman whose room, Troy Taylor claims, was located in what became the rhetoric room, which is now an office for graduate assistants. She manifests herself in typical fashion; flickering lights, doors that close on their own, etc..

The third floor of Lincoln Hall has its own ghost, but so does the ultra-modern Psychology Building. According to Taylor, "several years ago" a student threatened to kill himself by jumping from one of the upper floors overlooking the foyer. He survived the incident unscathed, but died a few years later. Some students claim that his ghost has returned to torment his analytical former classmates.

Even the YMCA cannot claim to be ghost-free. In an unlikely haunting, the spectral manifestation of Chief Illiniwek is said to roam the basement of this venerable building, which formerly hosted a painting of the university's mascot. Perhaps all the recent controversy has contributed to his unrest!

Despite these stories, many are skeptical. "An excursion through college records shows the tales of suicidal students and other campus violence are without merit," Thuma and Lower concluded. We may never know.

THE FALLEN INVESTIGATE

MAY 2

2:00 PM

62° F

The campus of the University of Illinois bustled with activity as the Fallen slipped into the crowd with relative ease. Unbeknownst to the young men and women around them, the five interlopers had come with motivations very different from passing a final exam.

Mike, Aurelia, Emmer, Greg, and Davin strolled down the sidewalk along the west end of the quad toward the English Building. Greg and Davin's eyes wandered from coed to coed. Neither paid much attention to what Mike was saying.

"As I was saying," Mike interjected with forced emphasis, "before I explain what we're doing here, Emmer has something to tell us."

"Yeah, okay, whatever," Greg muttered as a long-legged woman wearing a short skirt and tank top walked past.

Emmer cleared his throat. "You remember what we found at Sunset Haven and Bartonville, right?" he asked rhetorically. "Well, I managed to solve our coydog mystery right around the time those wannabe Satanists attacked us at Airtight Bridge. As it turns out, my hunch was right. Dr. Gale was crossbreeding coyotes and dogs in order to make a more perfect guard dog. He was going to sell the freak of nature to the highest bidder. Sort of a designer pet gone bad. The thing is, he must have been locked up before the sale could be made, then his creations escaped captivity."

"I guess that just goes to show that you shouldn't become a geneticist if you're insane," Greg chuckled.

Aurelia coughed. "So what is with this place?" she demanded impatiently. "I never thought I'd set foot on the grounds of a school again. This better be good."

"Ah," Mike said. "The U of I. This place supposedly has a number of ghosts. Up here is the English Building. The second floor is haunted by the ghost of a former student. There's also a number of other locations around here that are haunted too. I want to check them all out."

"Right," Davin interrupted. "I think I'm going to go check out some of those bars we saw on the way in. The bar age is eighteen here, isn't it?"

"Good idea," Greg chimed in. "I bet we can find some spirits there."

"Yeah, good luck," Emmer laughed as he joined Greg and Davin as they began to walk toward Green Street and the commercial strip near the university. "Let us know if you find any ghosts. I won't wait up for you."

"Jerks," Mike mumbled as the trio blended into the stream of students walking to and from class.

"Let them go," Aurelia said reassuringly. "They need a break. Besides, you know them. They'll only get in the way. We'll never find anything with Emmer around."

"We'll never find any ghosts, anyway," Mike added. He turned toward the gleaming white pillars of the English Building and began walking. Aurelia followed close behind until Mike threw open the heavy, wooden door. At the same time, a group of chatty Korean students exited the building. One of their over-stuffed book bags caught Mike in the side and he grunted. Aurelia laughed.

Inside, the hardwood floors creaked as the two made their way to the stairwell. Mike and Aurelia had to push past another group of students who congregated at the bottom of the stairs, but after several minutes they stood on the deserted second floor.

"I think this is where the grad offices are, and where the student committed suicide,"

ENGLISH BUILDING

Mike explained. "I'm not sure which room used to be the rhetoric room though."

"Maybe we should ask someone," Aurelia suggested.

"Nah," Mike said. "Why would we want to do that? We'll just find it the old fashioned way."

Aurelia grinned. "Isn't that where we wind up not finding anything at all?"

Mike ignored her comment and procured a crystal from his pocket. The crystal was attached to a long, black string. He held the tip of the string and dangled the crystal several feet from the floor. It slowly began to spin in a clockwise motion. "Hm," Mike said, "I'm picking up a faint trace of energy. What about you, do you sense anything?"

Aurelia closed her eyes and stood perfectly still for a few moments. Suddenly, her face began to register emotion. Her eyes jolted open. "The ghost is close by," she whispered. "The girl, I mean. I can feel her pain. I think she feels guilty about whatever happened."

"Are you sure?" Mike asked, but the look on his friend's face told him not to ask again.

Voices from down the hallway interrupted them and Mike pocketed the crystal. Moments later, a student and a professor appeared from inside one of the offices and walked in their direction. Mike and Aurelia nodded as the two passed.

Mike waited until he no longer heard footsteps and then whispered, "Which way?"

Aurelia pointed in the direction from which the student and professor had just come. That part of the hallway seemed to contract and became markedly cavernous. The dim, florescent lights flickered.

Mike swallowed and retrieved his crystal. As he cautiously walked down the hall, the crystal—already jolted by his movement—seemed to spin out of control.

The two had not traveled more than a few yards before Aurelia stopped dead in her tracks. "Oh, crap," she gasped seconds before the flyers and newspaper articles loosely taped to the office doors rustled and then tore free. The lights went dead for a moment and something hurled Mike against the wall. As his rear hit the floor, the lights returned to normal and the flyers fluttered slowly onto the hardwood.

A middle-aged lady with hefty glasses peaked out of her doorway. "Wow, that was some breeze!" she exclaimed. "Did someone open a window?"

"I don't know," Mike groaned as he attempted to stand.

The lady shrugged and disappeared again.

Aurelia grabbed Mike's hand and hoisted him to his feet. "I tried to warn you," she said, "but it happened too fast."

"It's okay," Mike assured her. "At least we know something is here."

"I think the ghost knows that we know she's here," Aurelia whispered. "She doesn't seem very happy about that."

"One thing is sure, she'll probably move to a different floor now. Should we track her down?"

"What are we going to do if we find her again," Aura inquired with a grin, "ask her to fill out a survey? You're just going to make her mad."

"We came all this way, we might as well introduce ourselves," Mike replied as he determinedly wrapped the crystal's black cord around his fingers and balled his hand into a fist.

Aurelia shook her head, but followed Mike back to the stairwell. The third floor, as it turned out, seemed even more abandoned than the second. Soft light beamed into the hallway from the windows that looked out onto the roof in the center of the rectangular building. Each window was nestled in a small corridor. Each corridor featured its own relic of the past—a desk, a heater, or even an old storm window. The Fallen checked each one with trepidation.

As they neared a window toward the end of the row, Aurelia clutched Mike's arm with a death grip that told him she had sensed

something. Despite the uncomfortable warning, his heart still leapt in his throat as he turned the corner and came face to face with a woman in her early twenties dressed in a drab blouse and long, dark skirt. Her empty eyes burned with fear and desperation. She opened her mouth to speak, but no sounds escaped.

Mike blinked and the apparition vanished. "Crowley's arse," he stuttered. "Was that her?"

"It's very likely," Aurelia whispered before taking a few deep breaths. "It's sad, you know. So much has changed since she died. I don't think she knows where she is anymore. I think we scared her as much as she scared us. She's fallen, just like us. She doesn't belong anywhere."

"I wish we could do more to help, now that we know the ghost story is real," Mike said. "Maybe when we finally open that astral gate we'll be able to enter her world and guide her home."

"Maybe," Aura replied, "but we still have to find it. I'm getting more certain by the day that the one we opened at St. James-Sag was a fluke, just a local portal."

"Me too," Mike added. "But in the meantime, we need to go find Greg and the rest of them. I could use a few drinks. They won't believe what just happened..."

INVESTIGATION FILE 018

CALVARY CEMETERY
Evanston, Illinois

Compared to Chicagoland's more notorious haunts, Evanston's Calvary Cemetery is barely a footnote, yet it is not so obscure as to escape the pages of most books on Chicago and Illinois ghost lore. This picturesque resting ground along the shore of Lake Michigan is home to a tale too strange to resist even brief mention. It is the tale of "the Aviator," or as he is sometimes affectionately known, "Seaweed Charlie."

The Aviator's ghost story appears in Ursula Bielski's *Chicago Haunts* (1998), Jo-Anne Christensen's *Ghost Stories of Illinois* (2000), Richard T. Crowe's *Chicago's Street Guide to the Supernatural* (2000, 2001), and Troy Taylor's *Haunted Illinois* (2004). Richard T. Crowe, as always, has done impeccable research on the tale and found its likely origin in a real event. Unlike most hauntings, that would make the story of Evanston's "Aviator" grounded in historical fact as well as geography and folklore.

The story begins along Sheridan Road between Lake Michigan and the eastern gate of Calvary Cemetery. During the day, there is hardly ever a break in traffic and bicyclists and joggers navigate the winding path along the boulders overlooking the lake. It is a charming scene. Between the late 1950s and 1960s, however, some passersby were treated to the alarming sight of a man drowning far out of reach in the icy waters. Even more startling was what came next.

Instead of disappearing under the waves to a watery grave, the man, usually disheveled but sometimes covered in seaweed, emerged from the lake and crawled over the rocks toward the gate of Calvary Cemetery before ultimately vanishing. This scene was replayed many times before finally, one night after cemetery caretakers accidentally left the gate open, the ghost disappeared forever. Despite this apparent end, sporadic sightings continued into the late '90s.

Richard T. Crowe speculated that the story could have an origin in a real plane crash that occurred 200 yards offshore, just east of Northwestern University, in 1951 during the height of the Korean War. Indeed, the *Daily Tribune* reported the crash on its front page in an article entitled "Hundreds See Jet Hit Lake; Pilot Missing."[25]

According to the Tribune, Lt. Laverne F. Nabours, a WW2 veteran and an instructor at Glenview Naval Airbase, suffered engine failure on his FH-1 Phantom and careened into Lake Michigan. The plane did not sink right away, rather, Laverne climbed on top of the wing and began waving for help. He then tried to swim ashore, but succumbed to the powerful waves. Several attempts were made to rescue him, but the lake's current prevented help from arriving in time.

Could this tragic event explain the origins of the tale of Seaweed Charlie? The timing seems right. The ghost did not appear until after the plane crash. If true, that would give this story an eerie authenticity few tales can match.

---

[25] *Daily Tribune* (Chicago) 5 May 1951.

The Fallen Investigate

JUN. 16

11:20 PM

72° F

Mike, Greg, Davin, and their anxious companion Emily stood on top of the boulders overlooking the deep blue waters of Lake Michigan. Despite it being the middle of June, an icy wind stung their cheeks. While two of the party seemed unaffected, Davin and Emily, who each wore outfits that looked like a Salvation Army outlet had exploded, shivered.

"Can you believe people swim in this lake?" Davin abruptly inquired in a tone that was more characteristic of a statement than a question.

"If it isn't August, forget it," Mike grumbled. "And even then, maybe."

Greg shook his head and ignored the topic. "So this ghost comes out over here, crawls across the road, and tries to enter the cemetery?" he asked.

"Yep," Mike replied.

"Well, where is he?" Greg insisted. "I don't have all day."

"Yeah, and why doesn't he just pass through the gate and go inside?" Davin added. "He's a ghost. He can't be stopped by solid objects."

Mike's cheeks turned an even darker shade of red. "I don't know," he hissed. "That's why we're here. To investigate the story."

"But it doesn't make any sense—"

Emily, who had been standing quietly next to Davin while the group bickered, cleared her throat. "Maybe we should just go back to the cemetery," she suggested sheepishly as a passing motorist honked his horn. "We might have better luck in there."

"Good idea," Mike said as he clutched a handful of Greg's shirt and pulled him down off of the boulders. Greg protested, but his small stature prevented him from doing anything about the involuntary dislocation. "We have a new toy too," Mike added. "Greg will show us when we're all across the road."

Greg finally tore free and straightened the collar of his tattered, olive green shirt that he wore no matter what the temperature, weather, or season. A pack of cars whizzed past along the street, followed by another. They seemed to be launched like boomerangs from somewhere beyond the curve from both the right and the left.

"Any minute now," Mike said as the gaps in traffic seemed to close as soon as they opened up. "...After the next car." Before he could set foot off the sidewalk, a wall of SUVs shot around the curve. "No, wait."

"This is ridiculous!" Davin shouted as he waded headlong into traffic. "I don't care if I get hit, this is taking forever." The rest of the group sprinted after him and found sanctuary on the concrete island that divided the four lanes of traffic. Seeing another opportunity, they bolted toward the cemetery gate and made it safely inside moments before a large van grazed Mike's heels.

Mike bent over, wheezing. "I... need to... start... exercising... again..." he gasped between breaths.

The van slowly turned and lumbered into the cemetery. The Fallen were forced to scatter as the driver honked his horn and swung over to the curb just inside of the iron gates. Mike groaned as soon as he saw who it was.

"We haven't seen these guys in a while," Greg sneered. "I was beginning to miss them."

A man in his early thirties, two middle-aged women, and one girl about the age of twelve dismounted the van and busied themselves removing equipment from the back. They didn't seem to notice the Fallen until Mike forcefully cleared his throat.

"Is there a problem?" the man asked as he removed a large video camera from an expensive carrying case.

"What are you guys doing here?" Mike demanded. "You know, we have some unfinished business, specifically regarding your association with those psycho-zealots who got us thrown in jail last year."

"For your information," one of the women, who was clad in a suit of denim, shot back, "we split from the Pan-Continental Paranormal Research Society. They wanted to start charging money for their services, so we formed the Greater-Midwestern Alliance for the Investigation, Inspection, and Research of Paraphysical Phenomenon, or G.M.A.I.I.R.P.P. for short. Can you imagine, charging people for our services?"

"Yeah I know, I think I'd feel ripped off for some reason," Greg muttered under his breath.

"Anyway," the man added brusquely, "we have an appearance on the Travel Channel in a couple of hours so we have to work quickly here, if you *kids* don't mind."

Mike looked as though he was about to say something that included a few, choice four-letter words, but he restrained himself.

"The Travel Channel, really?" Emily innocently exclaimed. "Are you presenting some new findings? MVPs?"

The man grinned and stopped unloading his camera. "That's EVP, sweetheart," he said. "As a matter of fact, we got a really good one yesterday." He turned toward one of his companions. "Get that EVP we recorded yesterday, will you?"

Mike closed his eyes and slowly massaged his temples.

"You can clearly hear someone say, 'Larry,'" the man continued as he snatched the tape recorder out of the woman's hands, turned up the volume, and pressed play. The tape recorder crackled and popped for a moment, then went silent. "Did you hear that?" he asked.

"No," Greg replied.

"Listen." This time a faint hiss came

LAKE MICHIGAN

across the tiny speaker.

"I think that said, 'Gary,'" Emily muttered.

"No," Davin interrupted. "It said 'Jerry.' Play it one more time."

"Crowley's arse!" Mike yelled. "We don't have time for this! It doesn't matter if it said 'Mrs. Butterworth.' You guys have never even seen a ghost, and you wouldn't know what to do even if you did."

The man scoffed and handed the tape recorder back to the denim-clad woman.

Disengaging from the interlopers, the Fallen walked a few yards away so that they stood close to the gate. Greg dug deep into his pockets and produced a small, round mirror that was painted black on one side.

"Now, do you see this?" Mike asked, gesturing toward the mirror. "The only real way to contact the other side is with simple, old fashioned parlor tricks.

"We're going to use this scrying mirror to try and see if we can find our friend Seaweed Charlie, and if it actually works, this might be able to help us finally locate the astral gate."

"Wait, you don't know where it is?" Emily asked with confusion. "Monk's Castle wasn't really the gate?"

Mike and Greg exchanged glances. "Don't worry about it," Greg snapped. "Even if we did know, *we wouldn't tell you.*"

Emily looked surprised, but clamped her jaw shut and stared at the ground. Davin, who had been standing next to her, took her hand in his to show support.

Greg shook his head and held up the mirror. He stared at it intensely for a few moments while everyone held their breath. "How the hell does this work?" he asked after a while.

"Give me that!" Mike exclaimed and tore it out of Greg's hands. As he held it up, the group gathered into a tight circle and concentrated on the glossy face of the mirror. After a few tense minutes, a mist began to manifest. Emily gasped as an image formed in the mist. The image seemed to be of a plane

streaking across the sky toward the murky lake. Davin instinctively looked up, but there was no plane in the sky above.

Greg broke the silence. "I don't get it," he said. "What's going on? What are you seeing?"

"You don't see that?" Mike asked.

"No," Greg replied. "What am I not seeing?"

"It looks like a plane falling through the clouds," Mike explained, but the conversation broke his concentration and the image dissolved.

"Point it at the gate," Davin suggested. "Maybe we'll see the ghost."

Mike complied, but after several minutes of staring at the reflection of cars whizzing back and forth, it became clear that nothing more was going to be revealed. Mike slipped the mirror into his pocket. "Well, I'd say that was somewhat of a success," he said.

"I suppose," Greg countered. "But what does this prove? Do you think this will help us find the gate?"

"It's worth a shot," Mike muttered. "Nothing else has worked so far."

Greg nodded, and the Fallen turned and walked slowly toward their car.

INVESTIGATION FILE 019

LAKEY'S CREEK
McLeansboro, Illinois

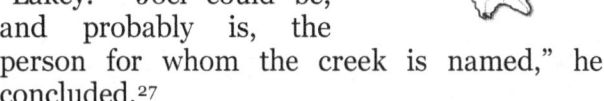

The headless horseman of Lakey's Creek is quite possibly one of the oldest ghost stories in Illinois. Passed down as an oral tradition until John W. Allen put the story on paper in 1963, the mysterious man named Lakey, as well as his untimely end, has been immortalized in the folklore of Southern Illinois. Like Seaweed Charlie, this ghost story may be preserving the memory of an unsettling event in local history.

Long before a concrete bridge spanned the shallow creek 1.5 miles east of McLeansboro, a frontiersman named Lakey attempted to erect his log cabin near a ford along the wagon trail to Mt. Vernon. One morning, a lone traveler stumbled upon Lakey's body. Lakey's head had been severed by his own ax, which was left at the scene. According to legend, his murderer was never found.

For decades after the murder, travelers reported being chased by a headless horseman who rode out of the woods along Lakey's Creek. "Always the rider, on a large black horse, joined travelers approaching the stream from the east, and always on the downstream side," John Allen wrote. "Each time and just before reaching the center of the creek, the mistlike figure would turn downstream and disappear."[26]

In the October 1973 issue of *Goshen Trails*, Ralph S. Harrelson published research in which he claimed to have learned the historical personage behind the Lakey legend. In a history of Hamilton County, he discovered a single sentence revealing that a man named Lakey—the same man who gave his name to the creek—had indeed lived near the ford, but more

tellingly, that he had been murdered by his son-in-law. After further research, Harrelson discovered that a man named Joel Leaky had owned a tract of land in that vicinity prior to 1824. "Leaky," apparently, was a variation in the spelling of "Lakey." "Joel could be, and probably is, the person for whom the creek is named," he concluded.[27]

The tale of the headless horseman of southern Illinois has graced the pages of many monographs on Illinois ghost lore since its first printing in 1963. Among others, Lakey's ghost has appeared in Beth Scott and Michael Norman's *Haunted Heartland* (1985), Jo-Anne Christensen's *Ghost Stories of Illinois* (2000), and Chad Lewis and Terry Fisk's *Illinois Road Guide to Haunted Locations* (2007).

Only Chad Lewis and Terry Fisk's work contains a contemporary encounter with the phantom. A local woman, who was familiar with the Lakey legend, told them about the incident. The woman passed over the bridge every day on her way to and from work. One evening, she saw something strange in the woods. "As the woman slowed down to get a better look at what she had seen, she almost crashed her car because of what was staring back at her," Lewis and Fisk related. "Perched on top of a large horse was a man with no head."[28]

We will never know if Washington Irving's famous tale of "The Legend of Sleepy Hollow" affected the legend of Lakey's Creek. It is possible that German settlers carried the tale from New England to southern Illinois. Stories involving ghostly chases, such as Gottfried Bürger's "The Wild Huntsman," were widely popular in the early 1800s. Then again, Lakey's black steed could have been sired right here in Illinois.

---

[26] John W. Allen, *Legends & Lore of Southern Illinois* (Carbondale: Southern Illinois University, 1963, 1973), 59.

[27] Ralph S. Harrelson, "History and Legend of Lakey," *Goshen Trails* (October 1973): 13.
[28] Lewis and Fisk, 263.

THE FALLEN INVESTIGATE

JUL. 11

1:10 PM

86° F

The summer sun created tiny mirages in the asphalt as the Fallen sped toward a concrete bridge just outside of McLeansboro. Manowar's "Return of the Warlord" blared from the speakers of their aging, dark blue Toyota Corolla, while the smell of tacos drifted from the backseat. Mike, who was behind the steering wheel as usual, eyed Greg, Davin, and Emmer munching down on a smorgasbord of hard and soft tacos in the rearview mirror. He cringed as bits of lettuce and cheese fell on the floor.

"If you guys don't knock it off, I'm going to turn this car around!" he threatened.

"Man," Greg replied as taco shell spewed from his mouth between words, "we're almost there. Look, there's the bridge. Isn't it?"

Aurelia, in the front passenger seat, inspected the crumbling map of Illinois that she gripped in her hands. "This is it," she confirmed.

Emmer cleared his throat. "What kind of ridiculous goose chase do you have us going on now?" he asked. "Zombies? Trolls? More things that only seem to happen when I'm not around?"

"A headless horseman," Mike said through clenched teeth.

Laughter erupted from the backseat.

"This is almost as bad as that Dug Hill trip last year," Emmer chuckled. "Southern Illinoisans sure do have an imagination."

"At least it's an interesting story," Greg interjected as Mike steered their Toyota off the road and onto a small gravel drive at the edge of a large field near the bridge. "But from what I

remember, no one has seen this ghost in decades, so what exactly do you expect to find?"

"Evidence of some kind," Mike replied. "An old well. Some spectral horse dung. I don't know. Something."

"Here we go again," Emmer sighed as the car came to a stop and he swung one of the rear doors open. "First a mysterious astral portal, now this. In a sane world you'd be locked up at the funny farm."

"Well, luckily for me we got rid of those," Mike said with a grin.

"Will you two shut up already," Aurelia interrupted. "You're giving me a headache. If we're going to find anything at all here we need to concentrate. We don't want to screw up now with all the success we've had lately."

"Yeah, that mirror thing really worked out well," Emmer said with a sneer.

After a few moments, the five congregated outside of their car. Ahead of them on their right stood the concrete bridge over Lakey's Creek. On their left stood a small, wooded area. A narrow gravel road followed the tree line on the opposite side of the creek. Oddly, a fire hydrant poked its head out of the tall grass in the field in which they stood. A large mound of dirt and debris was also noticeable.

"It looks like there used to be a house here," Mike observed. "You can tell because of that pile of crap over there. This empty field and that fire hydrant are also suspicious."

"Thanks, Dr. Watson," Aurelia said. "I thought I was queen of the obvious here."

Mike shot her an annoyed glare, but he continued on as though he had not heard the insult.

"Do I have to remind you that Lakey's cabin was built in the 1820s, if it was even built at all?" Greg said. "It definitely wouldn't have had a fire hydrant, that's for sure."

Mike led the group closer toward the tree line and the pile of debris. Even through the abundant undergrowth, it was apparent there was a path that cut through the woods along the creek. "You're missing the point,"

Mike argued. "Think about it. There used to be a house here, right next to the creek. Lakey's Creek. Right near the ford where the headless horseman was last seen. If we could find out who lived here, we might be able to talk to them and ask them if they ever saw or heard the horseman. Who knows, maybe the story itself originated here during some late night backyard bonfires."

"I guess that makes sense," Greg admitted. "So what do we do next?"

Before Mike had time to reply, Aurelia shouted from a few yards downstream. "Hey! I think I see something!"

Mike, Emmer, Greg, and Davin spun around just as a light flashed under the bridge. "I don't think we're alone," Davin whispered. Without hesitation, Mike motioned to Emmer and Greg to cross the road and come down into the creek bed on the other side of the bridge.

Mike and Davin raced to Aurelia's side. "What did you see?" Mike asked.

Aurelia rested her hands on her broad hips. "Something moved under the bridge. I'm not sure what it was, but I feel like something is out of place over there."

"You didn't notice anything more specific than that?" Davin demanded. "These hunches of yours aren't very helpful. Remember the time you thought you sensed something at Chesterville Cemetery, and it turned out to be woodpeckers?"

Aurelia crinkled her brow and dug her fist into Davin's ribs. Davin's knees buckled and he barely held himself upright as he gasped for breath.

"That's enough, you two," Mike hissed. "You're acting like a bunch of children."

"Humph!" Aurelia exclaimed and turned her back on her friends.

On the other side of the road, Emmer and Greg quickly moved into position. The duo hugged the side of the concrete bridge so that they could not be seen by whatever was lurking in the shadows. A recent drought had reduced the creek to a trickle, exposing a wide swath of

LAKEY'S CREEK

sediment on the creek bed. For a few moments, the two heard only the rustle of water and the chirp of nearby birds. Then, suddenly, the sound of stones grinding together alerted them to the presence of a being with obvious, physical existence.

Emmer and Greg exchanged nods and sprang into action, simultaneously jumping down into the creek bed. Their assault elicited a sharp cry of surprise from what looked like a teenage boy wearing baggy shorts and a Far Side t-shirt. The boy lost his balance on the loose sand and fell into a pile of gravel. A can of spray paint flew out of his hand and fell into the creek.

Both Greg and Emmer broke out into laughter. "It's just some dumb kid," Emmer shouted to Mike, Davin, and Aurelia, who had finally arrived at the opening on the other side of the bridge.

"He's a litter bug too," Greg added with a wide grin. "We better call Al Gore."

"Yo, who you callin' dumb, fool?" the kid spat at them. "This is my turf. I be taggin' this shizzle."

"Someone's watched a little too much MTV," Mike added. "Listen. We're the Fallen, and this location was the scene of an intersection of the astral and physical plane. So that means it's our turf."

"Wh...what?" the kid stammered. "Yo, you been huffin' or some shite?"

"No, he's always like this," Emmer sighed. "I usually just ignore him. Anyway, we don't care what you're doing. We thought you might be someone else."

"Some*thing* else to be exact," Greg added with emphasis.

"Yo. Yo. It's cool. I be just leaving. Peace out, yo." The kid pulled himself to his feet and carefully stepped out from under the bridge, leaving his can of spray paint behind.

"Hey, go read a frickin' book!" Greg shouted after him.

"I thought gangsta posing was out and girl-pants emo was in," Mike asked Davin, who shrugged his shoulders.

"How should I know?" he replied.

The Fallen waited for the kid to be out of sight before they reconvened along the road on the downstream side of the bridge.

"Let's get back down to business," Mike said as he pulled a digital camera out of the pocket of his cargo shorts. "We'll take pictures of the area as usual. Davin, you're on for the video. Aurelia, try to see if you sense anything else. Greg, audiotape. Emmer." He paused.

"I'll just go with Greg," Emmer said before Mike had time to finish his thought. "I doubt we'll find anything else here, but I'll go through the county records when we're done and try to find out who owned this property last. Who knows, maybe they can help us."

Mike nodded and went to work, while Emmer and Greg exchanged skeptical glances. "Do you really think we're going to find anything?" Emmer whispered.

Greg shrugged his shoulders and pulled out the tape recorder. "We might as well try," he replied.

INVESTIGATION FILE 020

PECK CEMETERY
Oakley, Illinois

Peck Cemetery is yet another of those cemeteries that developed a bad reputation in the 1970s and has since been rehabilitated. The cemetery itself is of the typical rural stock, formerly hidden in a wood at the end of a gravel road in the middle of nowhere. Things have changed a little in recent years.

People I have talked to who remember when the cemetery was at the height of its reputation tell me that the area has been dramatically transformed. Houses dot the pothole-filled road. The gravel path to the cemetery is now a driveway. "Beware of dogs" and "no trespassing" signs are prominently displayed. Passersby would never guess that Peck Cemetery is only about fifty yards away.

Troy Taylor has done much to publicize this place, but stories have circulated the Internet for years. Christopher D. Blickensderfer, one of these storytellers, maintains a website that includes his account of a trip to Peck Cemetery in the early 1980s.

Unlike cemeteries with similar claims, Peck Cemetery seems to have actually been a location of Satanic worship in the past. Hidden from view prior to the 1990s, it would have been the perfect place to hold nighttime excursions far from any prying eyes. The evidence of these practices included burnt candles, graffiti, headless statues covered in red paint, and even statements from alleged Satanists themselves.

Blickensderfer wrote that it was rumored the leader of this Satanic group installed a "devil's chair" in the cemetery, on which he would sit during the rituals. If anyone else sat on the chair, they would die within a year. There were many of these so-called Devil's chairs around central Illinois, and almost every untimely death of a teenager was accompanied by the rumor that he or she had dared to sit in the accursed chair.

The chair is no longer at the cemetery. The county sheriff, angered by what went on there, is rumored to have destroyed it with a sledgehammer. Like other monuments, however, it was likely to have been the victim of nihilistic vandals.

Troy Taylor lists "inexplicable cries," "whispers and voices," "hooded figures," "eerie lights," and "the sound of a woman's scream" as other phenomenon experienced at Peck Cemetery.[29] Cold spots can be added to the list, and car problems have also been reported.

One woman who grew up in the area told me that there used to be some kind of cabin or shed at the end of a long trail that ran through the woods back behind the cemetery. It appeared as though someone made campfires at the location.

Peck Cemetery is located north of the towns of Cerro Gordo and Oakley along Donavan Road. Today the cemetery is a quiet, peaceful place hidden behind a private residence. It took me four years to find it, even after learning of its exact location. Good luck!

NOTE

Peck Cemetery has recently been closed to the general public while it undergoes restoration. Relatives of the deceased may visit, but police will be called on trespassers.

---

[29] Taylor, *Haunted Illinois*, 170.

THE FALLEN INVESTIGATE

AUG. 23

5:34 AM

72° F

As the Fallen strolled down the gravel drive with Emily in tow, Greg walked ahead of the group like a tour guide, waving his hands in the air excitedly. "So get this," he said, retelling a joke he had probably found on the bathroom wall at a truck stop. "I knew this guy named Jim who met a freaky girl last summer. She worked at a carnival. She had a few missing teeth, but when she invited him back to her trailer, he figured, what the heck, why not?

"When he got there, he noticed a few strange things. First, he noticed that her hallway was filled with those 'funny mirrors' that make you look tall or short. He also noticed that her bedroom had shelves and shelves of stuffed animals. That was a little weird, but before he could ask about it, the girl had his pants around his ankles.

"He slept with her, and when he was done, he asked how it was. She goes, 'You can have anything from the bottom shelf, unless you want to try again for something from the middle shelf!'"

Davin snickered. "That was bad," he said.

Emmer gave him the 'thumbs down' sign and made a noise like an angry buzzer.

"Are you done?" Mike asked as he walked shoulder to shoulder with Aurelia, who was dressed in camouflage pants and a black wifebeater. Her dark brown hair was tied back in a ponytail.

"I'm sick of these cemeteries," Davin whined. "Sometimes literally. Remember what happened at Williamsburg Hill? I don't want to get hypothermia again in the middle of the summer."

"Oh, stop complaining," Aurelia sighed.

"We have serious work to do," Mike added as he adjusted his glasses. The group walked past two red traffic barriers into a brief corridor of trees. A few yards ahead, they could see a clearing and an old, rusted fence along the crest of a ridge that ran parallel to the drive. Mike picked up his pace and arrived at the cemetery entrance before the others.

"So this is the infamous Peck Cemetery?" he announced. "It doesn't look so scary."

"Yeah, well maybe that's because it's so early in the frickin' morning," Emmer yelled. "Tell me again why the heck we came here at five in the morning? I barely got any sleep last night."

Greg fished a miniature powdered doughnut out of the pocket of his ragged, green shirt and stuffed it into his mouth. "Yeah," he mumbled. "What's the deal?"

"I wanted to go here before it got too hot," Mike replied. "We'll go to IHOP after we're done, I promise. Besides, this is the perfect time for what I have planned."

"Oh geez," Emmer said. "Here we go."

The group stepped inside the rusted gates and waited while Mike scanned the area with the gaze of an experienced investigator. "There." He pointed at an empty patch of grass in the middle of the cemetery. "Aura, do your thing. Davin, I want you to help her."

Aurelia did what she was instructed, but Davin could not tear his eyes away from Emily, who wore a short, plaid skirt and a charcoal-colored blouse that was matted with sweat. She stood and smiled at him mysteriously.

Mike threw Davin an angry glance, and his friend finally stumbled after Aurelia. Emily followed.

"I don't get it," Greg said when the three were several yards away. "What are we doing here? You never mentioned this place might be a candidate for the location of the astral gate."

Mike grinned. "I know," he said quietly. "We'll see what happens in a few minutes. Maybe nothing. Hopefully something."

"I'll hold my breath and cross my fingers," Emmer said sarcastically.

Deep inside the cemetery, Aurelia pulled a dark blue pouch out of her pocket. She tore it open and scooped out a handful of salt. Inspecting Emily's face for any reaction, she began sprinkling it into the grass until she produced a circle that was invisible to the naked eye. She then pulled five quartz crystals out of her pocket and placed them at even intervals around the circumference of the circle. She bowed her head and began muttering in Latin.

"What is she doing?" Greg asked. Annoyance began to show in his voice. "What's going on?"

"You remember those zealots that we had so much trouble with last year?" Mike replied.

"Yeah," Greg said. "We haven't seen them around in a while."

"One of them wore a necklace with a six pointed star on it. I didn't think anything of it at the time, until I noticed that obese Satanist had one tattooed on his arm."

"It's a common symbol," Emmer interrupted. "The Chicago flag has several."

"Yeah, maybe," Mike said. "But is it a coincidence that both of those groups carry that symbol, and that both of them are trying to find the astral gate before we do? Something is up, and I'm going to get to the bottom of it." He tore his glasses off his face and wiped them clean with the hem of his black t-shirt.

About a dozen yards away, Aurelia had completed her preparations and was eyeing Davin and Emily contemptuously. The two hovered around each other like birds. Since they became acquainted at Airtight Bridge, they had spent every waking moment together. Aurelia was worried about what Davin had been telling Emily for all those months. He already had a tendency to disappear for weeks on end; she questioned his reliability.

No sooner had she signaled to Mike that the preparations were finished, two figures emerged from the nearby forest through a gap in the fence. One was wide and potbellied, the other, tall and thin. It was the Satanists. The rising sun caught two metal objects in their hands.

"Son of a—" Emmer began, but Mike cut him off.

"Aura, get over here!" he shouted.

Aurelia snarled, but before she could move, Emily tripped her and shoved her to the ground. It was only the element of surprise that protected Emily from an immediate reprisal.

Davin looked confused, but Emily grabbed his hand and pulled him toward the interlopers.

"Where is *he* going?" Greg demanded.

"Haven't you noticed that those guys show up every time we investigate a place we suspect might be the location of the astral gate?" Mike whispered.

"Do you think—?" his friend began.

Mike nodded. "Davin sold us out. You were right earlier. The only people I told about this place were Aura and Davin. There was no way those Satanists could have known unless Davin told Emily and Emily told them. She's been playing the innocent victim this whole time, all to get at one of us and break us up."

"Divide and conquer," Emmer said. "Clever."

"Not quite," Mike replied.

In defiance of her instincts to immediately go on the attack, Aurelia reluctantly joined Mike, Greg, and Emmer near the cemetery gate.

"It looks like they brought guns," Aurelia said. "Actual, blasted *guns*. What do you want to do?"

"What a bunch of scumbags," Mike said with a smirk. "It looks like there's nothing we can do."

By this time, the two Satanists, along with Davin and Emily, stood inside the circle Aurelia had made minutes earlier. The Satanists

PECK CEMETERY

pointed their pistols menacingly at the Fallen. "You know what we want," the obese man demanded.

"Wait... Are those BB guns?" Emmer whispered.

Mike produced a scroll out of the pocket of his shorts and tossed it to the Satanists, making sure that it fell short so they would have to bend over to get it.

"Just read this out loud and you should be able to open the portal," Mike yelled. "I hate to say it, but you really screwed us. We'll get out of here. We won't stop you."

The obese man made Davin retrieve the scroll and hand it to him. He licked his lips in anticipation as the Fallen backed out of the cemetery gates and retreated down the gravel drive.

As they passed beyond the far corner of the cemetery, Greg, Aurelia, Emmer, and Mike heard chanting coming from beyond the rusted fence, then nothing. Moments later, frantic curses and screams broke the silence and the Fallen ran toward their car.

Slamming the door, Mike made sure everyone was inside before he threw their Toyota Corolla into reverse.

"What did you give them?" Greg asked through ragged gasps for breath.

"Nothing," Mike said. "The scroll is nonsense, but that 'salt' Aura scattered was actually sugar coated in ant pheromones. They should be covered with thousands of them by now!"

Emmer and Greg broke out into laughter.

"This is far from over," Aurelia reminded them, but of that, everyone was already aware.

INVESTIGATION FILE 021

BLOOD'S POINT ROAD
Boone County, Illinois

Blood's Point is one of those locations that is well known to locals but has, to my knowledge, never been included in any book on Illinois ghost lore. The road and cemetery of the same name are home to a cornucopia of stories and myths, each one a variant or twist on the last.

The name of the road itself is enough to excite one's imagination. What kind of event would leave such a name upon the landscape? A gruesome murder or massacre? An ancient battle? Unfortunately, its origins are actually quite mundane. According to *The Past and Present of Boone County, Illinois* (1877), Blood's Point was named after a prominent local family, the Bloods. Arthur Blood was the first white settler in Flora Township; a pleasant area that derived its name from the abundance of flower-covered fields.

One could say that ever since its christening, the area has been stained by Blood (sorry, I couldn't resist). Both the Shadowlands Index of Haunted Places and Hauntedrockford.webs.com contain a myriad of tales relating to the cemetery and the railroad bridge that lies about a mile to the west. The road itself is said to be patrolled by phantom vehicles, most notably an old pickup truck, but also a big rig and a disappearing cop car.

NOTE

Hauntedrockford.webs.com is no longer a functioning website.

Depending on who you ask, around 4-8 people have hung themselves or have been hung from the railroad bridge; a witch, her children, three anonymous women, and even Arthur Blood along with his wife and their entire family! A busload of elementary school students is also said to have plummeted from the bridge.

In my opinion, one of the most interesting legends concerns a witch called "Witch Beulah" who (allegedly) lived in the area. According to Hauntedrockford.webs.com, Arthur Blood's children once encountered her under the railroad bridge and were enthralled by her ability to produce fire from her fingertips.

Afterwards, the locals grew suspicious of Arthur Blood's family and drove them to suicide. Other people say that Beulah hung her children from the bridge, or that she committed suicide in an identical fashion.

UPDATE

William Gorman wrote at length about Blood's Point in his book, *Ghost Whispers: Tales from Haunted Midway.*

On the Shadowlands Index, an anonymous contributor reported that a crumbling foundation exists in the woods off of Sweeney Road (which intersects with Blood's Point). Red lights supposedly dance around the area, and an old farmer chases trespassers off with a shotgun.

The cemetery itself is said to be visited by a wide variety of phenomenon, from orbs, to a phantom dog, to a vanishing barn, to the disembodied laughter of children and electrical malfunctions.

Some of these stories can be easily dismissed as transplanted urban legends, but some of them are detailed enough to, perhaps, have been rooted in fact. One thing is certain: naming an area "Blood's Point" is a good way to attract attention!

THE FALLEN INVESTIGATE

SEP. 10

9:30 PM

60° F

"**W**ith a name like Blood's Point, this area was just asking to be a paranormal focal point," Mike said as the Fallen cruised down the lonely rural avenue. The road was lit only by the light of the full moon and the dim headlights of their dark blue Toyota Corolla. The musical stylings of the Lord Weird Slough Feg emanated from the Corolla's speakers, while fog obscured the scenery on either side of the vehicle.

"So this school bus supposedly fell off a railroad bridge up here, the very same bridge where a witch was hung a hundred years before?" Emmer asked with a touch of skepticism.

"I guess you could say it was a *magic school bus*," Greg interjected, and the others groaned.

"There are a lot of layers to this place," Mike explained from behind the steering wheel. "Isn't it possible that over the course of several generations, a few traumatic incidents left their mark on this one stretch of road?"

"I'll believe it when I see it," Emmer replied.

Aurelia, seated on the front passenger side, examined a map under the narrow beam of a penlight and stayed out of the conversation. Her hair was tied tightly behind her almost cartoonishly round ears.

Suddenly, a pair of headlights lit up their rear windshield. Mike squinted as he tried to discern in the rearview mirror what type of vehicle the beams belonged to.

"Is that a cop?" Greg asked, straining to see over his shoulder.

"Better not be," Mike grumbled.

"He's coming up awfully fast," Emmer added with a touch of concern.

Indeed, the vehicle sped rapidly closer, and in a few moments, the Fallen plainly saw the outline of a large, white van behind them.

"It's some jerk," Mike said as he depressed the breaks. "I'll just let him pass."

The van sped forward until, as the railroad bridge loomed, its headlights practically pressed against the bumper of the dark blue Corolla, illuminating the bumper sticker that read "Necrophilia is Dead" in yellow, skeletal lettering.

"Look out!" Aurelia shrieked.

Mike covered his right ear and frowned. "What the heck?"

"Hey, isn't there also a legend about a car that chases you on this road?" Greg frantically asked as the bumpers briefly collided.

"Yeah, that's it, blame it on the ghosts," Emmer shot back.

"No, what if it's not a legend after all?" Mike said. "Crowley's arse! I'm going to try and throw him off."

Upon clearing the bridge, Mike jerked the steering wheel sharply to the right and braked. The Toyota's tires spit gravel and it lurched toward the embankment along the side of the road. If they had not been wearing seatbelts, Mike and Greg might have wound up in their friend's laps.

The van raced ahead into the night, but displayed break lights after less than fifty yards and made a tight U-turn. Mike carefully guided his car back onto the road, and the two vehicles sat facing each other menacingly.

"Did anyone get the license plate?" Emmer asked between gasps for breath.

"I think we have bigger things to worry about," Mike said as the van's tires squealed and it began to barrel toward the four investigators.

Then, without warning, a misty form materialized in front of the van. Its driver must have been startled by whatever had just appeared, because he or she slammed on the brakes and swerved into the opposite lane. Unfortunately for is occupants, but fortunately for the Fallen, the vehicle spun out of control and rolled off the road in a sickening tangle of steel and aluminum, before coming to a rest in the grassy trench along the border of a cornfield.

The mist in the road dissipated as quickly as it had congealed.

Greg broke the silence. "Uh, did you guys see that?" he asked.

"They must have blown a tire," Emmer said, still in shock.

"Tire my rear!" Aurelia yelled. "What was that thing in the road? And more importantly, where did it go? Is it coming after us too?"

"What are you talking about?" Emmer asked in frustration. "The mist? Hello—" He gestured wildly with his arms. "If you haven't noticed, we're surrounded by fog. I think the most important thing to do right now is find out if anyone in that van needs our help."

"What!?" Greg exclaimed. "Screw them! They tried to kill us!"

Mike drove cautiously toward the spot where the van had left the road. "No," he said. "I want to see who these guys are."

"Do I need to remind you that anyone within a mile radius is probably calling the cops right now?" Greg insisted. "Or that someone might drive by at any moment and see us next to the wreckage of a car that mysteriously flew off the road?"

"You have a point," Mike admitted, pushing down the accelerator.

"Isn't leaving the scene of an accident a felony?" Emmer asked, but he received no response as the Toyota Corolla rolled further down Blood's Point Road.

After another few minutes of listening to Slough Feg croon about ancient times, the silhouette of a cemetery appeared on the horizon.

"This is what we really came for," Mike announced.

"More phantoms?" Emmer asked in a haughty, dismissive tone.

"Nope," Mike replied. "Something nice and tangible. The remains of an Indian—er—a Native American chief. Well, one of his ribs, to be exact."

"Uh..."

"According to an old history of Boone County, a Pottawatomie chief named Big Thunder lived in this area in the late 1830s," Mike explained. "He died near present day Belvidere and was buried on a hill where the modern courthouse now sits. Well, buried isn't exactly the right word. He was placed on a chair facing to the west and a log structure was built up around him.

"Over time, the white settlers carried off his bones as souvenirs one by one, until nothing remained. Some of the locals tossed in old pig bones to play a joke on the curiosity seekers, so no one really knows where the original bones are. Except I have good information that one is buried up here in Blood's Point Cemetery. I did some mirror scrying and I think I know exactly where it is."

"Great," Emmer said. "Assuming it even exists, why do you want an old rib bone?"

"I think it will help us unlock the astral gate," Mike replied.

"Of course."

Their Toyota Corolla pulled over onto the road's narrow shoulder and the Fallen piled out. They stood for a moment and examined the cemetery's two gates in the darkness. A thick layer of fog obscured most of the grounds.

"Stay close," Mike ordered. "We can't use flashlights. Greg, you got the shovel?"

Greg nodded, and the quartet climbed over the red guardrail and entered the cemetery.

Mike tentatively led his friends toward the far left corner of Blood's Point Cemetery. On more than one occasion, he tripped over or collided with a headstone hidden in the fog-shrouded lawn, while Greg used his cane to distance himself from any such objects.

An old cinderblock shed loomed in front of them. Excited, Mike instructed Aurelia to shine the narrow beam of her penlight down at the grass while he dropped to his knees and felt around with his bare hands.

After a tense moment, he felt a small, box-like stone that protruded from the ground. "It's just like my vision in the mirror," he said.

"Are we supposed to dig?" Greg asked.

"No, look." Mike cleared the fog away from the stone with one swipe. It read, "B.T."

"I'll be damned," Emmer said.

Mike snatched the shovel out of Greg's hand and struck the stone with the sharp edge of the blade. To everyone's surprise, the stone was hollow and cracked open. Clearing the debris, Mike thrust his hand inside and removed an old, sun-bleached rib bone. He refrained from shouting in triumph.

"It's too bad Davin isn't here to see this," Aurelia muttered.

"I don't want to talk about him right now," Mike replied. "We've got what we came for. Let's get out of here before the cops show up."

Wading back into the murky haze, the Fallen disappeared into the night.

INVESTIGATION FILE 022

OLD UNION CEMETERY
Clinton, Illinois

A forgotten graveyard squirreled away in the cornfields of central Illinois makes for good storytelling, and almost every one has its ghostly tales. Old Union is no exception. This cemetery first received attention on Troy Taylor's website, Prairieghosts.com, and he later included it in *Weird Illinois* (2005).

Old Union Cemetery is one of Taylor's "secret cemeteries," the location of which he refuses to disclose to the public, making it difficult for anyone to independently verify his claims. Luckily for us, Old Union is clearly marked on cemetery and plat maps available to the general public through the DeWitt County Genealogical Society.

A history of the cemetery is difficult to find, and several sources appear, at first glance, to be fractional or contradictory. Troy Taylor provided a general overview on his website, but Genealogytrails.com, in an excerpt from an article entitled, "The Disciples of Christ History," filled in some of the details.

According to the article, Old Union Church was established 10 miles west of Clinton on October 13, 1831 near a large, white oak tree. The stump of the tree, and "the gravestones of the cemetery which grew around the house of worship" are "silent sentinels of faded joys and departed glories," the article opined.

The preacher at the church was a man named Hugh Bowles, a Kentuckian by birth and a friend of Abraham Lincoln while the future president ran a law office in nearby Clinton. Mr. Bowles died in 1846, and the article related that Old Union Church only remained open for fifty years because its attendees moved to Clinton when the railroad was built. According to Troy Taylor, however, a fire destroyed "Union Christian Church" in 1931.

The 1882 *History of DeWitt County, Illinois* cleared up why a name discrepancy existed between the two accounts. In Chapter 14, the book explained that "old Union Church" was organized in 1833, but had no formal house of worship until 1838. It was then known as "Union Christian Church" because its congregation recognized no particular denomination.

A second church, which had a seating capacity of 600 people, was erected in 1864 in front of the cemetery. "Springs of never failing water" flowed from the foot of the hill on which the new building sat. That second building must have been the fire-ravaged church that Troy Taylor described in his article.

As for the ghosts, Taylor maintained that he had obtained testimony from two cemetery workers and a sheriff's deputy that visitors had seen "glowing balls of light" in the cemetery at night. A private plot near the back of the cemetery, which is surrounded by an ornate fence and contains a single monument that is, contrary to Taylor's claims, clearly legible, was also accused of giving visitors "bad vibes."

Troy Taylor himself claimed to have seen a ball of light in Old Union during an investigation in daylight hours. He also described temperature drops of 40 degrees! So far, no one has stepped forward to offer any similar accounts.

THE FALLEN INVESTIGATE

OCT. 3

11:43 AM

55° F

The Fallen's dark blue Toyota Corolla splashed and skidded its way down the long, dirt road that was, currently, a sea of mud. Tall rows of unharvested corn flanked the vehicle on either side, making it virtually invisible to prying eyes.

"It's a good thing this car can take punishment," Mike said as he swerved to avoid the most obvious of the potholes. Even still, every few moments the Toyota hit one dead on and rocked violently.

"Watch out," Greg complained from the back seat. "I get motion sickness."

Suddenly, Mike slammed on the breaks. The tires swerved and the car came to a stop inches from a ravine that had opened up across the width of the road. A pool of murky water almost obscured the fissure from view, and driving a few more inches would have left them literally stuck in a rut.

"Well, this is where we get out," Mike announced.

Aurelia, Emmer, and Greg piled out of the vehicle while Mike popped open the trunk. The trunk hatch lifted up and Davin and Emily crawled out.

"Did you have fun back there?" Emmer asked sarcastically as Davin and Emily dusted themselves off.

"At least you don't have to clean the bathroom anymore," Aurelia laughed.

"Great," Davin grumbled.

Mike examined the crevice in the road and shook his head. "Man, that was close," he said. "I almost didn't even see that."

"Looks like we're going to have to go the rest of the way on foot," Greg added, tapping his cane for emphasis.

"Oh, look," Emmer interjected, peering down the lane at the fence in the distance, "another haunted cemetery. Aren't those a dime a dozen these days?"

"More like a nickel," Mike said. "But we have to check it out anyway. In a gallon of lies there might be one drop of truth."

Emmer snorted.

The group cautiously navigated around the crevice and slogged their way through the mud toward the tree line, beyond which lay the remnants of Old Union Cemetery.

Greg caught up to Mike and addressed him in a low whisper. "I can understand taking Davin back after his betrayal, but *that girl*? She's not one of us. What's up with that?"

"You're right," Mike replied. "Davin is one of us and Emily isn't."

"So what gives?" Greg demanded. "We can't trust her. Why let her come along at all?"

"We *won't* trust her," Mike explained. "Not now. Not ever. But I learned that one of the Satanists we've been having trouble with is her brother. That's why she keeps running back to them. We may not like her, but Davin does. Why sacrifice Davin just to get rid of her? Besides, this works both ways. We can use her to get at the Satanists just as much as they use her to get at us."

"I guess it sucks to be her," Greg chuckled.

"Until I get to the bottom of this, she might still prove to be useful," Mike added. "I don't have to tell you that we need all the help we can get at this point."

"Still, I don't like it. I'm going to keep an eye on her."

"I bet you will," Mike muttered under his breath.

"What are you talking about?" Davin yelled from the rear of the group.

"Nothing!" Mike shouted back. "Let's focus on why we're here. We have to investigate this place and then get out. We'll play it by the book."

As the six neared the edge of the woods, they heard growling coming from the trees to their left and froze in their tracks.

"What was that?" Emily asked frantically.

Mike dug into the pockets of his trench coat and produced a small pair of binoculars. He scanned the woods, which luckily were barren of underbrush since most of the weeds were dead, and noticed something moving in the newly fallen leaves.

"What is it?" Emmer asked.

"I don't know," Mike replied. "There's something moving around."

"Let's check it out," Greg said as he began moving in the direction of the sound.

Mike tried to protest, but his friends left him standing alone as they walked toward the woods. He shook his head and followed.

Greg entered the hinterlands of the forest and then stopped dead in his tracks. He was so startled by what he saw that he nearly fell over backwards and took Emmer with him.

Aurelia shoved her way past the two. A few yards ahead, a mangy dog growled and whined menacingly, but appeared to be stuck. The dog was covered by patchy, dark gray hair and seemed malnourished.

"What is that thing?" Emily asked, keeping herself strategically behind Davin.

"It's a dog," Emmer replied hesitantly. "I think it's trapped by something."

"Let's leave it alone," Mike said. "We have work to do."

Greg ignored his friend and crept toward the wounded animal. "Aw, who's a good dog?" he said in a baby voice. "Yes, you are. You're a good dog."

The animal whined and sniffed at its foot, which was caught in a metal trap and covered in dried blood.

"Hey, someone get a rag," Greg said, but Emily already had a bandana out and quickly handed it over. Greg knelt down beside the dog

and let it sniff his hand before he gingerly released the animal's leg from the trap. Its tail wagged and it licked Greg's face.

"Aw, it's a Kodak moment," Emmer said.

"Can we go now?" Mike insisted. "We still have work to do."

Greg finished tying the bandana around the animal's ankle and then stepped back. "All right, you're free," he said. "Go!" He pointed somewhere off in the distance, but the dog whined and limped toward him.

"I think she likes you," Aurelia said.

Mike threw up his hands in disbelief.

"We should give her a name," Greg suggested. "But I'm not sure what breed she is. I've never seen this before."

"I have," Emmer replied, matter of factly. "I'm pretty sure she's a coydog. Look at her snout and her ears. It's exactly like the pictures I found online."

"We should name her Casey," Greg said, "after Aura's boyfriend." He laughed. "Casey the Coydog!"

"Hey!" Aurelia fumed, but Greg ignored her.

"You can't be serious," Mike protested. "Look at that thing. It probably has fleas or rabies or scabies or Crowley knows what else."

"Didn't you just tell me that we need all the help we can get?" Greg replied. "Having a dog around would be great. She can sense things we can't, and she can even guard our HQ. Plus we can take her for walks and play fetch and brush her and—"

"Alright, alright," Mike said. "But she has to sit in the backseat on the way home. Davin and Emily go back to the trunk. But first we have to check out this cemetery. That's the reason we came all this way, remember?"

"What is it this time?" Emmer asked. "Weeping women in white? Mysterious vanishing houses? Orbs? The key to energy independence?"

"Ghost lights and cold spots near the back of the cemetery," Mike replied.

"Oh, that's original."

The Fallen, accompanied by their new companion, walked past the barbed wire fence and into the cemetery grounds. A small plot surrounded by an old, rusted fence lay in the far left hand corner.

"That must be it," Aurelia remarked as she marched toward the spot.

As the group neared, Casey the Coydog began to whine and growl, and she refused to approach the area.

"What did I tell you?" Greg asked. "I knew she would come in handy." He bent down and patted her neck. "Who's a good dog? Yes, you are. Yes, you are."

Mike rolled his eyes and turned toward Aurelia. "Do you sense anything?"

Aurelia closed her eyes for a moment and concentrated. "I think something is here, but I don't think it's human, or was human, anyway."

"Interesting," Mike said. "Let's document the area and see how the crystal reacts. We can't be sure until we confirm this from several sources."

"You are insane," Emmer said. "Nothing that you're 'feeling' here is evidence of anything. All you have is a wounded dog whining because it's in pain, and the testimony of someone who is going out with a guy who sells meth for a living."

Greg tried to suppress a smile, but Mike shook his head. *One day I'll show him his proof, he thought. One day very soon.*

Investigation File 023

Hartford Castle
Hartford, Illinois

"Hartford Castle" is the colloquial name for a mansion that formerly stood on a tract of land just outside of Hartford, Illinois, across the river from St. Louis. The mansion's actual name was Lakeview, but few besides the original owner referred to it as such. The original owner was a French immigrant named Benjamin Biszant, who built the imposing home for his bride, an Englishwoman whose name has apparently been lost to history.

Sparing no expense (which was certainly an impressive dollar amount in 1897), Biszant surrounded Lakeview with sprawling gardens, statuary, romantic gazebos, and, finally, a moat to keep out trespassers. According to Louie Haines, a neighbor who recalled helping to dig the moat with his father, the Frenchman stocked it with goldfish that interbred with local crappie, producing what he described as "unusual looking fish."[30]

Eventually, Biszant's wife died and, perhaps, the pain was too much for him to remain at Lakeview. He sold the mansion and moved west. A number of owners and tenants occupied the mansion until 1923 when a husband and wife from nearby Wood River purchased the property. They lived there until 1964, when the wife became a widow and decided to move to less lonely surroundings.

During that time, according to Bill Matheus of the *Lewis & Clark Journal*, local residents treated the property as if it were their own. Visitors frequently roamed the grounds and even invited themselves inside the mansion for tours! The mansion deteriorated during the late 1960s, and in 1971 and 1972 vandals ran wild.

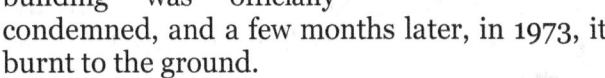

"Unknown persons... ripped mantels from the walls, crushed chandeliers, pulled supports from staircases, and took small sized telephone poles and used them to ram holes in the many rooms of the once beautiful 'castle,'" Matheus wrote. The building was officially condemned, and a few months later, in 1973, it burnt to the ground.

At least one ghost story came out of Lakeview during the time of its original ownership.

According to the *Lewis & Clark Journal*, the story started when a burglar entered the mansion and was scared away by the clinking of bamboo window curtains.

Benjamin Biszant himself claimed that was how the rumors of a ghost began. Troy Taylor, in what seems to be his only original contribution to the legend, asserted that the ghost of the Frenchman's wife has been seen on the property.[31]

Today, the Hartford Castle is nothing more than a hole in the ground, surrounded by concrete debris and a shallow moat. All of the gilded ornaments are long gone, and the beautiful gardens are no more. Soon, all that will remain are the memories of this once legendary spot.

---

[30] *Lewis & Clark Journal* (St. Louis) 25 March 1973.

[31] Taylor, Haunted Illinois, 121-122.

The Fallen Investigate

NOV. 28

3:25 PM

36° F

Leaves crunched beneath the feet of the Fallen as they trudged through the dense woods, while the rush of cars from the nearby highway partially obscured the sound of their movement. At long last, the quartet emerged into a clearing where the underbrush disappeared. Casey the Coydog panted excitedly and sniffed the ground.

Mike, Greg, Aurelia, and Emmer stood and faced what looked like a nondescript swamp, but what, in reality, was a wide moat that ringed an island that could only be seen in its entirety from the air. Somewhere on that island were the ruins of an old mansion.

"It's too bad Davin isn't here to see this," Emmer said, "and maybe that girl Emily too, I guess."

"*No it isn't,*" Greg shot back. "That—"

"That's enough," Mike said, interrupting his friend. "We have more important things to worry about right now, like how we're going to get across this moat."

"Isn't there a way around?" Emmer asked.

Mike scanned the area. For as far as his eyes could see, the water hugged the trunks of the trees. In some places, downed branches seemed to offer a ford, but it was doubtful whether any would hold a person's weight.

Casey the Coydog barked and began to trot along the shoreline away from the Fallen and toward the sounds of traffic.

"Where's she going?" Greg wondered aloud.

"Stupid mutt," Mike grumbled. "She's going to get hit by a car is what's going to happen."

"Forget about it," Emmer said. "How are we going to get across all this water?"

"We could build a bridge," Greg suggested. "Look at all these branches lying around. Mike, remember when we got stuck out in those woods and built a shelter out of whatever we could find? This is pretty much the same."

"We don't have time for that," Mike snapped. "This whole place is low ground—and flooded. It would take hours to get across. Crowley's arse!"

"Oh, for Pete's sake," Aurelia sighed. She shoved past Mike and Emmer and trudged straight into the water. Her boots sunk into the mud at the bottom of the moat, but the water was not deep enough to poor over the calf-high rim of her footwear.

"That's fine for you," Emmer laughed, "but what about us?" Mike, Greg, and Emmer were all wearing hiking shoes.

Greg shrugged. "For once I agree with Aura," he said. "It's the easiest way." Without skipping a beat, he joined Aurelia in the moat and made his way to the dry land a few yards away.

Exchanging glances, Mike and Emmer cautiously entered the freezing water.

After a few minutes, the four found themselves on the opposite shore, feet soaked, but otherwise in one piece.

"Since I'm probably going to get pneumonia, explain to me what was so darn important about coming here, and it better not have anything to do with imaginary beings, drunk high school kids, or this stupid portal obsession of yours," Emmer spat.

"Man, Emmer is really being a *wet blanket,*" Greg quipped, but the group ignored him.

Mike coughed. "It does have to do with the astral portal," he said. "We know a guy from France built this mansion, right? Supposedly for his English bride, who apparently never had a name? That is suspicious in and of itself, but why did he build the mansion right here? And where did his vast fortune come from? Why did he leave suddenly?"

"Maybe he was just a really private guy," Emmer said. "He left because his wife died and he got lonely. Why is everything a conspiracy with you?"

"Because sometimes it *is* a conspiracy," Mike countered. "And in this case, I'm convinced that this guy came here from Europe looking for the astral gate. And I think he actually found it. And I think it's nearby and he hid its location somewhere on this property. I think he tried to open the gate and it destroyed his life—cursing this property in the process."

"So why do we want to find this thing again?" Greg interjected.

Emmer ignored him. "What evidence do you have to back up this nonsense?" he demanded.

"I'll know it when I see it," Mike said.

Emmer threw up his hands, but joined the group as they trekked toward the center of the triangle of land that made up the grounds of the former mansion. Suddenly, the quartet heard barking coming from somewhere off to their right. They broke into a run, dodging branches and underbrush, until they caught a glimpse of a group of five adults dressed in white suits standing off in the distance near an old, crumbling gazebo.

"Darn it, I thought we got rid of those guys!" Mike exclaimed. In fact, the sharply-dressed zealots had not been seen in months.

"What are they doing here?" Emmer asked rhetorically. "Shouldn't they be in Haiti converting the dark and swarthy heathens or something?"

"I know what they're doing here," Mike said. "They're here for the same reason we are. I told you there was something to this!"

"Just because several people believe a delusion, doesn't make it any less delusional," his friend shot back.

As they closed the distance between them, the Fallen saw that Casey the Coydog had somehow circumvented the moat. Her mangy coat was bone dry, and she barked and growled at the dapper interlopers.

"Looks like you got here just in time!" the middle-aged, brown haired woman at the center of the group laughed as the Fallen came within ten yards.

She scrutinized them, noticing that they were soaking wet from the knee down. "What happened to you? Didn't you know there's a path from the highway to right where we're standing?"

"Shut up!" Aurelia growled. "What are you doing here?"

The woman laughed again. "Hypocrites! You claim the right to go wherever you want, but you won't extend that same right to us?"

"We're not *jerks*," Mike retorted. "What

HARTFORD CASTLE

have you found?"

"What do you mean?" the woman asked, feigning innocence. "There's something here to find?"

"You know what I'm talking about," Mike snapped.

The brown haired lady waved her hand and a balding, rotund man pushed a crumbling, stained book into her fingers. His hand bore a ring with a six-pointed star embossed on its surface. "Oh, you mean this?" she teased. "The journal that contains the directions to the astral gate, how to open it, and the ultimate secret to unlocking the world for our divine mission?"

"Yeah, that," Greg said.

"Give it to us!" Aurelia screamed and brandished her fists threateningly.

As the middle aged woman shook her head, two of the men behind her pulled small pistols out of their pockets and pointed them at the Fallen. "I assure you that unlike those idiot Devil-worshippers, these guns are quite real," the woman said. "I detest violence, of course, but even Yahweh was vengeful when He felt it necessary."

For a moment, Aurelia looked as though she was ready to test the zealot's resolve, but Mike firmly took her by the arm and began backing away. "We never pick fights we can't win," Mike whispered. "Trust me, it's better this way."

"If you only realized how ridiculous all of you look," Emmer interjected with a quick chuckle. "Don't even get me started."

The zealots threw him an angry glance, but slowly withdrew down the overgrown path, journal in hand.

Aurelia waited until they were out of sight before she swore and struck at the air, while Greg whistled for Casey the Coydog and embraced her when she trotted over by his side.

"Good dog," he whispered. "You did your best." He then turned and addressed the group. "Well, that's that, isn't it? All this work for nothing. Congratulations."

Mike stroked his prominent chin. "Not quite," he said. "I'm not a *complete* moron. I

thought there was a chance that they would get here before we did, especially since they seem to be working with those Satanists somehow."

"That still doesn't make any sense to me," Greg said. "Why would they help each other? They have exactly the opposite agenda."

"It's too bad neither heaven nor hell actually exist," Emmer, always the skeptic, interrupted.

"Whatever," Mike snapped. "The important thing now is that we stop them from opening that gate. Luckily for us, I think I figured out where it is without even looking at the Frenchman's journal, but we have to act quickly. Time is not in our favor."

INVESTIGATION FILE 024

CAHOKIA MOUNDS
Collinsville, Illinois

Cahokia Mounds State Historic Site is located near Collinsville, Illinois, around eight miles east of St. Louis. The site consists of dozens of prehistoric mounds constructed by American Indians around the time that Leif Ericson's longships landed in Vinland.

The most prominent feature of these mounds is Monk's Mound. Monk's Mound was the largest earthen structure north of central Mexico at the time of its construction. "Begun around A.D. 900 and completed 300 years later," Gene S. Stuart wrote in his book *America's Ancient Cities* (1988), "it has 4 terraces; rises 100 feet; covers some 16 acres with a base measuring approximately 700 by 1,080 feet, and contains about 22 million cubic feet of earth."[32] A large building sat at the summit of the mound.

The Cahokia Mounds were built by a group of people identified by anthropologists as belonging to the Mississippian Culture. Not much is known about them, other than the artifacts and earthen structures they left behind.

The mounds were a part of a large city, which reached the height of its power between 1000 and 1200 AD. A large stockade surrounded the central structures at the site, which the residents rebuilt several times. There is no evidence of battles or who their enemy might have been.

Cahokia stood at the hub of a network of "mound communities," which would have reinforced its role as a trade center along with its place at the juncture of the Mississippi, Illinois, and Missouri Rivers. It maintained that

position for several hundred years before the site was mysteriously abandoned around 1400 AD. In comparison, the city of St. Louis has been in existence for a little over 200 years.

Cahokia was not the only mound city in North America. According to Earl H. Swanson, in his book *The Making of the Past: The Ancient Americas* (1989), similar, but less extensive cities have been found near Spiro, Oklahoma; Etowah, Georgia; Moundville, Alabama; and Hiwassee Island, Tennessee. Many of these mounds were used for burial, and contain human remains, stone tools, weapons, pottery, and artwork.

At the time the first French explorers began to penetrate the Illinois territory, the native peoples had no knowledge of who had once occupied the massive site. In the 1800s, American archeologists believed that some earlier race, distinct from the Amerindians, constructed the mounds. They called them, appropriately enough, the "Mound People" or the "Mound Builders." They assumed that the Native American tribes had exterminated them some time in the distant past.

Many of the familiar tales of Illinois are only a few decades old. We must not forget that people have lived on this land for over a thousand years. The Cahokia Mounds are a reminder that every nook and cranny of this land is haunted by the past.

---

[32] Gene S. Stuart, *America's Ancient Cities* (National Geographic Society, 1988), 31.

THE FALLEN INVESTIGATE

DEC. 21

11:42 PM

18° F

With Primordial's "Empire Falls" echoing from the speakers of their rusted, dark blue Toyota Corolla, the Fallen raced down the deserted road toward Cahokia Mounds State Historic Site under the cover of darkness. Snow flurries trickled down from the sky as the urban landscape suddenly gave way to an open field and the massive silhouette of Monk's Mound appeared on the horizon.

"Where is this place?" Greg asked from the backseat. He clutched his gnarled, wooden cane anxiously. Beside him sat Emmer, a tall and lanky young man with a dour expression. Aurelia sat in the front passenger side. Mike, as always, sat behind the wheel.

"It's right there," Mike said, pointing his finger at the mound in the distance.

"What, that?" Greg asked. "That's it? I've seen sled hills bigger than that."

"*It's an ancient monument,*" Mike explained with naked agitation. "It's a sacred place."

"It looks like the Kenosha toboggan hill," Greg laughed.

Emmer grinned. "Well, I'm ready to see some fireworks," he said. "What's it been, over a year now you've been looking for this astral gate? I'd hate the whole thing to turn out to be a bone headed mistake on your part."

"I've got your bone right here," Mike shot back, but before he could continue, Aurelia pulled a weathered rib bone out of a backpack that had been laying on the floor.

"No really, he does!" she exclaimed.

It took a few moments for the quartet to settle down, but as soon as they saw the cars already in the parking lot of Monk's Mound, their demeanor sobered.

"Looks like we're a little late," Emmer grumbled.

Mike spun the wheel, and the Toyota lurched into the parking lot, driving over a chain that had obviously been cut. In a heartbeat, the gear was in park and the engine off. The Fallen stealthily piled out of the car.

"Just think," Greg whispered. "Millions of people are asleep in their warm beds getting ready for the Christmas season—or whatever. No one but us is awake right now. What a way to celebrate the winter solstice—climbing a wet, snowy hill in the freezing cold!"

"Bone me," Mike said, holding out his hand.

Aurelia slapped the long-lost rib bone of Big Thunder into his palm. Dark, ominous clouds gathered in the sky above and thunder shook the asphalt of the parking lot.

Step by step, the Fallen made their way to the stairs that led to the top of Monk's Mound. From that vantage point, it looked as though they would have to climb a thousand steps. By the time they made it to the top, they feared, their adversaries could have already opened the astral gate.

"Follow my lead!" Mike shouted under the roaring thunder. He tightened his black, leather trench coat around his waist and began the ascent.

The farther they climbed, the more clearly the four heard voices echoing from the plateau at the top of the mound. Wind whipped the noise down to their ears along with the freezing snow, which had quickly turned to icy rain.

Finally, after ten or fifteen minutes, the Fallen reached within a yard of the summit. They stopped there and sunk down to avoid detection. Greg peered over the edge and observed that the six zealots—their rivals for control over the astral gate—were joined with the Satanists, Davin and Emily among them.

They stood in formation in the shape of a hexagram, with the zealots standing at the points and Davin and the Satanists standing at the intersections.

"I don't believe my own eyes," Greg cursed. "How can those zealots and those Satanists be working together? It doesn't make any sense! And that bastard Davin... don't even get me—"

"The two are just different sides of the same coin. Get it?" Emmer hissed. His friend looked at him blankly, so he quickly elaborated. "Look, have you ever read *Nineteen Eighty-Four*? It's like Big Brother and Emmanuel Goldstein. They are both—"

"No," Greg blinked, cutting him off. "But I guess it doesn't matter. We have to stop them whatever the heck is going on." He turned towards Mike. "What do we do?" he asked frantically, readying his cane for a fight.

"Nothing—yet," Mike replied. "We have to wait for them to open the gate."

"Wait, isn't that exactly what we *don't* want them to do?" Aurelia interjected.

"Greg, remember when you were worried about keeping Emily around, because one of the Satanists is her brother and he was using her to get to us through Davin?" Mike asked rhetorically. "And remember when I said that worked both ways?"

"Yeah, but—" Greg protested.

"Just watch."

From the top of the mound the voice of the leader of the zealots, a middle aged matriarch with long, curly hair, rang out in low, clear decibels. Her hands were outstretched. "*O caput mortuum impero tibi per vivium Serpentem. Kerub impero tibi per Adam. Aquila impero tibi per alas Tauri. Serpens impero tibi per Angelum et Leonem.*"

The man at the head of the human hexagram added, "*I conjure thee Shax, in the name of Bileth and Beliall, their power and retribution and to their virtues and powers I charge thee Shax, that thou shalt not take leave from thy place and constraint, nor alter thy bodily image to deceive, nor any power shalt*

thou have of our bodies or souls, earthly or ghostly, but to be obedient to me, and to the words of my conjuration."

At that, the entire group began to speak in tongues—releasing a chorus of nonsensical phrases that spewed forth from their deep, trance-like state. In the sky above, the clouds slowly began to spin.

"All of you have officially gone off the deep end," Emmer trembled. "We should get off this hill before we get struck by lightning or something. This has gone far enough."

"Wait!" Mike yelled and reached out to restrain his friend, but as Emmer turned to retreat down the stairs, a fissure appeared in the clouds and a bolt of lightning struck the ground inches away. Emmer was thrown onto the side of the mound and rolled to a stop on a plateau midway to the bottom.

The crack in the clouds widened and electro-magnetic energy lit up the top of Monk's Mound. "I think I'm feeling some déjà vu!" Greg exclaimed as fingers of lightning crackled across the midnight sky.

"We have to close this gate forever!" Mike shouted over the whipping wind and stinging, icy hail. He turned the rib bone around in his hand to get a more balanced grip.

"What?" Greg asked with astonishment. "We came all this way and now that we found the gate *you want to destroy it?*"

"We don't have a choice," Mike argued. "Once the gate is in the wrong hands, there will be no going back. The world will plunge into slavery. There will be no freedom—only one thought, one herd, one faith, one world order." He stood up and shouted, "Davin, do it now!"

Near the middle of the enemy formation at the top of the mound, Davin sprang into action. Their leader had been momentarily distracted by the sudden appearance of Mike, so she was unprepared for the blow that came at her from behind. Davin launched himself at the woman and knocked her down with the brunt of his shoulder.

MONK'S MOUND

At the same moment, Mike hurled the bone of Big Thunder into the fissure in the clouds. Davin barely got to his feet—slipping and sliding on the icy grass—before a great roar pierced the air and lighting touched down in every direction.

Mike grabbed Aurelia and Greg and jumped off the side of the hill. They landed with a sickening thud, but their momentum carried them down the slope before they could be fried by the lightning.

The others were not so lucky. Both the Satanists and the zealots—along with Emily—were scorched by the searing heat. Davin, who fell on top of one of the larger men, narrowly escaped. As the swirling clouds above lurched to a halt and began to dissipate, he crawled over to Emily, but her lifeless eyes told him that he was too late.

By the time Davin reached the bottom of the hill, the other members of the Fallen had gathered a few yards from the parking lot. Aurelia and Greg carried Emmer, who was still unconscious.

"The *snoozepapers* will probably report this as some kind of tragic accident," Aurelia growled. "Probably use it as an excuse for a lecture on weather safety."

"It *was* a tragedy," Mike said as he reached the door of the dark blue Toyota. "The ancients hid this here eons ago to allow us to one day unlock the secrets of the cosmos. Instead of using it for knowledge, it was destroyed because of ignorance."

"Maybe there are more of them out there," Davin suggested. "All I know is that it's great to be back. I almost started to miss you guys." He grinned and joined the others in the vehicle.

INVESTIGATION FILE 025

LEBANON ROAD
Collinsville, Illinois

Late night drives are common wherever teenagers have cars, and many communities throughout Illinois have legendary roads that offer more thrills than most. Lebanon Road is one of the more interesting of these. On or around the road are seven railroad bridges, some no longer in use. All of them are heavily coated in graffiti—a testament to their popularity for nighttime excursions.

Local visitors have crafted a hellish tale around these seven bridges, which they dubbed the "Seven Gates to Hell." According to Chad Lewis and Terry Fisk's *Illinois Road Guide to Haunted Locations* (2007), these stories have been circulating in the area for at least 40 years.

The legend is that if someone were to drive through all seven bridges and enter the last one exactly at midnight, he or she would be transported to Hell. In some versions, the person entering the final tunnel must be a skeptic. In other versions, no tunnel can be driven through twice in order for the magic to work.

The tunnels, the stories say, are guarded by spectral hounds. "Often these 'dogs' are said to be dark black in color with glowing red or green eyes," Chad and Terry wrote. "Many witnesses report that the grotesque creatures are nearly transparent and often times vanish into thin air."[33]

In *Weird Illinois* (2005), Mark Moran and Mark Sceurman mentioned that a "source" claimed the bridges were once used by the Ku Klux Klan for lynchings. This source might very well be the anonymous author of a website called "The Abbey of St. Ulric the Eclectic" (http://tinyurl.com/awfpvq2).

On that website, the author claimed that the origin of the lynching story was none other than his or her friend, one Eric Miller. Eric had started the rumor as an experiment. "He created the bare bones of a story and told it [to] some people and waited to see 1. how long it took until he heard the story from someone else and 2. see how many variations of the story developed," the site revealed. "He was not displeased, several variations of the story have come back to him by people who swear to him they are true."

Directions to all seven gates, as well as a treasure trove of other information about Lebanon Road, are also available on that website.

Like Cuba Road in Barrington, an abandoned property near Lebanon Road has given rise to rumors of a "death house." A closed road or driveway is alleged to lead to an old house in which a family was murdered. Moreover, a group of Satanists are said to sacrifice animals and children at the location.

Mark Moran and Mark Sceurman wrote about another bridge along Lebanon Road, called "Acid Bridge," where a number of teens tripping on LSD are said to have crashed their car and died—an event that is supposed to reenact itself.

Lebanon Road and the Seven Gates to Hell is a wonderful trip and part of a dying tradition of roadside adventures. If you are near Collinsville, do not be afraid to see if the stories are true.

---

[33] Lewis and Fisk, 221.

The Fallen Investigate

JAN. 8

11:25 PM

15° F

As the Fallen's rusted Toyota Corolla sped down Lebanon Road, Manowar's "Brothers of Metal" blared from the speakers while Eric Adams' operatic voice crooned, "And if we all were not brothers of metal, *would we fall?*"

"*No!*" Mike, Greg, Emmer, and Davin cried out in unison.

Aurelia, who sat in the front passenger seat, rolled her eyes.

Greg piped up and turned toward Emmer, who sat next to him in the backseat. "Speaking of epic battles," he said, "it's too bad you were unconscious for most of that fight at Cahokia Mounds. You wouldn't believe it if we told you."

"You *did* tell me," Emmer replied, "and you're right, I don't believe it."

"It's too bad Emily *died* in that fight," Davin whined. "You guys don't even care. We loved each other."

"She was a whore," Aurelia shouted, and the cabin fell silent in shock. "Well, someone had to say it!"

"That's wonderful," Davin muttered. "I think I'm going back to bed for a few weeks. You can wake me when you're not being jerks."

"Forget about all that," Mike said from behind the steering wheel. "So two years of searching for the astral gate was all in vain. So we wasted thousands of dollars in gas. It's the journey that counts. It's the times we had along the way."

"You keep telling yourself that buddy," Emmer grinned. "I know I got a few laughs out of the whole thing."

Suddenly, the soft yellow headlights of the dark blue Corolla fell on the outline of a concrete railroad tunnel up ahead as the car navigated around a sharp curve in the road. A colorful variety of graffiti clung to the moistened walls of the tunnel.

"Ah, that's what we're looking for," Mike announced. "The first gate to Hell! Supposedly if we pass through all seven of these tunnels by midnight we'll be transported to the underworld."

"No wonder you wanted to stay out past your bedtime," Aurelia snorted.

"What's with you and seeking out portals and tunnels?" Emmer asked. "I think Freud would have something interesting to say about this."

"You shut up from now on," Mike said.

Their Toyota swept under the bridge and down the road. Its passengers were quiet for a while, until Greg piped up.

"Is everything ready for the Black Willow Grove expedition?" he asked eagerly.

"I think so," Mike replied as they shot around a tight curve. "I just got off the phone with the realtor. We can rent the two storefronts next to each other; one for my bookstore and one for Emmer's record store. Davin, did you get your job yet?"

"Yeah, whatever," Davin replied, his hand buried in his cheek.

"It's important," Mike stressed. "Being a pizza delivery guy will give you access to anywhere in town. It's the perfect cover for our investigation."

BEHIND THE SCENES

Black Willow Grove was to be the setting of a novel featuring the Fallen. Its plot ran parallel with Issues 25-36. A teaser chapter appeared in *Legends and Lore of Illinois: Case Files*, Vol. 1.

"Hey, look out!" Emmer abruptly shouted. "You almost missed another bridge!"

The blue Toyota screeched to a halt and began to slowly backpedal. Mike strained his eyes to catch the turnoff. Indeed, the second bridge lay just to their left along a side street. The car's rusted frame groaned as it turned and passed between the colorfully painted stone walls.

"Well, that's number two," Aurelia announced.

"Thanks again, queen of the obvious," Greg chuckled as Mike depressed the gas pedal and attempted to navigate the dark street. There were no lights there. Trees lined the road and the moon was obscured behind a dark cloud.

"Let's focus on the task at hand," Mike said. "We'll talk about Black Willow Grove when we get home later tonight. Right now I want to find these bridges and test this little story. We only have twenty more minutes before midnight."

"I'm beginning to worry that we're not going to be transported to Hell," Emmer said sarcastically from the backseat.

"It's too bad we couldn't bring Casey," Greg lamented, referring to the feral coydog the Fallen had adopted a few months earlier. "She would know if there were any Hell hounds lurking around here."

Mike sighed deeply as the forest became denser and an overgrown railroad bridge came into view in the Corolla's headlights. It was obvious from first glance that this bridge had not been in use for a long time. The steel rails of

the railroad tracks, if they were still there, were hidden under a layer of dirt and weeds. Small bushes and saplings grew on top of the bridge.

Suddenly, as they slowly crept through the tunnel, a sharp BANG pierced the air and Mike briefly lost control of the vehicle. "Crowley's arse!" he swore. "I think we blew a tire!" He guided the Toyota out of the tunnel and pulled to the side of the road.

Cutting the ignition, Mike stepped out of the car along with his four friends, who each examined one of the four tires using small electric torches. After a moment, they discovered that it was the rear, passenger side tire that had blown.

"Well, we're screwed now," Emmer joked. "We'll never get to Hell!"

Aurelia rolled her eyes and pushed him out of the way, waiting for Mike to pop the trunk before she dug out the spare tire. As this was going on, the Fallen hardly noticed the appearance of three interlopers; two plus sized girls and one fresh faced boy. None looked like they were out of high school. They were dressed in a variety of striped clothes—red and black, black and green, black and blue—all of which originated on the shelves of Hot Topic.

Greg and Davin laughed and pushed each other as they tried to keep warm in the January temperature.

One of the two girls cleared her throat. "Uh, excuse me," she whined. "What are you doing here?"

The Fallen stopped what they were doing and looked up, surprised to see anyone else on the road at night. "Where did they come from?" Mike wondered out loud. "Did we see them on the road on our way out here?"

"More importantly... who are they, more Satanists?" Emmer asked no one in particular. "I thought you guys said they were dead."

"We are dead!" one of the trio exclaimed. "We're the undead."

"Great," Greg grumbled, "*Twilight* has only been out of the theaters for a month and already junior high kids are pretending to be vampires. Didn't Anne Rice cause us enough pain already?"

"You know she's Catholic now," Davin interjected.

"That's old news!" Aurelia yelled as she tightened a bolt on the spare tire.

"Excuse me," one of the vampire kids whined. "I don't think you're taking us seriously."

Emmer laughed. "It's always the most ridiculous people who demand to be taken seriously!"

"All right," Mike said as he dug his hands into the pockets of his trench coat. "Suppose we take you seriously. There are five of us and three of you. Me and my friend Greg here have already killed a vampire before. A real one. Now you have to decide if you're going to take us seriously."

"You... you've killed a vampire, man?" one of the kids stammered. "Really?"

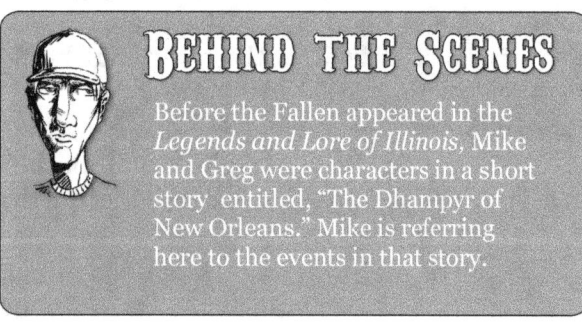

BEHIND THE SCENES

Before the Fallen appeared in the *Legends and Lore of Illinois*, Mike and Greg were characters in a short story entitled, "The Dhampyr of New Orleans." Mike is referring here to the events in that story.

"They say they have," Emmer said, dryly. "Are you gonna stick around to find out if they're telling the truth?"

"What are you doing out here in the middle of the night anyway?" Mike asked.

"Same thing you are," one of the two girls replied.

Suddenly, the eyes of the boy in the trio lit up. "Hey!" he cried. "I know who you are! You're the Fallen, right? Holy cow!"

Mike, Greg, Davin, and Emmer exchanged glances, while Aurelia ignored them. "You know of the Fallen?" Mike asked.

"You guys are legendary!" the boy replied enthusiastically. "I mean, I've only heard things... rumors on forums and in chat rooms... I didn't think you actually existed."

Greg grinned. "The Fallen don't exist," he said. "Now get out of here. We have to change this tire and go find the entrance to Hell."

"It's too late," Mike announced, looking at his watch. "It's five 'till. We'd never make it through all the gates in time."

"Darn," Emmer said.

The three kids looked at each other apprehensively. "Actually, could we get a ride home?" one of the girls asked. "It's freezing out here."

"What does this look like, a bus?" Aurelia replied from beside the car. She had just finished tightening the last bolt and was getting ready to put the tools back in the trunk.

"Sorry, there's no room," Mike said. "Five is all she can carry."

The vampire kids looked disappointed, but eventually turned and shuffled away while the Fallen piled back into their Corolla and drove toward a forth tunnel that appeared just around the bend.

"This is going to be an exciting year," Mike said. "I can feel it."

INVESTIGATION FILE 026

RAMSEY CEMETERY
Effingham, Illinois

Southern Illinois has a far more diverse topography than the rest of the state. Situated at the gateway to Little Egypt, Ramsey Cemetery in Effingham County is no exception. Its claim to fame is the "caves" (rock shelters) that lay nearby. Formed by thousands of years of erosion, generations of local residents have carved their names, alongside proclamations of love, into the sandstone walls.

Back in 2002, the Shadowlands Index of Haunted Places mislabeled this place "Kazbar Cemetery." The entry described it as an "old cemetery that has haunted caves." Eschewing details, it added, "a were wolf and a man in a black coat with red eyes is said to be seen there. Many weird things have happened there." Luckily for us, Chad Lewis and Terry Fisk rode to the rescue with a thorough background investigation in their book *The Illinois Road Guide to Haunted Locations* (2007).

NOTE

A reader later informed us that locals called the area around the rock shelters "the Kazbar."

One story they uncovered was the tale of a young man who allegedly committed suicide in Ramsey Cemetery. According to Lewis and Fisk, a small chapel existed on the cemetery grounds for the benefit of mourners from the 1920s until the 1960s when it was torn down due to vandalism.

"The story goes that one dark evening in the 1960s, a troubled young man drove out to the chapel," they wrote. "Once there he grabbed a shot gun from the trunk of his car, walked inside the chapel and blew his head off."[34]

Another version of the tale has the man hanging himself. The authors were not able to locate any evidence to substantiate the story.

The legend of the werewolf that inhabits the nearby caves is slightly more interesting, if not more fantastical. Like the rumors of the werewolf that wanders around the stone quarry in Coles County, this tale has very little background information. It may have origins in the unique history of the area, however.

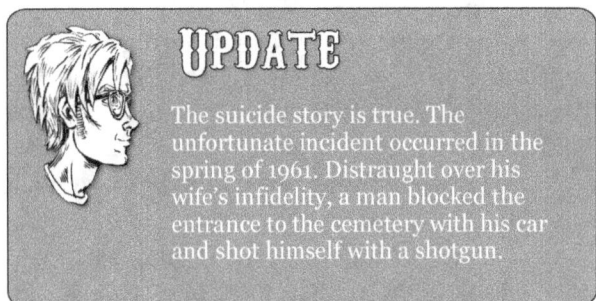

UPDATE

The suicide story is true. The unfortunate incident occurred in the spring of 1961. Distraught over his wife's infidelity, a man blocked the entrance to the cemetery with his car and shot himself with a shotgun.

According to several histories of Effingham County, the backcountry was always rough and tumble, and the roads and hills were inhabited by transients and brigands. Some of them may have occupied the rock shelters near Ramsey Cemetery. In the late 1800s, a wanderer called "Leather-man" made his home in the hills of western Connecticut. It is possible, if not unlikely, that the werewolf legend began with a similar man, living the life of a backwoodsman north of Effingham, Illinois.

And what to make of the black-clad man with glowing red eyes? His appearance might have something to do with the occult activity that is rumored to take place in the cemetery at night, or he might dwell in a more earthly realm—in the minds of local visitors. One thing is for sure, Ramsey Cemetery is one of the more interesting cemeteries in south-central Illinois.

---

34 Lewis and Fisk, 235.

THE FALLEN INVESTIGATE

FEB. 11

2:33 PM

29° F

The Fallen, absent Davin and Emmer, stood in a mud puddle facing a wide cleft in the hillside, which was caused by centuries of sandstone erosion. Moss-covered rocks jutted out from under the soil, and coils of tree roots poked their way into the open air. The temperature was just above freezing, making the ground a mix of snow and sludge, but the creek behind them had not yet swelled with the spring runoff.

"I can't believe we almost drove past this," Mike said, chastising himself.

"It's like in *Labyrinth*," Greg said. "You have to look at it the right way, otherwise it just appears to be a normal roadside ditch." He walked a few yards to the right and paused. "But if you look at it from over here, BAM, a whole new world of wonder is revealed."

"You do remind me of Hoggle," Aurelia teased.

Greg shot her a dirty look, but chose not to pursue the matter any farther.

The trio slogged past the rusted 'no-dumping' sign and entered the wide cleavage in the hillside. The gap gradually narrowed until, about fifty yards ahead, it came to a close at the point at which a small waterfall trickled down into a half-frozen basin. The rock shelters were more pronounced there, but clung to the sides of the entire crevasse for one hundred and eighty degrees. Aside from a few dark apertures, nothing resembling a cave appeared in their field of vision.

"Reality strikes again," Mike grumbled as he tightened his leather trench coat around his waist. Even in this naturally sheltered area, the wind blew fiercely.

"Don't be such a wet blanket," Greg said, sprightly climbing the various ridges and boulders with ease. "We just got here. Maybe we'll find something after all."

As the words left his mouth, he recoiled in surprise as a bundle of rags began to move inside the crevice near to which he stood. His feet slid on a patch of ice and he landed in a pile of leaves at the base of the ridge that led up to the rock wall. Mike and Aurelia rushed to his aid as a dirty face peered out from under the rags.

"Who are you?" a raspy, yet feminine voice demanded. Before Mike could reply, the homeless woman's eyes widened as she saw his black trench coat. "The man in black!" she shrieked, and a boney finger pointing accusingly at Mike. She threw the pile of rags and newspapers aside and attempted to flee, but like Greg, she slid on the partially frozen ground.

"Wait!" Mike yelled. "You got the wrong guy!"

"You hope she does, anyway," Aurelia added.

By this time, Greg had regained his footing and used his cane to anchor himself. He rejoined the group and the three cautiously approached the homeless woman.

Mike's assurances had not fazed the woman, because her eyes were still filled with fear and she held up her hands as if to fend off an attack. "What do you want?" she pleaded. "I don't have anything! I just sleeping here!"

"It's alright," Aurelia said in something that vaguely resembled a soothing tone. "We're not going to hurt you."

"I think you scared us just as much as we scared you!" Greg chuckled, but no one else indulged in his levity.

"Who is the man in black?" Mike demanded.

The woman's eyes darted from Mike to Greg to Aurelia, then back again. "I sees him sometimes at night. In the forest." She coughed and wheezed. "I sees his glowing eyes through the trees. He's a bad spirit. He dresses all in black, just like you."

"Well, unlike this thing, I'm alive," Mike muttered. "And how long have you been living here? It's freezing outside."

"I be here since the fall," the woman said, timidly. "Not any colder than anywhere else."

"Well, I guess that makes sense," Greg said. He pulled Mike aside for a moment. "Listen, why don't we go check out that cemetery, eh? There's obviously no werewolf here."

"You goin' to the cemetery?" the woman interjected.

"Uh, no," Greg coughed. "We're just gonna go somewhere else. *Anywhere else.*"

"The man in black lives in that cemetery," the woman said. "Any soul looks into his eyes will be stolen, that's what I thinks."

"Well, thanks for the help," Mike said, adjusting his glasses. "We'll come back if we have any other questions. Stay warm."

With that, the three took a few pictures of the rock shelters and walked back to their car, which was parked on the side of the road where they had first entered the cleft in the hillside. Mike and Greg shivered, but Aurelia seemed unfazed by the temperature.

"Aura, what do you think about what that lady said?" Mike asked. "What do you make of this 'man in black'?"

"She definitely saw something that scared her," Aurelia replied as she opened the front passenger door and sat down. "But I didn't sense anything unusual about that area. I guess we'll see what happens when we get to the cemetery."

"I don't want to sound like Emmer here, but that woman could be all kinds of nuts," Greg said from the backseat. "I mean, she's living in a cave. She's a *cave woman*. We can't even imagine what led up to her living there."

Mike started the engine and the Toyota's speakers ejaculated the wailing vocals of King Diamond as he sang "Twilight Symphony." With gas petal depressed, the vehicle groaned and started up the well-worn gravel road toward Ramsey Cemetery. After a few moments, trees became scarce as the crest of the hill came into view and white monuments grew larger and larger behind a barbed wire fence.

Picking a good spot to pull over, Mike turned the steering wheel and parked the car just outside of the entrance. A large, weathered oak tree stood nearby. Its trunk was covered in graffiti, and its barren limbs stretched outward like gnarled fingers. A barbed wire fence held up by bleached wood posts surrounded the graveyard.

Mike, Aurelia, and Greg exited the vehicle and drank in the scene as the chilly wind swept the crest of the hill. Nothing appeared out of the ordinary. It looked like every other rural cemetery they had seen on their journeys. Never the less, the trio felt uneasy after their encounter with the homeless woman.

"What do you think?" Mike asked, scratching the five o'clock shadow on his chin.

"This is less interesting than those caves," Greg replied, "but at least there are no crazy people here."

"You forgot about us!" Aurelia laughed, but the joke was short lived. As she passed near the old oak, she doubled over as though she had been hit by something unseen.

"Aura, what happened?" Mike shouted as he rushed to her side.

Aurelia clutched her stomach, groaned, and attempted to squirm away from the tree. Mike grabbed her and pulled her a few yards toward the car, after which she seemed to relax. It took her a few moments to catch her breath.

"It looks like there's more to this place than it seems," she gasped. "It's that tree. Something is protecting it."

"What do you think it is?" Greg asked, readying his cane for a fight.

"I don't think it's human, that's for sure," Aurelia grumbled, embarrassed at having been caught off guard. Mike tried to help her to her feet, but she brushed him off and pulled herself up. She closed her eyes and concentrated. For a long while, the only sound was the rushing of the wind across the lawn.

"Something happened there," she said at long last. "I can feel frustration and anger. Blind rage. Whatever it is lashed out at me because it knew I'm sensitive to its presence."

"Well, let's not bother it then," Mike said. "Obviously it's been through enough. We didn't come for that anyway."

"Agreed," Greg seconded and started toward the cemetery gates. He pulled out a camera and began to take pictures while Mike produced a video camera from his coat and began to film. Aurelia looked around nervously.

"Let's try to find out where that chapel was," Mike suggested. "Then when we go home tonight we can try to do some research on that tree."

"Yeah, I'm sure we'll find a lot of information on a tree," Greg muttered sarcastically.

"I wonder how Davin and Emmer are doing back at Black Willow Grove?" Mike said aloud. "What do they have on tap, the woods?"

"Yeah I'm sure they'll find something, Emmer and Davin together," Greg laughed. "Emmer will convince Davin anything that happens didn't really happen, and Davin will more than likely be drunk."

"I have a little bit more faith in them than that," Mike replied. "Let's just see what they come up with on their own. In the meantime, let's get back to work."

Greg shook his head, and the three began to explore the cemetery.

INVESTIGATION FILE 027

MANTENO STATE HOSPITAL
Manteno, Illinois

Manteno State Hospital, one of two such facilities in Kankakee County, opened its doors in the early 1930s. It took several years after the purchase of the property in 1927 for the sprawling mental hospital to be completed. Like Peoria (Bartonville) State Hospital, Manteno was laid out in a "cottage plan," which meant that the patients were housed in a series of separate buildings, rather than in one single institution. When it first opened, Manteno accommodated 5,500 patients and 760 staff.

It did not take long for tragedy to strike the hospital. In an incident that *Time* magazine referred to as the "Manteno Madness," 384 patients and staff came down with typhoid fever (47 died) in 1939. At first, Ralph Hinton, the director of Manteno State, believed the affliction to be nothing more than a common case of diarrhea, but state welfare agents stepped in as the number of ill dramatically increased. Panic gripped the hospital.

"Patients lay moaning in bed," *Time* reported. "Others, whipped by mad fear, beat against the screened windows, grappled with attendants... Every night kitchen boys and orderlies disappeared. Over 45 ran away in all."[35]

Kankakee County State's Attorney Sam Shapiro, who would go on to become governor of Illinois, dragged the director of the state's Public Welfare Department, Archie Bowen, to court over the incident in 1940 even though Bowen had sent a truckload of typhoid vaccine to Manteno at the onset of the outbreak. At first, Bowen was convicted, but the State Supreme Court overturned the conviction because, as the *Kankakee Daily Journal* reported, "Shapiro had failed to show that the epidemic was caused by polluted drinking water."[36]

The Manteno State Hospital was later renamed the Manteno Mental Health Center, and closed in 1985 along with many of the other such mental health facilities in Illinois. Its campus was divided up and sold off. The north side of campus became a veteran's home. Other buildings were consolidated into the Illinois Diversatech Campus and rented to businesses. The main administration building became a bank. Despite public health concerns, a housing project called Fairway Oaks Estates was recently built at the location.

Manteno has attracted many curiosity seekers since its closure, including its share of ghost hunters. "Over the years I have had many reports of people who entered the old buildings and saw nurses and doctors and even patients still dressed in their gowns," Chad Lewis recently told the *Daily Journal*.[37] Amateur investigators have taken dozens of strange photographs in the old buildings.

Only a small handful of abandoned buildings remain, and it is doubtful they will exist for much longer. The quiet town of Manteno has done its best to erase the memory of this place, but there will always be stories.

---

[35] "Manteno Madness," *Time*, 23 October 1939.

[36] *Daily Journal* (Kankakee) 31 March 2007.
[37] *Daily Journal* (Kankakee) 31 October 2008.

THE FALLEN INVESTIGATE

MAR. 7

3:19 PM

48° F

Aurelia parked her battered old Buick LeSabre across from the last dilapidated structure of the dozens that once made up Manteno State Hospital. Originally laid out in "cottages," each building had been either converted into a business, boarded up, or torn down—all except for this one. Aurelia had agreed to meet the rest of the Fallen there, having been delayed for about thirty minutes by a previous commitment.

The Fallen's dark blue, Toyota Corolla sat along the curb, empty. "Jerks," Aurelia grumbled. Her friends had apparently decided to begin the investigation without her. She slammed the door of her LeSabre and scanned the area with a hawkish gaze. Down the block, children laughed and played in the subdivision that had sprung up around the old hospital. The air was still chilly, but the sun warmed anyone who was under its rays.

Disregarding any concern for stealth, she yelled, "Hello? I'm here! Where are you?"

There was no reply.

Aurelia sighed and strolled toward the 'H' shaped building. The front of the one-story building was enhanced with a wide porch. The porch's roof was held up by a row of white pillars, and a plywood board covered every window.

If they aren't going to come out here, Aurelia reasoned, *I'll just have to go in after them.*

It was no use trying the main entrance; the doors were heavily chained, but Aurelia's curiosity led her onto the porch anyway. With a uniquely sensitive mind, she could imagine the more docile patients waiting for visitors. A profound sadness permeated the air, and the building itself seemed to exhale with the breeze. Aurelia could not sense how many souls wandered the grounds, but she could feel their presence.

She worked her way around the side of the building until it opened up into a small courtyard. A corridor, which connected the two sections, sat about fifteen yards ahead of her. The doors on either section were chained shut and large blocks of cement had been placed in front of them, but most of the windows along the corridor were damaged, allowing for easy access. There was no sign of Mike, Greg, Emmer, or Davin anywhere.

Cursing under her breath, Aurelia stomped over to the corridor, intending to enter the building there, but as she gained a foothold on the windowsill with her boot, she noticed some movement out of the corner of her eye. The motion came from a window located at ground level on the section to her left. A railing surrounded the window, which allowed light to spill into the hospital's basement. Aura paused and her eyes focused on the spot. Nothing stirred, but she felt a tingle run up her spine.

Hesitating, she turned and walked toward the other window. When she was halfway across the courtyard, she thought she saw a flash of light in the basement through the pealing window frame. "Hah!" Aurelia cried. "There you are. Bastards!" She rushed over and used the railing to swing down into the window sill. A thick grease came off on her hands, and she frowned.

"Gross," Aurelia said. She wiped her hands on some old, dried leaves and peered through the window into the basement of the hospital. "Hello?" she yelled. The echo of her own voice was the only reply. She wrinkled her brow and slid, feet first, through the window. It was about a yard drop to the floor. Landing without any difficulty, she dug into the pocket of her hooded sweatshirt and produced a small flashlight.

The beam revealed an empty, rectangular room. Small piles of debris littered the floor, but there were no furniture or markings to indicate for what the room was once used. As her flashlight fell on a narrow hallway, Aurelia remembered that Mike had rambled on and on about tunnels that linked all of the buildings.

A heavy thud suddenly echoed from somewhere beyond the range of the beam, and Aurelia jumped despite having been steeled by years of encounters with the unusual. She quickly looked around to make sure that no one had seen. In the back of her mind, she was beginning to believe that her friends were playing some kind of joke.

Or, at least, she hoped. She was still shaken up by her encounter outside of Ramsey Cemetery, and by her feelings about Black Willow Grove, the code name for the Fallen's most recent assignment. Mike had forbidden the group from using the town's real name. The feelings she got there were odd and ominous. She felt that now—a gnawing sense that something other than the spirits of the departed stalked these corridors. Even the dead seemed to flee from this unknown presence.

A musty smell like that of old newspapers wafted past Aurelia's aquiline nose. She sniffed defiantly and marched down the dark hallway, deep into the bowels of Manteno. Condensation dripped from the pipes overhead, and old bulbs sat lifeless in their sockets in the ceiling.

She was getting close to the source of her gnawing dread, but her flashlight revealed nothing but dirt and cobwebs. Curiosity drove her forward. If her friends jumped out at the last moment, she thought with amusement, she would quickly make them very sorry.

Before she could finish her thought, she felt a rush of ice cold air that almost knocked her down. She took a wide stance and braced herself as if she was entering a storm without an umbrella. Her flashlight flickered and threatened to be extinguished, but the battery held. Not that its narrow beam did any good—the shadows in the corridor seemed to congeal and absorb what precious little light the device emitted.

Wasting no time, Aurelia thrust out her hands and cried out, "*Eko, eko, Azarak! Eko, eko, Zomelak! Bazabi lacha bachabe! Lamac cahi achababe!*"

The shadows retreated for a moment, but returned in full force. A gust of wind burst through the tunnel and Aurelia fell to the ground. Her rear-end planted itself amongst the grime and broken bits of cement. Suddenly, a bright light illuminated the hallway directly in the path of the shadows. The luminescent glow burned away the darkness, and the howling wind fell to a whisper. Just like that, the light was gone, and the corridor returned to normal. The whole incident lasted only a few seconds.

That's twice I've been saved by something, Aurelia thought. *Once might have been a coincidence, but twice is a pattern.* She grudgingly thanked whatever it was, pulled herself up, and dusted herself off. Just then, she heard footsteps coming from around the bend in the hallway and she readied herself for another encounter. This time she would not be caught off guard.

Moments later, Mike, Greg, Emmer, and Davin appeared around the corner. They made a collective sigh of relief when they saw Aurelia, but it was short lived.

Aurelia marched over to the group, pushed Davin out of the way, and punched Mike in the face. Mike swore while Greg and Emmer laughed. Their laughter quickly died when Aurelia spun toward them with a menacing glare.

"Where the heck have you been?" she yelled. "I almost got killed down here."

"We didn't know where you were," Mike protested while checking his nose for blood. "We waited forever and you never showed up."

"I *told you* I was going to be late," Aurelia hissed.

"What happened?" Davin asked. "What do you mean you were almost killed?"

MANTENO STATE HOSPITAL

"There was something down here," Aurelia explained. "It attacked me. Luckily I was able to fight it off."

"What attacked you?" Greg asked with a grin. "A rat? A gaggle of goblins?"

"Some kind of dark spirit," Aurelia replied. "I can't quite explain it."

Emmer snorted. "So this thing just happened to disappear before we got here? Where did it go? What did it look like?"

"I don't know."

"Wait a minute," Mike said while bending his glasses back into their proper shape. "Tell us exactly what happened."

Aurelia explained everything that happened since she arrived, leaving out the part about being saved by a mysterious light.

"We should be more careful," Mike said. "I don't have a good feeling about this. Luckily Aura was able to fight this thing off, but next time either her or any of us might not be so lucky."

"Speak for yourself," Emmer replied. "I'm not afraid of the invisible. We've been through all of this before. Nothing I've seen or heard has been very convincing. I'm not going to jump at shadows."

Mike sighed. "Well, let's finish up here, but let's stick together, shall we?" he said as he pulled a camera out of the pocket of his trench coat. "I want to explore these tunnels. I know a lot of the buildings have been torn down, but maybe we'll find something down here."

"Or something will find us," Greg chuckled.

Aurelia grit her teeth and joined her friends as the five disappeared into the darkness.

Investigation File 028

Elmwood Cemetery
Centralia, Illinois

Elmwood Cemetery is located in the southern Illinois' town of Centralia off Gragg and Sycamore Streets directly west of the Raccoon Creek Reservoir. Originally called Centralia Cemetery (and sometimes referred to as such today), the graveyard was in use in the 1860s but not officially established until 1877. Its name was changed to Elmwood Cemetery in 1921. According to Centralia's own website, the cemetery is a resting place for around 17,000 former residents.

Deep inside Elmwood sits a large monument shaped like a tabernacle or an ancient Greek temple with only four columns. At the top of the monument stands a nearly life sized statue of a young girl with flowing locks of hair. In her hands she holds a violin. The statue depicts Harriet Annie, the daughter of Dr. Winfield and Eoline Marshall. Annie died in 1890, a few weeks after her eleventh birthday.

A popular local legend maintains that the sweet strains of a violin can be heard emanating from the cemetery at night. The origin of the ethereal notes is said to be none other than the statue of H. Annie Winfield, or "Violin Annie," as she has come to be known. According to a testimonial on the Shadowlands Index of Haunted Places for Illinois, Annie died of diphtheria, an upper respiratory tract illness that mainly affects children. The most gruesome version of the story claims that her own father (or mother) killed her with her violin.

This is unlikely, as she was greatly beloved by her family. Chad Lewis and Terry Fisk, in their book *The Illinois Road Guide to Haunted Locations* (2007), cite an obituary that read, in part, "The heart-broken parents have the sympathy of the entire city and community. The floral pieces were numerous and

beautiful."[38] A small companion stone on the left side of the Marshall monument reads, "Each year of your life was a new song more delightful than all before."

According to Lewis and Fisk, some locals believe that Violin Annie's statue glows on Halloween night. But that is not the only phenomenon attributed to this location. A group of visitors also claimed to see green tears coming from the statue's eerily-blue eyes. The "green tears" are most likely streaks of mold that have appeared in the crevices and indentations of the statue.

The violin that Annie used to impress friends and neighbors alike disappeared after her death. Chad Lewis and Terry Fisk were able to confirm that an antique violin case had been purchased from the estate of a relative, but the case was empty.

Alongside the two main entries on Annie and her mysterious statue, the Shadowlands Index of Haunted Places for Illinois also contains an entry erroneously placing her in Central City. Although Elmwood Cemetery borders Central City, which is a village located just north of Centralia, it is technically still part of Centralia.

Despite being a haunting and popular story, the mysterious music of Violin Annie has managed to stay out of most books on Illinois ghostlore. Thankfully, the majority of visitors have been respectful at the grave of Annie, and so her story can be enjoyed for years to come.

---

[38] Lewis and Fisk, 216.

THE FALLEN INVESTIGATE

APR. 13

3:30 PM

69° F

The sound of returning flocks of birds intermingled with the distant wail of sirens in the streets of Centralia. Mike, Greg, Aurelia, and Davin stood at the entrance to Elmwood Cemetery next to their dark blue Toyota Corolla, which sported a bumper sticker that read "Necrophilia is Dead" in yellow lettering. Casey the Coydog sniffed debris in the nearby curb, every few minutes stopping to scratch her patchy, grey fur.

"Emmer said he had to go to an Enslaved concert," Mike announced as he wiped the dust off his glasses and checked them in the glittering sunlight. "He said he couldn't miss it for anything, but I'm glad the rest of you decided to join me."

"What else would we do?" Greg replied. "There hasn't been anything good on TV since 1989. Besides, we picked the one nice day in April to come all the way down here."

"This is better than TV," Mike said. "This is real life." He paused and looked around. "Now, where is this statue?" he wondered.

"I'll give you two guesses," Davin interrupted as he pointed toward a black sport utility vehicle that sat deep inside the cemetery.

Casey the Coydog perked up and growled.

"Crowley's arse," Mike cursed. "Who is it this time?"

The quartet could not make out the letters on the side of the SUV, but the motivation of its passengers was obvious. They had not come to the cemetery to mourn the passing of a loved one or to admire the scenery. Indeed, the Fallen could see five figures unloading equipment of various sizes from the back of the SUV.

"Let's see what they're up to," Mike grudgingly suggested. He tucked his hands into the pockets of his black, leather trench coat and frowned.

Aurelia, who wore a long black skirt and a black hooded sweatshirt, smirked. "What do you think they're up to? They came here for the same reason we did, to investigate the story of Violin Annie."

"That and to get themselves on television," Davin added while attempting to straighten out his dirty white t-shirt.

The Fallen took off toward the SUV and its passengers as Casey the Coydog obediently followed. The other paranormal group hardly noticed, until the Fallen were about ten yards away and Casey began to bark furiously. The two groups squared off around the statue of a young girl holding a violin that sat at the top of a large monument.

The five paranormal investigators from the rival group all looked to be in their mid-forties to fifties, with one young man about eighteen. Three were women; all were overweight. The older man sported a horse whisker mustache and his hair was greasy and unkempt. All were draped in clothing that praised a certain paranormal investigative team on the Sci-Fi Channel.

"What is this, a LARP convention?" Greg snorted.

"Oh, son of a b— is that?" one of the women whispered when she noticed the Fallen approach. She tugged on the sleeve of her nearest colleague to get her to turn in the same direction. "The Pan-Continental Paranormal Research Society warned us about you!" she shouted.

"Oh yeah?" Mike replied. "What did they say?"

"They said to keep you away from all our locations. They reported you to the Paranormal Police, you know. You're in *big trouble*." The woman attempted to appear intimidating, but the various cameras around her neck only made her look like a tourist at Disneyland.

"*Oh no,*" Greg blurted, feigning concern. "Now we won't get put on the Christmas card list!"

Mike rolled his eyes. "Who are you?" he asked. "What gives you the right to tell us where we can and can't go?"

"We're the National Association for the Advancement of the Study of the Paranormal, or N.A.A.S.P. for short. We have over ten years of experience between us. We've gotten mountains of evidence, which is more than *you* can say."

"Oh, yeah?" Greg asked. "What evidence?"

The woman scoffed. "Well, we have hours of videotape."

"What's on it?"

"What?"

"What's on the tape?" Greg insisted. "What paranormal phenomenon have you captured on the tape?"

"Well, uh... we..." the woman stuttered.

"We have EVPs," the greasy haired man cut in.

"Lots of 'em. And Linda here is psychic. She's personally helped several spirits over to the other side, haven't you, honey?"

"I'm sure the National Academy of Sciences would be more than happy to review your evidence," Davin said. "Clearly you've made the discovery of the century. I can't wait to see what you find here." He scratched his head, partially as a mocking gesture, but mostly because he had not showered or left the Fallen's apartment in days.

"Mainstream scientists reject what they can't explain," the man spat. "Besides, *screw you.* We're the professionals here. We don't have to share our evidence with you or anyone else."

"Oh, yeah," Mike said with a hint of sarcasm. "Wouldn't want anyone independently verifying your claims. That's not part of the scientific process at all."

While this conversation was taking place, a strange black squirrel bounded out from behind the headstones and perched itself on a monument. It appeared to be listening intently, until Casey the Coydog caught its scent and took chase. The two fortean animals disappeared into the depths of the cemetery.

"The paranormal is spontaneous and other-worldly," Mike continued to argue. "By its very nature it is something unknown and hidden. You can't measure it with mechanical instruments. Not in any way that's ever going to stand up to scientific scrutiny, at any rate."

"Mike, Mike," Greg interrupted. "There's no use trying to reason with them. They're the experts, remember? I'm sure they've captured a lot of paranormal phenomenon on their gadgets."

Mike grinned and took Greg aside, ignoring the N.A.A.S.P. members who at this point were fuming with indignation. "Let's give them something that will blow their minds," he whispered.

With their backs to the crowd, Mike and Greg conferred secretly for another moment, and then turned and nodded at Aurelia and Davin. The two seemed to instinctually understand and the Fallen gathered around the statue of Violin Annie. They joined hands and closed their eyes.

"Hey, get away from there!" the greasy haired man yelled, but the woman next to him held him back. "What are you doing? We have to stop them. This is outrageous!"

As the Fallen began to hum in unison, a large cloud passed under the sun, blanketing the cemetery in shadows. The temperature dropped noticeably, and some of the members of N.A.A.S.P. tried to check their thermometers, only to find the numbers wildly fluctuating.

"*Bagahi laca bachahe; Lamac cahi achabahe,*" Mike, Aurelia, Greg, and Davin chanted. "*Karrelyos. Lamac lamec bachalyos; Cabahagi sabalyos. Baryolas. Lagozatha cabyolas; Samahac et famyolas. Harrahya.*"

As they repeated the incantation, the veil between this world and the next parted. A sweet, pleasant smell filled the air, followed by the sorrowful tones of a violin. The eerie music echoed throughout Elmwood Cemetery. As if close but yet coming from somewhere beyond, the laughter of a young girl filled the air.

The Fallen smiled and the spell was broken.

The other paranormal investigators stood silent and dumbfounded as the clouds broke and the temperature returned to normal.

"H... how did you do that?" the greasy haired man stuttered. "That's impossible!"

The Fallen broke contact and gathered back into a group on one side of the granite monument.

"Did you get *that* on video?" Greg asked with a smirk.

"W... what?" the older woman from N.A.A.S.P. replied.

"Aw, you missed it?" he teased. "That's too bad. Hey, guys, I'm kind of tired, I think we should go back to the motel."

"Yeah me, too," Mike agreed, pretending to yawn.

"Wait!" the woman yelled. "You have to do that again! You have to show us how you did that. I... I don't even believe it."

"You can report that to your Paranormal Police," Aurelia spat.

Greg looked around for Casey and whistled. After a few minutes, the coydog raced to his side. The Fallen left the five interlopers behind as they walked slowly back to their car.

ELMWOOD CEMETERY

INVESTIGATION FILE 029

MOON POINT CEMETERY
Streator, Illinois

Moon Point Cemetery is an old graveyard located just south of Streator in Livingston County. Like other rural graveyards, Moon Point became an object of folklore in the late 1960s and '70s when local teens, looking for a place to 'hang out' after dark, picked this isolated location to drink, spin yarns, and play pranks on one another.

According to the *History of Livingston County, Illinois* (1878), "Moon's Point" got its name from Jacob Moon who, along with his daughter and three sons, was the first to settle that particular area. Moon had fought in the War of 1812, and like other veterans of that war, moved west in search of cheap and abundant land. In 1830, the family settled along a winding creek near a wooded area in Illinois country that became known as Moon Point.

Moon Point Cemetery is located adjacent to Moon Creek, leading many to refer to the graveyard as "Moon Creek Cemetery." It is listed as such in the Shadowlands Index of Haunted Places for Illinois. According to the Index, Moon Point is haunted by the ghost of a "hatchet lady." This lady went insane, the story goes, after either her son or daughter died, and "each night of a full moon a spirit is seen running around the cemetery, tossing hatchets."

While there is no historical evidence for this hatchet lady, the *Times-Press* was able to verify that a man interred in the cemetery had been murdered with an ax in 1886, but it was during a "drunken brawl" at a local coal mine.[39]

Another tale associated with Moon Point concerns an abandoned house (previously owned by a witch, of course) that is also rumored to be haunted. I cannot help but wonder if the story of the witch and the hatchet lady are related, but never the less, many tales of séances and illicit trespasses have come from the location. "Quinn," commenting on Ghost-traveller.com, revealed that the house was actually an old barn located about 100 yards from the cemetery. Whatever it was, it seems to have been torn down.

A man named "Mark," also on Ghost-traveller.com, related his encounters at Moon Point during a film project in which he claimed to record colorful lights, whisperings, and "the grating of a large concrete object against another." Furthermore, he wrote that the hatchet lady, or some other spirit, whispered "get out" in his ear. Al Morris of the Midwest Ghost Hunter & Paranormal Investigators also added "children giggling" to the list of strange occurrences.[40]

The remoteness of the location is accentuated by the fact that a railroad track bisects the road leading to the cemetery, E 3150 N. It is said that anyone who is caught in the cemetery while a train passes will be trapped there. That much is actually true. According to legend, however, your car will also die and not be able to restart until after the train has gone.

The variety of legends associated with Moon Point Cemetery makes it one of the more interesting haunted cemeteries in Illinois. Feel free to visit, but pray that the hatchet lady has poor aim!

---

[39] *Times-Press* (Streator) 28 October 2001.

[40] http://www.ruhaunted.com

THE FALLEN INVESTIGATE

MAY 25

1:52 PM

75° F

The Fallen's rusted Toyota Corolla bounced over the railroad tracks along a country road as Vibeke Stene and Morten Veland's sorrowful and raspy vocals battled for dominance in the speakers. With the others held up by a separate investigation, Mike and Greg were the only two in the vehicle. Greg examined a map while Mike fiddled with the volume button on the tape deck.

"The map shows that this road connects up ahead, but it doesn't look like it does," Greg said from the front passenger seat with a hint of concern.

"No, it doesn't," Mike agreed as his eyes scanned the horizon. He spun the wheel as the driveway to Moon Point Cemetery appeared on his right. The cemetery was nestled in woods along a creek about a few dozen yards down that gravel road.

"Man, this is just like old times," Greg said out of the blue. "Just the two of us. Who needs those other guys?"

"They're part of the team," Mike replied. "There needs to be five of us, like the five points of the star."

"Save that esoteric crap for the others," Greg laughed. "What has Emmer or Davin ever contributed, seriously? And don't even get me started on Aura—"

"That's enough," Mike interrupted. "We're not getting rid of anyone." The undercarriage of the Toyota rattled as he pulled it over to the side of the road just just outside of the graveyard's iron fence. A 'no trespassing' sign was planted firmly at the entrance.

As the two got out of their car, their shoes were quickly soaked by a pool of water in the grass, which had absorbed several inches of rain the night before. Although the first leaves and weeds were starting to sprout, the area was still a muddy mess and the nearby creek was swollen to twice its normal size.

"I just got a really bad feeling about this place," Greg said with uncharacteristic sobriety.

"I know what you mean," Mike replied.

The two paused at the entrance to the cemetery, wondering if they should go inside. Nothing stirred aside from the occasional chirp of a bird and the whisper of the wind in the trees. It occurred to them that they were alone, and yet, they felt the presence of someone else. It was a hauntingly familiar feeling.

"Normally I'd say we should split up, but under the circumstances I think it'd be better if we stick together," Mike suggested.

"Agreed."

The two headed down the gravel drive into the cemetery. The driveway made a wide loop like a lasso around several trees and came back to the entrance, so Mike and Greg had to hike onto the damp lawn to access the rest of the cemetery. Broken branches from the spring storms littered the ground.

Mike pulled a crystal pendulum out of his pocket and suspended it a few feet off the ground. It swayed with every step, but, theoretically, it would begin to act irregularly if there was any disruption in the natural energy of the area. Emmer and Greg had always been skeptical of this instrument, but Mike swore by it.

"Have you ever found anything with that?" Greg asked as the two friends began to walk the periphery of Moon Point.

"Yeah, at the University of Illinois," Mike replied with a touch of bitterness. "Me and Aura tracked down that ghost in the English building and this led us right to her, remember? Oh yeah, that's right, you, Emmer, and Davin decided to go to a bar and drink instead."

Greg smiled. "Oh yeah, that was a good time. You should have gone with us. There were a lot of really hot women there."

Mike rolled his eyes and did not have time to notice that the pendulum in his hand began to swing wildly.

A slender hand caught it in midair, and Mike and Greg were jolted by surprise. A young woman blocked their path. She had long, black hair, and her faintly Oriental features gave her away as being a Roma, although her skin was unusually pale.

"It's the hatchet lady!" Greg blurted reflexively, but his first guess missed the mark by a wide margin.

Mike's heart skipped a beat. "Great Odin's raven!" he exclaimed. *Misa?* How did you get here?" He moved to embrace her, but her icy stare stopped him in his tracks. "It's been what, five, six years?"

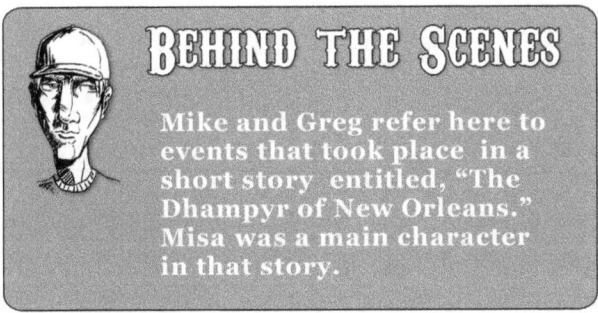

BEHIND THE SCENES

Mike and Greg refer here to events that took place in a short story entitled, "The Dhampyr of New Orleans." Misa was a main character in that story.

"You don't look like you've aged a day," Greg added, while not concealing his lack of enthusiasm for her sudden appearance.

"*Of course I haven't,*" the young woman replied. "What did you expect?"

"You ending up in a loony bin?" Greg replied, although he knew Misa's question was rhetorical.

"You're all in danger," Misa said, grimly. "You should not have opened the astral gate at Cahokia Mounds last December."

"We didn't," Mike replied, "those *jerks* did. Besides, we closed it right away. No harm, no foul, right?"

"I'm afraid not. You allowed something to escape."

"Wait a minute," Greg interrupted. "How did you get here? How did you know to meet us here on today of all days? I realize you're a dhampyr—or whatever—but you still have to obey the laws of physics."

"*This is important,*" Misa growled.

"Yeah, it's important," Mike parroted. "We don't have time for those kinds of questions. Do we?"

"No."

"So what is this thing then?" Greg demanded. "What escaped from the astral gate? Is this the same thing that's been attacking Aurelia lately? Not that I care, really."

"Your friend Aurelia will be fine," Misa replied. "It's both of *you* I'm worried about. You saved my life before, so I'm in your debt. I've been keeping tabs on you, making sure nothing happened to you. Those people who were after you last year—the zealots and the Satanists—they were unwitting pawns. They became food for the thing they unleashed; a primordial demon from the ranks of what some call 'the ancient ones.'"

"I guess Emmer was right for once, in a way," Greg mumbled. "They thought they were playing us and were, in fact, the ones who were played! Beautiful! So what does any of this have to do with us?"

"The acolytes of the ancient ones abducted your friend Davin and took him to an abandoned military base about sixty miles south of here. It just happened last night, during the thunder storm."

Mike frowned and pulled his cell phone from his pocket. Dialing Aurelia's number, he held the phone up to his ear and waited. After a few moments, Aurelia's shrill voice answered, making him wince. "It's Mike," he said. "Where is Davin?"

"I don't know, why didn't you call him?" Aurelia replied.

"He never answers his phone."

There was a pause, then Mike, Greg, and Misa heard Aura scream Davin's name several times. Mike jerked the phone away from his ear in annoyance.

"I don't know where he is," Aurelia said after a few moments. "He's not here. He's probably out getting drunk."

"Oh, I don't think so," Mike replied. "At least not this time."

"What do you mean?"

"Do you remember what I told you about me and Greg's trip to New Orleans the summer after we graduated high school? Remember that woman we met?" Mike glanced at Misa. "Well, it's a funny story. You see, she's back. We met her at the cemetery we're investigating. She says Davin was abducted." A pause. "No, not by aliens. By crazies who worship some kind of ancient gods."

Aurelia swore loudly enough for everyone to hear.

"I'll fill you in when we get back," Mike said and hung up.

"What, you didn't believe me?" Misa asked before Mike had time to drop his phone back into his pocket.

"I'll put it this way," Mike explained, "I don't believe anything unless I get at least a good second opinion."

Greg snorted.

Mike took a deep breath and folded his arms across his chest. "There's more to this than it seems," he muttered. "I don't like the way this feels at all. Misa, will you come with us and help get Davin back?"

Misa nodded. She seemed to have grown more confident in the years since Mike and Greg had last seen her, but the added confidence did not help make her more alluring. The nature of her breeding made her appear awkward and somewhat otherworldly.

The three took another look around the cemetery and decided that their work there was done. Mike, Greg, and Misa turned and walked back to their car. They hoped they would not be too late to save their friend.

INVESTIGATION FILE 030

CHANUTE AIR FORCE BASE
Rantoul, Illinois

Chanute Air Force Base opened in Rantoul in July 1917 and was a vital part of the local economy for nearly 76 years. After its closure in 1993, much of the base was divided up into residential and commercial properties, but most of the core buildings remain abandoned. The Chanute Air Museum moved into one of the old hangers, and its website offers an illustrated retrospective of the base's history. Inevitably, local kids exploring the abandoned parts of the base in the past few years have begun to bring home unusual stories.

Chanute Field, as the facility was originally known, opened as a result of the First World War. When the United States entered the war in 1917, our fleet of military aircraft was woefully inadequate. The War Department quickly allocated funds to open the Field and begin training an air corps. After the war, Congress bought the land around Chanute Field and authorized construction of nine steel hangers. Fires plagued the original base, since many of the buildings were made of wood.

Between 1938 and 1941, as the United States began modernizing its military, a "renaissance" occurred at Chanute. Buildings such as a headquarters, hospital, fire station, water tower, gymnasium, and even a theater were installed. The Works Progress Administration provided everything necessary for a permanent air corps to be stationed there.

At the outbreak of World War 2, thousands of new recruits flooded the base. According to the Chanute Air Museum website, the number of trainees at Chanute Field reached a peak of 25,000 in January 1943. After the war, however, the facilities deteriorated and the base gained a negative reputation. It became a joke in the Air Force that if someone needed to be punished, "Don't shoot 'em, Chanute 'em."

In the 1960s and '70s, Chanute Air Base played an important role in American missile development. It was the primary training center for the LGM-30 Minuteman ICBM and the Air-Launched Cruise Missile. In 1971, the Air Force closed the base's last remaining runway. In the following years, Chanute continued to be a training center for new aircraft pilots and engineers.

At the tail end of 1988, the Department of Defense recommended that the base be closed in order to save money. The end of the Cold War was the final nail in the coffin, and Chanute locked its doors and hangers for the last time on September 30, 1993. Most of the outlying structures of the base, including the officer's quarters and the barracks, are now occupied as residences. There remains, however, a portion of the base that is abandoned. While by no means properly maintained, it is heavily patrolled by local police. Visitors are free to tour the grounds, but not enter the buildings.

The presence of abandoned buildings anywhere is always an incubator for ghost stories. Chanute is no exception. Some visitors have, through the broken windows, reported seeing an officer working at his desk. Others say they have seen airmen strolling the weed-choked sidewalks.

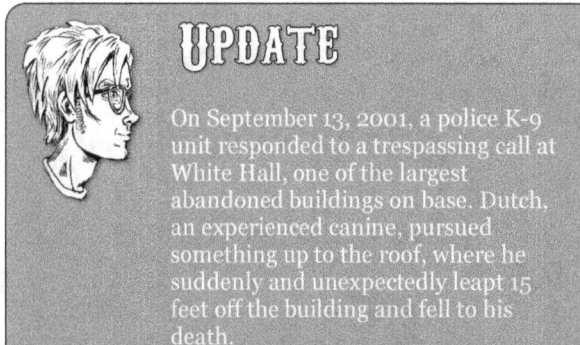

UPDATE

On September 13, 2001, a police K-9 unit responded to a trespassing call at White Hall, one of the largest abandoned buildings on base. Dutch, an experienced canine, pursued something up to the roof, where he suddenly and unexpectedly leapt 15 feet off the building and fell to his death.

The Fallen Investigate

JUN. 8

11:16 PM

78° F

The warehouse was dark, stuffy, and filled with stained boxes and machine parts. The only light penetrating the gloomy interior came from a few narrow windows high above. Davin could not move. Ropes bound his chest and his legs to an old plastic and metal chair. His mouth was not covered, partially because his captors knew he would not scream, and partially because it would not do any good if he had. For all Davin knew, he was in the middle of nowhere. He could have been in the Arizona desert. When they took him, his captors had covered his head with a black hood and drove for what seemed like an eternity.

There were two other men in the warehouse with him. Both were stocky and of average height. They kept their backs to him and their faces covered by ski masks. One sipped café mocha from a Starbucks cup. Every few hours they splashed water on Davin's face to keep him from passing out from the heat.

"Will you guys *please* just kill me already?" Davin pleaded. "We've been here for weeks. I told you my friends aren't going to come for me. They could care less."

"Shut up!" the mocha drinker yelled.

"Seriously, you guys are the worst kidnappers ever," Davin snapped back. "Aren't you even going to torture me a little? Look, I could help you out. Is there any rusted metal around here?"

"*What the hell is wrong with you?*" the other guard replied.

Suddenly, a hollow paint can tumbled to the cement floor with a crash, startling everyone. Something akin to the sound of footsteps followed briefly and then tapered off.

"What was that?" one of the guards hissed.

His companion gently lowered his café mocha and pulled a long, black flashlight from his belt.

*　　*　　*

Hours passed. Chanute Air Force Base was quiet aside from the chorus of insects and the dog that barked incessantly in the distance. Mike, Aurelia, Greg, Emmer, and Misa stole through the darkness, past broken park benches and empty windows. Misa led the way. Her eyes pierced the nebulous shadows cast by the glow of a handful of street lamps hitting the thick, brick buildings. Her ears heard the blood pounding in the veins of the Fallen.

"Now might be a good time to raise the point that we have no idea where Davin is being held," Emmer whispered.

"He probably hasn't showered in over a week," Misa replied. "When we're close, I'll smell him."

"There's nothing unusual about that," Greg chuckled.

Suddenly, a police cruiser turned onto the nearby street and shined a spotlight into the yard. The Fallen dropped to the ground, with the exception of Misa and Aurelia, who were close enough to the nearest building to disappear behind the wall. The squad car passed slowly, conducting its nightly rounds.

The core of the former Air Force base was laid out like a baseball field, with the administrative and classroom buildings in the diamond, the hangers and warehouses in the infield, and the airstrips in the outfield. The Fallen were currently hunkered down between home plate and first base, not very far from a majestic metal sculpture of a falcon taking flight. Mike, Greg, and Emmer waited for the policemen to disappear from sight before they joined Aurelia and Misa behind the building.

"You know," Greg wheezed from shortness of breath, "I think I had you all wrong, Misa. You've changed a lot from being that awkward, insecure dhampyr we met all those years ago. I think you and me ought to get together sometime."

"Please," Misa hissed. "What do you think this is, *Twilight*? Humans make me sick. You're like a cheeseburger to me."

"Uh oh, call the Anti-Defamation League," Emmer said. "We've got some kind of weird, nerdy interracial harassment going on here."

"Put your tongue back in your mouth, Greg," Mike ordered with feigned seriousness.

Misa tucked her thick, black hair behind her ears and peered into the distance. "I think we're close," she said. "We just have to get around that building." She pointed to a large, four story hall that formerly held classrooms. It wrapped around the western half of the diamond and concealed most of the hangers from view. Directly south, in one of the former warehouses, sat the Chanute Air Museum. The Fallen were pretty sure their friend was not being held in there. Only a handful of other options remained.

The group stealthily crossed the yard in front of White Hall and made their way north. This time, they pressed themselves against the dirty, brick wall as the police cruiser passed, heading in the opposite direction. "I don't like all these close calls," Emmer whispered. "If we're caught out here we'll never find Davin."

"That would be a shame," Greg mumbled under his breath.

"Keep it down," Mike whispered.

The group crept along the face of the building, past the front door, until they came to the northernmost corner. A handful of bats scattered from the windowsill. Greg playfully shoved Misa and pointed toward the creatures, but she was not amused.

"I sense something," Aurelia said suddenly. "I'm feeling a profound sense of duty. Like there is a soldier or an officer nearby."

Emmer rolled his eyes. "Like that cop that keeps driving past?"

"No, jerk," Aurelia replied. "It's a ghost."

Mike stroked his prominent chin and leaned forward. It was hard to tell in the dark, but it looked like the old hangers were over twenty yards away. The Fallen would have to cross a road, and there was no telling when the police cruiser would return.

"We're getting close," Misa replied to Mike's unspoken question. "I think Davin is in one of those hangers. The air is thick with perspiration... and cheap aftershave."

Mike looked around, embarrassed.

"Man, I'm so glad I'm out here instead of at home, drinking beer and listening to Opeth," Emmer grumbled.

Then, just as Mike had expected, the police car passed by again, this time at an agonizingly slow pace. It seemed as though the officer inside was looking for someone. He shined his spotlight into the windows of a long, white building across the street.

"Do you think he's looking for us?" Greg whispered.

"I hope not," Mike replied.

The group waited for the car to pass before they snuck across the road's cracked pavement. It was hard for five people not to make a sound, but they managed in spite of a proclivity on the part of Aurelia to throw caution to the wind. Just before they got within a few yards of the nearest warehouse, a loud rumble echoed from somewhere off to their left.

Mike, Greg, and Emmer turned toward Aurelia, waiting for her to make some kind of characteristically-obvious statement, but Misa spoke first.

"Something happened," she hissed.

Aurelia shot her the evil eye, and Greg suppressed a burst of laughter.

CHAUTE AIR FORCE BASE

WHITE HALL

Another clatter pierced the air. This time, the Fallen knew the noise came from the last building to their left. It sounded like empty canisters hitting the floor, followed by the scraping of metal. The quintet raced over to the warehouse, no longer concerned with keeping their presence a secret.

They were too late. Two masked men burst from the warehouse entrance and took off down the street in the opposite direction. The glass door slammed shut on the person behind them, and he or she fell backwards with a crash. Mike and Greg rushed forward and flung open the door. Davin lay on the other side, still tied to the chair. His two captors had left in such a hurry they had not bothered to free him.

"Get me the heck out of here!" Davin shouted frantically.

Mike pulled a pocket knife out of his cargo shorts and cut the rope that tied his friend to the chair, while Greg grabbed Davin's arm and pulled him to his feet. The group raced back across the street and gathered in the corner of one of the buildings.

"There was something in there with us," Davin gasped. "It scared the bejeezus out of us."

"What, the guys who abducted you were scared off by a ghost?" Mike asked. "What kind of evil acolytes are these?"

"They were just goons," Misa explained. "Do you think the acolytes would get their hands dirty with something like this? They were just trying to send a message."

"Well I'd say they failed miserably," Aurelia said.

Davin, having regained some of his composure, stared at Misa. "Who is that?" he demanded.

Mike looked up and down the darkened roadway. "We gotta get out of here before that cop comes back," he said. "I'll explain everything to you when we get home."

INVESTIGATION FILE 031

AUX SABLE CEMETERY
Minooka, Illinois

Aux Sable is a quaint, garden-like cemetery tucked in the woods near Aux Sable Creek in Grundy County. Despite an otherwise mundane existence, it continues to be a point of contention between local youth and law enforcement, with paranormal tourists often caught in the middle. The legends associated with the cemetery are of the usual stock: strange car trouble, the ghost of a young child, and rumors of a gate to Hell. Aux Sable has yet to appear in any books on Illinois ghostlore, but it has been discussed and debated at length on numerous websites.

According to a "History of Aux Sable Township and Villages" by D.A. Henneberry, Aux Sable Township was a hunting ground for Pottawatomie Indians before Europeans arrived. The first white settler in the area was Salmon Rutherford, a notable figure in pioneer Illinois. He arrived in 1833 and established the settlement of Dresden. The land around Aux Sable Creek provided fertile soil for farming, a bountiful harvest of timber, and a large population of wild bees, which supplied honey for the settlers. The honey was made into an alcoholic beverage called Metheglin (otherwise known as mead).

The nearby town of Minooka was platted in 1852, but did not experience much growth until after 1858. Aux Sable Cemetery was probably in use around that time. Referring to the local residents, Mr. Henneberry wrote, "religion has taught them to subdue any evil tendencies they may have ever had with very noticeable results."[41]

But this suppression of evil tendencies did not prevent rumors from spreading about satanic worship at Aux Sable Cemetery. In the 1980s, Satanists were feared to be hiding under every rock, so a remote cemetery, hidden from prying eyes and a favorite drinking spot for teens, was a natural incubator for such rumors.

The most notable story at Aux Sable concerns the ghost of a young girl that has been seen lurking around the cemetery. According to the Shadowlands Index of Haunted Places for Illinois, the ghost will only appear if you get out of your car. The story has generated a lot of discussion on Strangeusa.com, where contributors reported that, recently, someone removed the headstone of a six year old girl and left it on the playground of an elementary school. They allege the ghost belongs to this particular girl.

An anonymous visitor to Strangeusa.com, claiming to own the property around the cemetery, had this to say: "Whether your [sic] a 'paranormal investigator', hallunicnating [sic] drug addict or just kids looking for a fun time, please stay out of the woods." A search of the *Morris Daily Herald* shows that police have arrested visitors numerous times in the past few years.

The stories of Aux Sable are too many to list in detail here, but one thing is for certain, hundreds of people risk arrest to explore this remote location. Perhaps it is the perception of danger that keeps them coming back for more.

---

[41] http://tinyurl.com/az5g8jy

THE FALLEN INVESTIGATE

JUL. 21

8:06 AM

86° F

The Grundy County Sheriff's office was crowded for a Saturday. Three tan-shirted officers escorted the Fallen through the narrow hallway toward several empty rooms while the window mounted air conditioner worked overtime to combat the heat and humidity. Blue carpet, which had absorbed the moisture in the air and the condensation that dripped from the air conditioner, sloshed under their feet. Greg winked at the secretary before one of the officers shoved him into a room.

Aurelia kicked and screamed in the hands of two female deputies. She was the only one of the Fallen in handcuffs, and the deputies had to tie a rag around her mouth to keep her from biting them.

Mike shook his head as he watched. He knew he would have to bail Aurelia out of jail later, but he also felt sorry for the two deputies. They obviously did not realize that she would use every part of her body as a weapon. She had already been tased and pepper sprayed. They would have to sedate her before she would give up the fight. Aurelia's temper could be an asset, but most of the time it was a liability.

"You really f—ed up big time," Emmer whispered before he was also taken into one of the rooms.

Mike and Davin remained in the hallway, watched over by the sheriff himself—a burly man with a white mustache who chewed tobacco impatiently.

A deputy, with "Johnson" etched onto his nameplate, approached the trio. "None of these kids have any identification on them," he informed the sheriff. "We're going to have to throw the girl in a cell. We can't get her to stop resisting."

The sheriff turned to Mike and Davin. "How about it?" he asked. "You've got ten seconds to tell me your names."

"I told you already," Mike said. "My name is John Smith."

"What were you doing at Aux Sable Cemetery?"

"Bird watching."

"You better wipe that smirk off your face or I'll do it for you," the sheriff growled.

Just then, the officer who had gone into a room to interrogate Greg burst into the hallway, wiping his eyes. His arms shook.

"Bundy, *are you crying?*" the sheriff yelled.

"No... I... just have something in my eye," the officer replied, his voice choked.

Inside Room 103, Emmer sat behind a plain desk, across from a chubby deputy with short, frosted hair. The deputy, whose last name was Marx, looked tired, and like he had not been at his job for very long.

"Look," he said. "The worst thing we can charge you with is trespassing. Just tell me your name and what you were doing in Aux Sable and we can both get out of here."

"I want a lawyer," Emmer replied. "I'm not with those guys. I just wanted a ride to the gas station. They picked me up and took me to this cemetery. They're all nuts, especially the short one. You have to look out for him."

"Why did they go to the cemetery?" Marx asked. "Did they go there to tip headstones, smoke dope, break something, or what? You know we don't like kids back there."

"First of all," Emmer replied, "I'm probably older than you are. Secondly, they weren't doing anything illegal. They were just looking for ghosts. Don't ask me why. They think some dust particles are pictures of spirits or whatever. I don't believe in any of that stuff. I just want to get out of here and buy my lottery tickets."

Deputy Marx shot him a deeply skeptical glance. "So you've never met any of those guys before today, huh?"

In the room next door, Mike sat eye to eye with the sheriff, who kept a manila folder in front of him at all times and a waste basket at his feet for his chew, which he would spit into at intervals of one to two minutes. He was an intimidating man, the kind where even his scent was imposing. Each line on his face was like a tally of the criminals he had busted over his years in law enforcement.

"Cut the crap," he barked. "Tell me what you were up to before I bust your butt for obstruction of justice."

Mike raised his eyebrows. "You want to know the *truth?*" he asked. He did not wait for a reply. "The truth is that last year a group of zealots briefly opened a door to the astral realm, allowing some kind of ancient daemon to escape. A half vampire, half human girl my friend and I rescued years ago informed us that acolytes of this daemon were attempting to trap it and unleash its power for their own ends. We were in Aux Sable Cemetery because I believed something there might give us a clue to their whereabouts."

"Son, why would followers of our Lord and Savior Jesus Christ—if that's what they are—open a demonic portal?" The sheriff snorted before he ejected a huge wad of black tar from his mouth into the waste basket.

"*Don't ask me,*" Mike replied. "I never said it made sense."

"I think you're full of crap," the sheriff said. "In over thirty years with a badge, I've never heard anything so ridiculously stupid. Why don't you just tell me what you were really doing there? We're going to get it out of one of you. Why don't you stop wasting my goddamn time?"

At that point, Deputy Marx stuck his head into the room and called the sheriff over.

They conversed for a few moments, then the sheriff cursed loudly.

"Ghost hunting?" he growled. "Son of a bitch. We have a hundred things to do and this is how we spend the afternoon?" He turned toward Mike. "You're in deep trouble, son."

As Deputy Marx drove Mike, Greg, Davin, and Emmer back to their car, the sheriff stood outside the station with two other officers. He spat as he watched the police cruiser disappear down the street.

Deputy Johnson handed him a sheet of paper. "The fingerprint check came back," the officer said. "It looks like these guys were picked up in Lake County in August 2007 on a trespassing charge. There's nothing else on any of the males. The female has a record. Shoplifting. Disorderly conduct. That kind of thing. She has a number of aliases, the most recent being..." He flipped through the pages. "Aurelia. We've still got her locked up. We could probably charge her with resisting arrest and assaulting a police officer."

"Might as well go ahead," the sheriff said. "Make 'em post bail. They can pay for the damage she did to my station. I don't have time for this."

A sloppy wad of tobacco hit the blistering pavement before the three turned and walked back into the building.

While the police cruiser slowly bounced along the road to Aux Sable Cemetery, Deputy Marx engaged his passengers in idle conversation, attempting to bate them into confessing their identities. He did not believe anything they had said back at the station. In his short time at the sheriff's office he learned to trust no one, especially not some Goth freaks prowling around a cemetery.

"So, where are you guys from?" he asked.

"Uranus," Emmer replied.

They spent the rest of the trip in silence.

Deputy Marx dropped off the four near their car, which was still parked in Aux Sable Cemetery. He waited until they got into their vehicle and drove down the narrow, gravel lane toward the cemetery entrance before he followed them. He let his police cruiser idle near the entrance, making sure the four miscreants did not come back.

Behind the wheel of the Fallen's Toyota Corolla, Mike eyed the cop with distain. "Can you believe that guy?" he grumbled.

"You know, they probably would have let us all go a lot sooner if Aurelia hadn't thrown a tantrum," Davin said from the backseat. "They have our license plate number now."

"Yeah, and now we have to figure out a way to get Aurelia out of jail," Mike said.

"We do?" Greg, Emmer, and Davin asked in unison.

"Hey, do you remember when you made me ride in the trunk?" Davin whined. "You should make Aura do that."

"You're lucky you're riding up here right now," Greg laughed.

"Hey! Who saved your rear at—"

"Knock it off!" Mike interrupted. "We have more important things to worry about right now. The cops are onto us. We have to be more careful, especially with the Black Willow Grove investigation."

"Agreed," Emmer said. "Might I suggest the first thing we should do is sell this piece of junk car, and get one with a CD player in it."

Mike narrowed his eyes. "First let's get out of here and see if we can't spring Aura from the pen," he said, and he turned the car onto the highway.

INVESTIGATION FILE 032

CUMBERLAND CEMETERY

Wenona, Illinois

Cumberland Cemetery, located near the town of Wenona in Marshall County, is rumored to be the home of a headless lady, spook lights, and the ghost of a little girl. The cemetery itself is rich in history. It was the site of the first farm in Evans Township, and its rolling hills were once occupied by a fort built during the Black Hawk War to protect the nearby settlers from marauding Sauk, Fox, and Kickapoo Indians.

Marshall County was settled comparatively late. Illinois became a state in 1818, but the first white settler in Evans Township, Benjamin Darnell, arrived there in 1828. The book *Past and Present of Marshall and Putnam Counties* tells us that his nearest neighbor lived six miles away in what became Roberts Township. Benjamin Darnell had ten children, including a 14 year old daughter named Lucy (the date of settlement given here, including Lucy's age, is different than that given by Chad Lewis and Terry Fisk in the *Illinois Road Guide to Haunted Locations*. I believe my source to be more accurate).

Lucy took ill and died in 1829. Her family buried her on their farm, and her grave formed the cornerstone of Cumberland Cemetery. It is thought that the spirit of the first person (or animal) to be interred in a cemetery becomes its guardian. Perhaps that superstition explains the origin of the young girl's ghost reportedly encountered in Cumberland?

Immigration to Marshall County picked up between 1830 and 1832, but in 1832 settlers received word of an uprising of tribes under the command of Chief Black Hawk, who contested a treaty with the United States government which removed American Indians to the west of the Mississippi. The settlers, who had no legal claim to the land in Marshall County until 1835,

erected a stockade on the Darnell property and called it Fort Darnell. It was never used.

The main legend associated with Cumberland Cemetery involves a headless woman. There is no evidence to substantiate the story, but that has not stopped its proliferation. It goes like this: a long time ago, a farm occupied the land that would become Cumberland Cemetery. The farmer and his wife lived there happily tilling the fields and taking care of their animals. They were quite content on their own. After a time, however, more families moved into the area, along with quite a few bachelors.

The farmer never had any reason to suspect infidelity on the part of his wife before, but he began to suspect she was having an affair with one of the young men who now hung around his farm looking for work. Crazed with jealousy, the farmer cornered his wife in their barn and confronted her. Despite her pleas and denials, the farmer took his ax and chopped off her head. From then on, her ghost stalked the cemetery, searching for her missing head.

Or was she looking for revenge? Regardless, she is said to haunt the cemetery and, according to the Shadowlands Index of Haunted Places, a nearby barn. The ghost has been reported as far back as the 1950s. As usual, many locals have taken nightly trips out to the cemetery in hopes of seeing this and Cumberland's other spirits.

THE FALLEN INVESTIGATE

AUG. 6

12:11 AM

79° F

The moon sat low in the deep blue sky, while white pines teased its silhouette just beyond the entrance to Cumberland Cemetery. A thousand insects buzzed, chirped, and whistled in the nearby woods and fields. Mike, Greg, Aurelia, and Misa stood in the shadows beneath the pine trees. They spoke in low whispers.

"After being arrested for trespassing last month, *again*, do you really think it's prudent to be back in a cemetery at night?" Greg asked.

"We'll just have to be more careful this time," Mike replied. "Besides, this is where we agreed to meet our mysterious contact."

"Why?" Greg asked.

"Because otherwise it wouldn't be *mysterious*," Aurelia said matter-of-factly.

Greg cleared his throat. "Well, I hope that car back there didn't belong to him," he said, pointing in the direction of a white Ford Explorer partially hidden by overgrown weeds near the cemetery entrance. It looked like it had been sitting there for quite some time.

"It is awfully quiet," Misa purred in her characteristically breathless voice.

"I definitely sense someone—or at least something," Aurelia added.

Mike flicked a mosquito off his arm and then folded his arms across his chest. "Crowley's arse, that's all we need. It's bad enough that we have to be out here without Emmer and Davin, but I don't like running headlong into something that reeks of a trap without the entire team. I don't like it one bit."

"You know after what happened last month we can't afford to be in the same place at the same time," Greg interjected. "We can't afford to let them get all of us at once."

"I know," Mike said with a tinge of annoyance. "That's why I told Davin and Emmer to stay at home."

"We don't need them anyway," Greg laughed. "What have they ever done, really? Davin is great if you need someone to get himself captured or to cut and run—literally, in his case."

"That's enough of that," Mike said. "We all know you don't like him. This isn't the time or the place—we have to find this 'contact' and get the heck out of here before the cops show up again." An uneasy feeling developed in the pit of his stomach. *This is one of our darkest hours, but we'll get through it*, he thought with melodrama honed by hours of reading Victorian gothic tales.

"It sucks being hunted by everyone, doesn't it?" Misa asked with a touch of bitterness.

Without warning, the temperature lowered noticeably. Aurelia winced, but she did not sense anything threatening. Then, starting with a pair of worn-out, brown shoes and working its way upward, a man slowly materialized no more than a few feet away. He was gaunt, with greasy blonde hair and a wry smile. He wore what looked like a uniform—rough wool pants and a dirty white shirt under a butternut jacket. The entire form flickered and glowed like it had been projected from an old film reel, or for the Star Wars nerds among us, like Princess Leia's message to Obi-Wan.

The Fallen were startled. Greg reached for his cane and Mike's hand fell on the Ka-Bar he kept hidden in his waistband. Misa hardly flinched. She was accustomed to dealing with both the living and the dead.

"There's no need for that," the specter said, eyeing Mike and Greg's defensive postures. "Not that you could hurt me anyway."

"What do you want?" Mike demanded.

CUMBERLAND CEMETERY

"I'm the one you came here to meet," the ghost explained. "The name's Johnny. I've been watching you since you went to Decatur a few years back."

"Greenwood Cemetery?" Greg interrupted.

"That's right. I was one of those poor souls who met their end on the side of that hill. Buried alive I was. There's nothing worse, I can assure you of that, but the past hundred years or so has tempered my anger somewhat. That's the thing about being dead—gives you a lot of time to think." The ghost seemed to possess the usual gallows humor of those hurled into the afterlife against their will.

"So what do you want from us?" Mike asked, but before Johnny's incorporeal remains could respond, Aurelia answered for him.

"He's the spirit who's been helping me," she said, then addressed the ghost. "Haven't you?"

"Yes," Johnny replied. "I knew there was something different about you the moment I saw you. I figured you could use my help. I know what it's like to be hated and vilified for fighting for a lost cause."

Mike chuckled. "The odds are a thousand to one, but we haven't given up yet. We've still got a few cards up our sleeve. The trouble is every time we peel back one layer there's another conspiracy behind that. Not that what we've found so far makes very much sense."

"The world as you see it is a lie," the ghost explained. "Up is down and left is right. The people who profess to be good are often times the most evil. They cloak their crimes in virtue and they call the good, evil, and evil, good. It's too bad it doesn't get much clearer when you're dead. It's just another mystery."

This guy sounds like a dirty, New Age hippie, Greg thought, but kept his opinion to himself.

"That sounds depressing," Mike said. "But why should we believe you? How do we know you're not leading us into a trap? Why haven't you made your presence known before?"

"I didn't know how you would respond," Johnny said. "It's not every day you meet a ghost! But the more I learned about you the more I wanted to help. I figur'd I should show myself to you only under the gravest of circumstances, so you took me seriously when I did."

"What does a ghost do all day?" Greg asked.

"Oh, we just frequent our old haunts," Johnny replied.

"Now that we're introduced," Mike interrupted, clearing his throat, "tell us why you brought us here."

"Right to business, huh?" the ghost said. "Al'ight then. Word is you're stepping in the middle of something big. You're angering things you don't want to anger. Let me tell you—*you don't want to.*"

"Tell us something we don't know," Mike said, thrusting his thumb toward Misa. "She's already filled us in."

"Can't you be any more specific than that?" Aurelia asked. Her mind worked overtime, trying to detect anything from the ghost. Ghosts are notoriously fickle. Lacking the filter of a brain, their emotions are pure and sharp—uninterrupted by fleshly impulses. The living see and experience only a small fraction of existence, while a ghost is not confined by the senses. Aurelia's brain was more sensitive to energy than most, so she could feel thoughts radiating from the spirit of Johnny, but she could not determine whether or not he was being truthful.

"I heard down the line you opened some kind of door into our world and some mighty big players are angry about it," Johnny explained. "They'll be coming for you with everything they got, and from what I hear, you don't ever want to meet these guys."

"He's right," Misa said with a grin. "We're your only friends."

"Great—the dead and the undead!" Greg explained. "If we had any more friends we could reenact the 'Thriller' video."

"Forgive me, but I have to leave you for the time being," Johnny said. "It takes a lot of ectoplasm to materialize like this. I need to return to my world and regenerate, or I'll be no good to you."

"Be careful," Mike said. "We appreciate your help, and I'm sure we'll need you again soon."

With that, the ghost vanished as quickly and as mysteriously as he had appeared. Cumberland Cemetery returned to normal. Mike looked around at the faces of his friends before asking the obvious question. "Should we trust him?"

"At least we know who's been helping us this whole time," Aurelia chimed in. "I don't see what choice we have. We have to trust *someone.* It might as well be a dead guy. He doesn't have anything to lose by helping us."

Misa snorted.

Mike deeply inhaled the midnight air and caught a tinge of electric energy, like that preceding a thunderstorm. He knew it must have been an aftereffect of the ghost's appearance. He folded his arms across his chest. "We need to get back to Black Willow Grove," he said. "Emmer and Davin will be waiting there, wondering what happened to us. Emmer won't believe this, so I don't see any reason to tell him. He'll just think we're even crazier than before."

"Agreed," Greg and Aurelia said simultaneously. They exchanged suspicious glances, since they did not often agree, and joined Mike and Misa in walking stealthily back to their car.

INVESTIGATION FILE 033

ASHMORE ESTATES

Ashmore, Illinois

Ashmore Estates looms large in the minds of many Coles County residents, even if they have only heard the stories. It stood abandoned for nearly twenty years, until its new owners opened it as a haunted house in autumn 2006. Since then, the building has been scoured by paranormal investigators and will soon be featured in several television programs, including *American Horrors* and the Booth brothers' *Children of the Grave 2.*

The building (known as an almshouse) began as a part of the Coles County Poor Farm. It was built after the Auxiliary Committee of the State Board of Charities condemned the first almshouse. In January 1915, bids were placed for the construction of a fireproof building on the location. The contract for the new almshouse was awarded to J.W. Montgomery in March of 1916 for $20,389, and the cornerstone was laid on May 17, 1916. L.F.W. Stuebe was the architect who designed the building.

The modern poor farm operated for over forty years, until attitudes regarding public welfare began to change. Many of them were demolished and the land sold off to private farmers, but others were privatized as care facilities. Coles County sold its almshouse to Ashmore Estates, Inc. in February 1959. That corporation opened the building as a private psychiatric hospital, but it suffered from financial difficulties from the very beginning. In May of 1979, the Illinois Department of Public Health ordered the building closed after finding twenty-two safety code violations, but it remained open until November after a judge found progress in fixing the problems.

In the early 1980s, the building was used as a home for the mentally and developmentally disabled. The *Times-Courier* described it as a pleasant and caring environment where residents were happy, had their needs taken care of, and even pursued artistic interests. Ashmore Estates finally closed its doors in 1987. A few years later, Corrections Corporation of America wanted to buy the building for use as a mental health clinic for teenage boys, but the Ashmore Village Board denied them a zoning variance. There was also public resistance to the idea because area residents were concerned about what would happen if some of the boys escaped.

Unclear of the actual owner (a Champaign County resident named Paul Swinford had owned the building, but he released the deed to a real estate broker), and facing possible condemnation, Ashmore Estates went up for sale at auction in the summer of 1998 because of delinquent taxes that went back for two years. Arthur Colclasure, a Sullivan resident, bought the building for $12,500 and planned to turn it into his home, but vandalism thwarted his efforts.

In the summer of 2006, Scott Kelley purchased Ashmore Estates and opened it as a haunted attraction. For years, local kids had risked arrest to explore the building, finally they were able to venture inside and see the things they feared lurking there come to life. In recent years, Ashmore Estates has become something of an obsession for the paranormal community, but most are content to just sit back and swap stories about this fascinating building.

UPDATE

Ashmore Estates has since been featured on the TV show *Ghost Adventures* and more recently on *Ghost Hunters*. Your humble author had a chance to appear briefly in the *Ghost Adventures* episode.

THE FALLEN INVESTIGATE

SEP. 13

3:45 PM

66° F

The two story, red-brick building grew closer and closer, until the Fallen could see the remnants of last year's haunted house splashed across its façade. Gravel spun and crackled under the wheels of their dark blue Toyota Corolla as it slid up the driveway and came to a stop on the turf parking lot, jolting its passengers. Mike threw the gearshift into park and turned the key, but his companions did not wait until the car was off to start climbing out. Through the windshield, Mike saw a tall man stride toward the car, wearing a black t-shirt that sported "Ashmore Estates" in spooky lettering. A black and white Border Collie followed obediently at his heels. Across the yard, an employee busied himself clearing some debris.

Greg, Aurelia, Emmer, and Davin instinctively lined up behind Mike as he stepped out of the Toyota to greet the man, who he correctly assumed to be the building's owner. Mike, as usual, was donned head to toe in black, and his trench coat hung loosely from his shoulders. Aurelia knew the day might involve crawling around inside a dusty old building, so she wore a black tank top, camouflage pants, and combat boots. Her dark brown hair was tied up in a ponytail. Greg was decked out in an old Vietnam-era olive green shirt and tattered khaki shorts. Emmer and Davin were less imaginative, content with jeans and dirty t-shirts. Neither came out in public voluntarily, and they dressed accordingly.

The man shook Mike's hand, and he introduced himself as Scott, "spookmeister" of Ashmore Estates. "I'm glad you came," he said. "If you don't mind, I'd like to get right down to business. I've got a lot of work to do before the season begins."

Mike nodded. "Of course."

"We have here the most popular haunted attraction in east central Illinois," Scott explained. "Do you guys like haunted houses?"

The Fallen exchanged glances.

"Ok, well, we get over a thousand visitors every season," Scott continued without missing a beat. "You know this building is supposed to be haunted in real life, right? We've had a number of paranormal investigators in here over the past few years, but nothing's ever happened like this before. A bunch of key props have gone missing recently. A ladder to the attic fell, and yesterday I found oil on the stairs. I can't have that happening. I didn't know what to do until someone told me about you guys. They said you're different from those other paranormal groups. You better be, for as much as I'm paying you."

"Have your employees seen anything?" Mike asked, ignoring Scott's last comment.

Scott hesitated. "Joe over there." He pointed toward the young man who was working in the yard a few dozen feet away, near some horses. "He refuses to talk about it though. He got real shook up."

"We'll go check out the building," Mike said. "Whatever it is, we'll take care of it."

"Before you go in there, I have to ask you to sign these forms," Scott said with a wide grin. He thrust a stack of papers toward the Fallen. "Just in case."

One after the other, Mike, Aurelia, Greg, Emmer, and Davin signed the forms and filed into the aging building. Upon entering, they were confronted by a stairwell that led two floors up and one floor down. "Let's start in the basement," Greg suggested, and the others agreed.

A musty smell hit them as they arrived at the bottom of the stairs, and it became immediately clear that the basement was being used to store the props and other equipment for the haunted house. There was little space to walk around. Costumes, boxes, benches, and buckets lined the walls and filled the rooms.

"I think this used to be the kitchen and cafeteria," Aurelia said. "I can sense relaxation and satisfaction. I can almost hear the silverware scraping against the plates."

Emmer rolled his eyes. "Yeah, that and there's two windows in the wall where they would have served food through. That's a big clue."

"Let's keep going," Davin urged. "It's too damp down here."

The Fallen continued down the hallway toward the back of the building. At a certain point it became clear they had entered the newer addition. The distinction was obvious on the exterior, where the builders had not even attempted to preserve the original architecture.

Without warning, a small rubber ball began to bounce along the concrete floor toward the Fallen. Aurelia brought it to a stop with her boot, and the quintet fell silent. No one moved as their ears strained to pick up the faintest sound. For a few tense moments, they heard nothing but the wind and the chirping of birds floating through the open door at the other end of the hall. Then, a clatter from the stairs.

The Fallen bolted into action. Practically tripping over one another, they raced to the stairwell and climbed up to the third floor. "That definitely sounded like a person," Mike wheezed.

Davin, also winded by their short jog, fell on his rear end into the dust at the top of the stairs.

"Let's go!" Aurelia shouted, grabbing him by his shirt collar and hoisting him to his feet.

The Fallen spilled into a wide corridor that looked like it had been created out of some of the original rooms by way of knocking down the walls. A maze of heavy, black folding screens and black curtains filled the area. "You've got to be kidding me," Emmer said, giving Mike the evil eye. "You told me this was going to be easy."

Mike grinned. "This is the fun part," he said. Suddenly, the cackle of a maniacal clown filled the air—deflating his smile. "Not *that* fun," he frowned.

"*I hate clowns*," Davin said with a shudder.

Mike motioned to Aurelia and she instantly understood. She moved quickly to find the exit to the maze, while the other four entered it.

Inside the walls of the maze, vision was reduced to just a few inches. The only light came from the open window at the end of the hallway, and it barely peaked over the top of the black folding screens. Despite its confined area—or perhaps because of it—navigating the maze proved frustratingly difficult. Mike, Greg, Davin, and Emmer groped the walls and bumped into each other. More than once, they thought they caught someone, only to discover that it was one of their friends.

Meanwhile, near the exit, Aurelia waited with arms folded across her chest. She tapped her foot impatiently. "This is pointless!" she finally shouted. "Will you guys stop screwing around in there?"

As the last word left her lips, a section of the wooden screen collapsed and Mike and his companions spilled onto the floor, along with someone wearing a polka doted jumpsuit covered in red paint, with a twisted mask and rainbow colored hair. The clown sprang to his feet and bolted past Aurelia, who was too shocked to react.

"I knew it wasn't a ghost!" Emmer yelled. "Get him!"

But Aurelia was already gone. She chased the clown down the hallway, past rooms filled with props and seaweed-green walls covered with graffiti.

At the same time, Scott appeared at the top of the stairs. "I heard a crash," he said. "What's going on in here?"

The clown veered into the closest room to the stairwell, while Mike, Emmer, Greg, and Davin finally got to their feet and raced to join Aurelia. Mike grabbed Greg and pulled him into one of the rooms further up the hall, assuming the rooms might connect. He was right. Over the years, vandals had knocked holes through the walls, creating a passage from one end of the building to the other.

Aurelia, Davin, and Emmer plugged the doorway with their bodies, and when the clown saw Mike and Greg coming through the hole in the wall, he knew he was trapped. He climbed through the window and jumped onto the roof, but his baggy pants got caught on a nail, throwing him off balance. The clown plummeted to the ground and landed with a thud.

Moments later, Scott and the Fallen were down the stairs and on the front lawn. They surrounded the clown, who clutched his knee and groaned. "We think we found your ghost," Mike said, addressing Scott. "We chased him to the third floor. That's when you came upstairs."

Emmer grabbed the twisted clown mask and pulled it off, revealing the man who had been cleaning the yard when the Fallen first arrived.

"Joe!" Scott yelled. "Why would you do this?"

"He was creating accidents to try and scare you off," Emmer explained. "Probably wanted to take over the place himself."

"I would have gotten away with it too, if it wasn't for you freaks!" Joe spat.

As orderlies wheeled the disgruntled clown into the waiting ambulance, Mike approached him. "There's just one thing I can't figure out," he said. "How did you do that trick with the ball when we were in the basement? We didn't hear anyone else down there."

Joe looked back at Mike with a puzzled expression. "What ball?" he asked, and then he disappeared into the ambulance.

INVESTIGATION FILE 034

TWIN SISTER'S WOODS
Rockford, Illinois

Twin Sister's Woods is located in Rockford and is part of Twin Sister Hills Park—22.44 acres of recreational land complete with two baseball fields and three sled hills. It is a popular winter destination, when the snow is thick and area youths come out to careen down the hill slopes, but some locals claim this park is home to more sinister guests. The woods, they say, has been the scene of several murders, hangings, and even a drowning. Add feelings of dread, disembodied voices, and mysterious figures and you have one of Rockford's closely guarded secrets.

Twin Sister Hills Park is wedged between Keith Creek, 27th Street, and a shopping center called Rockford Plaza. To the south runs Charles Street. East High School—with its own resident phantoms—stands on the opposite side of that street. Many of its students grew up sledding on Twin Sister Hills, and as they grew older, appropriated the nearby woods for less than family friendly activities. Twin Sister Woods is 8-acres enclosed on three sides by a fence on the west side of the park. An imposing willow tree, which is the focal point of several legends, sits at the entrance.

The legends of Twin Sisters are varied and quite imaginative. First told among local high school students, they eventually found their way into the Shadowlands Index of Haunted Places for Illinois. "If you walk by the willow tree it is said that you have a strange desire to go into the woods," the index reads.

"There is an old hanging tree with some odd carvings on it. A little girl is said to be seen walking around." The little girl is the ghost of a child who allegedly drowned in nearby Keith Creek.

While the entry in the Shadowlands Index is not specific about which tree is the "hanging tree," Haunted Rockford (a now defunct website at Webs.com) points to the old willow. "Some believe that a satanic cult used this tree for sacrificial purposes and would carve ritualistic symbols into the trunk of the tree," it claimed. "Others believe that a young girl was hung from the tree." But with its high, vertical branches, a willow makes a poor hanging tree, and oaks are the traditional tree for ritual sacrifice.

Another legend involves the ghosts of three rape victims who haunt the woods. Their ethereal shadows duck in and out of the trees. While nothing substantiates these stories, it is easy to imagine that Twin Sister's Woods has been a crime scene. It is a claustrophobic area surrounded by urban blight, and if murders have not taken place within its boundaries, there have certainly been some nearby. There were 20 murders and 106 sexual assaults in Rockford in 2007, and as recently as August 29, a decomposing body was found in the backyard of a suburban Machesney Park home.

The legends of Twin Sister's Woods reflect the reality of life in metropolitan Illinois. As one of the only wooded areas in the City of Rockford, Twin Sisters has developed an undeserved reputation as a place of mystery and danger, and ghost stories naturally accentuate this titillating atmosphere for its visitors.

THE FALLEN INVESTIGATE

OCT. 15

12:05 PM

62° F

A crisp, autumn wind whipped across the freshly cut grass and broke against the three small hills at the periphery of the park. Emmer kicked an empty beer can across the chipped pavement of the parking lot, while Greg and Davin traded insults and pushed and elbowed each other like two birds of prey fighting over the same perch. Casey the Coydog waited patiently by Emmer's side, panting and occasionally gnawing at her shoulder. A narrow stream followed the edge of the parking lot and then wound its way toward a small, confined wood, which sat about fifty yards away.

Emmer massaged his forehead and sighed. "I never thought I would come back here," he grumbled.

"Twin Sister's Woods?" Greg asked.

"No, Rockford," Emmer replied. "It's a long story. I went out with a girl from Rockford once. She broke my heart."

"Ah, the plot thins," Greg chuckled.

Davin slapped Emmer on the back. "You gotta quit those Internet romances," he said. "Take it from one who knows."

"If Mike were here, he'd be telling us to get serious right about now," Greg said, then broke into an impression of his dour friend. *"We're here to investigate. There's no room for anything else."*

Emmer grinned. "Yeah, 'cause people who look for ghosts should really take their work seriously," he retorted. His eyes examined the nearby stream and followed it to the tree line, where a thick, gnarled weeping willow grew near the entrance to the wood. "Well, there's that willow tree Mike told us about."

Davin unfolded a stack of papers and began to read, but Greg snatched it out of his hands.

"Go fetch," he said and tossed the papers into the air. The wind blew them across the parking lot and into the nearby chain linked fence.

"Hey!" Davin protested. "Those were our instructions! Besides, haven't you ever heard of a little thing called littering?"

"We're being hunted like dogs, hiding out in some weird girl's attic, and my roommate looks at my neck like it's a value meal," Greg replied. "Mike can go screw his instructions. Why did he send us out here, anyway, to get rid of us for the day? What is he planning?"

"You know why we're here," Davin grumbled.

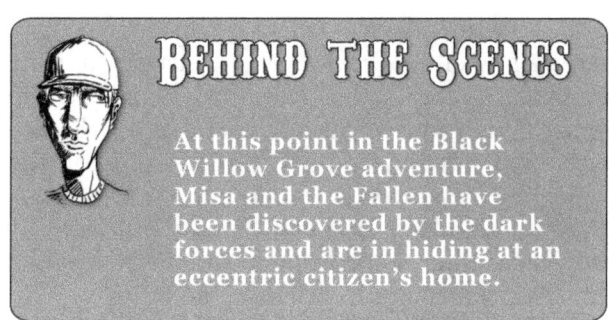

BEHIND THE SCENES

At this point in the Black Willow Grove adventure, Misa and the Fallen have been discovered by the dark forces and are in hiding at an eccentric citizen's home.

"Alright, let's just do this," Emmer said. "I'm getting hungry and I saw a Beefaroo on the way out here. Get the camera and the video camera. We have to document every inch of this place. I suggest starting with the woods, since that's where the story takes place. We gotta find this 'hanging tree.' It shouldn't be that difficult."

The trio retrieved their equipment from their car and set off toward the woods. By all indications, they were alone. They could hear only the traffic from the nearby road and the barking of a dog in the distance. Casey, however, behaved nervously. It was not the sound of the other canine that excited her—it was something nearby. She whined and scratched the grass.

"What's the matter, girl?" Greg asked the mutt. "Do you smell a ghost?"

Casey's ears perked up and she began to bark. She took off toward the woods and vanished from sight beneath the weeping willow.

"That was odd," Davin remarked.

"Oh please, don't start," Emmer said. "Just because that dog acts weird—it doesn't mean anything paranormal is happening. She could have smelled a squirrel or something."

"I know," Davin grumbled.

"I was just making sure."

By the time the trio was done arguing, they stood under the willow tree. A path led into the woods to their right and the creek lay just beyond the path.

Greg thoughtfully examined the tree, which was at least four yards in circumference and looked like it had been there for many years. "That's a willow alright," he said.

"Why are you so fixated on this thing?" Emmer asked, his back to the tree and his friends. He panned his camcorder from left to right, recording the field and adjacent parking lot. "What does it have to do with the legend?"

"I don't know," Greg replied. "I threw that crap away, remember?"

Davin and Emmer both scowled at him.

"I don't need to know the story," he protested, waving his hands wildly in the air. "All I need is my instinct. That's the problem with the way Mike does things. He thinks too much. Now, let's keep walking. I remember something about a hanging in the woods."

Casey, from somewhere up ahead, barked twice and the Fallen followed the sound to a clearing in the wood. Five teenagers, three guys and two girls, stood next to a graffiti-covered piece of concrete in the middle of the clearing. The young men stood and smoked while the girls knelt down and petted Casey. "Hey, is she yours?" one of them, who wore a High School Musical hoodie, asked.

"Come here, Casey!" Greg yelled playfully while he slapped his knees. The coydog responded immediately, its ragged, gray tail wagging furiously.

"What a useless guard dog," Emmer grumbled. "They could have been waiting here to kill us and she would be licking their faces."

"Shouldn't you be in school?" Davin asked the five teens while he motioned to them to pass their joint.

"We are," the girl in the hoodie responded. "Our school is right across the street. We snuck out here during lunch."

"And there, gentlemen, is the origin of your ghost stories," Emmer laughed.

"Did you say something about ghosts?" one of the young men asked as he took a drag. "You know these woods are supposed to be haunted, right? Tony has seen some stuff,

TWIN SISTERS WOODS

haven't you?" He thrust his finger toward a short, pudgy boy with curly red hair and something that looked like it could be a beard, if given a few more years to grow.

"Me and Maddy were here one night," Tony began, "and we see this light in the woods. We thought it was a cop, you know? So we head for those hills over there, figurin' we'd hide behind them. Well, when we come out of the woods, we see that there ain't any cars in the parking lot. We turned around and the light was gone."

"What kind of light was it?" Greg asked. "What color was it?"

"I don't know, man," Tony replied. "It was real bright. Like a spotlight."

"Maybe it was a spotlight," Emmer said.

"A lot of weird stuff happens in these woods," one of the girls insisted. "Sometimes you hear weird noises."

"It'll take more than some lights and weird noises to convince me," Emmer replied.

"Hey, what are you guys doing out here, anyway?" Tony asked. He took a hit from his joint and passed it to the girls. "You're not cops, are you?"

Greg laughed. "Do we look like cops? Nah, we're here looking for ghosts. Did any walk past here recently?"

"Oh, like T.A.P.S.?" one of the girls asked, becoming unnecessarily excited.

"Something like that," Davin replied. He handed her a card with his phone number on it. "If you ever see anything strange around here, give me a call."

The girl took it and blushed.

With that, the Fallen tromped farther into the wood, walking over discarded branches and around chunks of concrete. They picked a trail and followed it, hoping it would lead to something out of the ordinary. The path twisted between the trees, their autumn-colored leaves sprinkling the forest floor. Although the trio had not walked far, the voices of the high school students faded into the distance.

Davin became nervous. "Does anyone else feel odd?" he asked.

As if in reply, Casey the Coydog began to whine and refused to go any further. Greg, Emmer, and Davin looked up—they had wandered near the edge of the wood and faced an old, gnarled Black Willow tree that looked like it had been struck by lightning.

"Something isn't right about this tree," Davin said.

"For once, I agree with you," Greg replied.

Emmer just rolled his eyes and walked up to the tree. He kicked it and stared defiantly at his friends. "Look," he said. "There is absolutely nothing unusual about this tree. It's a fricken' tree. That's all."

A blast of wind sent brown leaves showering down, and over Emmer's shoulder Greg and Davin saw shadows slither up the knotted, twisted branches of the Black Willow, which emerged from the ground like fingers on a severely arthritic hand. Greg and Davin instinctively took a few steps backward while Casey barked and growled.

Emmer watched the color drain out of the faces of his friends and felt a chill run down his spine in spite of himself. He spun around, but saw nothing out of the ordinary. He allowed himself to smile. "I told you," he bragged. "It was just the wind."

Greg and Davin exchanged glances, but did not try to argue. "Let's just get out of here," Davin said. "I think we got all the pictures and video we need."

Emmer shook his head and took the lead as the three friends marched out of Twin Sister's Woods.

INVESTIGATION FILE 035

HARRISON CEMETERY
Buckner, Illinois

Located between the town of Christopher and the village of Buckner in rural Franklin County, Harrison Cemetery is home to two luminous phantoms, as well as haunting, ethereal tones. If you can get past the glowing ghosts of a man and a woman who are said to guard the cemetery, you will discover a small monument in the form of a piano. Although locked in stone, this unique headstone is said to be the source of the ghostly music.

Harrison Cemetery has served area residents for over 120 years and is named after one of the first families to settle Browning Township. The *History of Gallatin, Saline, Hamilton, Franklin and Williamson Counties* listed A. [Andrew] U. Harrison among the township's early settlers, most of whom arrived in the same year Illinois became a state: 1818.[42] Both Andrew Harrison and his wife Elizabeth are interred in the cemetery. They died in 1845 and 1846, respectively, but Harrison Cemetery was not officially chartered until 1907.

The village of Buckner grew up along the Illinois Central rail during the 1910s and flourished due to its proximity to a large United Coal Mining Company plant that churned out 4,000 tons of coal per day.[43] Workers at the plant and from the nearby mines converged on Buckner after their shifts. The village developed a reputation for its nightlife, and even today it is home to the only club in southern Illinois to stay open until 4am.

Many of the men who for decades pulled coal out of the earth were, at the end of their lives, returned to the earth alongside their families on the sloping hills of Harrison Cemetery. But some locals say that the souls of at least two of those people refuse to rest. According to an entry on the Shadowlands Index of Haunted Places for Illinois, the ghosts of both a man and a woman guard the graveyard. "The man usually shows up as an orange glow in a field beside the cemetery," the index reads. "The woman is usually a whitish glow. She usually shows up near a group of pine trees in a far corner of the cemetery."

This corner of the cemetery is also the home of a third legend, that of a piano that plays at midnight. This legend is clearly tied to an unusual looking headstone set apart from the others. With its oversized piano keys, it appears to memorialize a child, perhaps one with an interest in music, but there is no name or date to give any clues as to who it belonged.

Recently, Tracy DeVore interviewed the Southern Illinois Ghost Hunters Society on examiner.com. Speaking about their experiences at one section of Harrison Cemetery, they said, "it literally felt like an elephant was sitting on our chests and we were all getting very dizzy, and while all that was going on when we were standing still we could hear something running next to us and nothing was there."[44]

Whether you believe the stories or not, Harrison Cemetery certainly has an interesting place in the history and folklore of Franklin County.

---

[42] *History of Gallatin, Saline, Hamilton, Franklin and Williamson Counties* (Chicago: The Goodspeed Publishing Co., 1887), 342.

[43] *The Prospects of Franklin County Illinois* (Benton Commercial Club, 1912), 6.

[44] http://tiny.cc/6BpIR

THE FALLEN INVESTIGATE

NOV. 5

4:45 PM

43° F

It began with an over-determined squirrel, transporting one of the last acorns of the season to his hovel in the woods behind the cemetery. Casey the Coydog sniffed him out and raced to demonstrate her superiority in the food chain, but the squirrel proved to be too wily. Momentarily abandoning his prize, he bounded out of the way just as Casey's paws slammed into the dirt, and then scampered between her legs, scooped up the acorn, and fled for the nearest tree. With a blur of gray fur, Casey shook her mangy head in frustration.

Mike, Aurelia, Greg, and Emmer watched these proceedings with amusement while they stood next to their rusted Toyota Corolla at the base of the hill near the entrance to Harrison Cemetery. Mike shielded himself from the biting wind with his black leather trench coat, but Aurelia, in contrast, stood oblivious to the dropping temperature in a black t-shirt and skirt. Davin sat in the backseat of the car with his eyes closed and his face pressed against the window. A small trickle of drool ran down the glass from the edge of his mouth.

"Are we just going to let him sleep in there?" Emmer asked.

Without saying a word, Aurelia opened the passenger door and Davin spilled out, uttering a cry of surprise as he hit the lawn.

"What the heck?" he protested as he pulled himself to his feet.

"I told you not to drink so much last night," Mike said.

"You tell me a lot of things—" Davin brushed the dirt and leaves off his jeans while

his friends fished around in the Toyota's trunk for their supplies.

The sun was nearly below the horizon. Casey the Coydog paced the tree line, waiting for the squirrel to reappear. Emmer popped open the LCD display on his camcorder while Mike pulled a digital camera from the pocket of his trench coat. "I'm looking forward to seeing some ghosts this time," Emmer said. "There are two here, right? That means we have a 50 percent chance of seeing at least one of them."

"I don't think your math adds up," Greg chuckled, and then turned to Mike. "Hey, how long are we going to be down here? We should go back to the Cotton Club after this investigation. That bartender was smokin' hot."

Mike scowled. "Is that all you think about?" he replied. "As for how long we're going to be here, I figured we'd stay in southern Illinois for a couple of weeks and wait for things to calm down a bit. We'll hit a couple of other places, and then maybe we can slip back into Black Willow Grove unnoticed."

"Good luck with that," Aurelia said. "The town elders know what our car looks like. I'm sure they know who we are by now. We can't even go out in public without people whispering."

"How is that any different from before?" Davin asked with a grin. "I think every one of us is banned from at least three different establishments."

"Yeah, but the owners of those places weren't also trying to kill us."

Mike stepped in between Aurelia and Davin, interrupting them. "Can we focus for five minutes?" he pleaded. "We're not going anywhere until we get what we came for. As Emmer mentioned earlier, there are two different ghosts here. We're also supposed to be able to hear a piano playing. Our objective is to document the cemetery while there's still a sliver of daylight, then see if we can't encounter these ghosts ourselves. Who has the tape recorder?"

Greg, who wore tattered khaki shorts and mismatched socks, raised his hand.

"At midnight we are going to try and record this mysterious piano music," Mike continued. "Any objections?"

"Uh, yeah," Emmer said. "I'd much rather be back at the bar."

Aurelia slapped him upside the head, hard enough for his baseball cap to fly off.

"Didn't your parents teach you not to hit other people?" he yelled and quickly made use of Davin as a human shield.

Aurelia scoffed. "My parents kicked me out when I was nine years old," she said, her voice tinged with disdain.

After the group settled down, Mike and Aurelia went in one direction and Davin, Emmer, and Greg in another. They filmed the terrain and took pictures until the sun disappeared below the horizon and stars began to pop into view. Mike and Aurelia walked up the hill on the northwest quadrant of the cemetery, not bothering to turn on their flashlights. The sky was cloudless and the moon nearly full, providing just enough light to navigate between the headstones. When Mike reached the summit of the hill, he stopped and looked up at the sky.

"Look at all those millions of stars," he said. "There are things we can't even imagine out there, yet the distance that perplexes us the most is that between us and the people lying under our feet."

Aurelia turned and faced him, but said nothing.

Mike adjusted his glasses, and his mind raced from one subject to the next. "We certainly made a mess of things. If we can't fix it, I'm sure we'll be back here again in another life, and things will be even worse than before."

Laughter echoed up the hill from the direction of Greg, Emmer, and Davin, who had wandered across the road into a separate part of Harrison Cemetery. Aurelia fought back a grin while she slipped her arm around Mike's waist and rested her head on his shoulder. "At least we're all stuck here together," she said. "For now."

Mike shot a glance over at the dark shapes of his other friends at the opposite end of the cemetery. "Yeah. Great."

"I've been trying to work my way up the sauces at Buffalo Wild Wings," Greg said as Emmer snapped shut the LCD display on his camcorder. "I'm on Mango Habanero. It's like having a Hawaiian in a sombrero pour fire in your mouth. It's awesome."

"Mangos are from India, not Hawaii," Emmer said.

"Man, whatever. I'm the only here who has even been to both of those places."

Without warning, Casey the Coydog—who had been shadowing the trio since sundown—stopped in her tracks and began to whine.

"Turn the camera back on," Davin whispered.

Emmer looked like he was about to rain verbal abuse down on his friend for even suggesting that Casey's behavior might be abnormal, but before he could, a sphere of orange light roughly the size of a baseball appeared and rushed toward him. Davin and Greg dove out of the way, but Emmer did not move. His eyes grew wide, and the orange glow passed through his shoulder with a jolt—spinning him ninety degrees before it zipped back into the headstones.

Greg flipped open his cell phone and sent a text message to Mike, telling him to come quickly. He then got to his feet and ran over to Emmer, who looked more pale than usual. "Are you ok, man?" he asked in a low whisper.

Emmer's mouth moved, but no sound escaped.

Out of the corner of his eye, Greg noticed that the bright orange light was coming around for another pass. He shoved Emmer out of the way just as it burned the air about their heads.

On the other side of the cemetery, Mike's cell phone vibrated. He plucked it out of the pocket of his trench coat and accepted the incoming text. The message simply read, "H."

"They're in trouble," Mike said. He glanced in the direction of his friends, but they were too far away to see them clearly.

Mike and Aurelia wasted no time. They raced down the hill, dodging and weaving around the headstones as they went. After they crossed the road, it was only a few more yards before they reached their compatriots.

Aurelia knew what happened without needing to ask. She sensed the anger of the orange being and threw up her hands. She muttered a few arcane words and the air became still. Without missing a beat, Aurelia walked up to Emmer and slapped him across the face. "Snap out of it!" she shrieked.

Emmer shook his head and swore. "What the heck did you do that for?"

"What happened?" Mike asked.

"We were attacked," Davin said frantically. "By some kind of light. It hit Emmer."

"Are you ok?"

Emmer rubbed the side of his face, which still had a red imprint of Aurelia's hand. "Not anymore," he grumbled. "I don't know what the heck that was, but my shoulder is sore too. I feel like I got an electric shock."

"Let's stick together for the rest of the night," Mike said tentatively. "I don't want any more of these incidents. Did you get it on video?"

"No," Greg said. "Emmer turned off the camera right before it struck."

"Ok, from now on keep the tape rolling," Mike replied. "Aura, I want you to tell me if you sense that thing coming back. Let's wrap up the investigation and get out of here."

For once, no one argued.

INVESTIGATION FILE 036

AXEMAN'S BRIDGE
Crete, Illinois

There is nothing peculiar about the concrete bridge along Old Post Road two miles east of Crete. If a motorist were to drive past, over the trickling waters of Plum Creek on a pleasant summer day, not much would alert this passerby to the Axeman's gruesome story. In the woods a few yards to the northeast, however, sits a rickety steel bridge, currently collapsed into the water. It is tagged with graffiti. For years, local teens imagined that this was the scene of a gruesome axe murder. The remains of a home hidden in the trees and the closure of the road leading to the steel bridge have only fueled the legend.

Although landmarks set the stage for this story, the exact history of the area is difficult to determine. According to John Drury's photographic history, *This is Will County, Illinois* (1955), David Harner was the first white settler of Crete Township, and a large contingent of ethnic Germans followed. Early on in the history of Will County, the thick timberland along Plum Creek was called Beebe's Grove. It was named after Minoris Beebe, who arrived in 1834 along with David Harner. According to an old county plat map, a man named William Vocke owned the property around Axeman's Bridge in 1909. I have been unable to determine when this bridge closed.

To my knowledge, there are two books that mention the legend of Axeman's Bridge: *Windy City Ghosts* by Dale Kaczmarek and *Weird Illinois* by Troy Taylor. Both have competing accounts of the story, but neither is necessarily incorrect. In folklore, there is no "correct story," since the details change with every retelling.

In one version, told by Dale Kaczmarek, the Axeman (or Ax-Man) was a lonely old hermit who killed a pair of kids he caught trespassing on his property. Their friends, waiting safely on the road, had dared the two boys to run from one side of his bridge to the other. The version found on the Internet and related by Troy Taylor tied the Axeman's tale to the abandoned house in the woods. The man, who had a history of abusive behavior, chopped up his family and then set his house on fire. Online, others have added that the Axeman then murdered two sheriff's deputies who came to investigate the fire. When backup arrived, the police chased the murderer to the old steel bridge, where they shot him dead.

Since that time, some visitors have reported that their car has stalled on the bridge along Old Post Road, or that they have spotted the soft yellow lights of a house in the woods. Others have heard screams and the sharp ping of an axe hitting iron supports.

Old bridges and axe murders are staples of folklore, but rarely are the two combined. The legend of Axeman's Bridge is an interesting mixture of tropes that makes this location in particular so unique, and there is no doubt that people will continue to visit for years to come.

The Fallen Investigate

DEC. 11

10:30 AM

28° F

"**I**f you two don't knock it off, I'm turning this car around!" Mike threatened from behind the wheel of the wobbly Toyota Corolla as it sped down a rural avenue somewhere in Will County. The car's rusted frame protested against the near freezing temperature, and its paper thin tires tenuously gripped the icy road. In the backseat, Greg and Davin traded insults while Aurelia buried her forehead against her palm and rested her elbow on the passenger door. Emmer sat in the front passenger seat, reading a Tom Clancy novel.

Mike's eyes darted from the windshield to the rearview mirror. "Pay attention," he said. "I swear you two are like five year olds. I'm not going to explain this again."

Aurelia pinched Davin's arm to get his attention, and he yelled in surprise.

"This bridge we're going to is haunted by a man with an ax," Mike explained. "He allegedly killed his family before being gunned down by the cops."

"Do you have any evidence of this?" Emmer asked, never taking his eyes off the novel in his hands. "Any newspaper articles? Interviews? Channel 5 special reports? Court records?"

"No," Mike replied. "But we're hoping to get some evidence the old bridge is haunted."

"Good luck with that," Emmer muttered.

"Do you still refuse to believe in ghosts?" Greg asked, momentarily abandoning his determination to make Davin's life miserable. "Even after everything you've seen? How do you explain what happened to you at Harrison Cemetery last month?"

Emmer snapped. "*I don't know*, but it wasn't paranormal."

"Let's face it, Emmer will always be a skeptic," Aurelia said.

Greg laughed. "He's not a skeptic. He's paranormally-challenged."

Emmer put down his Tom Clancy novel. "I'll admit I've seen a lot of unusual things since I signed up with you guys," he said. "Most of it involves things you do. But the other stuff can be explained by idiocy. You want to believe it so badly—it's your first explanation for everything. 'Oh, that light was a ghost,' instead of the hundred other things it could have been."

"But you won't even accept that as a possibility," Greg protested. "I don't believe in anything unless I see it for myself, and I know I've seen a ghost or two in my life."

The Fallen's Toyota shot past a side street, and Aurelia pulled out the large-print map of Illinois. "Shut up, everyone!" she shrieked. "Mike, I think you missed our turn."

"What?" Mike glanced over his shoulder, but the street sign was long gone. "Crap," he muttered. "I don't know where the hell we are."

"You just have to stop and turn around," Aurelia said in a tone usually reserved for scolding children.

Up ahead, an old man wearing a lumberjack hat stepped out to the end of his driveway to check his mailbox.

"Why don't we just stop and ask that guy?" Mike inquired rhetorically.

"It could be the axeman!" Davin shouted.

"You're drunk again, aren't you?" Greg snapped at him.

Mike gradually brought the vehicle to a stop next to the old man and signaled to Emmer to roll down the window. Emmer complied, and a burst of frozen air filled the Toyota's interior.

"Excuse me!" Mike leaned over and strained to look through the window at the man's weathered face. "Excuse me! Do you know how to get to Old Post Road?"

AXEMAN'S BRIDGE

The old man inched up to the car and put a callused, leathery hand on the open window. "Did you say *Old Post Road*?"

Mike nodded.

"You aren't going there to mess around on that old bridge, are you? I would stay away from there, if I were you. It's dangerous there. Some of you might get hurt." The old man's lips curled into a smile.

"Thanks, we'll keep that in mind," Emmer said. "Could you just tell us how to get there?"

"Keep going straight. Then turn right as soon as you can." The old man began to step away from the car, but paused. "But don't say I didn't warn you."

The Toyota's tires spun angrily on the ice and gravel before they finally caught traction and the car jolted forward. Emmer quickly rolled up the window and Mike cranked up the heater. It only took a few more minutes for them to reach the intersection with Old Post Road.

"I guess we weren't really lost after all," Mike said as he turned the steering wheel. The car and its passengers entered an area of dense woods on either side of the road. Snow and ice hung from the barren branches, yet they seemed more foreboding than beautiful. After a few minutes, a newly paved, concrete bridge came into view. Mike pulled the Toyota over to the shoulder just before the aluminum guardrails poked out of the snow.

Doors slammed as the Fallen piled out of their vehicle and onto the road. Mike scanned the tree line, and his eyes fell on the twisted steel supports of a bridge upstream. "Looks like we found the right place," he said. "It kind of reminds me of Airtight Bridge."

"Yeah, but at least that legend was based on something that really happened," Emmer said.

Aurelia did not mention it, but she began to feel nervous. She could tell there was something wrong, but she could not put her finger on the problem. As the group neared the path in the woods, she felt a subtle shift in the atmosphere. Suddenly, a house stood about fifty yards past the tree line, and the bridge, which had been collapsed into the creek moments earlier, appeared to be structurally sound. Aurelia could not contain her feelings any longer.

"Did anyone notice that house appear over there?" she asked.

"Hasn't it been there the entire time?" Davin replied.

"Uh, no."

Mike, Greg, and Emmer all threw Aurelia puzzled looks, but before she could respond, the group heard blood-curdling screams coming from the dreary, white house. The Fallen bolted into action. Greg readied his cane while the quintet plowed off the road and into the pristine snow of the timber.

Suddenly, a woman burst from the screen door. "He's going to kill my babies!" she yelled frantically.

In what must have been minutes—but seemed like seconds—the Fallen closed the distance between them and the panicked woman. She immediately collapsed into Davin's arms. "Help!" she gasped. "He's going to kill them!" Her face was sweaty and smeared with grease, and her hair was tangled.

Mike only had to nod, and Greg and Aurelia were at his side. Mike cursed. "What the heck is going on?"

"I swear to you, this house was not here when we pulled up," Aurelia said.

"Doesn't matter," Mike replied. "We'll figure that out later. Now's the time to act."

Greg brandished his cane like a club, and Aurelia led the way into the small house. She tore aside the screen door and shot up the small set of stairs into the kitchen. She could not have picked a more opportune time: a man with an ax stood over the cowering figures of two children. He was about to strike, but had been distracted when the Fallen came pounding through the door.

Aurelia picked up the first thing she saw—a black rotary phone—which she tore off

the wall and hurled at the would-be murderer's head. It landed with a sickening crash and he crumpled to the linoleum. The two children, cheeks stained with tears, dashed past the Fallen and out the back door.

Mike gripped Aurelia's shoulder. "We better get out of here before the cops come," he said.

Outside, the two children, overcome by emotion, embraced their mother while Emmer and Davin looked at each other and shrugged. Neither one could explain what happened.

After a few moments, Mike, Aurelia, and Greg joined them. Mike ran up to Davin and Emmer and drew them in close. "We gotta go, now," he whispered. "Forget the investigation. Aurelia just bashed some guy's head in over there."

He did not need to say anything more.

As the Fallen retreated back down the old road and out of the woods, Aurelia looked back at the woman and her children. "Thank you," she heard the woman say, just before the three of them, along with the dirty white house, vanished.

"That guy must have been the son of the old man we ran into earlier," Mike remarked as he got into the car. "I might have imagined it, but they looked a lot alike..."

INVESTIGATION FILE 037

SEVENTH AVENUE DEAD END

Sterling, Illinois

Around the dinner table after a hard day's work, the residents of Sterling, Illinois have been known to whisper about the deaths that have occurred along the nearby railroad tracks and the banks of the Rock River. These deaths have occasionally left behind ghosts, the most famous of which is a wailing woman who wanders the tracks just beyond the Seventh Avenue dead end, searching for her missing children.

The City of Sterling was incorporated in February 1857 and is located across the Rock River from the town of Rock Falls. These twin cities are connected by the First Avenue Bridge. Sterling has long been a center of industry in the area, ever since the Union Pacific Railroad, the oldest railroad network in the United States, came through in 1856. Businesses like Northwestern Steel & Wire, Franz Manufacturing, and National Manufacturing followed at the turn of the century. Consequently, the city was once called the hardware capital of the world.

Over the years, the twin life-sources of Sterling—the railroad and the Rock River—have occasionally become a curse rather than a blessing. Some do not respect the silent power of the river and succumb to its undertow. Others, mainly children, have innocently wandered to their doom while playing on the bluffs along the river. According to the Shadowlands Index of Haunted Places for Illinois, there is a "blind corner" near the Dillon Home Museum between Tenth and Eleventh avenues, where the railroad tracks turn slightly north. Anyone walking on the tracks in that area would not be seen by the train conductor, and several people have been struck and killed.

It is difficult to imagine that such circumstances would not produce a ghost story or two, but over the years, one phantom in particular has captured the imaginations of locals. She is a young woman who has been seen wandering the railroad tracks and the riverbank past Seventh Avenue. Her story is similar to the legend of La Llorona, in which a beautiful woman drowns her children and is condemned to spend eternity searching for them. As she searches, she weeps and wails, earning the name "The Crying woman." It is unclear, however, why the Seventh Avenue ghost appears. It is said that her children are missing, but not why they are missing.

According to Trent Brandon's *Book of Ghosts*, the weeping woman is a type of ghost he calls "The Broken Heart." Having lost one dear to them, they are alone and desperately search for the soul of a dead child or lover. The ghost is overwhelmed with guilt and believes she must wander the earth endlessly until reunited, or until she has endured enough punishment to assuage her guilt.

Whatever the reason, the ghost story of the Seventh Avenue dead end stands as a reminder to residents who live near the river and the railroad, especially children, that they must always remain vigilant or suffer a similar fate.

THE FALLEN INVESTIGATE

JAN. 5

5:28 PM

19° F

The melodic tones of Woods of Ypres' "Years of Silence" filled the cabin of the Fallen's Toyota Corolla as it slid through the sludge and ice along the First Avenue bridge and into downtown Sterling. Mike managed to keep the vehicle on course as he popped cheesy tots one after another into his awaiting mouth. Aurelia sat next to him in the passenger seat and Greg, Davin, and Misa were stuffed in the rear passenger compartment. Davin sat in between Greg and Misa with his hands clutching the space between the headrest and the backrest of Mike and Aurelia's seats. He was not wearing a seatbelt.

In the left hand lane, cars crawled bumper to bumper while their drivers cursed and honked at each other. "It's a good thing I have a death wish, because otherwise I would be pissing myself right about now," Davin yelled over the music as the car swerved.

"Oh, relax," Aurelia replied. "If we crashed, the windshield would cushion the blow."

Davin laughed nervously.

"Hey," Mike cut in, "I've never gotten us into an accident. Not once in all these years, so pipe down."

Greg grinned. "Yeah, would you rather go back to riding in the trunk?"

"You guys are great friends," Davin said sarcastically.

The Toyota passed the sign for Second Street. "We're getting close," Mike said and slightly depressed the breaks. His eyes strained to see out the smeared windshield. It had been gloomy all day, but it seemed to be getting prematurely darker. Then, over the rooftops of a row of businesses to the northeast, he noticed a column of black smoke that combined with the cloud cover to block out the sun.

David Gold's voice, scratchy from being filtered through the tape deck and worn out speakers, cut through the momentary silence. *But what good are memories with no one to stand beside you? What good are memories if those you made them with despise you?*

Mike turned the corner onto Third Street and his vehicle crawled to a stop. Two police cruisers and a fire truck blocked the road, and there was an officer in a heavy coat detouring traffic north. Flashing emergency lights lit up the storefronts and fresh snow like lasers at a dance party, and flames licked out of an old warehouse in the middle of the block. Black and gray ash rained down and mixed with the snow.

"Unbelievable," Mike said. "We're going to have to find a way around."

"Yeah, let's get out of here before that traffic cop checks our license plates," Aurelia suggested with transparent urgency.

Mike carefully turned the car and began driving away. "We'll just go around to the other block and find a parking space on Seventh Avenue."

With Third Street blocked, the Fallen worked their way north, past Fourth Street—which was one-way in the wrong direction—all the way up to Fifth Street. There they turned right and saw the street was clear. By that time, Woods of Ypres was midway through "Deepest Roots: Belief that all is Lost." Misa sat silent and expressionless in the backseat, with Greg and Davin as far away from her as possible without becoming uncomfortably close to each other.

"Let's go over the case one more time," Mike said. "At the end of Seventh Avenue there are railroad tracks. The ghost of a woman has been seen there. She's a 'Broken Heart,' a type of ghost that is searching for a lost child or lover. Hopefully we can confirm the story."

"For what purpose?" Greg asked as the Corolla turned onto Seventh Avenue and headed south.

"What?"

"Well, who cares if the story is true?" Greg continued, gesturing wildly in his customary manner.

"We do, I guess," Mike replied.

"If the story is true, we might be able to learn something," Misa explained. "Whether she is aware of it or not, this ghost is in continuous contact with the netherworld, and will be able to tell us something about your… predicament. It's often the case with these ghosts that they find everything *but* the thing they're looking for, especially when it comes to information. They are kind of like metaphysical sponges."

"Yeah, what she said."

"When did you become an expert?" Greg demanded. "A decade ago you needed us to save your butt from your bloodsucking father. Now all of a sudden you're like a paranormal guru. And why don't we just ask Aurelia's imaginary friend? We wouldn't have had to drive three hours in the middle of winter."

"A lot's happened since New Orleans," Misa replied. "I've seen and done things you can't even imagine."

"Everything but take a shower," Greg shot back.

"That's *enough*," Mike said, and as he reached to take a friendly swipe at Greg, he did not notice the Plymouth Voyager that turned onto Seventh Avenue right in front of them. Mike slammed on the breaks, and his dark blue Toyota swerved in the newly fallen snow as he let out a string of obscenities. The Voyager cleared the intersection just in time, however, and the Fallen's Corolla slid on the icy pavement and was marooned on a snow bank just past the stop sign. The Voyager drove off, apparently unconcerned with what had just occurred.

"Well, here's where we get out."

The Fallen piled out of their vehicle. The Seventh Avenue dead end was in sight. On that final block before the railroad tracks, the street turned to brick and only about a half-dozen houses stood on either side. "There's the railroad tracks on the other side of that barrier," Misa said, pointing south toward the terminus of the street. "Let me do the talking."

As the quintet walked down the street, it occurred to Davin how odd and alarming their activity might seem to the folks living there. He could not imagine many visitors coming to that neck of the woods, let alone a group of five people dressed all in black in the dead of winter. His eyes darted from house to house, looking for any signs of movement.

It did not take long for the Fallen to reach the dead end. They hopped over the guardrail and waded through the knee-high snow to the railroad tracks. A few yards away, the Rock River crept along, weighted down by chunks of ice.

"So where is this ghost?" Greg demanded.

Not long after the words left his mouth, a blast of icy wind cut through the rail bed, rustling the tall, yellow grass on either side. At the same time, Aurelia was hit with a feeling of intense sadness followed by nausea. Her friends seemed unaffected, but all five witnessed the flickering specter that formed before their eyes. It was transparent and smoky gray in color, almost indistinguishable from the dirty snow and overcast sky.

She cried, but her voice was not audible. Instead, it echoed in the minds of all those present. "Where are my babies? Do you know what happened to them?"

The Fallen exchanged glances to confirm they had each heard the same thing.

Misa spoke up first. "Yes," she said. "I know where they are. But first you have to tell us what we want to know."

The ghost gave no response, and the air became still.

SEVENTH AVE DEAD END

"I know you have felt the terrible thing that was unleashed on this world exactly one year ago," Misa continued. "You have felt the cold dread of its presence, and the determination of its followers. My friends here need to know how to send it back from where it came. You have looked everywhere for your missing children. Surely you stumbled on something that can help us. Tell us, and I'll give you what you are looking for."

"You know where my children are? You can help me?" the ghost asked, frantically.

"Yes," Mike replied, although he knew that was a lie.

The specter dissolved, and for several moments, the quintet believed she was not coming back. "We *don't know* where the heck her kids are," Greg whispered. "How are we supposed to help her?"

"It doesn't matter," Misa replied. "The only thing that matters is fixing your mistake by sending that thing back through the astral gate."

"But we closed the gate," Mike protested. "You know that. I don't feel right about this."

Misa did not have time to respond before the ghost of the woman reappeared, holding a folded piece of cloth. "Take this," she said and quickly handed it to Mike. "On it, you'll find the information you're looking for. Now, where are my babies?"

"We will come back with them before the year is out," Misa said, then whispered an incantation and waved her left hand through the air. The ghost vanished.

"Let's get out of here," Davin said.

Mike agreed. He stuffed the piece of cloth into the pocket of his trench coat, and the quintet walked back to the street.

"We will reunite them," he said. "The Fallen never go back on their word."

"Suit yourself," Misa replied. "But right now we have much bigger fish to fry.

INVESTIGATION FILE 038

WILLOW CREEK FARM
Shannon, Illinois

Willow Creek is an unassuming farm in rural Carroll County, just outside the town of Shannon. In recent years, it has been the subject of at least a dozen different paranormal investigations, all of which have uncovered a treasure trove of mysterious phenomenon both of the visual and auditory variety. The farmhouse itself is said to be haunted by at least seven ghosts or spirits. Since Albert Kelchner, its current owner, moved there in 2006 to get away from the big city, he has kept a careful record of all the unusual events that have happened in the past several years.

The farm has a long history, dating back to the 1830s when the Boardmans settled on the property. William and Mary Boardman came from England in 1835 and made their way to Rockford when the future city was merely a trading post along the wagon trail from Lake Michigan to the Mississippi River. In 1838, William staked out a claim in Section 10, Cherry Grove Township in Carroll County and built a log cabin. This log cabin was still standing in the 1920s. William then left to retrieve his family, who had stayed in Rockford. Unfortunately, a claim jumper got wind of William's activities and rode ahead on horseback. He arrived in Dixon before William and stole part of the claim.

William and Mary had many children, among them was a daughter named Mary, who married a man named David Holmes, who was born in Leistershire, England. The two had a daughter named Margaret Etta Holmes. Margaret married Frank Zier on December 31, 1889. The Zier family remained in possession of the farm until they went bankrupt in the 1980s. The property then went through several owners until Mr. Kelchner bought it in 2006 and christened it Willow Creek Farm.

According to records, the farmhouse dates to 1878, however, there is reason to believe it was built as much as a decade earlier, since it appears on an 1869 plat map.

Mr. Kelchner, with the help of several psychics and mediums, has identified and named seven distinct ghosts, including several others lacking a strong presence. The main otherworldly inhabitant of the farm-house is a woman named Sarah. She wears a blue floral print dress with an apron, and is sometimes seen wearing the kind of lady's black boots fashionable in the 1800s. There is no question as to whether she is the matron of the house. Another often-felt presence is that of an African American man called "Joe" who inhabits the basement under the family room. He is said to hide under the stairs.

Probably the most disturbing presence is that of the "creep" or "creeper." He was a reverend or doctor in life, and exibits a powerfully negative energy, especially to women. He has been felt in the northwest bedroom, where some psychics believe he might be imprisoning another ghost—a 10 to 12-year old boy named "Robbie." Robbie is thought to have died of a prolonged illness.

Much could be written about Willow Creek Farm, but this much is certain: it has caught the attention of many paranormal investigative groups from all corners of Illinois. We are likely to hear a lot more about this mysterious place in the future.

THE FALLEN INVESTIGATE

FEB. 7

4:45 PM

31° F

The sun was already in its descent by the time the Fallen's car pulled into the driveway, and after several hours drive, the team had finally arrived at Willow Creek Farm. A white, two story farmhouse stood to their right, and a fallow cornfield to their left. From behind the steering wheel, Mike frowned. With one hand on the wheel, he shuffled through a pile of printed Google maps. "I knew we should have turned right," he muttered.

"Maybe you want to think about getting a GPS," Greg suggested offhandedly from the backseat while Emmer, Aurelia, and Davin suppressed grins.

"This car still has a *tape deck*," Emmer said. "Do you think Mike is going to get a GPS?"

"I doubt a GPS would even work out here," Mike replied defensively.

The Toyota passed beneath a large, golden willow tree and came to a stop a few yards from the farmhouse. As the quintet got out of the car, Al, the farm's owner, greeted them one by one with gregarious handshakes. He was a stout man who wore a checkered shirt and a tattered baseball cap and spoke with his hands. He took particular interest in Aurelia, until she met his friendly smile with a scowl.

"Don't mind her," Greg said. "She reacts that way to everyone."

Al brushed off the snub, and the Fallen followed him through the open garage into the kitchen. The kitchen was unfinished, as was the dining room. A section of the floor was concrete, and a stairway to the second floor was immediately visible. A stove sat in the middle of the kitchen, and a large table stood a few feet to the left. Mike, Greg, Aurelia, Davin, and Emmer fanned out across the room, staking their places where they would remain for the next few minutes.

"Well, I'm glad you came," Al said. "I've heard a lot about you. Not all of it was positive, but hey, do I know you? No, but I'm willing to see what you can find."

"You did the right thing by calling us," Mike said. "I suppose one of the other groups you had here was the P.C.P.R.S.? We've had run-ins with them before. I'm sure they had nothing good to say about us. The feeling is mutual, I can assure you."

"The Pan-Continental Paranormal Research Society? Yeah, they tried to warn me away from you, but I can make up my own mind. None of us are experts when it comes to this. I was mostly a skeptic until I moved here, and I can tell you, this stuff is real. I've had at least a dozen different groups in here and every one of them experienced something."

Mike glanced at Emmer, who rolled his eyes. "Emmer over here is our skeptic," he explained. "If something happens that can convince him, I'd be impressed."

"I'm here to keep Mike from going totally off the deep end," Emmer retorted.

"I can't guarantee something will happen," Al said. "All I know is that this is a very active place. But I'm just going to let you guys explore the place and see what you find. I'm not going to tell you anything until later—to see if you come up with some of the same conclusions that other groups have."

Davin, who looked like he had just spent the past 24 hours in a Chinese prison, slapped Aurelia on the shoulder. "Aura here is one of the best psychics around," he said with a smile. "I'm sure she'll be very accurate. Isn't that right?"

Aurelia returned the gesture with a look of death, but Al mashed his hands together in satisfaction.

"Good," he said. "I'm looking forward to your report."

Mike seized the moment. "I don't want to waste any time then. We'll break into two small groups. Me and Greg will walk the property while it's still light out, and Aura, Emmer, and Davin will check out the house. You know the drill."

"Great," Al replied. "I've got some work to do, so I'll get out of your way."

Just like that, the Fallen were alone. Al walked out the kitchen door into the garage, and Mike waited to speak until he could no longer hear Al's footsteps.

"Ok," he said. "You all know what we're really doing here."

Emmer folded his arms across his chest. "What are we really doing here?"

"The weeping woman of Seventh Avenue in Sterling gave us a list of things we need to find in order to send that... creature... we accidentally unleashed back into the abyss from whence it came."

"I see," Emmer said in a voice dripping with sarcasm. "And what happened when you woke up the next morning?"

"*It wasn't a dream.* Aura, Greg, Davin, and Misa were all there. They saw it."

"It's true," Greg said. "It's still even hard for me to believe, but she was there."

"So what's the plan?" Davin asked.

"The same as what I told our gracious host," Mike replied. "We have to make it look like we're conducting a routine investigation. In fact, as I have heard, some psychics who have visited this farm claim the land here is some kind of paranormal gateway."

"Not this again..."

"The Indians living in this area in the early 1800s knew of its power—that's why they made this a sacred meeting place. Now, the ghost at the Seventh Avenue dead end told us a peace pipe is central to the ritual we need to conduct in order to send that demon back into the void. It *was* an ancient Indian burial mound where we accidentally released it, after all."

"As I recall," Davin interrupted, "we didn't open the gate. It was those zealot jerks, and my girlfriend died because of it."

Greg could hardly contain his disgust. "She was just using you," he spat.

"Ok, we get it," Mike said. "None of that matters right now. For some reason the followers of this thing have targeted us, and so we need to destroy it. It's as simple as that. I have reason to believe that the Indians who met on this land buried some artifacts that could be useful toward those ends. At least that's what the ghost told us."

Emmer chuckled. "Have fun with all of that."

"That's why you're staying here with Aura and Davin," Mike replied through clenched teeth. He thrust his hands deep into the pockets of his trench coat. "Now let's get started. We don't have any time to waste."

Mike and Greg left the farmhouse and headed south past the barn, following a wire fence through a fallow cornfield. "Do you really think we're going to find anything here?" Greg asked.

"Ye of little faith," Mike replied. "I was right about the astral gate, wasn't I?"

Greg winced. "Yeah, and look how that turned out. Look, why don't we take what money we have left and get out of here? We can just live off the radar, like we used to."

"You really think we can outrun this thing?" The question was rhetorical. "No. We have to defeat it here in Illinois, then we can disappear."

The two friends reached a break in the cornfield where the fence turned left to cordon off the pasture. A grand old oak tree stood about twenty yards in that direction, joined by the stumps of several others. At some time in the past, these trees formed a row at the south end of the pasture.

"This is the place," Mike announced. "I can feel the energy."

"Me too."

"Now, if you were an Indian living over a hundred and fifty years ago, where would you hide something out here?"

Mike and Greg looked around, but saw nothing out of the ordinary. The duo climbed over the gate and entered the pasture next to the trees.

"How old do you think these trees are?" Greg asked.

His friend glanced over at the tree rings of the nearest stump. The surface of the stump was weathered, cracked, and had been feasted on by insects. A deep gouge had opened up in the center, which was at least a foot in radius. The entire stump was at least two times that size.

"It's really hard to say," Mike replied. "You're the expert in Druidry, you tell me."

Greg smirked. "Man, I'm our expert in everything. Besides, that only works if the tree is alive." He approached the tree stump and climbed up on the exposed roots to get a better look inside the crevasse. "I'll be damned," he said. "Look at this." His hands fished through the crumbling organic matter until they seized the handle of something firm. "I need some help."

Mike pulled out his KA-Bar and dug the blade into the tree core. After a few moments, he carefully dislodged a long pipe from inside the wall of the stump. Greg and he exchanged glances. "Mission accomplished, eh?"

"They must have attached this to the tree over a hundred years ago, and the tree grew around it," Greg gasped. "Unbelievable."

Mike carefully brushed off the organic residue and stuffed the pipe into the interior pocket of his trench coat. "Let's go tell the others, and then finish up this investigation."
Greg agreed, and the two began their long trek back to the farmhouse.

Investigation File 039

Illinois State University
Normal, Illinois

Founded in 1857 and originally a teacher's college, Illinois State University is currently home to around 23,000 students and faculty, as well as one tenacious ghost. This ghost is said to be that of Angeline V. Milner, or Ange for short, a librarian who remained with her books long after she passed from this world. As head librarian for 37 years, she was so beloved by the school that Illinois State University named its library after her.

Angeline Vernon Milner was born on April 9, 1856 in Bloomington. By all accounts, she seemed to be destined for the work which would become her legacy. According to Charles W. Perry, who assisted the famed librarian for several years and wrote her biography, she learned how to read before she was four-years-old. Ange began her fated job at the university library on February 1, 1890, and the Normal School Board was so impressed with her skill and dedication that they appointed her as the sole and head librarian in the fall of that same year.

"Aunt Ange," as the students called her, died in 1928. According to legend, she collapsed while organizing a section of biology books. She was buried in Bloomington's Evergreen Cemetery, but for whatever reason did not have a headstone until a short time ago. In April 2006, former Governor Rod Blagojevich, along with Mayor Chris Koos of Normal, issued dual proclamations declaring April 10th "Angie Milner Day."

In 1917, the university moved its library from the Old Main Building to North Hall, where Miss Milner worked until she died. North Hall served as the library until 1940, when a new building was constructed and christened "Milner Library" to honor Normal University's beloved Aunt Ange. In 1976, the old Milner Library became known as Williams Hall and most of the university's books were moved into the new Milner Library, located on the north side of campus. Many of the older books, still with call numbers hand written on the binding by Ange Milner herself, remained on the third floor of Williams Hall.

Since at least the 1980s, staff members working in the Williams Hall archives have reported encounters with what they believe is the ghost of Ange Milner. Employees have reported eerie feelings, sightings of mist or fog, and even discovered books that inexplicably fell from the shelves. A psychic even claimed to see a "purple column of light."

In 2004, a former employee named Joan Winters told the *Daily Vidette* that she had witnessed a full-torso apparition of the former librarian while working in the archive in 1995. She described it as "a five-foot tall elderly woman in a floor length dress wearing her hair in a bun."[45] The fact that Miss Milner never set foot in Williams Hall has led observers to conclude that her ghost haunts her books, not a particular location.

The haunted books have recently been moved again, to a brand new storage facility much better suited for their preservation. Has Ange Milner's ghost followed them to their new location, or has she finally found peace? Only time will tell.

---

[45] *Daily Vidette* (Normal) 27 October 2004.

The Fallen Investigate

MAR. 13

3:12 PM

37° F

The Fallen stood on a bridge over College Avenue just outside the Bone Student Center eating ice cream while twenty-somethings strolled past, seemingly unaware of the five interlopers. "I love universities," Mike said between scoops of mint chocolate chip. "So many young minds, all eager to absorb knowledge."

"What universe do you live in?" Davin retorted. "When we were at college the only thing anyone learned was how to play flippy-cup and extend their tolerance for various substances."

"That's probably why you were kicked out," Aurelia said with a snort. With back arched and arms folded across her black blouse, she tried to stand aloof from her surroundings, but could not conceal her discomfort. It was not that the cool spring afternoon contrasted with her attire, but that the passing crowd, clad in bright pinks, blues, and yellows; chatty with beaming smiles, made her acutely aware that she did not fit in.

Davin became visibly agitated. "I dropped out, along with Greg, to join you guys, remember? It hasn't helped my social life or my employment prospects—or my health, for that matter."

Greg looked like he was about to respond, but Emmer cut him off. Emmer was a head taller than anyone else in the group. He wore a Cubs baseball cap, jeans, and a black Green Carnation hoodie. "Far be it from me to bring up something relevant, but what are we doing here?"

"We're eating ice cream," Greg replied.

Mike cleared his throat. "We're here to find a book. It's an old English translation of a manuscript written by French missionaries about the religious practices of the Indians they encountered. It contains detailed rituals. As far as I know, there's only one copy and it's here in the archives."

"I suppose there's some ghost story you want to check out here too?"

Mike smiled. "Of course." Motioning to the others to follow, he finished the last scoop of his ice cream, strolled over to the garbage bin, and tossed in the empty container. "But our primary goal is to secure this book. I'm looking forward to reading it—and not just because it might save our lives. The subject fascinates me. Algonquin religion was very Manichean."

"English, please," Aurelia interrupted.

"They believed the world was divided between good and evil, but that those spirits, or manitou, were all around us, inhabiting every rock and every living thing."

"Sounds just as crazy as every other religion," Emmer scoffed.

"Have a little faith," Mike said, mainly because he knew the phrase would get under his friend's skin, but if he succeeded, Emmer gave no reaction.

The Fallen walked through the quad, past Moulton and Hovey halls, until they came to the red brick, neo-Georgian façade of Williams Hall.

"Let's make this nice and painless," Mike said. "There's no reason we can't just get this book and spend the rest of the evening relaxing at a bar." He swung the door open and the quintet ascended the winding stairs to the third floor, pushing their way through crowds of students in the process. Finally they came to a glass door that marked the entrance to the university archive. Beyond it was a large desk, and a lanky, freckle-faced young man sat beyond that. His eyes were transfixed by the flat screen computer monitor at his station.

Mike cleared his throat. "Excuse me," he said. "*Excuse me.*"

The young man looked up, disinterested. "Yes?"

"I was hoping you could help me find a book." Mike placed his hands flat on the counter and leaned forward. "It's a book of old American Indian rituals. I'm not sure who the author is. It would be one of the oldest books in your collection."

Fingers pecked at a keyboard, and the freckly young man became annoyed. "Can you be any more specific?" he snapped, but did not wait for an answer. More pecking, and then, "I think I found it. Can I have your ID?"

"My what?" Mike asked, feigning innocence.

"Your student ID? You are a student here, aren't you?"

Greg stepped up to the desk. "We don't have an '*ID*,'" he said, "but Alexander Hamilton has an ID." He slowly rubbed his thumb and index finger together.

"Who's Alexander Hamilton?"

"What my friend is saying," Mike explained, "is that we would be willing to compensate you for your troubles if you would simply get us the book and allow us to photocopy some things out of it."

"Sorry, I can't," the student said. "It's *archive policy*." His eyes went back to the computer screen, no doubt preoccupied with Farmville or some other Facebook game.

Temporarily defeated, the Fallen backed out of the room to regroup. "Ok, that didn't go how I planned," Mike whispered.

"We need someone to seduce that guy," Greg suggested. "He looks like he hasn't gotten laid in... ever." He hesitated. "Now which one of us could do that?"

All eyes fell on Aurelia, and then immediately found the floor, the ceiling, or any other place to look. "Any other ideas?" Greg asked.

"Humph!" Aurelia exclaimed, offended by both the suggestion and by her friends' immediate rejection of it. Her voice echoed far down the corridor.

"Maybe we should just go home," Davin said.

Mike looked around the hallway and through the glass window into the archive. The third floor appeared to be under construction, and there was a hole in the ceiling where a security camera would normally have been. "I have an idea. Greg, do you have that rope?"

"Why do you carry rope around with you?" Emmer asked, but was not sure if he wanted to hear the answer.

Greg smiled and pulled a length of cord out of the cargo pocket on his tattered, green shorts. "You never know when it's going to come in handy."

With grim determination, the Fallen marched back into the university archive. Mike, Emmer, Davin, and Aurelia formed a wall in front of the desk—blocking the view of anyone who happened to pass by—while Greg climbed over the top of the desk and tackled the unsuspecting grad assistant. Pens and paper clips flew, but after a few moments, he had the young man tied up next to his chair, with a sock stuffed in his mouth. "Sorry, buddy," he said. "It's nothing personal. We just really need that book."

Mike spun the computer monitor around and looked at the search results that the G.A. had retrieved a few minutes earlier. "Ok, I found it," he said and wrote down the call number. "Emmer and Davin, come with me. Aura, if anyone asks, tell them the guy is helping you find a book and won't be back for at least 15 minutes."

Mike, Emmer, and Davin raced around the desk and into the archive. The space between the shelves was tight, and a distinct smell emanated off the books despite the room's regulated temperature. An exhaust fan rattled in the background. Mike glanced down at the piece of paper in his hand and back up to the numbers written or printed on the book bindings. "It's around here somewhere," he whispered.

Without warning, Davin—who was walking behind Mike and Emmer—plunged into

WILLIAMS HALL

their backs. The trio stumbled forward, but remained on their feet.

"Watch where you're going!" Emmer snapped, but a confused look on Davin's face greeted his rebuke.

"I feel sick," Davin said. "I think something pushed me."

Mike never took his eyes off the shelves. Excited, he stopped and ran his hand along the spines of the books on the second shelf down from the top of the bookcase. His fingers stopped. "This is it!" As he removed the box that contained the centuries old volume, however, several books fell from the top shelf and struck his head and shoulder. He jerked back in surprise and the hairs stood up on the back of his neck.

"I have a feeling we should get out of here," Davin suggested. His voice was shaken and he edged slowly backward.

"I agree," Mike said without missing a beat. He shoved the book under his arm and followed his friends toward the exit.

"Remember when we get outside, we're just students like everyone else. Don't do anything that will raise suspicions."

Emmer grinned. "Oh, you mean like dress all in black and burst into the university archive like we're in the frickin' Matrix?"

"Exactly."

Outside in the foyer, Greg had just finished untying the grad assistant and educated him on how it would be in his best interest to forget about what had just happened. Mike signaled to Aurelia and he, and in another moment the Fallen were heading down the stairs.

"We're one step closer to finishing this thing," Mike said as the group strolled across the campus of Illinois State University toward their car. "Let's hope our luck holds out."

"Luck?" Greg parroted. "Please. We're just that good. We'll be back in New Orleans in no time, and it'll be just like old times..."

Investigation File 040

Rockford College
Rockford, Illinois

Rockford's first college, established before the city was even chartered, was Rockford Female Seminary. Jane Addams, who would go on to fame as a social reformer and co-founder of Chicago's Hull House, was a graduate of the seminary in 1881. In 1892 RFS became known as Rockford College, which remained a predominately female academy until 1958. In 1964 the campus was moved from its home along the river to its present location along State Street.

While rich in history, Rockford College is also rich in ghostlore and the origin of a wide variety of alleged haunts. No less than three buildings are said to be home to restless spirits, along with one memorial arch, which was built using materials from the original Rock River campus. Blanche Walker Burpee Center, Adams Arch, and the Clark Arts Center run the gambit of ghostly phenomenon, from disembodied voices, to moving objects, to phantom reflections, and a whole host of other unexplained things.

Out of all of the buildings at Rockford College, the Clark Arts Center, which contains both Cheek and Maddox theaters, is thought to be the most haunted. Ancient frescos depicting figures in various stages of celebration, often playing instruments, line the hall outside Maddox Theatre. Their cherubic faces, it has been said, change expressions and even watch the audience as the guests filter in for a performance. Aboriginal artifacts from Africa, as well as a collection of Hopi Indian kachina dolls, are also on display in the hallways that lead to the class and practice rooms. For many years, these fragile bowls, masks, and dolls were locked in a storage room. Reports of heavy, ominous feelings made sure no one ever entered there alone.

Cheek Theatre, named after Mary Ashby Cheek, is a much smaller theater located on the ground floor opposite of Maddox. The walls are painted black, giving it a gloomy appearance that compliments its resident ghost. Before some performances, theater students say they have seen a shadowy figure, which they assert is the ghost of a former music teacher who died in a car accident.

A few yards south of the Clark Arts Center rests a scenic memorial known as Adams Arch. On certain evenings, when the air is very still, visitors have reported hearing the laughter of young women in its vicinity.

Blanche Walker Burpee Center, another allegedly haunted building, serves as the college's welcome center as well as the bookstore and the offices for administrative services. Some students and storytellers maintain that the basement formerly held a radio station that was the scene of a man's suicide. No one is quite clear about who this man was, whether a student or employee, but individuals who find themselves in the building after hours report hearing doors slamming shut, footsteps, and a man's disembodied voice in the basement.

Despite not being as well-known as other haunted colleges, Rockford certainly is in the running for one of the most haunted in Illinois.

THE FALLEN INVESTIGATE

APR. 16

1:50 AM

48° F

Mike smelled the sun-bleached musk of stale wood as the giant skeletal horse, constructed from driftwood and now animated by some unknown force, pressed him against the wall in the foyer of the Clark Arts Center. The petrified "bones" of the creature rattled in his ears, and his muscles strained to hold back its assault. As he fought for his life, his mind involuntarily wandered to thoughts of Saint Sebastian College in Maine—where all this trouble began—perhaps searching for an explanation for how he might end up crushed by an elaborate piece of modern art.

He recalled finding "the book," just before Saint Sebastian burned. The book was similar to the one he had just acquired at Illinois State University, only it was written in Latin and brought over from Europe by a sect of rogue monks. Its contents led the Fallen to Illinois in search of a portal that opened to the astral plane. That was more than three years ago. All they had to do was find the portal buried among the haunted places of Illinois. How difficult could it have been? But a group of zealots had gotten there first, and even though the Fallen had thwarted the zealots' effort at the summit of Monk's Mound, they accidentally unleashed an ancient demon that was now on a mission to destroy them.

Suddenly, he snapped back to the present, and the petrified horse collapsed before his eyes. As the wooden pieces clattered to the floor, he saw Aurelia standing in the hallway with a queer grin on her face.

"Simple animation spell," she said. "Pretty easy to remove." She wore military-issue camouflage pants, black combat boots, and a black tank top. Her dark brown hair was cropped short, but tied up in such a way that it looked like a giant paint brush was sticking out of the back of her head. Mike affectionately referred to this as her "poof."

A door slammed. "What are you doing?" Misa yelled as she burst into the hallway from the direction of Maddox Theater. "You're wasting time!" Her long, black hair was carefully tucked behind her misshapen ears, and her eyes burned with uncharacteristic intensity.

"*Calm down,*" Mike said as he brushed the dust off his black t-shirt and faded jeans. "Take a deep breath."

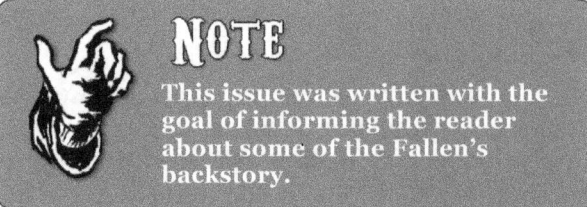

NOTE

This issue was written with the goal of informing the reader about some of the Fallen's backstory.

Even Aurelia arched her eyebrows as Misa perched her hands on her hips like a stereotypical Irish housewife scolding her children. Misa weighed 100 pounds soaking wet—when Mike and Greg met her in New Orleans, she had not displayed one iota of fortitude. She used to be terrified by every shadow, but that was nearly a decade ago. She had been forced to fend for herself after Mike and Greg slew her vampirous father. Alone, she worked her way up the Mississippi River to Memphis, where she began to hear rumors through underground channels that a group calling itself the Fallen had appeared in Illinois and was stirring up trouble. Curious, she tracked them down and was surprised to find that Mike and Greg were its organizers. Still feeling herself in their debt, she decided to warn them of the dangerous forces gathered against them. A year later she was in Rockford, feeling like a babysitter.

In the lobby of Maddox Theater, in the shadow of a half-dozen mannequins donned in Shakespearean dress, Emmer, Greg, and Davin carefully made their way toward the door that opened into the theater itself.

"Was I not clear in October about how little I wanted to come back to Rockford?" Emmer asked rhetorically as the trio entered the theater and began walking down the aisle toward the stage. The room was dark except for the emergency lights and the red exit signs above the doors.

"Don't you have more pressing concerns than some girl who dumped you over a year ago?" Greg retorted.

Emmer grumbled, "Considering the circumstances, I wish I didn't."

The three froze as they heard a crash, but they could not tell from what direction it had come. Their eyes and ears played tricks on them in the darkness, and at times it seemed as though the shadows moved on their own.

Emmer, of course, knew that was an illusion. There were times when he wondered why he kept coming on these adventures, especially when they were hazardous to his health. He was nearly struck and killed by lightning on Monk's Mound, just after he had finished giving his friends a mouthful about how much nonsense Mike's notion of the paranormal was—a lecture that he found himself giving more frequently ever since Misa showed up. She was convinced, and had Mike and Greg convinced—apparently—that she was a dhampyr, a half-vampire. Emmer knew it was crazy. Still, they were his friends. He could not imagine the trouble they would find themselves in without someone to knock sense into them. Now they were all risking arrest by being in this building at night—something Mike swore only a few months ago they would never do again.

The faint ring of a bell broke the silence. This time, Emmer, Greg, and Davin knew this particular sound came from backstage. They nodded to each other and cautiously ascended the steps to the proscenium, just in front of the heavy, red curtains. Props were set up on stage for an upcoming performance. The three friends weaved between a fake plant, a park bench, and a cardboard streetlamp. They strained their ears, but it was not long before they heard the sound again. This time, the jingle was louder and more distinct.

"I know you heard that too," Davin said, directing his assertion toward Emmer. "I'm not imagining that."

"I hear it," Emmer whispered. "The question is, what is it? I'll bet you a hundred bucks it isn't a ghost."

Greg, who wore his usual attire of frayed cargo shorts and an olive green shirt, hesitated. "I've got a bad feeling about this," he said. "I think I'd be more worried if it turned out to be something that was alive." The three never had a chance to find out. Greg's cell phone vibrated in his pocket. It was a text message from Mike.

[Mike] Get the heck out here, right now. You won't believe what just happened.

"We just got new marching orders," Greg announced with a touch of sarcasm. "Mike wants us out in the hallway. I think he might have an explanation for that crash we heard a couple of minutes ago." Emmer, Davin, and Greg took one more look backstage to see if they could detect the source of the sound of the bell, but gave up after a few seconds and headed back down the aisle to the lobby. There they met Mike, Misa, and Aurelia, who were standing over a pile of driftwood.

Mike smiled. "Would you believe me if I told you this giant sculpture of a horse came to life and attacked me?"

His friends were speechless, but Emmer raised one eyebrow in a defiant, "No."

"Something is definitely trying to keep us away from here," Aurelia said.

"Yeah, *common sense*," Greg replied.

"We came here for a purpose," Misa growled. "Stop screwing around. We have to get some of those ceremonial tools they have stored here. My contact says they are in a storage room in the basement, but she didn't know which one."

ADAMS HALL

The Fallen followed Misa down the hall to the stairs, and Mike flicked on his electric torch. "Crowley's arse," he cursed. "I can't see a darn thing." As if to emphasize the point, Greg stumbled into Emmer, nearly bringing the entire group down with him.

"That better have been your flashlight back there," Emmer said after he regained his footing.

After a few minutes, the group found themselves in another hallway. This time Aurelia took the lead. She paused at each door to feel the vibrations from the other side. Finally, she came to one that nearly knocked the breath out of her. "This is it," she said. "This is definitely the room."

Mike tried the handle, but it was locked. Impatient, Greg pulled a small sewing kit out of his cargo shorts. Wires and paperclips of various sizes were inside. He selected a few that looked promising and went to work picking the lock, with Mike providing the illumination. What seemed like an eternity passed before he heard the lock click. Greg threw open the door, and the Fallen poured into the room.

"Be really careful," Mike said. "We need to take a ceremonial bowl and one of those dolls, but it can't look like we were ever here."

Misa examined the centuries-old items that had been filed in drawers, wrapped in newspaper, and stacked in boxes. At long last, her gangly fingers found a clay bowl with several strange symbols painted on the side. She motioned for Aurelia, who hesitantly came over and stared at one of the kachina dolls. After mumbling an incantation, she wrapped it in a specially prepared cloth and placed it in Greg's backpack.

Mike breathed a sigh of relief. "Let's get out of here before campus security notices," he said, allowing himself to smile. "We're closer than ever to the end of this thing, and the end couldn't come soon enough."

Finally, Emmer found a reason to agree.

INVESTIGATION FILE 041

BISHOP-ZION CEMETERY
Bishop, Illinois

Nearly a half-century ago, the smoldering embers of a rural church gave birth to a legend—a legend that has since been passed down among the residents of Mason County. The church's former preacher, it is said, was buried in the nearby cemetery under a tree, where he could forever tend his flock. Anyone brave enough to walk to the back of the cemetery and knock on the tree would be treated to the sound of the preacher's voice calling out from the grave.

Mason County was carved out of Tazewell County and established on January 20, 1841. According to *Pioneers of Menard and Mason County* (1902) by T.G. Onstott, the land around Bishop-Zion Cemetery was not settled until 1840, when a man named A. Winthrow built a cabin there. Peter Himmel, A. File, Henry Bishop, and Stephen Hedge followed. There are at least two dozen descendants of Peter Himmel buried in Bishop-Zion Cemetery. Ultimately, however, the cemetery and nearby village came to be named after the Bishop family.

Henry Bishop, we are told by the *Portrait & Biographical Record of Tazewell & Mason Counties, Illinois* (1894), was brought by his parents from Hanover, Germany to St. Louis, before ultimately settling on pristine land in the heart of Mason County. According to the *Portrait & Biographical Record*, "He was a member of the Evangelical Association... and aided in building Zion Church." His son, John H. Bishop, was a prominent member of the local community and owned a grain elevator. John H.'s wife, Maggie, was the daughter of John Bowser, who is buried in Bishop-Zion Cemetery.

Zion Church evidently was built sometime between 1855 and 1885. According to Chad Lewis and Terry Fisk, in their *Illinois Road Guide to Haunted Locations* (2007), the church was removed from the deed to the property in 1955, leading them to believe that it burnt down prior to that date. However, there is no evidence that any parishioners died in the fire, as legend maintains.

Locals, drawn by the cemetery's unique history and its remote location, have visited this spot for many years, but the tale of the immolation of Zion Church is not the only story. Some visitors report hearing the laughter of children—particularly of adolescent girls—dancing in and out of the nearby woods. Moreover, anyone who enters the cemetery through its white gates will be greeted by an icy chill that seems to follow them throughout the grounds.

The most prominent tale is that of the preacher's grave. Like the person interred in the alleged witch's grave of Chesterville Cemetery, this individual's resting spot is marked by a tree. Teenagers dare each other to walk to the back of the cemetery at night and knock on the preacher's tree. Only a few are brave enough to make it, but those who do are supposedly rewarded with shrieks from beyond.

Like many rural cemeteries, Bishop-Zion has attracted its fair share of legends, but its historical background is what makes this one unique.

The Fallen Investigate

MAY 8

11:46 AM

79° F

"We knew it would happen eventually," Aurelia said from behind the wheel of her steel blue Buick LaSabre as she navigated it down the dirt road just outside the tiny village of Forest City. All the usual suspects rode along, with one conspicuous absence. Greg sat in the front passenger seat, and Davin, Emmer, and Misa sat in the back.

"It was *your* fault," Misa hissed at Emmer. "If you had taken this more seriously..."

Emmer waved his hand dismissively. "Don't blame me, whack job. You weren't even there."

"It's no one's fault," Greg said in a mediating tone. "The cops have been after us for months. It was only a matter of time before they pinched one of us."

"Yeah, but *Mike*?" Davin asked. "What are we going to do without him? We're totally screwed." He pulled at the collar of his cheap, white undershirt that was stained with months of dried sweat, dirt, and marinara sauce.

Behind the Scenes

At this point in the Black Willow Grove adventure, Mike has been arrested on false charges.

The Buick lurched to the right, bounced over several depressions in the road, and came to a stop a few yards before the white gate of Bishop-Zion Cemetery. "All of you, calm down,"

Aurelia said. "We're *not* screwed. We still have the list of things we need to find, so we don't need Mike to tell us where they are. As far as he is concerned, as soon as the judge has the bail hearing, we'll find out how much we have to pay for the cash bond and then we'll get his rear end out of jail. In the meantime, we have a mission to take care of."

Emmer rolled his eyes. "You're not serious, are you? We need to get the heck out of here. This little fantasy is over."

Aurelia slammed her fist into Greg's headrest and her friends jumped. "*We're not abandoning Mike,*" she said through clenched teeth. "We're not giving up. *Does everyone understand?*"

Greg, Davin, Emmer and Misa nodded in silent agreement.

Aurelia threw the gear into park and got out of the car without saying another word. The others followed tentatively. They approached the cemetery gate and scanned the area. Large flocks of gnats hovered above the grass, threatening to be accidentally inhaled at any moment. Oddly, the insects ignored Misa, whose pale, clammy skin seemed even more unnatural in the afternoon sun. Her charcoal gray jumper hung off her like she was more mannequin than human being.

Greg pulled a clipboard out of his backpack and flipped through the attached papers. "It says in the report that a church adjacent to the cemetery burnt down with everyone inside. Clearly—according to Mike, at any rate—this was a paranormal event precipitated by dark forces. What we need to do is find the remnants of this church and gather up some of the ashes. It should work as a powerful catalyst when we perform this ritual to send that demon back across the barrier into the astral realm."

Emmer scoffed.

"Hey, I'm just reading what it says on the paper," Greg said defensively.

Davin brushed gnats away from his face. "If that's what we're here to do, then let's do it," he said. "I'm tired of you guys whining about everything. Mike was right about that astral gate to begin with. If you have a better idea about how we can get rid of this thing that's trying to kill us, let's hear it. We already have the peace pipe, the ritual book, the bowl, and the kachina doll. We only have a few items left on the list. We might as well see if this works before we just decide to give up."

The others were taken aback at Davin's sudden assertiveness, but Greg demanded the final word. "It won't do any good if we turn on each other," he said and started toward the cemetery gate. After a few steps, he hesitated and took a second look around the cemetery. "Now, if you were the charred remains of a church, where would you be?"

"We'll split up," Aurelia suggested. "I'll take Misa and Davin around to the right. Greg, you and Emmer take a look at the left."

"Right," Greg agreed. "Both groups will sweep the perimeter and we'll meet in the back. If you find the ashes, fill up one of these baggies." He handed a quart sized Ziplock to Misa, who held it disdainfully. "I'm sure the site will be overgrown with weeds. Look for a place where there are no trees. There might be pieces of blackened wood too. You never know. A lot of time as passed."

Aurelia nodded and the Fallen separated into two groups to begin their search. Greg and Emmer headed into the woods and put some distance between themselves and the others before they started talking. Even still, they spoke in low whispers.

"You know I'm right," Emmer said. "We should have split town months ago. This Black Willow Grove thing has become another one of Mike's crazy obsessions."

"I tried telling him that," Greg replied after clearing his lips of gnats. The tiny insects swarmed everywhere—there was no escaping them. He continued, "I argued with Mike about it when we were investigating Willow Creek Farm. He wouldn't listen to me, but in a way he probably has a point. We can try to run from this thing, but for how long?"

"This is insane," Emmer grumbled. "I don't know why I keep sticking my neck out for

you guys. I had a job back home. People weren't trying to kill me. Life was good."

"Yeah, but you know it was really boring," Greg replied with a smirk. Suddenly, his feet hit hard ground and he looked down. "What have we here?" He kneeled and parted the weeds.

Emmer joined him and pulled put a pair of eyeglasses from his shirt pocket. He grabbed a nearby stick, poked the dirt, and immediately hit pavement, which was hidden under what they at first thought was a thin layer of soil. "This looks like a foundation," he whispered.

"This stuff is too powdery to be dirt," Greg said as he played with a palm full of the material. "It's got to be ashes. Look at the splinters of wood around here. This is what we've been looking for!" He could not keep himself from shouting triumphantly. He whipped out the plastic baggie, filled it with several handfuls of ash and burnt debris, then wiped the remainder on his shorts. "Suck on that, Aura!"

"You really don't like her, do you?"

"Are you kidding? That woman terrifies me."

The two made their way back to the front of the cemetery, where they noticed a white, two door sedan parked next to Aurelia's Buick. Alarmed, they picked up their pace and burst out of the tree line. There, in front of the gates, they saw a man in the advanced stages of baldness, dressed in khakis and a polo shirt, talking with Aurelia, Davin, and Misa. He held a microcassette recorder in his hand.

"The name's Fess Parker," the man said enthusiastically when he saw Greg and Emmer emerge from the woods. He held out his hand, but no one took it. "Can I ask you guys a few questions? I won't take up much of your time."

Greg glanced over at Aurelia. "*Who is this guy?*"

"A reporter," she replied with a touch of disgust. "From the... what was it? The *Paranormal Review and Gazette*?" She folded her arms across her orange tank top, the hem of which just touched the waistline of her ankle length, red skirt.

Greg's eyes fell on the reporter, who was obviously trying to hide his nervousness behind his barrage of questions. Greg went on the attack. "How did you find us?" he demanded. "Did you follow us here?"

The man ignored Greg's questions. "Are you members of the Fallen too? What are your names? What are you hoping to find at Bishop-Zion Cemetery?"

"Look, man," Davin interrupted. "We already told you. We stopped here because my friends had to go take a leak. We're on our way to a Phish concert in St. Louis."

"Yeah," Greg said. "Found a great spot too. It was just what we were looking for."

"We should probably get going then," Aurelia suggested.

The reporter stepped in front of the quintet, blocking the path to their car. "Look, I wasn't born yesterday," he said. "You guys gotta give me something. This is the third time in as many years that one of your members has been picked up by the police—is that right? It was Mike this time, right? If you don't tell me, I'll get it out of the cops. I bet they wouldn't be happy to learn that you were sneaking around here either."

The Fallen shoved their way past the reporter to Aurelia's 1989 Skylark without saying another word, and he made no attempt to stop them. Misa had a curious smile on her face as her shoulder bumped up against his for a brief moment. She made a mental note of the scent of his aftershave, and heard his heart beating in his chest.

Davin, once in the backseat, leapt up and patted Aurelia on the shoulder as she settled in behind the wheel and secured her seatbelt.. "Let's get out of here," he said frantically. "Make sure to go back in a confusing route so we can lose this guy."

Emmer let out a deep breath as Aurelia started the ignition. *"We are so screwed."*

INVESTIGATION FILE 042

VISHNU SPRINGS
Colchester, Illinois

A once-thriving resort community, Vishnu Springs has captured the imagination of Illinoisans as much in its afterlife as it did in its heyday. What remains of its three-story hotel, once majestic and full of exuberance, has become a haven for students from Western Illinois University looking for a thrill. Some of these unwanted visitors have returned with stories of harrowing encounters with the unknown (as well as with law enforcement, who routinely patrol the grounds). Many are unaware of the location's rich history.

In the 1860s and '70s, a farmer named Ebenezer Hicks began to notice the unusual taste and mineral quality of an artesian well flowing in a forest on his land north of the town of Colchester in McDonough County. Attracted to the natural spring's healing properties, a Doctor named J.W. Aiken attempted to sell the water as a cure-all to local coal miners, but made a negligible profit. After the landowner passed away, his son, an entrepreneur named Darius Hicks, inherited the land and built a hotel he called the Capital Hotel, which opened in 1890.

Others soon arrived to live and work there, but the isolated nature of the resort impeded its growth. Darius named the place "Vishnu Springs" after the Hindu god Vishnu, who is said to support and sustain the universe. At its height, the resort contained a few dozen houses, a carousel, a pond, sports fields, and even a small race track. During the early 1900s, several deadly incidents and scandals tarnished the community, and when Darius Hicks committed suicide in 1908, no one remained who was willing to invest their energy in the resort.[46]

---

[46] www.vishnusprings.org

During the 1970s, a group of hippies made a short lived attempt to turn Vishnu Springs into a commune. Today, all that remains is the old hotel. Some visitors have reportedly seen the ghost of a lady in black wandering the grounds. Olga Kay Kennedy, a Western Illinois University alumnus, inherited Vishnu Springs from her grandparents and gifted it to the university in 2003. According to her wishes, all 140 acres will be turned into a wildlife sanctuary.

According to Troy Taylor, Vishnu Springs is home to a number of restless ghosts. It is rumored that Darius' wife, Maud, died in childbirth in one of the rooms of the Capital Hotel, an event that left an "impression" behind. Aside from the woman in black who wanders the grounds and vanishes when approached, in *Haunted Illinois* (2004) Taylor claimed "Visitors also told of sounds from Vishnu's past, echoing into the present." These sounds are remnants of earlier, happier days. Since the late 1890s, visitors, including a former state senator, have written their names into the wooden walls of the Capital Hotel.

NOTE

According to a local folklorist, Troy Taylor mistakenly associated the ghost of a lady in black with Vishnu Springs after the folklorist accidentally included that story in papers about Vishnu Springs he sent to Troy Taylor.

While the site has become a perennial subject for the *Western Courier*, preservationists have so far prevented the hotel from being demolished. Donations have been raised, and not even threats of arrest and fines have not abated the public interest in this fascinating place.

THE FALLEN INVESTIGATE

JUN. 21

11:30 PM

79° F

As Greg, Davin, and Misa walked down the lengthy dirt and gravel trail through the woods with only the moonlight to illuminate their path, Greg and Davin repeatedly glanced over their shoulders. Misa walked ahead of them—her eyes much more accustomed to the darkness. A branch snapped, and Davin froze in his tracks.

"If I thought that was anything other than an animal, I'd let you know," Misa said, her words stressed with impatience.

"Mike has only been out of jail for a couple of weeks," Davin said. "Forgive me if I'm a little cautious. We can't afford to bail anyone else out. Definitely not all three of us."

"At least Mike finally came to his senses and split us up," Greg interjected. "Especially for this expedition... from what I hear, they don't look too kindly on trespassers."

Davin hurried to catch up with the others. "How many places have we gone where we weren't supposed to be?"

"Yeah, but we were never this close to the end before. We can't afford anymore slipups. All we have to do is find this 'healing spring' and get a sample of the water. Then everything will be ready."

A moment of silence followed while the trio continued deeper into the woods, and then Greg began to whistle. Every few minutes, Davin smacked the mosquitoes that landed on his neck and forearms. The insects did not seem to bother his two friends. As twigs, stones, and dirt passed under their feet, the trail appeared to go on forever. Finally, it curved to the left and began a steep descent into a valley, where Greg, Davin, and Misa could hardly make out the top

of a roof silhouetted by the moon. Darkness obscured most of the structure, but it was unmistakably what remained of the former Vishnu Springs Hotel. In the distant past, the hotel would have been lit up by lanterns, and the chatter of the guests would have echoed in the valley. Today, its graffiti covered walls stood silently in the moonlight.

"It's about time," Davin grumbled. "I thought we would never find this place."

The trio rushed as fast as they could down the hill, avoided tripping over any fallen branches, and sloshed through a shallow stream that flowed over the path. Greg got to the clearing first, and thinking it was safe to do so, he flicked on his flashlight. He scanned the area for any sign of the fabled spring. Finally, the beam from his electric torch fell on a shallow pool of water about twenty yards away, which was coated in green with a layer of thick algae. *This looks just as likely as any other spot*, he thought, and he signaled to his friends to join him. As Davin and Misa caught up, Greg stuffed his flashlight into the pocket of his cargo shorts, pulled out a small jar, unscrewed the lid, and knelt down to dip it in the water. As he did so, Misa froze. She heard what the others had not—under the chorus of insects and the whisper of the wind blowing through the trees, the wheels of a car slowly cracked and popped the gravel on the trail.

"Do you remember how I said I would tell you if there was anyone else here?" she asked. Without waiting for a response, she added, "*Someone's here.*"

Davin cast a worried look at the others. "Do you think it's the cops?"

"Who else would it be?" Greg replied. "Damn it! We just can't catch a break." Cupping his hand over the mouth of the jar to strain out most of the algae and debris, he quickly dipped it into the pool of water, and looked around for a place to hide. The woods were dark, but appeared foreboding.

Misa and Davin were one step ahead. Misa grabbed Greg's shirt collar, pulled him to his feet, and the trio raced toward the old Vishnu Springs Hotel just as the headlights of a sheriff's cruiser crested the top of the hill. For

CAPITOL HOTEL

once, they were in luck; the door to the hotel had been pried open by trespassers long before they had arrived.

Greg, Misa, and Davin—repressing fear and adrenaline—felt their way into the inky blackness of the building's interior. Suddenly, the headlights of the cruiser struck the side of the hotel, and light poured in through the windows, illuminating a doorway at the top of the stairs that led to the second floor. The Fallen quickly decided to go deeper into the building and find somewhere to hide.

"They must have seen our car on the side of the road," Davin whispered. "I told you we didn't park far enough away."

"There's nothing we can do about it now," Greg replied as he groped the wall and led his friends past the stairs and a large, metal bathtub (clearly out of place) into the main hallway on the first floor.

"This reminds me of the time we went to Sunset Haven and we almost got caught by that groundskeeper," Davin said. "Remember?"

Greg eyed him disapprovingly. "Let's reminisce later, ok?"

Misa, hearing a car door slam shut, grabbed Davin and Greg and pulled them under the stairs. There was enough room to stand, and so the trio pressed up against the wall. Misa, by virtue of having led them into the hiding place, now found herself behind her two companions. It was uncomfortable, but adjusting would have made too much noise. Already, they heard footsteps approaching the building, and light from two high-powered flashlights shown through the cracks in the stairs. The garbled static of a radio pierced the air.

"So far nothing on those trespassers," one of the deputies said in a deep voice. "We're going to check the building."

"*Ten-Four*," the radio crackled.

As the footsteps of the deputies came closer, Misa smelled the salty perspiration spreading across the back of Davin's t-shirt. Her stomach rumbled, and blood pumped through the veins just under the surface of Davin's neck. Pressed up against his shoulders, she felt his heart beating rapidly. She closed her eyes and started to count to ten.

The footsteps stopped. "I'll check upstairs," one of the deputies said. "I haven't heard anything, but do a sweep of this floor anyway, just to make sure. The kids probably heard us coming and ran off into the woods. Who would be dumb enough to try to hide in here?"

His partner laughed. "This would be so much easier if we had a K-9 unit. If nothing else, the dog would scare the little creeps."

As the heavy thump of boots rained down on the stairs above their heads, Davin felt Misa's teeth press against his neck near his jugular vein, and he tugged on Greg's shirt. At first, Greg brushed him off, but sensing his friend's urgency, he turned his head just in time to see what was happening by the faint glow provided by the sheriff deputy's flashlight. The deputy, by that time, stood parallel with the staircase, just a few feet away. Using the noise from the ascent of the deputy's partner as cover, Greg backhanded Misa in the forehead. *God, I've wanted to do that for a while*, he thought. Misa jerked back in surprise and released her hold on Davin.

The sheriff's deputy had not heard a thing. He walked past the stairs and entered the main hallway, and Greg and Davin breathed a sigh of relief. Misa, although clearly upset, regained her balance and bit her tongue. If *she* got caught, she knew even more than Greg or Davin, or even Mike, it would mean spending the rest of her life in a hospital, fed a steady diet of *Thorazine*. Furthermore, she knew she *had* temporarily lost control, and if Greg had not acted, being caught trespassing would have been the least of their worries. Still, it took all her willpower to stop from lashing out in retribution.

As the footsteps of the deputies disappeared deeper into the interior of the abandoned hotel, the Fallen allowed themselves to relax. They shifted position, so that Misa stood in front of Greg and Davin. Davin rubbed his neck bitterly, and checked his hand to make sure no blood had been drawn. Finally, after a

moment, Greg gently pushed Misa and whispered "let's go," in her ear.

The deputies, one on the ground floor and one on the second, chatted through their radios as they searched one room after another. The Fallen crept slowly through the darkness toward the door, careful not to make a sound. Once outside, they made a beeline for the trail.

"*What the heck was that?*" Davin hissed between ragged breaths as the trio jumped across the stream and began to walk up the steep incline.

"*I'm sorry*," Misa replied. "I haven't eaten in days."

"We could have gotten caught," Greg lectured. "You know what that would mean. How could you do that?"

Greg checked his pocket to see if the small jar of pond water was still there. It was. "At least we got what we came for. Let's get the heck out of here before those cops catch up to us."

Davin and Misa both nodded in agreement, and the Fallen disappeared into the night.

INVESTIGATION FILE 043

CRYBABY BRIDGE
Monmouth, Illinois

Many years ago, as lightning flashed and storm clouds swirled overhead, a young unwed mother—driven mad by the pain of abandonment, regret, and the fear of being ostracized—hurled her week-old baby boy over the trestles of this rural bridge into the swirling water below. Ever since, passersby have heard the spine-tingling cries of a baby struggling to breathe. Or so the story goes.

This one-lane, steel bridge spanning Cedar Creek three miles northwest of Monmouth is one of many christened a "cry baby bridge" because of its alleged connection to an incident like the one just described. Another popular story told is that an elementary school bus plunged off the side of the bridge during a flood. All the children drowned, but should your car break down while crossing the bridge, their ghosts will push it safely to the other side.

As a result of these stories, otherwise mundane rural bridges have become the focus of intense local curiosity. Few residents of Monmouth have never heard of their cry baby bridge.

Charisma, 27, had her own interesting encounter as a friend and she tested the legend. "I grew up in Monmouth, living there most of my life, and of course had heard all of the stories about crybaby bridge," she told us. "A few years ago, I met someone who had just moved to town and we got to talking about the bridge and all of the 'happenings' out there. Both being quite skeptical because it sounds a lot like an urban legend, we decided to check it out one day. We got in the car and headed out to the small, hidden road off of US 67-N where the bridge is located. The actual bridge is at the bottom of a relatively steep hill that you would come to after going around a sharp curve to the left. It's also a very narrow road that only one car will fit down.

"At the bottom of the hill, we stopped to investigate a bit. The area of the road where the actual bridge sits over the shallows of cedar creek is completely flat with no slope whatsoever. Putting the car into neutral, it started to slowly inch forward until the end of the bridge, then it just stopped. Thinking that there must have been an environmental cause for the whole thing, we went up the hill on the other side and turned around to come back down and test it going the other way.

"Again, we got to the bottom of the hill and stopped the car completely before putting it in neutral. Instead of rolling backwards like we were expecting, it rolled forward again. All the way to end of the bridge and just stopped. I'm not sure how to explain what happened, and I don't necessarily believe any of the stories surrounding it, but my experience at crybaby bridge still baffles me to this day."

Many have had similar experiences, yet few are sure of the actual history of the bridge. One of the only clues on the scene is an inscription of "Dec. 4, 1941" in the cement foundation. But the history of the bridge has little bearing on the stories told. According to authors Chad Lewis and Terry Fisk, several eyewitnesses swear they have heard crying near the bridge. We may never know the origins of these ethereal sounds, but they are an ingredient of a great night-time excursion.

THE FALLEN INVESTIGATE

JUL. 2

2:30 PM

89° F

With In Ruin's "Four Seasons of Grey" issuing from the Toyota Corolla's speakers, Mike alternated his gaze from side view mirror to windshield, to rearview mirror and back again. Dust kicked up by the vehicle's tires obscured the road behind it, and the thin layer of white chalk coating the foliage was evidence that dozens of cars had come down that road before.

"Where the heck are we?" Mike asked everyone and no one.

Aurelia, her tanned arm bouncing outside the open window along with every pit and pothole, seemed just as frustrated. "Why couldn't we just meet them at Taco Bell like we usually do?" She spoke of their three friends and compatriots: Greg, Davin, and Misa, who had finished their mission at Vishnu Springs and who had agreed to meet Mike, Aurelia, and Emmer outside of Monmouth, which was about 40 miles north of there. Emmer was asleep in the backseat, his Cubs hat tilted down over his eyes.

"They wanted to meet at a nondescript location," Mike replied. "Can you blame them? They said they almost got caught out at Vishnu, and the way Greg tells it, Misa is becoming unstable. She almost attacked Davin when they were hiding from the cops. That's the last thing we need to happen in a public place."

"Greg says Misa is unstable? There's the pot calling the kettle black," Aurelia said. "Besides, we have everything we were looking for. Why don't we just get rid of her if she's becoming a liability?"

Mike turned his head toward Aurelia and said nothing for several long seconds. "Are you serious?" he finally asked. "She's our *friend*. Well, she's mine, anyway. I don't betray friends. She saved our butts, remember?"

"She saved *Davin's* butt," Aurelia corrected, "before she decided he was a Happy Meal. We'd be fine without him anyway."

Mike ignored Aurelia's last comment. "Whatever," he replied. "We need to figure out where we are."

As the last words left his lips, the dark blue Toyota entered a wooded area and approached a short, steel bridge that spanned a creek. The bridge was covered in graffiti. As the wheels of the Toyota left the dirt and gravel road and began to cross, the engine sputtered and died.

"Crowley's arse," Mike cursed. "You've got to be kidding me." He turned the key in the ignition, but it did nothing but click. Frustrated, he punched the hard plastic steering wheel. "Damn it! This is all we need."

Emmer stirred in the backseat. "Are we there? What's going on?"

Ignoring Emmer, Aurelia opened the front passenger door. "Pop the hood—I'll look at it." The moment she stepped out of the car, however, she hesitated. The hairs on the back of her neck stood on end. "There's something odd about this place," she announced as the latch on the hood snapped open.

Acting quickly, Mike stuck his hand into the air. "Hand me that catalogue in the backseat."

Emmer, grumbling a few inaudible words, fished around on the floor until he found a black binder. He pushed it into Mike's hand and then fell back against the seat cushion. "Why did we stop?" he asked.

"I don't know," Mike replied halfheartedly while he flipped through the well-worn pages of the binder. His finger fell on 'M' and he quickly found the listing for Monmouth. "Ah-ha!" he exclaimed. "I knew there was something odd about this place."

Aurelia sighed.

Mike continued. "It says here there's a crybaby bridge outside of town. I guess we found it."

"I thought those places were just an urban legend," Aurelia said.

"Every place we've ever been was an urban legend," Emmer protested. "Yet you guys still continue to think something paranormal is happening there."

"Urban legends are usually based on a real event somewhere down the line. Maybe this is the real thing."

"What is this, the show *Supernatural*? I don't see some helpless woman in distress anywhere around here."

Aurelia sneered. "You got that right!"

"Even if nothing paranormal is going on," Mike said, "we're still stuck on a bridge in the middle of nowhere. What are we going to do about that?"

Aurelia slammed the car door. "I'm telling you—I sense something, but whatever. Don't listen to me. I'll just look at the darn engine..." Her voice faded as she made her way around to the front of the Toyota Corolla and lifted the hood.

Mike and Emmer sat in the car in silence for a few moments before they simultaneously decided to get out and join Aurelia. The summer sun beat down through the trees, but the shade provided some relief from the heat. In all appearances, the woods were bucolic. A chorus of birds and insects serenaded the Fallen, and the sounds of civilization were far away.

Hands moving over the engine and through wires like a pro, Aurelia checked every conceivable part. Finally, Mike spoke up. "Emmer will think I'm nuts, but—"

"You're probably right," Emmer interrupted.

"But since this is a crybaby bridge, why don't we try to put the car in neutral and see what happens? It's better than just twiddling our thumbs."

Emmer chuckled. "I actually agree with Mike for once. We should put the car in neutral and push it to the nearest mechanic."

Mike scowled and climbed back into the driver's seat, and while Aurelia slammed the hood shut, he shifted the gear into neutral. Aurelia and Emmer stepped to one side of the bridge and folded their arms across their chests.

There they awaited the outcome of Mike's experiment. Much to everyone's surprise, the car began to move forward. It rolled slowly across the bridge until it came to a stop on the opposite end. Cautiously, Mike turned the key in the ignition. The engine rolled over and sputtered to life. As Aurelia and Emmer rushed to get back inside the car, Mike threw the gear shift into park and turned off the engine.

"What the heck are you doing?" Aurelia demanded.

"Send Greg a text message," Mike said. "We're going to meet them here. I want to look around a bit." He glanced at Emmer. "How do you explain *that*?"

"Easily," Emmer said as he flipped open his cell phone and typed out a quick text message to Greg. "This is an old, piece of junk

car and we've been driving around in the country in the hottest month of the year. The engine obviously overheated or something, and it cooled down here in the shade. As for the car moving across the bridge; it's obviously on an incline."

"Why don't we turn the car around and see if it rolls across the other way, smartass?"

"Ok, fine."

Mike started the engine once again and executed a flawless 3-point turnaround a few yards up the road from the bridge, while Emmer and Aurelia leaned against the steel trestles. The dark blue, Toyota Corolla came to a stop and Mike put the gear in neutral. At first it did not move, but then, slowly, it began to coast to the other side of the bridge. "Is the bridge angled both ways?!" Mike yelled out the open window.

"That doesn't prove *anything*," Emmer replied. "It's a bridge. It could be slightly arched."

"Does it look arched?" Mike protested. "It's perfectly flat."

"It could be so slight you don't even notice."

"Whatever."

At this point, Emmer was smiling widely. He loved to get Mike agitated.

Mike got out of the car and slammed the door. "Did you text Greg?"

"He should be here any minute," Emmer said. No sooner did those words leave his mouth, the trio heard the steady rumble of motorcycle engines coming down the road.

In a few moments, two unfaired, black and chrome Suzuki GS500Es appeared around the bend. Greg piloted one; Misa the other. Davin sat behind Greg in what was undoubtedly an uncomfortable configuration for the both of them. None of the three wore helmets, so they were instantly recognizable. They drove slowly over the gravel until they came to a stop in a dirt clearing at the edge of the woods, just a few yards from Mike's rusted, unwashed Corolla.

"You just missed some paranormal activity," Emmer announced with a hint of sarcasm. "We put the car in neutral and it drifted across the bridge—*both ways*."

"Call me impressed," Greg replied. "This is almost as exciting as the time all those ants attacked at Peck Cemetery."

"Don't remind me," Davin grumbled. Mike cleared his throat and waved his hand to quiet the group. "We have all the items we were looking for," he said, cutting to the chase. "We got the peace pipe from Willow Creek Farm, the ritual book from ISU, the ritual bowl from Rockford College, ashes from Bishop Zion Cemetery, and water from Vishnu Springs. There's just one more thing we need to do: we made a promise to that lady at the Seventh Avenue dead end that we would find her missing child. I intend to keep that promise."

INVESTIGATION FILE 044

DEATH CURVE
Cambridge, Illinois

Less than a mile outside of Cambridge sits Timber Ridge Road. As motorists travel west along Timber Ridge, they encounter a sharp curve marked by a Mulberry tree and an old, rustic fence that divides two cornfields. This bucolic scene hides a dark history, a history that few would remember if it were not for the ghost stories.

In 1896, Julia Johnson married a man named Clarence B. Markham, and the young couple settled on a farm in Andover Township outside of Cambridge. In nine years of marriage, Julia Markham gave birth to seven children, an average of one every 15 months. There were four girls and three boys, aged from between five months to eight and a half years. On the morning of Saturday September 30, 1905, while her husband labored in a neighboring field, Mrs. Markham, to quote the *Cambridge Chronicle*, "committed one of the most dastardly deeds that has ever occurred in Henry County."

At around 11 o'clock, Julia sent her two eldest children to a nearby spring to retrieve water. While they were gone, she took an ax and swung it at the heads of her five youngest, killing them instantly. When her eldest returned, she dealt with them the same way. Julia had carefully planned the massacre and tried to commit suicide afterward, but the knife that she used to cut her throat was too dull. Wounded, she laid her children out on a bed and doused them with coal oil. She lit the oil on fire and the entire house went up in flames.

Meanwhile, the Markham's neighbors saw smoke billowing from the house and rushed over. Intending to save the children, they instead stumbled upon a terrible scene. "Mrs. Markham stayed in the burning house until practically all her clothing was burned off, and then crawled out doors," the *Chronicle* reported. A Doctor on the scene informed her that she did not have long to live. Seeing the end was near, she confessed and died at 3 o'clock that afternoon.[47]

Decades passed, and the ruin of the Markham's home was plowed over. Their aging, red barn remained, however, and became a focal point for local teens who grew up hearing stories about the murders. Facts blurred and people began to report seeing the ghost of Julia Markham along the roadside. They blamed accidents at the curve in Timber Ridge Rd. on her ghost.

On May 19, 2007, the Moline *Dispatch* reported one eyewitness account of the haunting from 18 years earlier. The Markham's barn was still standing at the time, and two young women drove out there looking for a place to hang out. As they neared the curve, they caught sight of something unexpected. "On the fence, you could see something white floating off into the cornfield," one of the women told the newspaper. "It was white with long flowing hair..." But a translucent phantom was not the only thing spotted along the road. Paranormal researchers Chad Lewis and Terry Fisk spoke with one woman who told them that she had seen a spook light floating near the old fence.[48]

Today, there is nothing unusual about the curve in Timber Ridge Road, even less so now that the barn is gone. Aside from a few articles on dusty microfilm reels, nothing tangible remains that would remind passersby of the unspeakable acts committed outside the village of Cambridge that fateful day in 1905. Yet the act of a mother murdering her own children—something so anathema to our basic values—is a stain that will not be so easily removed. The spirits of Julia and her children cry out from the grave.

[47] *Cambridge Chronicle* (Cambridge) 5 October 1905.
[48] Lewis and Fisk, 135.

THE FALLEN INVESTIGATE

AUG. 19

10:24 AM

82° F

Mike knew the Fallen were going to run into trouble when he first saw the black van parked on the side of the road near the Cambridge "Death Curve." Sure enough, as he got closer, he saw the letters "P.C.P.R.S." stenciled onto the side of the van in big yellow and orange letters. He clutched the steering wheel until his knuckles turned white.

"Oh no," Greg, who smelled like orange soda, said from the backseat of Mike's dark blue Toyota Corolla. "Is that the Pan-Continental Paranormal Research Society's van?" Greg's hair was unkempt and pressed forward by hand, yet it was short enough to appear styled, and his face was weather-beaten and pocket marked. It was a face that had felt a dozen different climates, from deserts to the icy tundra.

Davin, who sat next to Greg, was pale and clean-shaven. He looked like a man who was accustomed to living a sedentary life. He wore a simple undershirt and jean shorts, both of which were soaked with sweat. Emmer, a foot taller than the others, rounded out the trio in the backseat. The prominence of his Adam's apple was only rivaled by the prominence of his nose, which jutted out from under the brim of his Chicago Cubs' baseball cap.

"It is, unfortunately," Aurelia replied from the front passenger seat. In contrast to her companions, Aurelia did not look like she had slept in her clothes the the previous night. She wore a red and black striped tank top, urban camouflage pants, and dog-eared combat boots. It did not seem to matter to her that the temperature was nearly a ninety degrees Fahrenheit outside, with high humidity.

"What are *they* doing here?" Greg asked, referring to the occupants of the black van, without expecting an answer.

After a few moments, the Fallen could make out the features of two men and two women wearing black t-shirts who stood along the side of the road at the apex of the curve. They were chatting with a man wearing a periwinkle polo shirt and khaki shorts who was furiously jotting down notes in an I-Pad he held in one hand.

"Who is that?" Mike asked when he failed to recognize the man in the polo shirt.

"Isn't that the reporter we ran into at Bishop-Zion Cemetery?" Aurelia replied. She snorted. "*It is.*"

Greg leaned forward eagerly. "What do you want to do? Do you just want to come back another time?"

Mike took his Toyota Corolla around the curve and pulled over as soon as he found room on the shoulder. "Heck no," he said as he unfastened his seatbelt. "We have as much a right to be here as they do."

"Which is probably very little—" Emmer interjected.

The Fallen's arrival did not go unnoticed. The four members of P.C.P.R.S., along with Fess Parker (from the *Paranormal Review and Gazette*), stopped talking and stared at the dark blue Toyota as it approached. Their eyes betrayed an equal measure of envy and hatred. Although the Pan-Continental Paranormal Research Society had chalked up countless interviews and television appearances, the Fallen had an uncanny access to paranormal phenomenon. Everywhere they went, potential clients spoke of the Fallen in hushed tones somewhere between fear and curiosity. Keith, president of P.C.P.R.S., *knew* this mysterious quintet were nothing but *amateurs*—kids who had never even been invited on a Blog Talk Radio show. Then there were the rumors of illicit activity—trespassing, theft, arson, destruction of property, and even (worst of all) *charging for investigations*.

"Shouldn't you *kids* be out playing roll playing games or whatever it is you do?" Keith said as soon as the Fallen got out of their vehicle. He chuckled and bumped fists with the other man in the P.C.P.R.S..

Mike could not help but laugh as well, but for different reasons. "Look," he said as he laid his hand on Aurelia's shoulder to let her know it would be Ok. "We just want to get done what we came here to do. That's all. We'll get out of your way and then you'll never hear from us again." Inside, he cringed. He hated to be nice to the P.C.P.R.S., with whom the Fallen had feuded ever since they came to Illinois, but there were more important things to worry about now.

"I'm afraid that won't be possible," Keith replied. He wielded his potbelly like a weapon and positioned himself like a boulder in front of the Fallen's path. "This is *our* investigation site. You're disturbing the energy pattern, and we won't be able to get any EVPs if you're here talking all the time."

Emmer rolled his eyes. "How many EVPs have you ever gotten?"

Suddenly, the reporter stepped forward. "How was that Phish concert?" he asked sarcastically.

"*What is he talking about?*" Mike whispered to Greg.

"It happened when you were in jail a couple of months ago," Greg replied. "We told him we'd stopped to take a leak on our way to a Phish concert when he cornered us at Bishop-Zion Cemetery."

"Nice."

"You can forget about that interview," the reporter snapped. "Keith here has been telling me all about your group, and frankly, you disgust me. You actually *charge* for investigations? That's really unprofessional."

"First of all," Mike said as he abandoned any pretense of politeness, "it's none of your business what we do. Secondly, I can't think of a professional anything who *doesn't* charge for their services. That's the definition of a professional. If you do it for free, it's a hobby. Finally, we never wanted to do an interview with you anyway, so piss off."

Greg cleared his throat and Mike regained his composure.

Davin, who never liked confrontations, hovered near the passenger door on the opposite side of the car. "Why don't we just come back tomorrow?" he muttered.

"Why don't you listen to your friend?" a member of the P.C.P.R.S., a middle aged woman with a buzz haircut wearing stonewashed jeans, spat. She waved a thick arm wildly through the air and pointed down the road.

"You are getting dangerously close to stepping over the line," Mike replied, and a curious smile grew across Aurelia's face.

Keith pressed his fingers against his chest and began to shout like an out-of-control guest on the Jerry Springer Show. "What are you going to do, huh? What are you going to do?"

Mike stood quietly facing down his opponent as Greg, who had maneuvered into the man's peripheral vision, pulled a Taser out of the pocket of his cargo shorts. With a quick pull of the trigger, a pair of sharp electrodes embedded themselves into Keith's neck and delivered a shock of 1,200 volts and .04 amps a second until he collapsed onto the dirt at the roadside.

"*Oh my God!*" the two middle-aged women screamed. They covered their mouths with their hands and stumbled backward while the reporter dropped his I-Pad in shock.

Greg quickly ejected the Taser cartridge and replaced it. He then pointed the non-lethal weapon at the other members of the P.C.P.R.S. while they scrambled for cover behind their van. "We warned you!" he shouted. "We're not playing around this time. Get in your van and get the heck out of here!"

"W... We're calling the cops!" Keith stuttered as he got to his feet and headed for the van. The reporter and the rest of the P.C.P.R.S. quickly threw their equipment bags inside and followed right behind without worrying about where they were going to sit, fastening their seatbelts, or even closing the door. Keith threw the van into drive and peeled away while clutching his neck and uttering a string of obscenities.

Emmer scooped up the reporter's I-Pad, which had been left on the pavement, while Mike and Aurelia hurried to the fence post just beyond the curve in Timber Ridge Road. "I'd say we have about ten or fifteen minutes before the county sheriff shows up, so do what you have to do and let's get out of here!" he yelled after them.

Laughing, Greg put the Taser back into his shorts. "Man, I've wanted to do that for a really long time. It felt great."

"It was reckless," Emmer chastised. "I hope Mike finds whatever it is he's looking for here. I hope this is worth it."

"If we can find it—it will be. It'll lead us like a beacon right to the missing child of the Seventh Avenue ghost." As the words left Greg's mouth, he heard Mike shout triumphantly and saw him wave something in the air. "Looks like a success."

"It seems stupid to risk getting arrested again for helping out someone who isn't even alive," Davin said.

Greg shrugged. "We never break a promise."

Investigation File 045

Western Illinois University
Macomb, Illinois

For years, students and faculty in Western Illinois University's Simpkins Hall have told stories about phantom children. Many other odd occurrences are attributed to "Harold," a former janitor or graduate assistant who lurks among the classrooms on the third floor. After classes finish for the day, the disembodied sound of keys jingling, doors opening and closing, or a typewriter clicking, rattle the nerves of even the most seasoned educator. In addition to Simpkins Hall, several of the campus dorms—Bayliss just to name one—are also rumored to be haunted.

Nestled in the small town of Macomb, Western Illinois University began as a teacher's college. Originally called Western Illinois State Normal School, its classes were confined to one building, now known as Sherman Hall. Sherman Hall was originally known as "Main Building." In 1937, the university built a new training school adjacent to Main Building. Local children enrolled in the Training School and were taught by the students at the college.

In the 1960s, as Western Illinois State Normal School became Western Illinois University, the Training School building was given to the Department of English and Journalism. The children went elsewhere to accommodate the deluge of incoming college freshmen from the baby boom generation, but closets with tape still bearing the names of the last occupants, rows of green lockers, tiny desks, and wooden loudspeakers remained. With such a unique past, Simpkins Hall, as it was christened in 1968, was a natural incubator for ghost stories.

Compared to Simpkins Hall's phantom child, Harold is a relatively recent ghost. Randy Smith and Judi Hardin, who have both been at the university for decades, told *Western Courier* reporter Sarah Cash that they first heard the Harold stories in the 1980s. Miss Cash believed the story might have its origins in the experience of a former teaching assistant who heard typing early one morning as she lay down to rest her eyes in the Writing Center. Exasper-ated, she yelled, "Harold, knock it off!" She did not hear the mysterious sounds again that morning.

Bayliss Hall is haunted by the ghosts of two suicide victims. The first, a freshman girl, allegedly became pregnant and delivered the baby in her dorm room. In a panic, she threw the baby—along with any evidence of the delivery—down the garbage chute. She then hung herself in the closet. Some students claim that the cries of both the girl and the baby echo through the hall. In the second story, the roommate of a young woman suffering from severe depression left her alone over the weekend and she ended her life in the closet. Today, residents of that particular room report strange noises and electrical disturbances.

The tale of the roommate's suicide in Bayliss Hall serves as a dramatic morality play, warning students to look after their fellow classmates. There are lessons in all of these stories, and such events are the dark underside to the culture at our universities, a culture (and history) that is reflected in contemporary campus folklore.

THE FALLEN INVESTIGATE

SEP. 8

1:00 AM

72° F

"**D**on't you think it's risky for the five of us to appear at a major university like this?" Emmer asked from the backseat, his baseball cap tilted over his eyes. Emmer, along with Mike, Greg, Davin, and Aurelia, traveled east down University Drive in Mike's battered Toyota Corolla, windows open, with Wintersun blaring from the speakers to drown out the hip-hop emanating from a platinum-colored SUV in the other lane.

"We're not 'appearing' here," Davin replied with a hint of annoyance. "It's not like it's an announced visit. I'm just seeing my friend one last time before we have to leave the state."

Greg, who sat next to Davin, gave him a shove. "You mean your first and only visit?" he teased. "Where did you meet this girl anyway, the Internet? Does she know you're a member of a super-secret organization that investigates the paranormal and is hunted by crazed cultists?" He paused for dramatic effect. "Wait, was that your *selling point*?"

"All right, leave him alone," Mike said from behind the steering wheel. "At least *one* of us has a social life." He grinned. "Besides, this campus is supposed to be crawling with ghosts, and when Davin is chatting with his girlfriend, I'm going to be checking it out. Who's with me?"

Greg, Aurelia, and Emmer gave a few half-hearted cheers.

Emmer suddenly sat upright. "Hey, isn't this supposed to be a party school?"

Mike cut him off. "No—we're not going to have a repeat of what happened at the University of Illinois. You guys left to go drink and me and Aura had to deal with that ghost by ourselves." He looked over his shoulder at Emmer and recalled how Emmer's skepticism tended to suppress paranormal activity. "On second thought, maybe you *should* go off on your own."

"Slow down or you're going to miss the turn," Davin said as the car passed Brophy Hall. "There's a parking lot on your right. I think we can park there. Tessa lives in Bayliss Hall, which I think is up ahead in this group of dorms."

Greg laughed. "Her name is *Tessa*?"

The lot was large and filled with a sea of vehicles of every type. Ignoring the signs on which parking sticker requirements were posted, Mike drove up and down the aisles until he found an open space. The Fallen got out of their car and waited while Davin whipped out his cell phone. After some polite chatter, he snapped the phone closed and began walking toward the tall, black residence halls that resembled an inner-city housing project. "Tessa is going to meet us downstairs," he said, and Mike, Greg, Emmer, and Aurelia followed.

With the exception of Davin, who wore his usual white t-shirt and blue jeans, and Greg, who wore his usual olive green shirt and khaki shorts, most of the quintet was dressed in black. They stood out like sore thumbs against the backdrop of 20-somethings wearing polo shirts, sandals, visors, white baseball caps, colorful sweatpants, or clever t-shirts. Neck beards were everywhere. Some of these students pointed and covered their mouths to hide their laughter as the Fallen walked past.

It was not long before they stood at the entrance to Bayliss Hall, and after a few minutes, Tessa appeared out of the elevator. Blushing, she was short and chubby, with curly hair, a snub nose and pleasant features. She wore pink capris and a yellow t-shirt that featured a cartoon squirrel. Davin and she recognized each other instantly, and they hugged. She eyed the other members of the Fallen suspiciously and with a hint of distaste. "Are *these* your friends?" she asked.

SIMPKINS HALL

Davin laughed nervously but did not reply.

Mike laid his hands on both Davin and Tessa's shoulders and smiled. "So, why don't you show us around campus?"

*   *   *

"So, here we are again," Mike said as Aurelia and he wandered Simpkins Hall alone. "I can't believe the other guys would rather go out and drink with a bunch of nubile, free spirited college girls than look for ghosts."

Aurelia snorted. "I know I wouldn't!"

"Do you sense anything in this building?" Mike asked as he dangled a crystal from the end of a black cord as he walked. "I'm not getting any response from the pendulum."

"I sense something, but it's more like a blanket of emotions. I can't really single out one particular person or entity."

"For once, I don't think there's anything substantial here. Let's get out of here before the janitor comes back."

"Ooo, maybe it will be *Harold*," Aurelia said, laughing.

Suddenly, Mike's pocket vibrated. He retrieved his cell phone and examined it with a skeptical eye. "It's Davin," he announced. "He says they're in Tessa's dorm room and Emmer is passed out, so they're going to experiment with the Ouija board."

"Uh oh, we better get over there."

Mike nodded, and the two friends exited Simpkins as quickly as they could without being noticed. Outside, the campus was dark aside from the occasional lamp, and laughter and shouts echoed from nearby fraternity houses.

It took fifteen minutes to get from one end of campus to the other, because Mike and Aurelia had walked to Simpkins earlier that evening. When they arrived at Bayliss Hall, they were sweaty and exhausted. Davin and Tessa met them downstairs and the four snuck past the night assistant to the elevator.

Tessa's room was on the ninth floor. Her roommate, a tall and pudgy sophomore who wore clothes several sizes too small, introduced herself as Sam. As they stepped inside, Mike and Aurelia noticed the Ouija board was already laid out on the linoleum floor. Emmer was laying, face down, on Sam's "Shrek" comforter, and several empty bottles of Pucker sat on the desk.

"How did it go at Simpkins Hall?" Greg asked as Mike and Aurelia found seats on the floor in the already cramped space. Aurelia took care to avoid sitting on or near anything pink, but her efforts proved useless.

"It was a bust," Mike replied, "but hopefully we'll have better luck here. What's the story again?"

"I heard several girls committed suicide in this dorm," Sam said. "*Maybe even on this floor.*"

"*Maybe even in this room,*" Aurelia said, mockingly.

"Oh my God, do you think so?" Sam replied, completely missing the tone of Aurelia's remarks.

Mike cleared his throat and scooted near the Ouija board. "Who wants to start?" He placed his fingers on one side of the planchette, and Davin and and Tessa followed suit. They waited quietly for several moments and concentrated on breathing deeply. Then, when the trio was relaxed, Mike began asking questions. "Is there someone else in here with us?" He glanced at Aurelia, and she nodded in the affirmative.

Slowly, meticulously, the planchette moved toward "yes" on the board.

"What's your name?" Sam blurted.

Mike opened his mouth to chide her, but the plastic pointer slid toward the "S." More quickly this time, it spelled out "S-a-l-l-y."

Sam giggled and began clapping wildly.

Tessa turned and shushed her roommate.

"Thank you," Mike said under his breath, and then he turned his attention back to the Ouija board. "Were you a student here?"

A door slammed in the hallway and Sam screamed. She reflexively covered her mouth as everyone's eyes fell on her. Suddenly, the bulb in the desk lamp burnt out.

"Mike," Aurelia said. "I think this is a bad idea. I'm getting a hostile vibe."

"Give me a one minute," Mike replied. "Did you die here? What do you want?"

"R-E-V-E-N-G-E," the planchette spelled out.

Aurelia jumped to her feet. "Mike!"

"*Give me one more minute.*"

All of a sudden, Emmer was violently dumped from the bed and landed with a thud on the floor next to a large plush elephant. His eyes shot open and he cried out in surprise as soon as he hit the cheap linoleum.

Mike, Davin, and Tessa all let go of the planchette at the same time, and it spun around several times before coming to a stop on the Ouija board over the word "bye." Mike grinned.

"What happened?" Emmer groaned. "Stop messing around."

There was no reply, but Greg turned to him and smiled. Sam and Tessa were in shock—they had never seen the other side as the Fallen had time after time. There was no going back from that, but the Fallen could not concern themselves with easing the qualms of two college girls—they had to keep moving.

Sam and Tessa chatted about the incident all night, but in the morning, after a quick dining hall breakfast of burnt bacon and powdered eggs, the Fallen disappeared.

INVESTIGATION FILE 046

ARCHER AVENUE
Willow Springs, Illinois

Archer Avenue begins at S. State Street in Chicago and travels steadily west until merging with Route 171 in suburban Summit. There the road turns sharply southwest and passes through Justice and Willow Springs before ultimately entering scenic Lemont. Starting with Resurrection Cemetery and ending at St. James-Sag Church, this section of Archer Avenue forms the northern border of a triangle of forest preserves, lakes, trails, and burial grounds that could easily be described as the most haunted place in Chicago.

Encompassing most of the Cook County Forest Preserve District's Palos Division, this triangle is defined by the Calumet Sag Channel to the south, Archer Avenue and the Des Plaines River to the north, and S. Kean Avenue to the west. It is a hilly, wooded area filled with over a dozen small lakes and sloughs. This area has a well-deserved reputation built upon generations of strange encounters, which make it a favorite for ghost tours, paranormal researchers, and curiosity seekers alike.

In addition to Resurrection Cemetery, Archer Woods Cemetery, Maple Lake, and St. James-Sag Church and Cemetery, there are at least seven lesser known locations in the vicinity with equally strange and fascinating stories: Bethania Cemetery, the Why Not drive-in, the Justice Public Library, Healing Waters Park, Fairmount Hills Cemetery, the intersection of 95th and Kean, and Sacred Heart Cemetery.

Bethania Cemetery borders Resurrection Cemetery. Although less well-known, Bethania has its own reputation for the unusual. In October 1989, the *Southtown Economist* reported the arrest of two young men inside the cemetery in the early morning hours. A day earlier, police had discovered an altar made from a marble cross—probably stolen from a monument—in a wooded area of the cemetery. The cross had been placed inside a circle drawn in the ground, and the police found evidence of a fire at the location.

On the opposite side of Route 171, along Frontage Road, sits the Why Not drive-in, a greasy spoon that recently closed down. According to Dale Kaczmarek, a local legend maintains that a ghost named Debbie appears on foggy nights to lure unsuspecting men on a futile chase through the streets of suburban Justice.

The Justice Public Library is located a few blocks north of the Why Not drive-in, along Oak Grove Avenue. Built in 1995, the new building replaced Justice's older and much smaller library, which Richard T. Crowe, purveyor of Chicago Supernatural Tours, reported to be afflicted with poltergeist activity. When the library moved to its new location just across the street, the ghost moved as well.

Across Archer Avenue, on the other side of the Des Plaines River and the Chicago Sanitary and Ship Canal, lies Healing Waters Park. The park, which consists of a small pond and a row of boulders 92 yards in length, is the last vestige of the area's prehistory. Long before the first Europeans set foot on the land that would one day become the village of Willow Springs, the Algonquian peoples traveled to this area to drink from springs that reportedly possessed healing powers.

Back across the river, exactly one mile southeast of Healing Waters Park nestled between 95th, 104th, and Archer Ave, is Fairmount Hills Cemetery, also known as Willow Hills Memorial Park. Fairmount vaguely resembles the state of Idaho in shape and breaks up the topography of the Archer Avenue "triangle." It is a scenic, garden-like cemetery plotted on rolling hills, but it has not escaped from the area's enigmatic pull.

MAPLE LAKE

According to Dale Kaczmarek, visitors discovered the body of a young woman inside Fairmount Hills in February 1981. She had been beaten and strangled, but there was no evidence of a robbery. Stranger still, someone broke into the funeral home where her body was awaiting burial and placed a rose and a love note nearby. The case went cold for a year until the woman's ex-boyfriend turned himself in for the crime.

The most frequently retold story associated with the cemetery is that of the mysterious music of the White mausoleum. The mausoleum, which no longer exists, was a simple, rectangular structure perched at the top of a hill with a small staircase that led up to its rusted door. Over the past few decades, several visitors reported hearing eerie music there. On one visit in 1982, a woman named Valerie told Richard Crowe that, "All of a sudden, faint but quite clear, a harpsichord began playing." Both Valerie and her niece heard the ethereal music, but it stopped abruptly when her sister joined them at the steps of the mausoleum. Unfortunately, the White mausoleum was

heavily damaged in a fire in 2003 and has since been torn down.

East of Fairmount Hills Cemetery along 95th Street lies an inconspicuous intersection allegedly haunted by some unusual apparitions. According to a variety of eyewitnesses, ghostly animals have been seen at the intersection of 95th and Kean Avenue near Hidden Pond Woods. The Palos Trail winds its way through these woods between Route 20 and Kean Avenue, and popular opinion holds that a number of horses and their riders have been killed trying to cross 95th Street.

On one particular night in 1979, a couple named Dennis and Sandy told Richard Crowe that they narrowly avoided striking a ghostly procession of horses and riders that were illuminated by an eerie glow. Sandy described the figures as "glistening," and told Crowe that she did not remember seeing their hooves touch the ground.

Horses are not the only animals to make this intersection their otherworldly home. Just inside the woods at the entrance to the Palos

Trail at 95th and Kean sits a small, marble headstone inscribed with the name "Felix." Felix was the beloved mascot of the local fire station who helped save many lives during his tenure with the department. According to Dale Kaczmarek, the ghost of Felix has been seen near the intersection on several occasions.

Last but not least, there is the strange tale of the "gray haired baby" of Sacred Heart Cemetery. Sacred Heart is a small graveyard dating back to the time when this area was still dotted by farms. It is located along Kean Avenue in Crooked Creek Woods south of the haunted intersection. 103rd Street dead-ends in front of the cemetery. Out of all the stories in the Archer Avenue "triangle," Sacred Heart might be home to the most incredible. It is the story of the "gray-haired baby," a feral man (some say a werewolf) who stalks the woods and horse trails nearby.

According to Richard Crowe, the legend began in the 1950s when, allegedly, a man and his wife were killed in a car accident near Sacred Heart Cemetery. Their baby was thrown from the vehicle and somehow survived in the forest preserve, feeding off the local wildlife. On moonlit nights, passing motorists occasionally caught a glimpse of a hairy creature in their headlights, and equestrians riding on the nearby trail reported that their horses would be spooked by something unseen.

There are many theories as to why this area attracts such a variety of unusual phenomena. In Ursula Bielski's book *Chicago Haunts*, she explored the possibility that this section of Archer Avenue runs alongside a ley line, metaphysical lines in the earth that intersect at "nodal points." These points were said to attract and concentrate paranormal energy.

It is more likely that these stories cropped up along this stretch of Archer Avenue because, like Cuba Road north of Chicago, the area developed a reputation for the mysterious among urban residents who came to the lakes, trails, and forest preserves to "get away" from the big city.

It is a place where visitors encounter cemeteries tucked inside the woods, lakes that seem to glow in the moonlight, and an old limestone church that looms above the surrounding landscape. In the darkness of night, one could easily imagine hearing the frantic hooves of a phantom black carriage barreling toward Archer Woods Cemetery.

There are haunted locations scattered throughout the City of Chicago, but no one place that is sufficiently remote enough to become a breeding ground for those tales. The Archer Avenue "triangle," at the periphery of the collective consciousness of Chicagoland's 9.5 million residents, is such a place.

The Fallen Investigate

OCT. 21

7:46 PM

41° F

The underbrush snapped and shuffled as Davin crawled up next to Aurelia. Dressed in camouflage pants and a black t-shirt, she was laying in the woods behind a partially decayed log two yards west of a horse trail that emptied out into a street a stone-throw away. A small, burgundy colored monument, inscribed with the name "Felix," sat at the mouth of the woods about halfway between the pair and the street. They watched the stoplights at the nearby intersection turn from red to green, and then Aurelia pointed her binoculars toward the well-worn Toyota Corolla parked along the curb on the other side of the intersection.

Inside the vehicle, Emmer gestured with his fore and index fingers, and a flash of light answered from the woods. He rolled his eyes and turned up the volume on the cassette player. Orphaned Land's "His Leaf Shall Not Wither" issued forth from the speakers. *This sound quality is terrible*, Emmer thought.

"I have a question," Davin whispered. "Why are we crawling around like this? I'm pretty sure that anyone passing by will be able to see us."

Aurelia tilted her binoculars and stared at Davin. Without saying a word, she got to her feet, grabbed him by his shirt collar, and pulled him up. "We've been here for thirty minutes without anything to show for it," she grumbled as she brushed off the front of her t-shirt. "I wonder if Mike and Greg are having any better luck."

"Now, we're back where it all started," Mike said, referring to southwest suburban Chicago, where the Fallen had first began their investigations in Illinois nearly four years earlier. He stared out over Maple Lake as the sun began its descent. The maple trees were just beginning to show their autumn colors, and the air was still. Greg nodded approvingly. Behind them, in the small pull-off, sat two unfaired, black and chrome Suzuki GS500Es.

"What are we going to do when it's all over?" Greg asked while massaging the few precious hairs that sprouted from his granite chin.

"I don't know," Mike replied. "We can go anywhere we want—*once we've destroyed that thing.*"

"Do you think it was worth it? It seems like it would have been a lot less trouble if we never found that portal to begin with."

"Those zealots would have found it eventually," Mike said mater-of-factly. "God knows what they would have done with it. At least we don't have to worry about that anymore."

Greg shot Mike a glance that asked, "who was worried?" and a long moment of silence followed. The moon began to show in the rapidly darkening sky. "Where the heck is this ghost light?" Greg finally exclaimed.

"I don't know, but we should check on Aura, Davin, and Emmer. They should be done at 95th and Kean. I wonder if they saw anything."

Greg chuckled. "I doubt it, with Emmer there. As for me, I can't wait to go to Chet's Melody Lounge. At least Davin is old enough to drink now... legally anyway."

"Hang on—I'm getting a text from him right now."

[Davin] OMG - You guys will never believe what happened

[Mike] Stay there. We r coming.

Mike perked up. "Let's get out of here. Davin says they saw something."

As Greg and Mike turned their backs to Maple Lake, an orange ball of light, about a foot in diameter, flickered in the middle of the lake, just above the reflection of the moon. It sat there, steadily, as Greg and Mike mounted their GS500Es, then it vanished as quickly as it had arrived.

The pair made their way through the deserted streets of Willow Springs, turned down Kean Avenue, and pulled into the parking lot of Hidden Pond Woods. The woods were just a few yards north of the intersection of 95th and Kean. Aurelia, Davin, and Emmer stood next to Mike's dark blue Toyota Corolla. They were chatting, laughing, and gesturing excitedly as Mike and Greg stopped their motorcycles in an adjacent parking space. As soon as they cut the engines, Davin blurted, *"You guys just missed the most incredible thing you've ever seen!"*

Emmer, who had been trying to maintain a straight face, burst out laughing.

"That's real funny, guys," Mike grumbled. "Did you really see something?"

"Not a darn thing—just as I expected," Emmer replied in a tone that resembled gloating.

Mike spat. "We better get out of here then, before the cop shows up to chain the parking lot. The forest preserve closes at dusk."

"What's next?" Aurelia asked. "Fairmont Cemetery?" She paused. "What happened at Maple Lake? Did you see the light?"

Greg smiled. "Nope. I think it's just an urban legend. Maybe headlights reflecting off the lake or something like that."

"Maybe we need to stay at these places longer," Davin suggested. "All of these reported sightings happen at random times—they don't happen every day. If they did, they wouldn't be mysterious or paranormal. They would just be *normal*. We've been lucky with the things we have seen, but these things aren't going to appear just because we show up."

The others ignored him.

"What's next on the list?" Aurelia asked impatiently. "We've seen Archer Woods, St. James-Sag, and Resurrection Cemetery already. I want to go somewhere new."

Greg agreed. "We might as well hit up as many places as we can before we leave the state." He paused. "We are leaving, right? As soon as we banish that *thing* back to the other side? You haven't changed your mind—I hope."

"We don't have much of a choice," Mike said. "And with the Black Willow Grove operation over, we don't have any reason to stay. We're already wanted in this state for God only knows how many crimes." He grinned. "You can thank Aura alone for most of that."

Aurelia gave a half-hearted curtsy.

From there, the Fallen decided to go to Fairmont Cemetery, and they left their vehicles on the side of the road where—they hoped—no one would drive past.

"I hope you realize we're taking a huge risk," Davin whispered as the quintet crossed the unfenced boundary into the cemetery.

"Oh, like we're going to get caught tonight out of all the other nights we've done this," Mike retorted.

Greg sneered. "This is coming from a guy who was sitting in jail as little as three months ago…"

Mike shrugged off the comment and led the Fallen deeper into the cemetery, all the while avoiding the main paths. After a short period of time, it became clear that they were not alone. Faint laughter and whispers echoed in the rolling hills among the moonlit headstones.

The Fallen ducked and froze. "I don't think we're alone," Aurelia said with a characteristic flair for the obvious.

"It sounds like a bunch of idiots," Emmer said.

With a signal from Mike's hand, Greg dashed to the right and Aurelia to the left, leaving Mike, Davin, and Emmer in the center. After exactly fifty paces, Greg and Aurelia stopped and the entire group began to slowly advance. Their eyes were adjusted to the darkness, so they had no trouble recognizing shapes in the moonlight. After a couple of yards, they crested a hill and saw four figures rocking a monument back and forth. Discarded aerosol cans lay in the grass.

Mike grinned and nodded. Without warning, the Fallen broke into a sprint and rushed toward the vandals from three directions. The vandals, who looked like typical teenagers, screamed and fled in terror. Mike, Greg, Aurelia, Davin, and Emmer arrived at the desecrated monument at the same time—all of them laughing hysterically. But their fun was short lived.

A police cruiser's spotlight swept past, and two headlights reflected off a pair of nearby monuments. Mike cursed and the Fallen ducked.

"I think it's time for us to leave," Aurelia whispered. No one argued or (for once) pointed out the obviousness of her statement.

The quintet began to run toward the nearest hill, hoping to avoid the cops until they drove past. They were not that lucky, however. A second police cruiser pulled up on the other side of the hill and shown its spotlight directly on the Fallen. It seemed like they were trapped.

"Evade! Evade!" Mike shouted. "Let's get out of here—we'll rendezvous at Site 23 and pick up the car and our bikes tomorrow."

The whole episode lasted a few seconds. Greg, Aurelia, Davin, and Emmer shook their heads affirmatively and dashed in opposite directions. By the time the police stopped their cars and began to yell, the five members of the Fallen had disappeared into the darkness.

The Willow Springs police officers scoured the hills of Fairmount Cemetery, but all they found were a couple of empty aerosol cans.

INVESTIGATION FILE 047

STARVED ROCK STATE PARK

Utica, Illinois

Situated along the southern bank of the Illinois River near Utica, Starved Rock State Park is the most visited park in Illinois. Its most prominent feature is a large, sandstone butte that stands high above the shoreline. Visitors flock to hike its 13 miles of trails and explore its 18 canyons, but while the park offers beautiful scenery, many do not realize the strange history and events that took place there.

The landforms themselves are thousands of years old, and copper clovis points found at Starved Rock indicate human habitation as early at 8000BC. The Kaskaskia tribe lived there in the early 1600s, but they came into conflict with the Iroquois, who moved into the area in 1660. The French soon followed. In 1673, famed explorers Louis Joliet and Father Jacques Marquette passed Starved Rock on their way back up the Illinois River.

LaSalle, another French explorer, built Fort St. Louis on the butte, but the fort was abandoned several decades later and there are no remnants of it today. Sometime in the early 1770s, Ottawa and Potawatomi Indians attacked a band of Illini living in the area. The Illini fled to the butte, where they starved to death. The area has been known as Starved Rock ever since, even though little physical evidence supports this story.

A tale of buried treasure comes from this period. Between 1685 and 1702, Henri de Tonti was the most powerful man in central Illinois. He was a character of legend, even though most people do not remember him today. He accompanied René-Robert Cavelier, Sieur de La Salle in his exploration of the Illinois country, and La Salle left him to hold Fort St. Louis when he returned to France. During his time in the Illinois River Valley, he is rumored to have accumulated over $100,000 in gold, which he buried around Starved Rock. He told a priest about the gold just before he died, but it has never been found despite search attempts in the 1750s by the French and the Potawatomie.

Starved Rock hides other, more sinister events. In March 1960, three middle-aged women (Frances Murphy, 47, Mildred Lindquist, 50, and Lillian Getting, 50) were murdered in the park, and their bodies were found in St. Louis Canyon. Two of the women were raped. When the women did not show up back at the lodge for the evening, a search party was organized. It took several days to find the bodies, which had been buried under a thin layer of snow. Their faces were bludgeoned until unrecognizable. The crime attracted national attention, and even *Time Magazine* covered the story. Eventually, a man named Chester Weger was convicted of the crime. Steve Stout, a photographer and author, has written extensively about the murders.

Troy Taylor claims that visitors to the park have heard groans and other disembodied voices amidst the rock formations, and ghosttraveller.com has reported that staff have heard doors slamming and felt cold spots in the lodge.

Starved Rock is a beautiful destination any time of the year, but just remember that even in its most remote canyon, you may not really be alone.

THE FALLEN INVESTIGATE

DEC. 21

12:00 AM

25° F

A full moon illuminated the thin layer of snow that coated the rocks, valleys, and crags of Starved Rock State Park, causing a bluish hue to be reflected off the naked and dormant branches of the deciduous forest. Despite recent snowfall, the temperature was crisp but bearable. The air was perfectly still. Heavy footsteps tromped through the frozen underbrush without regard for the noise—the travelers moved like they were on a mission and were far enough from the nearest dwelling to care.

Misa, a gangly young woman dressed in a flowing, knee-length coat, led the way. She moved swiftly but awkwardly; dodging and weaving through the trees like she was always off balance. Her appearance was deceptive, however, because she was neither helpless nor directionless. Her senses were honed for navigating in the dark. She heard the rustle of the owls in the trees and smelled the strangers who had tracked her friends since they left their car.

Aurelia was also keenly aware of their pursuers, but not through any of her five senses. She felt their power—*their rage*. The feeling soaked into her bones, and it got stronger the closer they came to the cliff.

Mike, Greg, Davin, and Emmer were oblivious. They moved with caution, instinctively locating sure footing on the snow-covered forest floor. Still, they lagged several yards behind Misa and Aurelia.

"Are you absolutely *sure* this plan is going to work?" Greg asked between heavy breaths. Fog puffed from his mouth.

"I didn't spend a year preparing for this to let it fail," Mike replied. His thick, black leather trench coat was tied tightly around his waist. "There are two parts to my plan, which I guess I have to explain to you again because you were asleep last time." He paused to see if Greg would lodge a protest, but none came. He continued, "First, we need to attract this *thing*— this demon or whatever it is—and let it know that we're here. It'll come after us, of course, and that's when we'll vanquish it."

"How come all your plans risk getting us killed?" Davin asked, but Mike ignored him.

"Man, no one said this was going to be safe," Greg replied with a chuckle.

"Not to throw a wrench in your little delusion you have going on here," Emmer interrupted while racing to catch up with the others, "but if this thing escaped at Cahokia Mounds two years ago, and it has been trying to destroy us this entire time, how come it hasn't done it yet? I mean, what's it waiting for? This is the worst demon ever."

"We're just that good," Greg said. "I mean, *I am*, anyway."

"It isn't strong enough," Mike said, not trying to disguise his annoyance. "Its abilities are muted here in the physical world, that's why it needs acolytes to do its bidding. Spiritual entities have a difficult time interacting with physical things, since they're technically in another dimension."

Emmer wanted to laugh uncontrollably, but he held his tongue.

Greg leapt over a log and ran to Mike's side. "Why did you pick *this place*?" he asked. "Why not go back to Monk's Mound, where it all started?"

"First of all, this is more remote," Mike explained. "Cahokia Mounds is too close to the city—there's too much of a risk of someone interrupting us or of civilians getting hurt. Secondly, it doesn't have exactly what we need for my plan to work." He grinned as the trees opened up to reveal a sandstone cliff, which had been formed millennia ago by the inexorable course of the Illinois River. Misa, who had arrived at the spot moments earlier, stood at the edge of the cliff, bathed in moonlight. Her skin appeared almost perfectly white.

Greg put down his backpack, pulled out a blanket, and spread it out on the ground. Carefully, he removed a weathered book with silver lettering pressed into the cover, a clay bowl, a plastic bag filled with ash, and a borosilicate glass beaker filled with murky water, and laid those items out on the blanket.

Alongside these items, Mike added a calumet pipe, which he had been keeping in his trench coat. Five eagle feathers dangled from the head of the red pipestone at the end of its stem. "So, a whole year's worth of searching has led to this," he whispered.

Every member of the Fallen, even Emmer, let out a long, slow breath.

"Let's get started," Aurelia said. "We don't have much time. Those guys will be here any minute."

"What guys?" Davin demanded.

"The acolytes that have been after you—they followed us here," Misa replied, matter-of-factly. "You didn't think they would let you do this without a fight, did you?"

"Don't worry," Mike said. "We need them. There's a very specific reason why we're here at this cliff."

"Isn't this 'lover's leap'?"

"Exactly. A demon of this size needs blood and death to maintain its presence in this realm. It needs it, like you and I need food. That's why it hangs out here, at Starved Rock. Have you ever wondered why it was called Starved Rock? Because an entire tribe vanished here, but you don't sense their spirits anywhere, do you? Add to that the murders in 1960 and all the young couples who have thrown themselves off this cliff. Why do you think they chose this cliff out of all the others?"

"Because it's a long way down?" Emmer interrupted.

"They were subconsciously drawn here by the demon so it could feed off their souls."

Emmer rolled his eyes and mumbled, "That's the most *logical* explanation, of course."

Mike brushed off the comment and began to push his companions away from the precipice. "Aurelia is right, we need to get going. Emmer, Greg, and Davin, take off down that trail for a few yards and find a good hiding spot. If you hear me yell, come running."

In the past, the three would have argued, but they all heard the determination in Mike's voice. They quickly obeyed and disappeared into the trees. Meanwhile, Mike, Aurelia, and Misa prepared the ritual circle in a clearing a few yards in front of the sandstone bluffs.

From the perspective of the eight cloaked figures that slowly emerged from the trees, they had cornered two of their prey: a young man dressed in a black leather coat and a young woman wearing a dark blue dress and a black tuxedo tail jacket. The two stood at the edge of the cliff with their backs to the open air. It would only be a matter of time before the acolytes caught the others, who had most likely ran off down one of the trails. A series of perverse smiles grew across their lips, which was all that was visible under their thick, brown hoods.

Misa crouched like she was getting ready to fight, and she watched the acolytes slowly advance. At the last moment, she threw herself backwards off the edge of the cliff.

Enraged, the acolytes rushed forward to seize the man in the leather coat, but he vanished as soon as their hands fell upon him. They heard a shout, and the next thing they saw was the open air and the rocky shore of the Illinois River rushing toward them. Spinning around, one caught a glimpse of the young woman in the tuxedo tail jacket suspended in the air by a nylon cord. She waved right before the world went black.

The Fallen stood at the edge of the precipice and looked down. At the last moment, they had rushed from their hiding places and pushed the acolytes to their deaths. Now, Greg,

Davin, and Emmer went to work hauling Misa up while Mike lit the calumet pipe and Aurelia opened the ageing, leather bound book. In a short time, Misa stood with the others, brushing off the front of her dress.

The sandstone cliff began to shake, and a deep, primordial groan echoed in the river valley. Stones and dirt shook loose and tumbled down into the darkness.

Standing in a circle, each of the Fallen puffed deeply from the calumet pipe as it was passed around. Aurelia read an incantation from the book, while Mike mixed the ashes from the Bishop-Zion Church fire with the healing water from Vishnu Springs in the ceremonial bowl. Purple and black smoke began to pour from the concoction, and it burst into flame.

In the best French accent Aurelia could manage, she chanted, "*Ce qui est foncé soyez rempli de lumière, enlèvent cet esprit de ma vue! Enlèvent cet esprit de ma vue!*"

A gust of wind seemed to carry the smoke up to the stars, and the low groan turned into a horrifying scream the likes of which none of the Fallen had ever heard. Aurelia repeated the line for a third time, and the flame in the ceremonial bowl exploded in a coruscating burst of green and red.

Calm spread over the Illinois River valley.

"*Factum est.*"

The ghost of a Confederate soldier appeared in the clearing with a curious grin on his face.

"Thanks for pretending to be me back there, Johnny," Mike said. "We couldn't have done this without you."

"It's the least I could do," the phantom replied. "I've felt a bit useless since I died, and well, you're my only friends."

Mike nodded. "We'll be leaving Illinois soon," he said, "now that the danger has passed. Who knows when we'll meet again."

"Good luck," Johnny said, and he faded away just before the Fallen strolled into the dark forest.

INVESTIGATION FILE 048

MUNGER ROAD

Wayne, Illinois

Like Barrington's Cuba Road, Munger Road sits at the periphery of the Chicago Suburbs and has attracted a number of strange legends. The road itself penetrates deep into Pratts Wayne Woods and until recently was fairly remote and not very well traveled. Rumors of abandoned houses and occult practices abound. Motorists have also reported being chased by a wolf with glowing red eyes as well as a vanishing Oldsmobile.

Perhaps the most famous legend centers on the now-defunct railroad tracks that intersect with Munger. The legend is a familiar one: three children pushed a baby carriage across the tracks just in time to save it from a passing train. Unfortunately, the children were killed. Today, if your car happens to stall on the tracks, phantom hands will push it to safety. While that is a common rural legend, a train did in fact derail nearby.

According to a former forest preserve employee interviewed by author Ursula Bielski for her book *Chicago Haunts 3*, an old abandoned house also sat north of the railroad tracks. Its owners left after a fire, and vandals and curious teens moved in. Naturally, they claimed the house was inhabited by Satan worshippers. The house was demolished in 2000. "There was a hole in the floor where a fire had ruined the house for its inhabitants…" the forest preserve employee said. "There were numerous signs of vandalism and the discarded packages of masks and things which someone had used in a lame attempt to scare someone else." He described the house as being two stories, white, and surrounded by large oak trees.

As mentioned earlier, rumors of a train derailment turned out to be true, although the old man who lived in a shack next to the railroad tracks was not crazed and his family was not killed, as some claimed. When the train derailed, it came to a stop against his home, but no one was injured.

The many legends of Munger Road were the backdrop for the 2011 horror movie of the same name, written by Nicholas Smith and produced by Kyle Heller. In the film, two police officers from St. Charles hear about four teenagers who have gone missing while investigating the story of the children killed at the train crossing. They fear that a serial killer is involved in the disappearance of the teens.

According to locals, Munger Road used to be closed to traffic. Teenagers would venture down there to explore the abandoned houses and nearby woods. Today, the road is nicely paved and there is a steady flow of traffic. That has not stopped the fascination with this place, however, and visitors remain convinced that ghostly children will push their cars safely over the railroad crossing. If you visit, you just might catch a glimpse of these phantoms in your rearview mirror as you pass over the tracks.

The Fallen Investigate

JAN. 14

11:40 PM

16° F

Munger Road was eerily serene. The air was calm, and snowflakes trickled down from a few scattered clouds too thin to obscure the bright buttery moon. Hugging the tree line, five figures stole through the darkness at the edge of the road. Not a single vehicle passed. The five had parked their car on the side of the road under the cover of trees and walked toward a railroad crossing at the crest of the hill. There, they would investigate the area for any truth to the legend of the deadly train wreck that took the lives of one unfortunate family.

Mike, a broad-shouldered man with light brown hair and glasses, lead the way with a night vision camera in hand. His black leather trench coat was wrapped tightly around his waist.

Behind him stomped a determined young woman named Aurelia, whose Aquiline nose sat prominently on her face. Everything about her demeanor gave off the impression of a bird of prey, especially her distant gaze. She seemed to be moving forward as if being led along, although her friends knew that she was simply too busy concentrating on detecting subtle disturbances in their surroundings to care where the road was. She would get where she was going because she trusted her friends to take her there.

Suddenly, Mike stopped dead in his tracks, causing Aurelia to do the same. The three men following closely behind her ran into each other, eliciting a few sharp cries of surprise.

"For crying out loud!" Greg shouted angrily. "Why don't we have flashlights?" Greg was about a head shorter than everyone else in the group. His dirty blonde hair was barely visible under his knit cap, and he wore baggy cargo shorts despite a temperature that was in the low teens.

"I told you," Mike replied, "no one can know we're out here. We don't want to attract attention."

"Any idiot driving by can see us," Emmer, who was following Greg, protested. Emmer was the tallest of the group, and his lankiness made him appear even taller than he was. He refused to wear any head covering other than a tattered Cubs baseball hat. Earlier that day, when Mike suggested that he wear something a little less conspicuous, he rolled his eyes.

Davin, the youngest of the quintet, spoke up. "Do you really think it's a good idea to be out here at night when we just spent a year away from Illinois on account of being wanted in several counties?"

"That's never stopped us before," Greg replied with a wide grin.

Mike thrust out his hand to calm the group. "Knock it off!" he hissed. "I thought I saw something up ahead." The trees to the side of the road were thin and widely spaced, offering a view of the clearing beyond, and the layer of freshly fallen snow seemed to glow in the moonlight. Not even a leaf stirred.

"No one is out here but us," Emmer said. He quickly added, "No one would be dumb enough to be out here at night but us."

"No," Aurelia said. "There is someone else out here. Can you hear that?"

The group fell silent as everyone strained their ears. Faintly, they began to hear a distant noise that sounded like an animal squealing or whining. They had not heard it over the shuffle of their feet on the gravel roadside.

"What is that?" Davin whispered.

"I wish we had brought Casey," Greg said, referring to the coydog they had adopted during a visit to Old Union Cemetery several years before. She was a scrappy, gray coated crossbreed between a wild coyote and a feral domesticated breed they still had not identified. Mike did not want her to come on the expedition to Munger Road because her barking might have alerted the neighbors to their presence.

"Where is it coming from?"

"Let's keep walking and see if it gets any louder," Mike suggested. "The railroad crossing is still about fifty yards away. There were supposed to be a couple of abandoned houses in woods too, if I'm not mistaken."

"I think they were torn down," Emmer said.

"Regardless, let's keep moving."

The quintet started walking again and the strange noise disappeared behind their footsteps and the rustle of their clothing and equipment. They soon reached a grassy clearing that meandered back to a large field. The park district had erected a metal cable covered with yellow plastic to block the entrance to the clearing, and a green sign announcing "Pratts Wayne Woods – Brewster Creek Wetland Restoration Site" stood beyond it.

Mike wiped snot away from his nose and inhaled deeply. "Does anyone else smell that?" he asked. "It smells like something burning. Incense, maybe?" He pointed his video camera toward the park district sign and zoomed in. A faint mist passed across the glowing green viewfinder.

"I smell it too," Greg said. "Where is it coming from?"

Everyone looked at Aurelia with an unspoken question. "Don't look at me," she protested. "I said I can sense ghosts and other entities—I never said I had a great sense of smell. It isn't a ghost, I'm 100 percent sure of that."

"So am I," Emmer said, chuckling. Emmer was the skeptic of the group. Despite everything he had seen during his time with the Fallen, he remained unconvinced. He swore he would stick with the group until they had

proven—to his satisfaction—the existence of the paranormal.

Mike led the group around the cable barrier. The further they got from the road, the stronger the strange smell became.

"I don't hear that noise at all anymore," Davin whispered. "Do you think the smell and that noise have something to do with each other?"

"We're about to find out."

Down the grassy path, near the sign for Pratts Wayne Woods, the landscape dipped down so that a sizable rectangular area lay outside their line of sight. The smell seemed to be coming from over there, and every gust of wind brought with it a small puff of smoke. The Fallen crouched and crept toward the edge of the embankment. They found it steep but shallow. There seemed to be something glowing down there, but what it was could not be discerned until the Fallen got a little closer.

Suddenly, an icy chill washed over the group. Lying in the snow in the middle of the depression was what looked like a large doll dressed in tattered clothes. Nearby, several glowing embers flickered around a collection of objects barely visible in the mix of mud and snow. There were footprints and drag marks all over the bottom of the rectangular depression, and enough snow was missing from the sides to reveal the cement edges of a house foundation.

At first, no one said a word. Then Greg spoke up. "Please tell me that isn't what I think it is," he said.

Davin covered his mouth and turned an even lighter shade of pale than usual.

Aurelia growled, shoved her way past Mike, and marched down to the bottom of the depression, but even she was not prepared for what she saw. It was the body of a child, as they had all feared, but its eye sockets were empty and filled with black residue. There were large gashes across its right leg and both of its arms, as though someone had been attempting to saw off the limbs, but had been interrupted. Steam rose from the fresh wounds.

MUNGER ROAD

"It looks like we interrupted whatever was happening here," Mike said. He joined Aurelia, but deliberately turned away from the corpse and examined the glowing embers and pile of debris. The embers, which lit up the ends of several fat sticks of incense, turned out to be the source of the scent they had smelled earlier. Most of the debris was unidentifiable—sticks, rocks, and pieces of organic matter. There was, however, a small stone statuette spattered with blood, surrounded by feathers of some kind. The statuette was unusual. It appeared to represent a man or monkey with large ears, bulging eyes, and a toothy grin sitting in a squatting position. Its arms were folded across its chest. Mike handed it to Greg. "Wrap this up and put it in your backpack," he said.

Greg hesitantly took the statuette and held it away from his body like it was diseased.

"This must have just happened," Emmer said. "*Jesus*. The perpetrators might still be around. They could even be watching us right now."

"Emmer is right," Mike said. "We need to get the heck out of here. I filmed enough of it so we can go back and try and figure this out later."

"What's there to figure out?" Greg said. "This is a police matter. I don't want to get dragged into it."

Mike gave his friend a scolding look. "You saw that statue, the incense, and the cuts. Don't tell me this doesn't look like a ritual to you. Not to mention whoever did this picked this particular spot near Munger Road. Why would they do that? This is definitely occult related, and that falls under our area of expertise."

"Mike is right," Aurelia said. "I have a bad feeling about this. I mean, for beyond the obvious reasons."

Without further discussion, the Fallen retreated to the road and hurried toward their car. In the darkness of the woods, several pairs of eyes watched and waited until they were gone.

INVESTIGATION FILE 049

WINSTON TUNNEL
Elizabeth, Illinois

The entrance to the Winston Tunnel, covered with iron bars like a gatehouse in a medieval dungeon, sits deep in the woods several miles southwest of Galena near the tiny community of Elizabeth. It has been abandoned since 1971, and nothing but the rattlesnakes that make their nests in the damp and murky interior have ventured inside.

At 2,493 feet, the Winston Tunnel was the longest railroad tunnel in Illinois. It was built in 1888 for the Minnesota and Northwestern Railroad, a line that ran from Chicago to Minneapolis, Omaha, and Kansas City. It took 350 workmen (and $600,000) more than nine months to complete the tunnel. Shortly after, the Minnesota and Northwestern became known as the "Chicago Great Western Railway." At least one worker is known to have been killed during construction of the tunnel, which was so long a pump house had to be built to ventilate it. In fact, it is said that the ghost of this Finnish laborer still haunts the site to this day. Two engineers, one stationed at the east entrance and one at the west entrance, stood watch.

Today, the Winston Tunnel is not easy to find. The east entrance has been covered over with dirt and debris, and the west entrance is quite a walk. To get there, you must park in a gravel parking lot off Blackjack Road (County Road 8), a mile or so north of Rocky Hill Road. There is a trail that leads from the parking lot to a grassy clearing next to a creek. Do not follow this trail too far. The abandoned ruins of the watchman's house will be on your right. Just south of there, along the creek, there will be a large amount of concrete blocks and debris leading up the side of a steep hill. Believe it or not, these used to support a bridge that spanned the creek and the small valley. Head up the path located on the right side of these concrete blocks.

Once you climb to the top of the remnants of the bridge, you will face a long, straight trail where you will have to walk over the old wooden ties mostly hidden under the grass. In a few years, visitors will hardly notice that trail used to be a railroad bed. As you travel down the trail, slowly but surely a white sign will appear in the distance, seeming to hover in a small area of darkness. This is the entrance to the Winston Tunnel.

The old pump house is gone now. It was torn down in 2007, but the bricks used to build its walls still remain. The path from there is full of pitfalls, rusted steel supports, and rotting timber. It is very dangerous – if you go, make sure to wear jeans and good hiking boots. The opposite side of the embankment is much easier to navigate (if you can get over there). Seeing the entrance to Winston Tunnel is worth all the trouble. I would not recommend trying to get inside, but I'm sure some foolhardy souls have attempted it. The site is currently maintained by the Illinois Department of Natural Resources, and is subject to their rules and regulations.

THE FALLEN INVESTIGATE

FEB. 9

2:10 PM

30° F

In front of the duo was an endless tunnel of darkness. Behind them, the tunnel entrance glowed almost unbearably bright, the bars that covered the opening only very briefly interrupting the sunlight. Greg and Davin slowly clawed their way forward, using the slippery cement wall as a guide. Davin clutched at Greg's shirt sleeve, but Greg, who was about a head shorter, brushed him off.

"I really think we should wait for the others," Davin said nervously. "Who knows what's down there? Not us, I'll tell you that."

Greg, who wore a ragged, olive green U.S. Army shirt from the Vietnam War with the sleeves rolled up, sighed in frustration. "Where is your sense of adventure? Why don't you get out of the basement every once and a while and live a little?"

"I *am* out of the basement," Davin grumbled. He jumped as his foot hit something long and thin—a branch that had been carried into the tunnel and deposited there during a heavy rain. "Man, there could be snakes in here and God knows what else."

"Snakes are cold-blooded, so they need to warm their bodies by being out in the sun," his friend replied. "I doubt we'll run into any in here."

"What? There are snakes that live in caves—" Davin was unable to complete his thought before several figures interrupted the light coming from the tunnel entrance.

"Good, Mike and the others finally made it," Greg said and quickly turned to give his friends a verbal lashing for taking so long to get there. When he turned to face the tunnel entrance, however, he saw only the outlines of three figures, each about six feet tall and two feet wide. They seemed to be absorbing all light, like deep black silk. An icy chill ran down his spine.

Earlier that day, the Fallen had left their car in the parking lot at the entrance to the forest preserve and walked into the woods past the sign that read "WINSTON TUNNEL." A dirt path wound up and down the uneven, hilly terrain until it suddenly opened up to a long grassy field. A creek flowed along the right side of the field, and a steep, wooded ridge jutted out of the landscape just beyond it. Mike, Greg, Aurelia, Davin and Emmer paused to take in the scenery.

"Do you see the tunnel anywhere?" Mike asked as he unfolded a map and examined it. He alternated his gaze between the map and the valley several times and ended with a puzzled look on his face.

Aurelia tore the map from his hands. "Give me that!" she shrieked.

"What is that over there?" Emmer interrupted. He pointed toward several large blocks of cement near the creek. "Maybe this is the entrance that was sealed off?"

"No," Mike said. "That was on the other side... I think."

The group walked over to the creek and examined the debris on the side of the ridge just beyond it. Aside from the blocks of cement, there were exposed rebar supports and a generous helping of gravel, but no tunnel.

"Let's keep going," Mike suggested. "This clearly isn't what we're looking for."

Up ahead, the valley narrowed, the woods closed in, and the field turned into a path that led deeper into the forest preserve. After about ten minutes of walking, the Fallen spotted the ruins of a large house in the woods off to their right. It was constructed of timber and yellowish limestone blocks. Greg rushed toward it excitedly like a kid whose babysitter had taken him to a new park.

Mocking him, Aurelia sang, "Now don't run too far!"

"We don't have time for this," Mike said. "We didn't come here to see an abandoned house." He was compelled to come along, however, when the rest of his friends voted with their feet and joined Greg in exploring the ruins.

After they had all settled down, Mike gathered them together. "We're burning daylight," he said. "We need to split up. Greg, go with Davin and see if we missed anything back by the creek. The rest of us will continue down this trail and see where it goes. Whoever finds the tunnel first will radio the other group."

Everyone shook their heads in mutual understanding and set off in their respective groups. Because they did not have to go far, Greg and Davin reached their destination rather quickly. Nothing had changed—there definitely was not a tunnel hidden along the ridge. "Why do we always get the crappy assignments?" Davin complained.

"Speak for yourself," Greg replied, examining the ridge. "Hey, how much you want to bet I can beat you to the top of this thing?"

A glance was all it took to signal the start of the race. The two friends scrambled to climb over the pieces of cement and up the steep incline. Greg reached the top first and jumped to his feet triumphantly. He hardly noticed the long trail that led from the top of the ridge straight back through the forest.

"Hey," Davin said when he finally reached the top. "Look behind you. Doesn't this look like an old railroad bed? I bet the tunnel is at the end of this trail."

Greg smiled. "Screw those other guys, let's get there *first*."

*   *   *

Aurelia immediately sensed the presence of the shadow creatures upon approaching the tunnel. Without any hesitation, she proceeded to descend the steep embankment, avoiding logs, holes, and other hazards as she went. Leaves and loose dirt gave way under the heavy weight of her boots, and Mike and Emmer followed closely (if not more carefully) behind.

It was not long before the trio felt the cold, wet sediment in front of the tunnel entrance beneath their feet. Now only yards away, they could plainly make out the quivering, Stygian shades against the bars. The shadows seemed to react to their presence by withdrawing further into the darkness. Greg and Davin were pressed up against the opposite wall, nearly out of sight.

Mike tried to take the lead, but Aurelia shoved past him again. "Get out of my way!" she shouted. She drew a quartz crystal from her purse and tossed it at the shadow that was closest to the entrance, hitting it dead on. The crystal seemed stuck for a moment, suspended in midair while the shadow drained away. After a few seconds, it clattered to the ground. Its once translucent pink surface was now black as coal.

The other two shadows seemed to be confused and drew closer to each other until they were nearly fused into one large mass. Then, without warning, Aurelia fell backwards into the muck at the bottom of the embankment, as if pushed by an unseen force.

As Aurelia crawled over the wet sand and rocks to get out of the way of the psychic attack, Mike pulled a pouch filled with kosher salt out of his pocket. He grabbed a handful of the salt and threw it at the shadows. Like a shotgun blast, the tiny pellets tore a hundred holes in their shimmering, atramentous ectoplasm. They promptly dissolved.

Greg and Davin rushed to the hole in the iron bars that covered the tunnel entrance, desperate to escape. Mike, Aurelia, and Emmer, however, were eager to get *into* the tunnel. They carefully squeezed through the gap in the bars and tried to reassure their friends that the threat from the mysterious interlopers was gone.

As soon as the reassuring was over,

however, Aurelia decided that a thorough scolding was in order. "Why didn't you wait for us?" she demanded. "We agreed that we would meet at the tunnel *before* we went in."

Mike, also irritated by his friend's recklessness, gave Greg and Davin the evil eye as he carefully located and then wrapped a cloth around the tarnished quartz. "Let's take this back with us and analyze it. It might be useful again someday."

"Does anyone want to explain to me what just happened?" Emmer said with a nervous laugh. "I couldn't see what was going on from back there. You guys act like you saw something—was it a snake?"

"Unbelievable," Greg said. "You were standing right there and you still missed it. Didn't you see those shadow people that Mike and Aura just got rid of? I mean, they weren't bothering me, but Davin was terrified."

Emmer shook his head. "*Shadow people?* Give me a break. You know your eyes start to see things that aren't there when exposed to, oh, a pitch-black tunnel for several minutes, right?"

"We weren't seeing things—" Davin began to protest, but he knew it was hopeless.

"Come on and help," Mike said. "Get the camera and start filming what you can. We need to get as much data as we can before someone else comes along and reports us to the park rangers."

Shaking off their strange encounter, the Fallen set to work exploring the area around the Winston Tunnel, but none of them—even Emmer—was willing to go much farther into its cavernous and foreboding interior.

INVESTIGATION FILE 050

SOUTHERN ILLINOIS UNIVERSITY
Carbondale, Illinois

Southern Illinois University in Carbondale has had a long and colorful history. Its mascot, the Saluki, is an ancient Egyptian dog breed and a salute to the region of southern Illinois called "Little Egypt." Nearly every campus building is said to be haunted, from the lost girl of Faner Hall to the ghost of "Henry" in Shryock Auditorium. The campus even boasts a labyrinth of underground tunnels.

Southern Illinois University was founded in 1869 as Southern Illinois Normal College, and its cornerstone was laid on May 17, 1870. Originally a small teacher's college, the university grew to over 23,000 students by 1980. Enrollment has remained relatively consistent ever since.

While noted as a research institution, SIU has also been popularly known as a "party school." During the late 1990s, Halloween celebrations broke out into riots, forcing the University to close its campus on Halloween weekend. A 15-year-long city ordinance that prevented three popular bars on Carbondale's main strip from doing business on Halloween and the following weekend was finally lifted for a one year trial period in 2013.[49]

Wheeler Hall, Faner Hall, Anthony Hall, Shryock Auditorium, and Mae Smith Residence Hall are all home to macabre tales.

Scott Thorne, owner of Castle Perilous Games, told author Bruce Cline that Wheeler Hall has been the scene of poltergeist activity. According to Thorne, a popular legend maintains that a woman working in the hall late at night was disturbed by chairs thrown by unseen hands.[50]

Faner Hall is one of the strangest buildings on campus. Designed in Brutalist style using bare concrete, Faner opened in 1972. Its corridors are deliberately confusing in order to discourage student rioters from taking over the building. In *Haunted Illinois* (2004), Troy Taylor related the campus legend of a young woman who became lost in Faner's maze-like interior and died. Some storytellers say she fell from a window shortly after the building opened. The coed's ghost is said to wander the halls, appearing confused and disoriented. When students approach her to help, she disappears.

One of SIU's most famous legends is that of Henry, the ghost light of Shryock Auditorium. The $135,000 auditorium opened in 1918 and was named after then SIU President Henry William Shryock. On April 13, 1935, Shryock died suddenly just before a morning assembly. Since his death, a stage light has mysteriously turned on and off at will. Students have nicknamed it "Henry." There are other reports of missing items, doors opening and closing, and phantom footsteps. According to Bruce Cline, a shadowy figure has been seen near the stage and pipe organ.

The ghost of a broken-hearted resident assistant supposedly haunts Mae Smith Residence Hall. Another female ghost is said to haunt Anthony Hall. She was reportedly a secretary who died on the job. Since then, people have reported hearing the sound of fingers tapping at a typewriter and file drawers sliding open.

Finally, maintenance tunnels crisscross SIU's campus, and they are rumored to be home to one or more students who were unfortunate enough to become trapped down there. Some parts of the tunnel system have not been visited by maintenance staff in decades. What gruesome discoveries await their return?

49 *The Southern Illinoisan* (Carbondale) 17 July 2013.
50 Bruce and Lisa Cline, *History, Mystery, and Hauntings of Southern Illinois* (Rockford: Black Oak Media, Inc., 2011), 79.

THE FALLEN INVESTIGATE

MAR. 10

6:30 PM

39° F

Deep in the bowels of the Faner Building, Professor Kenneth Pangloss scrutinized the wayward band of five that eyed, poked, and prodded their way through his office. His office was located in a back corner of the Anthropology Lab.

Aurelia, Emmer, Davin, and Greg examined the strange bric-à-brac that lined the shelves or hid behind glass doors. In stark contrast, Mike stood still. His gaze was fixated on the professor.

Professor Pangloss was a peculiar man. In his late 60s, he had a crescent of white hair around an otherwise bald head. He was dressed in brown corduroy pants and a plaid shirt.

"I wouldn't be asking for your help if I could figure this out on my own," Mike said, almost pleading.

"That may be so," Pangloss replied through clenched teeth, "but would you please ask your friends to stop manhandling my artifacts."

Mike turned to scold his curious companions. "Hey guys, knock it off!"

The others froze. Greg was caught in mid smirk as he gently set a fertility statue back on the dusty shelf.

Mike turned his attention back to the professor. "Professor, you are the foremost Midwestern scholar on ancient North America. I did some research on this totem, but couldn't come up with anything conclusive. Would you please just take a look at it?"

Pangloss squinted. "Where did you say you found this?"

"A construction site up north," Greg interjected. "We were getting ready to lay the foundation for a house when our friend here dug this out of the sediment." He slapped Davin on the shoulder.

"You are construction workers?" the professor asked, skeptically. Most of the five young people in his office were pale and thin. That was especially true for Davin and Emmer, who looked like they rarely ventured outside.

Greg, of course, was lying. The Fallen had discovered the artifact at a crime scene in the ruins of an old house along Munger Road. It was surrounded by feathers and spattered with the blood of a freshly-executed victim.

Professor Pangloss shrugged, pulled on a pair of latex gloves, and removed the totem from a plastic sandwich bag. It was a stone statuette representing a man or monkey with large ears, bulging eyes, and a toothy grin sitting in a squatting position. Its arms were folded across its chest. Dark stains covered much of its surface. He brought it over to his desk and examined it under a large magnifying glass. The anticipation in the room was palpable. The professor made a few sounds, then set the totem on his desk and removed his gloves with authoritative ease. "Well, my friends, you've been hoodwinked," he said.

"What do you mean?" Mike asked. He was obviously taken aback.

"I mean someone played a prank on you," Pangloss explained. "Probably someone who didn't want the construction project to proceed. Have any tree huggers been bothering you lately?"

"I don't understand," Mike said. "What is it? Why do you think it's a fake?"

"First off, it's nearly impossible to tell how old it is, but it does not belong to any Amerindian culture north of Mexico. This is an Aztec artifact—specifically Mictlantecuhtli, a god of the dead and the underworld. The only way for this to have gotten to your construction site was if someone brought it there recently. Secondly, you cannot simply buy a genuine Aztec artifact on Ebay. That makes me think this is a clever copy—not from a souvenir shop necessarily, but someone chiseled this by hand. It is actually quite good. They spattered it with some kind of paint, varnish, or oil, probably to scare you into thinking it's covered in blood."

Mike glanced at Aurelia. That was one fact they knew the professor had gotten wrong. All members of the Fallen had seen the victim's lifeless body and smelled the pungent aroma of death.

"That's good enough an explanation for me," Emmer said as he turned to leave.

"Wait!" Mike nearly shouted. He looked panicked, breaking his usual composure. "Is there any *other* explanation? Are there any present day cults that use this imagery?"

"Boy, have you lost your mind?" Professor Pangloss replied. He pointed to his doctoral diploma on the wall. "Do you see this diploma? Does it say 'cult expert' on it? Now, you asked me to identify this artifact and I did. I have a hundred tests to grade, *if you'll excuse me.*"

Mike looked like he was about to protest, but Aurelia clutched his arm and began to drag him away. He used the Ziploc bag to grab the totem and joined his companions as they made a hasty exit. Just before walking out the door, Mike heard the professor mutter something. "Probably just some apocalyptic cult," he thought he said.

"What was that?" Mike asked.

"It's the *Mayan* calendar that ends in 2012, not the *Aztec*. Idiots."

The Fallen winced as their eyes hit sunlight on the campus of Southern Illinois University. Across the quad, some students were hurrying to class, while others pulled their jackets tight and snuck a drag off dwindling cigarettes. The sun was going down.

"The professor said something about an apocalyptic cult as we were leaving," Mike volunteered. "Something about the Mayan apocalypse."

Greg corrected him. "He said it was an Aztec figure. Why would Mayan cultists conduct a ritual using an Aztec figure?"

"It's the same thing," Aurelia said.

Emmer agreed. "Aura has a point. Cultists aren't usually very intelligent."

Davin, who had been quiet the whole time, rubbed his right arm nervously and staired at a group of coeds as they walked past. "Geez, guys," he said. "I'm getting really tired of chasing psychos, *and being chased by them*, all over the state. I thought you said we were finally going to settle down? I'm in the prime of my life over here. What if I wanted to go back to college?" Davin's friends stared, their mouths hanging open. Saying something affirmative about his life—suggesting there was something to live for—was uncharacteristic. He continued. "I've been kidnapped, arrested, locked in a trunk, and nearly bitten by a vampire— *dhampyr*, or whatever. The point is, I'm tired of it, and I quit."

Before Mike could respond, Emmer spoke. "Davin has a good point," he said. "You know I've enjoyed these little adventures, but I have no desire to spend another year fighting idiots who think they're summoning some ancient god or bringing about the end of the world. I'm with Davin. I'm out of this one."

Mike's face slowly turned a brighter shade of red. "Greg, what do you think?"

"I hate to say it, but both of them have a point."

Mike turned to Aurelia. "I have nowhere else to go," she said. "If you think we should pursue this, then I'm with you."

"Sorry, Mike," Greg said. "You know you're like a brother to me, and we've been doing this longer than I can remember, but it's time to take a break. No one ever said we were going to do this forever."

"Yeah, the world's not going to end," Emmer said. "Really."

Defeated, Mike shoved his hands deep into his pockets, and the Fallen walked slowly into the sunset.

BEHIND THE SCENES

There are a variety of competing factions and groups all trying to gain access to haunted and forbidden places in Illinois, all with suspect intentions. Some seek fame, others knowledge, and still others seek the power those places might bring. The average reader, caught in the middle of this struggle, might have a difficult time sorting it all out. The following are just a few of the groups featured in the *Legends and Lore of Illinois*.

GROUPS AND FACTIONS

THE FALLEN

Our antiheros formed at St. Sebastian's College in Maine in 1998 to investigate the strange history of that school. They quickly found that dark forces were waiting to reemerge, and took steps to vanquish them. In the process, the college was destroyed by fire for a second time, but not before Mike rescued an old book from the library. This book, written by French missionaries in the early 1700s, claimed that an astral portal was hidden somewhere in the backwoods of Illinois.

The Fallen

Fleeing from New England, Mike, Aurelia, Greg, Davin, and Emmer travelled across the country until they reached Illinois. There they established themselves and began investigating the state's many haunted places, hoping to find the astral portal before anyone else. Their adventures in this state are chronicled in the *Legends and Lore of Illinois*.

The Fallen derive their name from the fact that each member is a social outcast, driven from society by their eccentricity and their interest in the macabre. Being in this position has its advantages, however, because it allows the Fallen to act as emissaries between this world and the next. Although they do not appear to get along, their loyalty to each other is unshakable.

Alignment: Chaotic Good

PAN-CONTINENTAL PARANORMAL RESEARCH SOCIETY (P.C.P.R.S.)

The Pan-Continental Paranormal Research Society is Illinois' most experienced and professional paranormal investigation team, or so they believe. Held in high regard by other 'ghost hunting' groups for their one-time appearance on the SyFy Channel, the P.C.P.R.S. utilizes the latest technology to investigate the paranormal. They also have matching t-shirts.

The P.C.P.R.S. is a constant thorn in the Fallen's side. Its members believe the Fallen are amateurs who give other paranormal investigation teams a bad name. They are not free of their own detractors, however. The Greater-Midwestern Alliance for the Investigation, Inspection, and Research of Paraphysical Phenomenon (G.M.A.I.I.R.P.P.) splintered from the group after the P.C.P.R.S. began charging for its services.

Alignment: Lawful Neutral

ZEALOTS

The origins of this group are mysterious, but their motivations are well-known. The Zealots are a fanatically religious cult whose members are convinced that they are serving everything good and holy. They despise the Fallen and will stop at nothing to beat them to the astral portal.

Because many of their members are prominent in society, they often use their positions of power to play one group off another. In their quest for the portal, they formed a secret and uneasy alliance with the Satanists, who they view as lost souls to be pitied and manipulated rather than a real danger.

Alignment: Neutral Good

SATANISTS

During the 1970s and '80s, concerned parents and some evangelical Christians believed satanic cults were lurking around every corner. These "Satanists" turned out to be nothing more than bored teenagers looking for something exciting and dangerous to do on a Friday night. A handful of these teenagers, more serious than most, have been enlisted by the Zealots to follow and harass the Fallen on their quest to find the astral portal.

Alignment: Neutral Evil

ACOLYTES

First encountered at St. James-Sag, the Acolytes are truly dangerous, as they serve a bloodthirsty demon god. The Acolytes have tried for centuries to resurrect their master, which has slumbered in the caverns of Starved Rock. When the Zealots were killed after finally succeeding in briefly opening the astral portal, the demon was awoken by its power. The Acolytes desperately seek to destroy the Fallen, because they are the only ones with the knowledge to vanquish their master and send it back to the netherworld.

Alignment: Lawful Evil

FAN BOYS (AND GIRLS)

Whether inspired by the *Twilight* series, *Hairy Potter*, *Interview with a Vampire*, or TV shows like *Charmed*, *Buffy the Vampire Slayer*, and *Ghost Adventures*, fan boys and girls acquire most of their knowledge about ghosts or the paranormal from fictional universes. These fans may dress like their favorite characters, or even claim to be wizards, vampires, or paranormal investigators. Occasionally, they will accidentally run into something genuinely paranormal. Mostly they just like to have fun, and that is okay as long as they do not bring their fandom into the workplace.

Alignment: Chaotic Neutral

LAW ENFORCEMENT

Local police and sheriff's departments are frequently mentioned in the *Legends and Lore of Illinois*. These guardians of law and order are simply trying to keep miscreants away from abandoned places, cemeteries, and other allegedly haunted sites. They enforce rules and arrest trespassers. Mostly skeptics, they are frequently perplexed at why so many people seem to be interested in these locations and are annoyed to be distracted from more serious crimes.

Alignment: Lawful Good

THE FALLEN CHARACTER PROFILE: MIKE

Age: 25
Height: 5'6"
Weight: 168 lbs
Eyes: Blue
Hair: Light Brown

Role: Fearless Leader
Year Joined: Founding Member
Investigations in Illinois: 48

Attributes

Strength: 07
Perception: 06
Endurance: 05
Charisma: 05
Intelligence: 07
Agility: 05
Luck: 04

Katie Conrad

History

Along with Greg, Mike was one of the founding members of The Fallen. Greg and Mike met in high school and became fast friends. Citing a mutual interest in the paranormal (as well as a mutual exclusion from even the lowest rungs of the social ladder), they decided to form the group after an ill-fated trip to New Orleans in which they vanquished a vampire at the behest of the vampire's half-breed daughter.

Mike and Aurelia have an even longer history. They were friends at a very young age, before Aurelia was sent off to a reform school. More than ten years later, Mike and Aurelia were reunited at St. Sebastian's College, where they decided that their fates must be intertwined.

Always searching for truth, Mike has been known to go to great lengths to acquire even the most obscure knowledge. He has developed a healthy distrust of authority and is prone to believing the fantastical over the mundane.

Mike's obsession with the unseen has been both a help and a hindrance, since he is eager to attribute almost everything to a supernatural origin. The other members of the group often have to steer him back to reality. Despite this flaw, he remains the group's compass and often determines where investigations will take place.

THE FALLEN CHARACTER PROFILE: GREG

Age: 24
Height: 5'1"
Weight: 126 lbs
Eyes: Blue
Hair: Dirty Blonde

Role: Cryptozoologist/Adventurer
Year Joined: Founding Member
Investigations in Illinois: 45

Attributes

Strength: 05
Perception: 07
Endurance: 06
Charisma: 08
Intelligence: 07
Agility: 07
Luck: 08

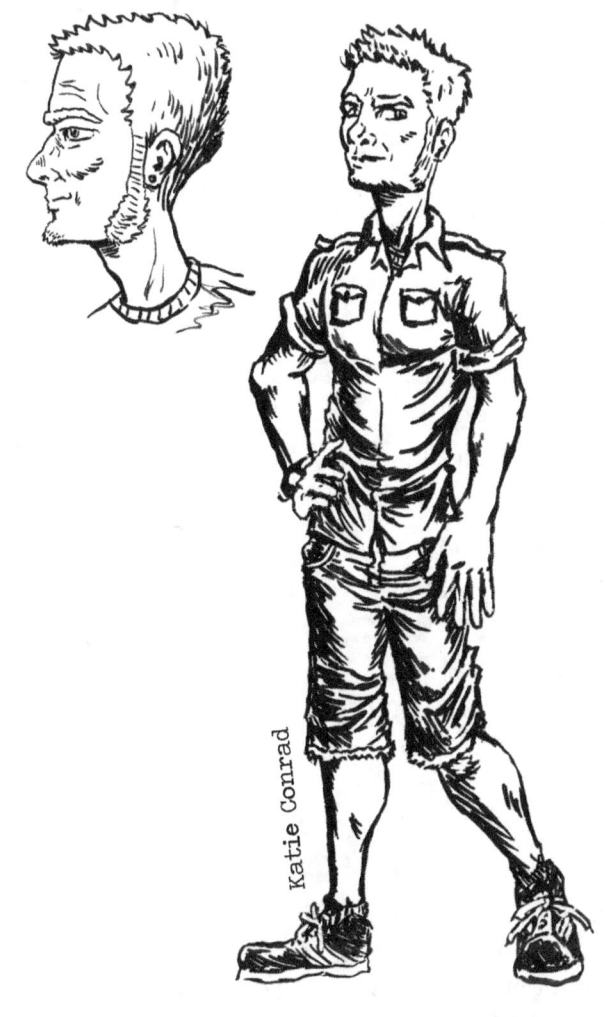

Katie Conrad

History

Along with Mike, Greg is one of the founding members of The Fallen. Many years ago, the two of them took a trip to New Orleans because they had heard it was one of the most historic and haunted cities in America.

While they wandered Bourbon Street one afternoon, they ran into a mysterious girl who claimed to be a half-vampire who was being terrorized by her full-blooded vampire father. Greg, fancying himself an expert on the subject, offered to help out. The rest is history. Greg and Mike vanquished the vampire and bid goodbye to their mysterious friend. From there, they traveled America where they eventually enrolled in St. Sebastian's College and met Aurelia, Davin, and Emmer.

Unafraid of adventure, Greg has been on many fortean investigations and has tracked down a number of priceless artifacts, which he has then proceeded to sell to the highest bidder. On a trip to Aruba, he discovered a rare spider; the venom of which he believed would cure paralysis.

Greg is a dynamic figure with an enormous ego. He is always ready to find the humor in any situation, especially if that situation is fatally serious. Well-read and well-traveled, he is usually prepared to handle any situation. The Fallen could not exist without him.

THE FALLEN CHARACTER PROFILE: AURELIA

Katie Conrad

Age: 25
Height: 5'3"
Weight: 130 lbs
Eyes: Green
Hair: Brunette

Role: Magician/Psychic-Medium
Year Joined: 1998
Investigations in Illinois: 44

Attributes

Strength:	07
Perception:	05
Endurance:	09
Charisma:	05
Intelligence:	06
Agility:	08
Luck:	07

History

Aurelia and Mike have known each other since their days in elementary school. Unfortunately, Aurelia, or Aura for short, never got along well with her classmates and was shipped to a reform school on account of her uncontrollable temper. Aurelia and Mike did not see each other again until they unexpectedly ran into each other at St. Sebastian's College over ten years later.

A student of magick, Aurelia makes Fairuza Balk's character in *The Craft* look like Mother Teresa. Discarding the warnings of more conventional Wiccans, she chose to study both the white and the black arts. Nine times out of ten, however, she prefers to rely on her fists rather than a spell to get even. She can also sense the presence of ghosts, spirits, and creeps. Her boyfriend, who wants nothing to do with the group unless he is looking for bail money, is frequently in trouble with the law. This has been a source of tension between her and Mike for many years.

Aurelia has been on nearly all of The Fallen's missions since she joined the group and is generally known as the navigator. Whenever Mike gets the group lost, Aurelia usually leads them to their destination. She has an uncanny ability to sense when they are near to the source of a mystery. Some have said this is the result of help from beyond. On more than one occasion, a mysterious spirit has appeared to help the Fallen. Aurelia has no explanation as to why this spirit might be following her, but she is grateful for its presence.

THE FALLEN CHARACTER PROFILE: DAVIN

Age: 22
Height: 5'7"
Weight: 151 lbs
Eyes: Gray
Hair: Light Brown

Role: UFO-ologist/Urban Explorer
Year Joined: 1998
Investigations in Illinois: 39

Attributes

Strength: 04
Perception: 06
Endurance: 04
Charisma: 06
Intelligence: 07
Agility: 06
Luck: 06

Katie Conrad

History

Davin's parents dumped him at St. Sebastian's College hoping that he would turn over a new leaf, since his high school years had been fraught with apathetic social involvement and nihilistic musings. Instead, Davin joined the Fallen after Greg and he became roommates his freshman year. Polar opposites, they enjoyed a contentious relationship. Greg antagonized him at every turn, until Mike realized Davin's potential.

When he was not playing computer games and writing expiration dates on his arm, he enjoyed reading about UFOs and other mysterious phenomenon. As a kid, Davin had witnessed a series of strange lights that hovered over his suburban neighborhood. His only interest became peering through his telescope and absorbing books on astronomy and alien abductions. Mike and Greg quickly recruited him to do their dirty work, and he has been a member of the team ever since.

Davin dropped out of college to pursue a life of paranormal investigation, self-loathing, and debauchery. Mike and Aurelia look on him as the dysfunctional adopted son they never had. Without their constant intervention, he is prone to bouts of drinking and substance abuse. Despite these failings, he can be charismatic and is the only one in the group to be readily accepted by the outside world. Despite having been roommates for a time (or perhaps because of that fact), Davin and Greg do not get along very well, but at least he has found a home.

THE FALLEN CHARACTER PROFILE: EMMER

Age: 24
Height: 5'11"
Weight: 174 lbs
Eyes: Blue
Hair: Blonde

Role: Skeptic
Year Joined: 1999
Investigations in Illinois: 35

Attributes

Strength:	05
Perception:	08
Endurance:	05
Charisma:	03
Intelligence:	08
Agility:	05
Luck:	06

Katie Conrad

History

Mike and Greg met Emmer at a bar on a weekend excursion into town during their tenure at St. Sebastian's College. Overhearing their conversation about spirits and the afterlife, Emmer challenged the two to prove the rumors that his father's bar was haunted by the ghost of its previous owner. While Mike and Greg claimed to obtain photographic evidence of the ghost, Emmer dismissed the mist on the photos as "just a bunch of steam or something."

During their investigation, the three discovered that they had many other common interests, and Emmer decided to join the Fallen in order to offer a rational voice to counter Mike's frequent assertions of paranormal discovery. Emmer and Mike are both music aficionados, while Emmer and Greg share an interest in poking fun at the other members of the group.

A staunch atheist and self-professed disbeliever, he wears his skepticism like impenetrable armor. He always finds a way to dismiss anything the Fallen uncover on their journeys. He has yet to be convinced by anything that has happened during his tenure with the group, and manages to be absent during times when most paranormal phenomenon is manifest.

Despite his abrasive nature, and regardless of his assertions that he "only goes on these trips out of boredom," his love of the usual side of American culture has won him lifelong friends among the rest of the group.

THE FALLEN CHARACTER PROFILE: CASEY THE COYDOG

Katie Conrad

Age: Unknown
Height: 2'
Length: 2'7"
Weight: 21 lbs
Eyes: Prussian Blue
Hair: Smokey Gray

Role: Tracker, Guard Dog
Year Joined: 2008
Investigations in Illinois: 12

Attributes

Strength: 04
Perception: 10
Endurance: 06
Charisma: 05
Intelligence: 05
Agility: 09
Luck: 07

History

Casey the Coydog is a cross breed between a female domesticated dog and a wild male coyote. Coydogs are extremely rare. Although good human companions, they still retain some of the unpredictable and wild nature of their paternal lineage. During their adventures, the Fallen discovered that Illinois coydogs may have been the product of a mad scientist's attempt to create the perfect guard dog. The scientist was later committed to Peoria State Hospital and his research was lost, but not before some of his puppies escaped.

The Fallen found Casey in the woods near Old Union Cemetery. Her paw was caught in a trap and Greg rescued her. Since then, Casey has been a loyal companion of the group. True to form, Greg gave her the name "Casey" as a joke. He named her after Aurelia's boyfriend—an all-around loser whose tendency to end up in jail annoys the other members of the Fallen, especially Mike.

Casey the Coydog has a keen sense for both the seen and unseen. On more than one occasion, she has alerted the Fallen to the presence of something otherworldly. Although they do not know her age, the Fallen hope she will be by their side for a long time.

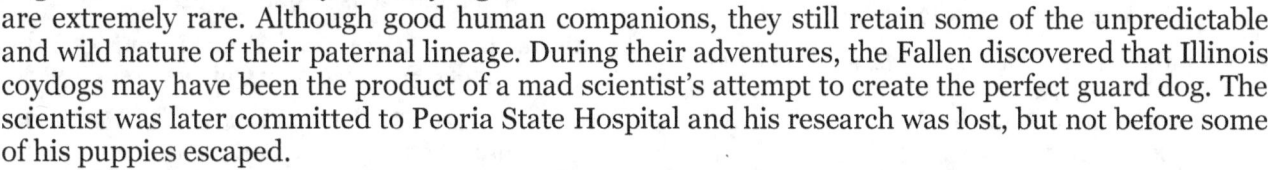

COMPREHENSIVE BIBLIOGRAPHY

The following is a close-to-exhaustive list of books on the folklore and ghost stories of Illinois. If any title has been omitted, it was purely by accident. Books are arranged alphabetically by author. Many of these were consulted in writing the *Legends and Lore of Illinois*, but it would be impossible to cite each individual instance. Instead, my readers are encouraged to enjoy each of these books on their own terms, as each one adds something to our understanding of Illinois history and ghostlore.

Adams, Len. *Phantoms in the Looking Glass: History and Hauntings of the Illinois Prairie*. Decatur: Whitechapel Press, 2008.

Allen, John W. *Legends & Lore of Southern Illinois*. Carbondale: Southern Illinois University, 1963, 1973.

Allen-Kline, Margaret. "'She Protects Her Girls': The Legend of Mary Hawkins at Pemberton Hall." M.A. thesis, Eastern Illinois University, 1998.

Bielski, Ursula. *Chicago Haunts: Ghostlore of the Windy City*. Chicago: Lake Claremont Press, 1998.

_____. *More Chicago Haunts: Scenes from Myth and Memory*. Chicago: Lake Claremont Press, 2000.

_____. *Chicago Haunts 3: Locked Up Stories from an October City*. Holt: Thunder Bay Press, 2009.

Brandon, Trent. *The Book of Ghosts*. Galloway: Zerotime Publishing, 2003.

Brooks, Rachel. *Chicago Ghosts*. Atglen: Schiffer Publishing, 2008.

_____. *Ghosts of Springfield and Southern Illinois*. Atglen: Schiffer Publishing, 2009.

Brunvand, Jan Harold. *The Mexican pet: More "New" Urban Legends and Some Old Favorites*. New York: W.W. Norton & Company, 1986.

_____. *The Vanishing Hitchhiker: American Urban Legends and Their Meanings*. New York: W.W. Norton & Company, 1981.

Burrows, Russell and Fred Rydholm. *The Mystery Cave of Many Faces: First in a Series on the Saga of Burrows' Cave*. Superior Heartland, 1992.

Christensen, Jo-Anne. *Ghost Stories of Illinois*. Edmonton: Lone Pine, 2000.

Clark, Jerome. *Unnatural Phenomena: A Guide to the Bizarre Wonders of North America* (Santa Barbara: ABC-CLIO, 2005).

Cline, Bruce and Lisa. *History, Mystery, and Hauntings of Southern Illinois*. Rockford: Black Oak Media, Inc., 2011.

Cline, Bruce. *More History, Mystery, and Hauntings of Southern Illinois*. Rockford: Black Oak Media, Inc., 2012.

Cline, Bruce and Tracey Todd Bragg. *Even More History, Mystery, and Hauntings of Southern Illinois*. Rockford: Black Oak Media, Inc., 2013.

Cole, Fay-Cooper, et al. *Kincaid: A Prehistoric Illinois Metropolis*. Chicago: University of Chicago Press, 1951.

Committee on State Charitable Institutions. *Brief History of the Charitable Institutions of the State of Illinois*. Chicago: John Morris, 1893.

Corliss, William R. *Handbook of Unusual Natural Phenomena: Eyewitness Accounts of Nature's Greatest Mysteries*. New York: Arlington House, 1986.

Carlson, Bruce. *Ghosts of Rock Island County, Illinois*. Fort Madison: Quixote Press, 1987.

Crowe, Richard T. *Chicago's Street Guide to the Supernatural*. Oak Park: Carolando Press, 2000, 2001.

Emerson, Thomas and Barry Lewis. *Cahokia and the Hinterlands: Middle Mississipian Cultures of the Midwest*. Urbana, Illinois: University of Illinois Press, 1991.

Frantz, Kevin J. *Naperville, Chicago's Haunted Heighbor*, Vol. 1. Naperville: Unrested Dead Publishing, 2008.

Gorman, William. *Ghost Whispers: Tales from Haunted Midway*. Rockford: Helm Publishing, 2005.

Graczyk, Jim and Donna Boonstra. *Field Guide to Illinois Hauntings*. Alton: Whitechapel Productions Press, 2001.

Guiley, Rosemary Ellen. *The Complete Vampire Companion*. New York: Macmillan, 1994.

Hauck, Dennis William. *Haunted Places: The National Directory: Ghostly Abodes, Sacred Sites, UFO Landings, and Other Supernatural Locations*. New York: Penguin Books, 1994, 1996.

Heise, Kenan. *Resurrection Mary: a Ghost Story*. Evanston: Chicago Historical Bookworks, 1990.

Henson, Michael Paul. *A Guide to Treasure in Illinois and Indiana*. Dona Ana: Carson Enterprises, 1982.

Hucke, Matt and Ursula Bielski. *Graveyards of Chicago: The People, History, Art, and Lore of Cook County Cemeteries*. Chicago: Lake Claremont Press, 1999.

Hyatt, Harry Middleton. *Folk-lore from Adams County, Illinois*. Alma Egan Hyatt Foundation, 1935.

Johnson, Raymond. *Chicago's Haunt Detective*. Atglen: Schiffer Publishing, 2011.

Kachuba, John B. *Ghosthunting Illinois*. Cincinnati: Clerisy Press, 2005.

Kaczmarek, Dale. *Illuminating the Darkness: The Mystery of Spook Lights*. Oak Lawn: Ghost Research Society Press, 2003.

_____. *Windy City Ghosts: An Essential Guide to the Haunted History of Chicago*. Oak Lawn: Ghost Research Society Press, 2000, 2005.

_____. *Windy City Ghosts II: More tales from America's most haunted city*. Oak Lawn: Ghost Research Society Press, 2005.

Kleen, Michael. *Haunting Illinois: A Tourist's Guide to the Weird and Wild Places of the Prairie State*. Holt: Thunder Bay Press, 2011.

_____. *Legends and Lore of Illinois*. Vol. 1-4. Charleston/Rockford: Black Oak Press, Illinois, 2007-2010.

_____. *Legends and Lore of Illinois: Case Files*. Vol. 1. Rockford: Black Oak Press, Illinois, 2009.

_____. *Legends and Lore of Coles County, Illinois*. Issues 1-9. Charleston: Black Oak Press, Illinois, 2006.

_____. *Paranormal Illinois*. Atglen: Schiffer Publishing, 2010.

_____. *Tales of Coles County, Illinois*. Rockford: Black Oak Media, Inc., 2004, 2013.

_____. *The Legend of Pemberton Hall*. Charleston: Black Oak Press, Illinois, 2008.

Ladley, Diane A. *Haunted Aurora*. Charleston: The History Press, 2010.

_____. *Haunted Naperville*. Chicago: Acadia Publishing, 2009.

Lewis, Chad and Terry Fisk. *The Illinois Road Guide to Haunted Locations*. Eau Claire: Unexplained Research Publishing, 2007.

Lisman, Gary. *Bittersweet Memories: a History of the Peoria State Hospital*. Victoria: Trafford Publishing, 2005.

Markus, Scott. *Voices from the Chicago Grave: They're Calling. Will You Answer?* Holt: Thunder Bay Press, 2008.

McCarthy, Stephanie E. *Haunted Peoria*. Chicago: Arcadia Publishing, 2009.

McCarty, Michael and Connie Corcoran Wilson. *Ghostly Tales of Route 66: from Chicago to Oklahoma*. Wever: Quixote Press, 2008.

Moffett, Garret. *Haunted Macomb*. Charleston, SC: The History Press, 2010.

_____. *Haunted Springfield, Illinois*. Charleston, SC: The History Press, 2011.

Moreno, Richard. *Illinois Curiosities: Quirky Characters, Roadside Oddities & Other Offbeat Stuff*. Guilford: Globe Pequot, 2011.

_____. *Myths and Mysteries of Illinois: True Stories of the Unsolved and Unexplained*. Guilford: Globe Pequot, 2013.

Morris, Jeff and Vince Sheilds. *Chicago Haunted Handbook: 99 Ghostly Places You Can Visit Around the Windy City*. Covington: Clerisy Press, 2013.

Neely, Charles, ed. *Tales and Songs of Southern Illinois*. Menasha: George Banta Publishing, 1938; reprint, Carbondale: Southern Illinois University Press, 1998.

Norman, Michael. *Haunted Homeland: A Definitive Collection of North American Ghost Stories*. New York: Tor Books, 2006.

Nowlan, James D. "From Lincoln to Forgottonia." *Illinois Issues* 24 (September 1998): 27-30.

Osborne, Stephen. *Ghosts of Northern Illinois*. Atglen: Schiffer Publishing, 2012.

Perry, Charles William. "Angeline Vernon Milner." *The Alumni Quarterly* 13 (May 1924): 2-10.

Pohlen, Jerome. *Oddball Illinois: A Guide to 450 Really Strange Places*. Chicago: Chicago Review Press, 2000, 2012.

Rowe, Bill. "Was Byron's Barefoot Phantom Merely a Masquerade?" *Rockford Magazine* 11 (Fall 1996): 24-25.

Schwartz, Alvin. *Scary Stories Treasury: Three Books to Chill Your Bones*. Vol. 2, *More Scary Stories to Tell in the Dark*. New York: Harper Collins, 1984.

Scott, Beth and Michael Norman. *Haunted Heartland: True Ghost Stories from the American Midwest*. New York: Barnes & Noble Books, 1985, 1992.

Selzer, Adam. *The Ghosts of Chicago: The Windy City's Most Famous Haunts*. Woodbury: Llewellyn Publications, 2013.

Shults, Sylvia. *Fractured Spirits: Hauntings at the Peoria State Hospital*. Tiskilwa: Dark Continents Publishing, 2013.

Stanton, Carl L. *They Called it Treason: an Account of Renegades, Copperheads, Guerrillas, Bushwhackers and Outlaw Gangs that Terrorized Illinois During the Civil War*. Bunker Hill: by the author, 2002.

Stout, Steve. *The Starved Rock Murders*. Utica: Utica House Publishing, 1982.

Taylor, Troy. *Beyond the Grave: The History of America's Most Haunted Graveyards*. Alton: Whitechapel Productions Press, 2001.

_____. *Flickering Images: The History & Hauntings of the Avon Theater*. Alton: Whitechapel Productions Press, 2001.

_____. *Ghosts of Millikin: The History & Hauntings of Millikin University*. Alton: Whitechapel Productions Press, 2001.

_____. *Haunted Alton: History & Hauntings of the Riverbend Region*. Alton: Whitechapel Productions Press, 1999.

_____. *Haunted Decatur Revisited: Ghostly Tales from the Haunted Heartland of Illinois*. Alton: Whitechapel Productions Press, 2000.

_____. *Haunted Illinois: Travel Guide to the History and Hauntings of the Prairie State*. Alton: Whitechapel Productions Press, 2004.

_____. *Weird Illinois: Your Travel Guide to Illinois' Local Legends and Best Kept Secrets*. New York: Sterling Publishing, 2005.

_____. *Where the Dead Walk: History & Hauntings of Greenwood Cemetery*. Alton: Whitechapel Productions Press, 2002.

Thuma, Cynthia and Catherine Lower. *Creepy Colleges and Haunted Universities*. Atglen: Schiffer Publishing, 2003.

Watson, Daryl. *Ghosts of Galena*. Galena: Galena/Jo Daviess County Historical Society, 1995. Reprint, Dubuque: Welu Printing Company, 2005.

Wilson, Larry. *Chasing Shadows: Investigating the Paranormal in Illinois, Missouri, and Iowa*. Rockford: Black Oak Media, Inc., 2011.

_____. *Echoes from the Grave: Exploring the Mysteries of the Supernatural in Illinois, Indiana, and Kansas*. Rockford: Black Oak Media, Inc., 2012.

Zeller, George Anthony. *Befriending the Bereft*. Peoria State Hospital: by the author, 1938.